CW01471672

Dark of Night
A Story of Rot and Ruin

JournalStone's DoubleDown Series, Book VIII

By
Jonathan Maberry and Rachael Lavin

JournalStone
San Francisco

JOURNALSTONE
YOUR LINK TO ARTISTIC TALENT

JournalStone books may be ordered through booksellers or by contacting:

JournalStone
www.journalstone.com

ISBN: 978-1-942712-91-6 *(sc)*
ISBN: 978-1-942712-92-3 *(ebook)*

Library of Congress Control Number: 2016933401

Printed in the United States of America
JournalStone rev. date: April 22, 2016

Cover Art and Design: Robert Grom
Author Photo: Sara Jo West
Photo Credits: Blood splatter © Mrspopman1985/shuttstock, Hands in bus window © murengstockphoto/shuttstock, Bus door © Skodadad/istock

Edited by: *Aaron J. French*

Author's Note

This story is a collaboration on several fronts.

It is first a collaboration between two writers, myself and talented newcomer Rachael Lavin.

It is also a collaboration—or perhaps collision—of three of my fictional worlds. Story threads from my Zombie Apocalypse duology, *Dead of Night* and *Fall of Night* lead us into the tale, but that thread quickly becomes entangled with elements from my *Rot & Ruin* novels and also with the Joe Ledger thrillers. You do not need to read those books first, however, in order to read and—hopefully—enjoy this tale of survival in the days following the rise of the living dead.

For those who have read some of all of those books, and for those who enjoy knowing where something falls in the proper chronology, this takes place fifteen years after the Joe Ledger books, and six months after 'First Night'—the events described in *Fall of Night*. Those events took place fourteen years before *Rot & Ruin*.

—Jonathan Maberry

Dark of Night

~1~

Dez Fox

"They're coming!"

The child's voice was too loud, too shrill and Desdemona Fox moved quickly to clamp a hand over the little boy's mouth. The boy struggled, panicking because of what was outside—what was *always* outside—and because of Dez's hold, her strength, the sharp stink of her unwashed body, the blood and dirt on her hands. The gun in her other hand.

But Dez pulled the boy close, pressing him against her breasts, curving her shoulder around him as if that could keep him safe.

Inside the bus the other children were frozen in postures of listening, their faces transformed into masks of fear and uncertainty. No one made a sound. Everyone held their breath as they listened and waited.

The only sounds were outside.

Those sounds.

Those awful sounds.

The slow, artless shuffle and thud of feet against the blacktop. The hiss of cloth as bodies brushed past the sides of the bus. The low, endlessly desperate moans that spoke of bottomless hungers.

In the grass alongside this stretch of highway even the birds and crickets had fallen silent. It had been half a year since these moans began to fill the air, and the animals had learned their lessons. The incautious—insect, bird, and mammal—died. The cautious few who survived had learned to be quiet, to be still. To be unheard and unseen.

The children inside the bus knew that lesson, too. Even the little boy who now clung to Dez, fearing her less than he feared the things passing by. He did not speak again. He barely breathed.

The moment stretched and stretched, becoming excruciating. *How long this time,* wondered Dez. *How many?*

And what was happening inside the other busses? She strained to hear, but there were only the dead sounds from outside. The *wrong* sounds.

No screams. No gunfire.

Thank god.

For now…thank god.

Then…

Nothing.

A silence that at first felt filled with promise like a cocked fist, and then emptier. Emptier and then finally empty.

Dez sagged back, exhaling the air that had burned to poison in her lungs. The little boy looked up at her, his eyes huge and filled with ghosts.

"Are they gone?" he said, more mouthing the words than speaking them aloud.

She pushed him back gently, handing him off to one of the older children, a girl of eleven. Dez put a finger to her lips and turned so that everyone on the bus saw the gesture. They nodded. Those who could nod. Those whose minds could process the signal.

Dez rose and moved toward the back of the bus. The creatures had been going that way, past them, heading south along the highway. All of the windows on the bus were blocked out, covered with pieces of cloth or cardboard held in place with duct tape. Sloppy but effective. She waved the kids away who crouched on the rear bench seat and they moved without comment, casting frightened looks at the opaque window behind them. The only other adult on the bus, Biel, a former math teacher with a pinched face and a bruised cheek that was fading from purple to yellow, also moved away from Dez. Biel's eyes met hers and immediately flicked away. He was silent. The bruise on his face was a reminder of the least of things that could happen to noisy people. He'd seen Dez kill someone who couldn't keep quiet. Not a kid, though; it had been an adult who they'd picked up along the way but who was a noisy troublemaker, whiner and complainer. The kind of person who couldn't hold his tongue even when it meant drawing the attention of the dead. Dez Fox had warned him twice. On that third time she hadn't said a word but had dragged the man to the door of the bus, drove a Buck hunting knife into his heart and threw him out into the road. The following morning, when the caravan had started up, they'd driven over what was left of his bones.

Dez moved past the math teacher and knelt on the bench seat. The thick cardboard covering the glass was loose at one corner, held in place with a tiny square of weak Velcro. She peeled it back, careful to minimize the sound, and then peered out.

There were at least forty of them.

Mostly men, a few women. All clad in the bloodstained shreds of forest camouflage battle dress uniforms. Their weapons and gear hung from belts and harnesses, or trailed behind them on straps. A few still wore helmets. They all wore the traces of the wounds that had killed them. Savage bites that had stolen their lives and futures away along with flesh and bone.

Every single one of them was a soldier.

National Guard, thought Dez. Coming from the north.

Her heart had long since broken, but now the pieces sank to a lower place in her chest. She resealed the window, turned and sat heavily on the bench, lowering her gun. Dez rubbed her tired eyes and felt the wetness of tears. She looked at her fingertips. Then she felt the weight of other eyes and looked up to see so many pale faces staring at her. A few were empty of anything except a lingering and vacuous shock, but most of them held some sparks of hope in their fearful expressions. No one spoke but those expressions asked the questions.

Are they gone?

Are we safe?

How could she answer? How could she even speak?

Dez felt immensely weary. She'd been at the heart of this thing, there from the very first bite. She and her partner, JT Hammond, had been the officers responding to the first attack. They'd tried to contain it, but even then, even when it was small, it was already racing out of control.

When everything fell apart, Dez and a handful of adult survivors had bundled a couple of hundred kids into a convoy of school busses and lit out for Asheville, North Carolina, where there was a rumor of a safe zone. But they'd had to detour time and time again, losing days, then weeks, and finally months. Jammed roads, forest fires, destroyed bridges, washouts, floods, and massive swarms of the hungry dead had forced them to find alternate routes. And then there were the nuclear wastelands created when the military dropped bombs to try and contain the spread. *Dumb fucks,* thought Dez. All they'd accomplished was to kill the last of the living in those cities and turn them into more of the dead, except now they were radioactive zombies. It only reinforced Dez's belief that humans were too goddam stupid to survive.

She'd lived this long because she was too mad at God to lay down and die. And because there was hope. Thin and threadbare, but there.

Now this.

This…

Dez knew where those soldiers had come from; knew it as surely as if they had spoken to her with their dead voices. The Appomattox River rescue station was twenty miles up this road. Dez didn't want to look at the skeletons of the four horses and six cows they'd used to pull the bus all these months. The animals had made it to within an easy day's walk of the rescue station and then a swarm of the dead had come out of the woods. Dez and Biel had fought them, but only for a while. They'd killed thirty-six of the dead, but as that day wore on more than two hundred zombies were drawn to the sound of gunfire.

They didn't have enough bullets to win that kind of fight. The horses and cows all died.

So, during a lull, Dez and Biel dragged the corpses of the ones she'd killed over to the bus and did her best to stack them around the vehicle. Then they wrapped rags around their own mouths, used bunches of weeds as paintbrushes, and painted the sides of the bus in the black worm-infested blood of the zombies. They were careful not to get any on their skin. It was horrible work and then only abandoned it after a fresh wave of the dead came staggering out of the woods.

The presence of the rotting corpses and the stink from the tainted blood kept the fresh waves of dead away from the bus. Those creatures were not attracted to putrescence. They only hungered for warm, living flesh.

Dez kept her kids safe in the bus and the nights and days passed in silent horror. They lived in that bus—stretching out their food, trying to ignore the stink of all those kids using buckets for toilets. Enduring. Weeping silently. Screaming into bunched-up jackets so as not to draw down death.

In the darkest parts of the night, as wave after wave of zombies passed by, Dez wondered—as she always did—about the other busses. Had any survived? If so, how many?

Had Billy survived?

Her on-again-off-again boyfriend, Billy Trout, had been in one of the other busses during the storm. She hadn't seen him in more than five months. Three times wandering refugees had told her about seeing groups of children walking with adults along the road. Or about busses blackened by fire or splattered with blood. She had no idea if the refugees were mad or accurate, or if these were even the children from Stebbins. Everyone who was alive was fleeing, and a lot of people were headed to Asheville.

If the safe zone there was even real.

If any of it was real.

The Appomattox River rescue station was supposed to be real, though. Too many people swore to it. There were signs, freshly painted, all along this road.

But now this.

The National Guard station had been their only beacon of hope. It was supposed to be maintained by a strong unit of soldiers who had food, shelter and medical care, and all of it under the protection of tanks and heavy weapons. A fortress that not even the dead could overwhelm.

It was up this road.

It was in the direction where this pack of zombies had come from.

Dez saw the hope in all of those young eyes.

She wanted so badly to scream.

~2~

Rachael Elle

It was quiet.

If there was one thing that Rachael had to identify as the part about the end of the world that she didn't expect, it was the silence. In video games and horror movies there was always music to announce something bad was going to happen. Bad guys had theme songs, and ambient music to build anxiety to big climaxes. She didn't realize how much background noise existed in real life until it was all gone.

She didn't realize how alone she was.

Now she eagerly waited for the scarce sounds of birds and other animals, anything to keep her company as she walked silently down the freeway. Anything to fill the silence.

Anything but the moans of the dead.

Those were the sounds she heard in her nightmares. Those were the sounds she heard while she was awake.

Nervously checking her weapons again, she scanned around. The road she was walking down was empty on her side for a while, with abandoned cars stacked up bumper to bumper across the median. Wrecked cars, smashed and burned out in some cases, littered the edges of the road. The wind whistled through the metal, rattling car doors left ajar and fluttering scraps of paper and plastic like leaves.

And bodies.

There were more bodies than she could bear to count. She avoided getting to close to any of the clusters of cars, the piles of dead. She didn't want to deal with something grabbing her when she wasn't expecting it. It was harder traveling in this world without someone having her back.

Rachael wished she'd asked someone to come with her, but she couldn't risk any of them on this trip. They were safe in the hospital. It was probably only going to be a temporary shelter for her group, but it would do. For now, at least. They had the supplies they needed, people around, a defense system. Plus, when she came back she needed a definitive place to meet them. A rally point. If they were wandering, she'd never find them again.

Brett wasn't happy she was leaving. In the two months it took them to get to out of New York and make their careful way south they'd taken on being co-leaders for the group. They weren't voted in or anything as formal as that; it was just something that had happened naturally. They'd been friends for so long, they were in sync. Even when fighting they had each other's backs.

But she couldn't ask him to leave the group. The group needed him to be there. He was big and powerful, he *looked* like a hero, and that calmed everyone else. It made them feel safe. Without Brett, Rachael knew, there would be panic and chaos. He would keep the group safe; he would keep them all together.

However Rachael knew that Brett was as terrified as everyone else, but she also knew that he was trying to act brave for her. She also knew that acting brave was sometimes enough. Fake it 'til you make it. She hoped that by leaving him in charge he would man up, get more confident, *become* tougher. Like her and some of the others, Brett still wore the hero costume he'd made for Comic Con. Thor, prince of Asgard. All leather and lightweight chainmail. Rachael wore her warrior woman costume, also made of leather reinforced with metal. At first they kept their costumes because it was nearly impossible to bite through those materials, but now they made a statement. To the others in their party and to each of them.

"Stay alive."

That's what Brett had said to her before she left, hugging her tightly as if he'd never see her again. She promised him she'd come back alive and in one piece.

Nice promise, easily said.

Rachael's hands nervously traced the ridges in her sword as she cast around, walking quickly and silently. In the last months, her sword hadn't left her side. It wasn't the one that had been part of her costume. This one had been scavenged from the hotel room of one of the event's vendors. He'd been a knife smith who sold everything from Klingon *bat'leth* to steel katanas to perfect replicas of the swords from each of the *Lord of the Rings* movies. The vendor hadn't been in his room and Rachael had no idea what happened to him. When she and Brett had begun to raid the other hotel rooms for supplies and food, they'd found the cache of weapons. It had been a godsend. Truly. Rachael had collapsed on the floor, clutching an armful of sheathed swords to her chest, and wept.

Now she carried one of those swords, an exact but functional replica of the sword carried by the elf lady Arwen in *The Fellowship of the Ring*. It was a real weapon with a razor-sharp edge, and she had the matching daggers as well. She kept them oiled and honed and ready, and those weapons had saved her life too many times to count. She was not an expert fencer, but that didn't matter. When you're fighting Orcs you don't need finesse and fancy footwork. Rachael favored slashing and working fast, taking them out with shots to the head as quickly as possible. Or chopping through their legs and letting the less skilled members of their team finish them with blunt force trauma to the head.

Orcs. That's what her group called the hungry dead. Easier to think of them as movie monsters, because the heroes could always cut their way through armies of Orcs. Heroes always won.

Right?

Yeah…maybe. But not always. They'd lost most of their friends in the first day. The rest didn't make it out of New York. There were other cosplayers that had made it out of the Avengers Tower—the hotel where they'd barricaded themselves the first few weeks—and civilians. Lots of civilians. Besides the group of thirty-two they'd gotten out of the hotel at New York Comic Con, they'd picked up more and more survivors as they took the trek to New Jersey.

But there were more people out there. There had to be. For the few months that they had been at the hospital they'd sent out small groups, looking for survivors, trying to bring them to safety. After the fall, civilizations had scattered. Cities were dangerous, and from what they could tell any survivors had vanished into the countryside.

There were rumors that there were camps of survivors further out, that the government had safe places they'd set up that hadn't fallen. Survivors meant more people. But no one could give her a definitive answer on where.

That's why Rachael had left Brett, had left the group behind at the hospital. It was safe there, hopefully. There was food and power, enough beds for her people, and they'd managed to clear out all of the Orcs. It was their haven, at least for now.

And she'd send people back. With the world in chaos, there needed to be a safe place for survivors.

But she couldn't make this trip with all of them. It would have taken them too long to try to find any survivors and get back, and she couldn't risk their lives. They weren't warriors, the people that they'd saved. They were scared. They would slow her down, and the more people there were, the larger the chances that they would lose some of them. Better she went out alone, find the camps, see if she could find any refugees that she could bring back to the safety of the hospital or, in turn, make sure there was a safe place that her and her group could stand a chance of starting their lives over again.

For someone who never played as a lawful good character, she really cared too much about saving people.

The sound of her boots was muffled against the pavement, and she was keeping a quick pace. Moving alone meant she could travel quickly, rest for shorter times, and hide easily, and since she'd left the hospital she'd covered a lot of ground. There were roaming hordes of Orcs on the road, though whether they were migrating somewhere together like geese or just happened to find each other when the world ended Rachael didn't know. All Rachael knew was that she wasn't taking on a horde alone.

So now she was traveling south as quickly as she could, on a fool's errand. She could tell that's what Brett had thought, though he never said it. Why should she go south, to the unknown, and leave their safe place behind? They had plenty of people here, plenty of food and supplies. How would she ever get back? Would she come back?

He didn't say it, but she could see the pain in his eyes. They'd lost everyone else. Now he could lose her too.

The wind carried the faint sound of a groan and the smell of death, and Rachael cast around, drawing her sword from the scabbard on her belt. She squinted into the sunlight ahead, eying the hazy silhouette, the hunched shape of a broken body that limped along the cracked pavement. She only saw one, though that didn't mean more weren't out of sight.

One she could take. She couldn't let these Orcs roam, hurt people, so she cleared them as she could.

Rachael walked towards the figure calmly, sword out and ready. It was a solo Orc, with tangled hair and half of her face tattered to shreds, which lunged at her the moment she got close, a bone chilling, inhuman sound escaping its throat the moments before Rachael sliced her sword through its head.

And then she was alone again in silence.

She couldn't think of those Orcs as what they'd been before. Rachael was not a killer. Rachael was a survivor, and she was doing what she had to do, but the moment she thought of these things as human beings she knew she would hesitate. And hesitation would be her death.

They were not human. They were monsters, like a video game villain's minions of darkness.

Except real.

That was the hardest part about all of this. After a life spent role-playing heroes and aliens, after years of live-action role-playing against Orcs, monsters, mutants and bands of killers in handmade costumes, this was real.

Real.

God.

Real.

~3~

The Ranger and the Dog

"What is it, boy?" murmured the big man.

He came to the edge of forest wall and squatted down next to where a huge dog stood. The animal was a mix of white shepherd and Irish wolfhound. One hundred and fifty pounds of muscle and fang, wrapped in strips of leather that were studded with heavy metal washers. Bite proof. The leather was oiled and worked to make it as silent as possible, and the dog—like the man—knew how to move without a sound. A helmet of thick iron-studded leather was buckled onto the dog's head. It made the animal look like one of the fighting dogs from ancient times.

The man was tall, in his fifties but muscular, with coarse blond hair that was going gray and blue eyes surrounded by crow's feet. He wore combat fatigue pants and a utility vest over a black t-shirt. The logo of the Army Rangers peeked above the vee of the vest.

The dog leaned slightly toward the road. His way of pointing. And the ranger narrowed his eyes to peer through the gloom of the woods and the bright sunlight of the midday road. The landscape was in a thousand shades of leaf green, bark brown, shadow gray and macadam black. But there in the middle of it was a bright yellow bus. Filthy, streaked with mud or possibly dried blood.

The ranger said nothing for a long time, watching the bus. If it had been empty and derelict the dog would not have hung back out of sight of the road. Something was in there. Alive or dead, but unseen.

A sound. Muffled, a furtive metallic creak.

Someone was opening a door on the far side of the bus. In the still air the creak sounded loud and alien. The hinges needed grease and whoever was on that bus needed his ass kicked. Might as well ring the damn dinner bell.

The dog stiffened and the ranger's hand slid to his hip and drew the long knife from its sheath. It was a Marine Corps Ka-Bar fighting and utility knife with a seven-inch straight blade with a clip point. The knife, like the man and the dog, was no virgin.

There was another sound. Very soft this time. A faint scuff of a shoe on the blacktop. The man and dog remained absolutely still.

A figure stepped out from the other side of the bus, moving with caution, creeping around the end of the bus, looking right and left, up and down the empty road. The figure was slim, dressed in filthy ragged clothes.

A girl.

The ranger guessed her as thirteen or fourteen. Young, but with visible swell of breasts and hips. Maybe pretty in a different version of the world. Now she merely looked young, and lost, ragged, and absolutely terrified. He could read that in her jerky, uncertain movements, in the birdlike jerk of her head as she tried to look in every direction at once.

Scared.

The dog uttered the smallest of whines, only loud enough for the man to hear. There was blood on the girl's face, and her shirt was torn, revealing the strap and part of a cup of a functional bra. The ranger tried not to read an even worse story into the state of her clothes. There were a lot of ways in which someone's clothes could get torn out here. Snagging it on a crooked branch, evading the clutching fingers of the dead. Lots of ways.

He did not want to calculate all of them. His heart was scarred enough already.

The girl looked over her shoulder, back at the bus, then with a small cry she broke and ran. Running across the road, away from the bus. Not running toward safety. No. She was fleeing from that bus.

"Shit," growled the big man.

And then he was up and running.

The girl was headed almost toward him, though he was sure she hadn't seen him or the dog. She was bolting for cover and a second later it was apparent why.

A man's voice punched its way through the still air.

"The bitch is getting away. Get her!"

The bus rocked on its springs as heavy bodies moved within it, and then four men came running around the end of the bus.

"There!" cried one, pointing, and they tore after the fleeing girl. The men were even filthier than their quarry, each of them dressed in soiled jeans, grimy t-shirts, sneakers. One wore a John Deere billed can swung backward on his tangled black hair. They had knives on their belts, and one had a machete in his hand. He was the one who'd spotted the girl and he waved his buddies on with the big, flat blade.

The girl shrieked and ran faster, veering away from the forest now to try and gain speed on the flat road. It was a bad choice, but then there seemed to have been a lot of bad choices in this kid's life. All of the good choices had been taken away from her by circumstances, bad luck, and men like these.

All the hair stood up along the dog's back and he bared his fangs. His powerful body trembled with savage need.

"Baskerville—*go*," snapped the ranger. "Hit, hit, hit!"

The dog burst from the woods onto the road and galloped toward the closest of the men. Not barking, not howling. Making no sounds but the clicking of its nails on the hardtop. The four men did not see the dog until it was almost on them. Then the last man in the string jerked around, seeing the gray monster bearing down on him. He screamed a warning as he tore a hunting knife from his belt.

The scream was too late. The knife, too small.

Baskerville struck the man like a missile, crushing him backward, slamming him down, tearing at him, tearing new screams from him.

The other men whirled, seeing the dog and then seeing the figure that was running directly toward them. The man with the machete slapped one of the others on the shoulder.

"Joey, get the bitch," he snarled, unimpressed by the middle-aged man. "Zucco and me'll dance this motherfucker."

Joey, a twenty-something with fresh scratch marks on his cheeks, pointed to the dog and its victim. "Holy shit, Bob, lookit Hank!"

"Screw Hank," growled the leader. "He was never worth shit anyway."

He used his machete to point to the girl, who was running up a hill two hundred yards down the road.

"Go drag that slut back here. We ain't even had a chance to break her in yet. Now git!"

Joey, his face ashen as he stared at Baskerville and the red thing on the ground, backpedaled a few paces, then turned and ran off. He was very fast.

The ranger slowed to a cautious walk, and one of the other two men tapped the leader.

"I got this, Bob," said Zucco. He was a bull of a man with heavy shoulders, tattooed arms and a heavy red beard. "Whyn't you go see about that damn mutt."

The ranger smiled. He had thick blond hair, blue eyes, and a smile that made him look like the guy who used to play Captain America. "This is the part where I'm supposed to tell you to lay down your weapons," he said as if this was a reasonable conversation. "This is the part where I'm supposed to appeal to your human decency and try to talk you off the ledge so you can reclaim your humanity."

Zucco said, "What…?

"But here's the thing," said the ranger, "I already used up today's whole ration of 'give a shit'. So…basically it sucks to be you."

"You crazy or something?" growled Zucco.

"It's come up in therapy." The ranger stopped and glanced up the road. Joey was gaining on the girl. "Shit." He clicked his tongue and the dog suddenly raised his head from what was left of Hank's throat. The ranger pointed with his Ka-Bar. "Save."

It was all he said.

The dog barked once and then leapt over the corpse and ran. Bob tried to chop him with the machete, but the dog jagged sideways to avoid the blade and tore past him, racing to catch up with the man and the girl.

The ranger turned back to face the remaining men. Zucco was on his left and Bob on his right. Both men were big and strong, both were decades younger, both were armed with heavy blades.

The ranger was still smiling. "You put your hands on that girl?" he asked. "You rape that kid?"

"Not yet," said Bob, grinning to show yellow teeth, "but the day's young."

"Just caught her," agreed Zucco. "Still fresh off the shelf."

"You her old man?" asked Bob. "Or you looking to tear off a piece for yourself?"

The ranger's smile, bright as it was, did not reach as far as his eyes. They were cold, blue stones in his weathered face. He nodded toward the bus. "You have any other kids in there?"

"What's it to you?" demanded Bob.

"Where'd you get that bus? It has Pennsylvania plates."

Zucco shook his head and took a threatening step toward the ranger, who did not flinch or even move. "Why are we talking to this dickhead?"

The ranger ignored him and addressed Bob. "You boys running with the NKK?"

"We're not with them," said Bob quickly.

"Really?"

"Bob," warned Zucco, "look at him, he's military. He's with that team out of Farmville. Those Free Scouts."

"Not exactly," said the ranger. "But they're stand-up guys. Met a bunch of them last week and they said there were two or three teams of NKK dickheads working this stretch of highway."

Bob said nothing, but Zucco actually put his left hand behind his hip. It was a bit late, though. The words NU KLUX KLAN had been visible through the dirt on his skin.

"For the record," said the ranger, "'Nu' Klux Klan is probably the stupidest name I've ever heard, and I've heard some real corkers."

"Yeah? Well kiss my ass," snapped Bob. "It *means* something."

"It means what, exactly? Please, tell me, I'm fascinated."

Bob sneered. "People think the world went all to hell because of some plague or bioweapon, but that ain't it. This is God testing us. He saw us fuck everything up by letting kikes and niggers and wetbacks take over, and this is how He's going to set it all right. He shook things up, just like when that flood thing happened. When this is all over, there ain't going to be nothing but pure whites running this world and we'll live like kings."

The ranger burst out laughing. "Holy shit. Seriously? You *believe* that shit or are you messing with me?"

"It's the way it is," growled Zucco. "It's the way it should be."

"You're saying that inbred mouth breathers are the meek who are supposed to inherit the Earth?"

"We ain't meek. We're the chosen people."

"Oh, so you're Jews?"

"What?"

"Jews. They're the chosen people. I seem to have read that somewhere in a book." He snapped his fingers. "What was it called now? Oh yeah, the Bible."

"You mocking us?" asked Bob, brandishing his machete.

"Um…yes? I thought that was clear," said the ranger. "What with my mocking tone and all."

"You're going to laugh out of the other side of your face," began Bob, but his words were cut off by the sound of a terrible high-pitched scream that came rolling at them down the road, it was chased by the echo of a deep-chested howl of red triumph.

"Oh, Jesus…," murmured Zucco. "Joey…"

"Personally," said the ranger, "I doubt you cats have Jesus on speed-dial."

He moved into them. The Ka-Bar rose, blurred, became fluid, moved like light as it knocked aside the other blades and filled the air with glittering rubies. Bob and Zucco simply ended. One moment they were there, big, deadly, feral, and the next they were disconnected pieces of meat that no longer looked human.

The smile never left the ranger's face. And it never reached his cold, blue eyes.

He stepped back and went still, listening to the air. The echo of Baskerville's howl had not even finished bouncing off the trees. The killing of these two men was nothing, a moment out of his life, and he turned away from them without further thought.

He ran to the bus, circled it, saw the open door, and went inside.

There was no one else in there.

However there was a line of eighteen human scalps hung above the driver's seat. Some of the hair was fine, the way a child's hair is.

The smile leaked away from his face and he sagged against the dashboard.

"Ah, Christ," he breathed.

Then he backed off the bus, turned and ran up the road to find Baskerville. And to find the girl.

~4~

Dez Fox

Dez heard Biel step down from the bus.

"Were they...?" began the math teacher, then he faltered. Dez turned to watch him as he looked at the retreating backs of the dead soldiers and then looked the other way, toward the Appomattox River rescue station. Dez waited for him to say something else, but all she heard was a tiny noise that might have been a whimper.

She scanned the woods. Route 625 ran through dense woods but the last six months without road crews cutting back the weeds had resulted in a riot of growth. Weeds, creeper vines, kudzu, and tall grasses grew all the way to the edge of the blacktop, and sprouted up in every crack. If things didn't turn around then this road would vanish completely in ten years. Mother Nature was a hungry and relentless bitch, she knew. Then she wondered if that would be a good thing or bad. Ever since the fucking brain trust in the military dropped all those nukes, which in turned hit everything with electromagnetic pulses, none of the vehicles worked. The fleet of busses she'd taken out of Stebbins were dead. One here, and the others God knew where. They'd been separated during a bad, bad night long ago. A storm raged throughout this part of the state, and the bombs—nuclear and fuel-air had chased tens of thousands of people into their path. The drivers of the other busses had panicked as rivers of people and zombies swept toward them. Some of them took side roads, some just disappeared...and then all the engines died as the EMPs played their dirty backstabbing trick.

The zombies were gone now and the road was clear. The woods were still, too. If it wasn't for all the rotting corpses it would be a pretty day in the country, she thought. Blue sky, sunshine, a few puffy white clouds.

Appomattox was twenty miles from here. She could make it in less than six hours. Dez was leaned down to rawhide and whipcord. She could haul ass and even dumb as he was, Biel could defend a closed bus for a day. There were smart kids on that bus, and they'd learned how to be quiet. Could she risk leaving them for half a day? That had been her plan, to button up the bus and head out alone, find some buff young guardsmen and get them to come back with lots of balls and bullets to rescue the kids and save the day.

"Shit," she said.

Biel came and stood next to her. "What do we do now?"

Dez sighed. It was noon or a little after. Lots of daylight left. She could make it to the rescue station long before dark.

But why bother?

Why frigging bother?

"Dez...?" prodded Biel.

She wanted to slap him. Not because he was speaking out of turn—he wasn't, it was a reasonable question—but because it might make her feel better.

"I don't know," she said.

"We have to do something."

"Let me think," she said quietly.

But before she could come up with anything resembling a plan there was a sound off to her left. She and Biel turned. It was there, deep in the woods, still hidden by the tall weeds.

Even unseen, though, they knew what it was. They heard it. The crashing of heavy bodies moving clumsily through the overgrown foliage, and the moans.

Those terrible moans, lifted from a dozen dead throats.

No...more than that.

Dozens.

Or...hundreds.

Dez closed her eyes. If the kids weren't in the bus, if they didn't need her, there were ways to shut off those sounds. Rush into them and tear down as many as she could before there was nothing left of her. Or ride a bullet into the big black.

There were always doorways out.

Staying alive had fewer options. Even when there was no real hope left.

Dez Fox opened her eyes, turned, and gave Biel a shove toward the bus. "Go," she said. He did. She followed.

And the dead came.

~5~

Rachael Elle

Night.

Rachael found a sheltered spot with good concealment that also allowed her good lines of sight and escape. She strung trip wires, caught and cleaned a young rabbit, found water from a stream, and built a fire. The woods were filled with sounds, which she took as a good sign. Silence meant danger.

But night meant waiting. Night meant another day away from Brett during which something could have happened, another day their group could have been attacked, another night that the world would fall further into chaos. The longer this trip took, the more she was beginning to lose hope, though she wouldn't voice it to herself out loud. She hadn't seen any signs of survivors after leaving the hospital, and now she was somewhere in the middle of Nowhere, Virginia, though exactly how far through the state she wasn't sure. The map she'd found in a rest stop was confusing to read, and she was used to navsystems and Google maps. Reading old-fashioned paper maps was never a skill she'd thought she'd need to learn.

She would keep following 95 all the way to North Carolina, and then she'd turn back, find a different route home, and try to see whom she could find.

Alone during the long hours of darkness, trying to keep her mind from pulling her down into negativity, her thoughts drifted to the past. To her family.

"We're… your aunt and I….we're headed south… North Carolina."

That fractured message, distorted by failing phone signals, was the last thing Rachael had heard from her mom. Rachael had tried to call her the day the world went to hell, and after the third try had managed to get through. But the connection was bad and the call got dropped quickly.

Rachael had been left with a dead line and "I love you, Mom," left on her lips. It had been six months since her phone battery had died. Everyone else had ditched their phones. They were useless now. Rachael hadn't been able to give hers up. She kept holding onto the hope that they'd find somewhere with power, that the towers would work again. It was silly and pointless, but her phone was her lifeline in the world before, and here in the world after she wouldn't leave it.

Rachael played with her iPhone absentmindedly, flipping it over between her hands as she stared into the small fire she'd built. The last birds dove through the air, reveling in the early spring. It was still just cold enough that she needed to wrap herself in the wool and fur cloak she'd found in one of the rooms in the Avengers Tower, and days of exhaustion from walking and uneasy sleep were adding up, weighing her lids. She needed to find somewhere to sleep; somewhere with doors that locked, but that sounded like it required more effort than she wanted to give that moment. So instead she closed her eyes, just for a moment, wishing she had a shot of espresso or a five-hour energy. She was going to make sure she grabbed those the next time she saw any.

She conjured images of her mother in her mind. The ache was immense and even all this time hadn't dulled the pain. She tried not to cry in front of Brett or the others, but now…alone, out here where no one could see…the tears came in a flood. Sobs broke in her chest with the intensity of bare-knuckle punches. She caved forward with her face in her hands and wept for all that she had lost.

She missed the change in the woods. She did not hear the birds fall silent. Rachael was unaware of anything until the dead weight that slammed into her from behind and the pinch of teeth on her arm.

~6~

The Ranger and the Dog

The ranger left the dead behind and ran up the road, following the baying of his dog. Baskerville could sound a lot like a wolf when he wanted to. The hound was mostly silent in the heat of a fight, but when the killing was done he liked to tell the world. It was the dog's only bad habit, but in a world of the savage dead and even more savage living, it was a habit that the ranger was trying very hard to break.

He climbed up the steep slope of the highway and plunged down the other side, but slowed to a quick walk within a hundred yards of the crest. What was left of Joey littered the center of the road. Baskerville could act like a puppy and sometimes like a clumsy goof, but not in combat. Like the ranger himself, there was a switch that doused all interior light and left only something dark and predatory. Something more savage than the dead. Not cruel, but thorough in its desire to destroy. In that way Baskerville was very much like both of his grandparents—a combat white shepherd and a fierce but strange Irish wolfhound. The shepherd—whose name had been Ghost—had walked through the valley of the shadow with the ranger on countless missions. Back when the ranger had been a captain in a covert special ops group called the Department of Military Sciences. The wolfhound, Banshee, had been bred by a group of women called Arklight, and they had bred some bizarre qualities into the dog. The pups of Ghost and Banshee had each been powerful and individual, and each of them had gone into combat, too. Baskerville was still young, but all of the intelligence, instinct and ferocity of his forebears was fully alive in him.

As alive as Joey was dead.

The ranger flicked a quick look at the corpse, noting the type of damage Baskerville had done, looking for what he called 'recreational' damage as opposed to wounds inflicted to win the fight. There was definitely some of that. Baskerville sometimes went too far, dismembering a kill even if it wasn't food. It was something the ranger would have to work on, and for a couple of reasons. First and foremost, he wanted the dog to be a soldier and not a monster. And, second, he needed to trust the animal. He knew from dealing with his own personal damage and inner demons that the killer within needed to be kept on a leash.

Baskerville stood on the shoulder of the road, body pointed toward the woods, head turned to watch the ranger approach. The hound did not wag his tail or romp around. He stood like a statue, eyes fixed, mouth smeared with fresh blood.

"Where?" asked the ranger.

The dog turned and looked off into the forest and then back at the ranger.

"Find," said the man. "My pace."

The dog whuffed once, very softly. He always did that, a habit from his grandfather. Ghost had been able to understand a huge number of verbal commands and always seemed to answer with that *whuff.* A strange and wonderful animal, and Baskerville had all of his best qualities. And some of his grandmother's more dangerous and enigmatic traits. A weird dog for a weird world, mused the ranger.

The dog began to move, but then the ranger said, "Wait."

He knelt beside the animal, tore off a thick handful of grass and used it to wipe most of the blood away from the animal's muzzle and fur. Baskerville endured it with all of the bad grace of a child getting chocolate wiped from his face. He even contrived to roll his eyes with exasperation.

"Stop it," complained the ranger. "You want to scare that kid even more than she is?"

He finished and stood, then clicked his tongue once. Baskerville moved off immediately. The ranger looked up and down the road once more and then followed.

~7~

Rachael Elle

Rachael was stunned for a moment as she hit the ground hard, but she reacted as adrenaline surged, using her legs to push the Orc off, twisting her arm out of its teeth.

It struggled to its feet, but she was faster, rolling over her shoulder into a crouch, dragging her dagger and holding it ready. She lunged forward, swinging her arm down to try to drive the knife through the Orc's skull, but her sharp metal blade bounced off, slicing through rotting skin but not penetrating the thick bone. Crying out in frustration as the Orc reached out for her with ragged nails, not phased by her attack, Rachael struggled to push it back, this time driving the dagger down hard through the softer bone at the top of the skull.

As it slumped to the ground so did she, hands shaking from adrenaline. Then she sat up, her hands running over her arm with feverish intensity to make sure that her leather bracer had held. The teeth marks were indented in the thick leather, but nothing broke through and she almost wept with relief.

But she couldn't sit long. One Orc meant more were close behind. She'd learned early on that Orcs seemed to find each other, traveling in hordes, a wave of disease and death washing over the world.

Using her boot to shovel dirt over the fire, Rachael tugged her bags back over her shoulders then buckled her knives and swords back on. She took a moment to stare down at the Orc, the rotted skin peeling back from the mouth and forehead, unseeing eyes staring past her face into the unknown. It didn't feel real. It still felt like a video game, like she was in a very realistic virtual reality, that when it got to be too much she could press start and go back to reality.

Her cellphone had fallen into the dirt and she picked it up gently, brushing the dust from the screen and tucking it into a pocket on her bag. One day she'd leave the phone behind. One day she'd give up her hope to return to the world before.

Today was not that day.

Back on the road, Rachael tugged her bag up over her shoulders, eyes casting around as she tried to find a sign for where she was, what direction to head in. Some of the signs on I95 had suffered significant damage, and she constantly had to compare her old paper map with fallen signs and old landmarks.

Rachael had driven this road a couple of times over the years, on family road trips or trips with her friends. Things looked so different from car windows, like a movie. Rachael passed a rest stop, a flicker of a memory from long ago, a kid from a different life peering out the dark car windows over her Gameboy. There was trash scattered around here now, fallen fences and abandoned cars. It looked so different, like something she recognized but also unrecognizable. Like that feeling you get in a dream when you know something but it's not exact.

There were a handful of Orcs wandering around, and Rachael cleared them quickly, her sword a blur as it hissed through the air, bodies slumping to the ground.

Inside the rest stop there was nothing standing, though bodies of fallen dead scattered around in heaps. Stepping around them carefully, Rachael grabbed a few bags of chips and some candy from the store, tucking a few five-hour energies into her pack.

Turning to leave, she noticed something written on the wall of the information center. It was hard to see, though it looked like it had been purposely wiped off and distorted. Half of a map taped to the sign was ripped, a few pieces lying around the floor. But it looked like the start of a circle, or some sort of writing on the map. Maybe that's where there were survivors? Could the information center be the place that someone had posted directions to a safe zone?

Squinting at the wall, the smudged out letters, she could make part of the words. *Appoma- Ri-er Re- Stati-.*

Picking up the few pieces of map papers she could find, Rachael pieced them together carefully on the table. Some of the crucial pieces were missing, but she could tell a general direction. Somewhere off the next exit there seemed to be something. She could see the edges of a circle drawn on the map, though what city or landmark they identified was lost. But maybe there would be more signs as she headed that way.

She pulled out her map and scoured it for anything that might contain the words written on the wall. The font was so small it was hard to read, and she pulled the map as close to her face as possible as she looked for anything, any hints at all.

Finally something caught her eyes. *Appomattox River Rescue Station.* That had to be it! It was in about the same place that the shredded map had indicated something. Copying as much of the information onto the new map as she could, she tucked that into a pouch at her waist, heading back onto the road and looking for a sign of an exit.

She wasn't sure how long that information had been there. She had no proof that it was actually legitimate, but for now she had nothing else to go on. This was the first sign of possible life, first hint of a location of people, and she was going to take it and hope for the best.

Turning off the next exit, avoiding the pileups of cars and bodies cautiously, she turned her eyes to the horizon. There was, at least, a chance—a chance of survivors, a chance there would be someone out there.

She just hoped she wasn't too late.

~8~

Dez Fox

It took half an hour for the swarm of dead to pass by. It felt like ten hours. Biel huddled down with the kids, both giving and taking comfort, while Dez crouched by the front of the bus and peered out through a peephole. Some of the dead came down the road from the direction of the rescue station. More soldiers, but also quite a few ordinary folk. Farmers and people dressed in whatever clothes they wore when they died. There was no uniformity to what the citizens wore either, nor was there any particular variety. In movies about the end of the world there were usually people dressed as clowns, as nuns, as bakers, as convenience store clerks. Like that. Each different so that the filmmakers could make some kind of statement. Not here. These zombies were just people. Unique in that they had each been an individual with a life, a future, a past, an identity, but turned homogenous in death. They were all hungry, all torn, all ragged, all beginning to rot, all undead.

And all of them would have battered their way through the cracked windows of the old school bus if they knew what was inside. From the oldest to the youngest, the strongest to the weakest, they would become an attacking army. Only the rotting flesh of their own kind made them pass by without pausing, without noticing, without knowing.

These thoughts shambled through Dez's mind with the same slow, deliberate gait as the zombies. She had never been the top student in her class, except in the Army and the police academy. In school she'd been a C student cruising the edges of frequent suspension and likely expulsion. But that did not mean she was not a thinker. The long hours of the nights since the fall of man had given her so much time to brood and ponder that she now considered herself a philosopher on the nature and specifics of the apocalypse. A new field of study and one in which she could hold her own as an expert against anyone.

That thought, though, made her immediately think of Billy Trout. He'd broken the story of the rogue bioweapon that had caused all this. His live broadcasts, placed on YouTube and blasted through social media, had focused the eyes of the world on Stebbins County. His pleas for mercy had kept the town from being thoroughly sterilized, including the school where the last of the living had been hiding. And, afterward, when the convoy of busses had set out, he stopped several times each day to give updates on the fall.

This is Billy Trout, reporting live from the apocalypse.

It had almost been a joke except that no one thought it was funny.

Where was Billy? He was the real thinker. He was the one who had always been in touch with his emotions. More so than Dez, who'd always mocked him for it.

She would give so much to have him back here right now. To hear his voice, even if he was saying something that made her mad. She'd even sit through a whole day of his liberal politics if it meant having him back. If it meant knowing he was alive.

Damn.

Outside a last zombie staggered out of the woods, a fat woman walking on a shattered foot, limping slower than the others, straggling behind.

"Come on you stupid cow," muttered Dez, too quiet even for the huddled kids to hear.

The dead woman fell to her knees, took an excruciating time getting back to her feet, walked five steps, fell, got up. Rinse repeat.

It took nearly fifteen minutes for the crippled corpse to walk to the crest of the hill.

Dez relaxed by very slow degrees. She went to the back of the bus to watch the lame zombie vanish over the hill, then to the front again to make sure that one really was the last.

It was.

For now, at least.

The children sat in silence, none of them visibly reacting the end of the immediate threat. They were becoming too weary to even show their fear. More than half of them had fallen asleep. A naïve person, Dez knew, would look at those sleeping bodies and think that it was a sign of the resilience of youth. Dez would want to smack that person for being an idiot. These kids were so deep into habitual shock that they were retreating into exhausted sleep, and that sleep was in no way refreshing.

Dez moved past the small bodies and tapped Biel on the shoulder and nodded to the door. He followed her outside and they walked a few paces away from the bus.

"Look," she said, "there were a bunch of farmers in that last batch, and I saw some yesterday, too."

"So what?" asked Biel.

"So this is farm country, or near enough to it."

"Again…so what? If you're thinking about holing up inside a farmhouse then you're nuts. It didn't keep the farmers from getting killed."

"Maybe," she said, "and maybe they tried to make a fight of it. Or went running to help neighbors and got bit. Whatever. This bus is getting rank and we're nearly out of food. Most farmers have stores of stuff, and they have rain barrels. And a barn could be reinforced pretty easily. They're stronger than houses and don't have as many windows."

"So, you're suggesting what? That we take the kids on a class trip to some hypothetical farm somewhere? Those woods are full of the dead."

"No, Einstein, that's not what I'm saying," she snapped. "I'm saying *I* go looking for a farm. Me. I can move faster alone. I can scout around and come back."

"What if you don't find anything?"

"Then I'll try a different direction tomorrow morning, and somewhere else tomorrow afternoon. And I'll keep trying until I find something better than a rusting tin box on an open road."

Biel looked badly shaken at the thought. "You'd leave us alone?"

"Not for long. I'd be out a couple hours at a time. You stay here and keep the bus buttoned up. You can do that, can't you?"

"I--."

"You *can* do that," she repeated, putting a more encouraging stress on her words. "C'mon, man, you've done this a lot of times. You're a pro. And I won't be far away. If the shit really hits the fan fire a shot and I'll hear it. But...*only* do that if things are going totally south. Don't do it just because you get spooked, you hear me?"

He nodded. It was a quick, nervous, uncertain nod, though.

Dez flashed him her very best smile and patted him on the shoulder. "That's my man."

Biel actually blushed.

Dez went back to the bus, stuffed the last two full magazines for her Glock into a pocket, slung a water bottle over her shoulder, and left without saying a word. The kids didn't even seem to notice. Or care.

Or anything.

At the edge of the forest she turned and waved to Biel, who stood in the doorway of the bus. He lifted one uncertain hand and then fled inside and closed the door.

"Jesus," Dez breathed, "what am I doing?"

She turned and ran into the woods.

Dez wasn't sure what to expect, or if there would be anything worth finding. Most of this area was state forest. But there had been farmers. A lot of farmers.

There had to be farms.

The sun scorched a hot line across the afternoon sky as she put mile after mile between her and her kids.

~9~

Rachael Elle

After a few long hours spent walking off of the exit, Rachael stopped to rest. She shrugged off the backpack and let it fall and then slumped down with her back to a burned out shell of a state police cruiser. The woods and road were quiet except for insect and bird sounds. That was good, that was safe.

Her rest period lasted less than a minute. The quiet was suddenly shattered by the frantic sound of whinnying, which was nearly a scream in the silence. A horse?

"God," she cried as she jumped to her feet, grabbed her bag, and instantly took off running after the sound. There was something else alive in this area besides her, and she was going to find it.

It didn't take her long to track the sound. It was close and it was in trouble. Rachael knew that she was running into danger, but the cry of that horse mattered more. It touched something deep inside her.

Not far beyond the trees were acres of fenced fields, the long grass rustling in the wind. Ducking under the posts, Rachael moved swiftly towards the barn in the center, scanning around nervously for possible threats. She could see movement along the side of the barn, and pulled one of her daggers, creeping closer silently. There were Orcs, though she couldn't tell if the smell was from them or from the barn, a handful of them that were trying reach through the open barn windows. There was no way they could get into the barn—the fields were fenced and gates locked, and the big barn door led directly into the fields. There was at least one horse in the barn though, Rachael could hear it, though why it didn't just leave the barn she wasn't sure.

Using the pommel of her dagger she banged it against the metal gate, the hollow clanging unnervingly loud.

"Over here, you ugly lumps!!" Rachael yelled, continuing to hit metal on metal. The Orcs, distracted by the sudden and new sound, turned to stumble towards her, lunging with moldy hands reached out for her, flesh and sinew hanging from bone. Pulling her elven dagger out of her belt, she waited until the first one was within arm's reach, then drove the dagger into the back of its skull. It crumpled to the ground as the second and third one reached the gate. She cleared the group without any problems, holding her breath as the rancid smell washed over her, breathing out her mouth and fighting to keep down the power bar she'd eaten earlier. Wiping the thick black blood on the grass, she kept it in hand, just in case, and moved over to the barn cautiously. The frantic cries of the horse had stopped, though she could still hear the hooves against the hard floor and deep snorting.

Could a horse become infected? Rachael hadn't come across many animals since New York, and a mental image of a half decomposed horse carrying an Orc across a field as if it were riding into battle flashed across her eyes. It was almost comical, something absurd from a corny movie, but she shook that off quickly. This wasn't a movie, and if animals could become infected there was a whole lot of new problems they were going to run into. Dead humans were bad enough; dead wolves were terrifying.

She peeked around the corner hesitantly, worried about what she might find. The horse was halfway down the barn, watching her with wild eyes. *Living* eyes.

Tucking her knife into her belt, she put her hands up in front of her, trying to calm the horse. It tried to back away, but the lead kept it in place. Rachael didn't need to imagine the horrors that this horse had seen in the last year. It probably thought she was going to try to hurt it.

"Shhhhh...it's okay." Rachael slowly inched her bag off her back and reached in, scouting for an apple. Taking a bite out of it and putting it in her hand, she moved closer to the horse, hand out, trying to tempt it with the treat. Its nostrils were flaring, watching her with panic, but it let her come closer.

"Look… look… it's an apple. You remember apples?" she asked in a calming voice, standing still with her hand out. The horse's ears flicked forward at the word apple. Rachael didn't move, letting the horse come to her. Its brown hair was matted and fur caked with mud and dried blood, but it looked to be in one piece—no gashes, cuts or bites.

Pablo—she already mentally named him Pablo after a horse she'd rode when she was a kid—shifted back and forth nervously, ears flicking, watching her every move, but let her approach, taking the bit of apple and munching on it eagerly.

"This isn't going to be easy," she said to him quietly. "It's going to be scary and dangerous. It's not a good place out there anymore. But I'm going to find survivors, and I'm going to find a safe place for everyone, okay? And we're going to make it a good world again."

Pablo nickered softly and she stroked his neck. Gently, calming him.

Rachael was relieved. Luck was on her side today. On horseback she could move faster, cover more ground. She could find survivors, and get back to Brett and their group easily.

"It's okay. See, we can stop the world from ending. We'll make it all okay."

~10~

The Ranger and the Dog

They moved through the wood with practiced ease, the dog leading and the man following. They went as fast as caution would allow, and not one step faster. There were no screams in the forest, which was encouraging.

But Baskerville suddenly stopped and looked off to his left. Not in the direction they'd been following. The ranger drew his fighting knife and crouched beside the dog, touching the animal's side in order to read the degree of tension. Baskerville was trembling. The dog did not fear the living. Not at all. But when there were zombies around the animal shivered like this. Even Baskerville feared the dead, and the ranger could understand why. Unlike human enemies, the dog could not use its fearsome fangs against the zombies. Canine instincts—or maybe it was some kind of prescience, the ranger didn't really know—made the dog fear the blood of the zombies. There were parasites in that black blood; tiny threadlike white worms, and they were the true monsters of this apocalypse. Genetically-modified larva that carried a chemical witch's brew cooked up in a Cold War bioweapons lab long ago. *Lucifer 113*. Conceived by Soviet scientists and then remodeled by a deranged prison doctor here in the U.S. Madness on all sides, and when the devil had slipped its chain the world was consumed.

Baskerville could not know or understand any of that, but it had a strong reaction to the presence of the dead. It would smash into them, knock them down, but it wouldn't bite. And the dog was even careful not to walk in spilled black blood. It's why Baskerville was still alive.

It's why the ranger was still alive. They were a team.

Baskerville was the best weapon against living human foes or against the packs of feral dogs that roved these woods. But it was the ranger who fought and killed the zombies.

The ranger tapped the dog's shoulder once. A question. *Close?*

Baskerville did not react, which was the answer. *No.*

Or at least not close enough to be an immediate threat. Nearby, though. The dog shivered, wanting to get away, so the ranger rose and used his knee to gently nudge the animal back toward the path they were following. Baskerville lingered a moment longer, giving an uncertain look to the dense forest, and then turned, sniffed to recapture the girl's scent, and took off.

The ranger slid his knife back into its sheath and followed.

The forest was a series of densely wooded hills with a few small streams cutting through it. The slopes and gullies were nothing to the dog, but the man felt his leg muscles begin to burn as he moved. He was fifty, not twenty, and this kind of thing was a young man's game. Once upon a time he would have run twenty miles of this for fun, but as he saw it that ship sailed, hit an iceberg, caught fire and sank. Now he felt every one of his years, every inch of scar tissue, every bit of calcification on broken bones. The kid they chased, though, must have been a marathon runner before the damned apocalypse. She was well ahead and seemed able to go through holes in the shrubbery where a rabbit wouldn't have tried.

Great natural athleticism will do that. So will stark terror.

Baskerville suddenly shot forward faster as the ground leveled out into an overgrown farm cornfield. As the ranger raced to catch up he saw the clear marks of small sneakered feet in the dirt. Ahead there was a rustling of something moving fast through the tall weeds and

"Circle," he called out and Baskerville cut suddenly left and really poured it on. He vanished into the corn but went wide to try and get in front of the fleeing girl. The girl was fast but the dog was faster. The ranger heard her voice rise in a sudden shriek. The girl had encountered the dog.

The ranger moved into the cornfield but he slowed his pace, then paused to call out.

"Girl," he said, pitching his voice to be heard but keeping urgency out of it. "Hey, kid…don't be afraid. My dog won't hurt you and neither will I."

There was no sound, no answer.

"Those guys back there…they can't hurt you anymore."

Nothing.

"I'm a soldier," he called. "My name is Captain Joe Ledger. My dog's name is Baskerville and he will not hurt you. We just want to help."

There was silence in the cornfield but the ranger—Ledger—thought it was different. A *listening* stillness.

"Please," he called. "I know you're scared. You're smart to be scared. I'm scared, too. But I'm a soldier and a father and I won't let anyone hurt you."

More silence except for the soft rustle of the corn.

Then a voice spoke. Young, trembling, frightened. Female.

"Leave me alone."

Ledger inched forward. "I can't, sweetheart. You're alone out here and there are more of those NKK freaks out there. You're safer with Baskerville and me."

"I can take care of myself," she said, and there was some iron mixed in with the fear.

"Not alone, kid. Heck, I don't even travel alone and I used to be with Special Forces." He had her exact location pegged now. Forty feet in and slightly to his right.

"Go away!" she yelled.

"Can't do it, darlin'," he said. "We good guys have to stick together."

"I don't need your help."

"Yeah, you do. There's some shamblers in the woods and they're coming this way. And when the rest of the NKK nutbags see what happened to their boys they're going to come hunting."

"I didn't do that. *You* did."

He moved closer, but he lowered his voice a little to disguise the fact. "Sure, I did that. But they won't know that. They're going to come looking for someone to hurt."

She sobbed. "Please…why can't you people just leave us alone?"

Us.

Did she mean the innocent? Or women in general? Or was she with a party? Ledger guessed that it was a bit of all three.

"Look, kid, I'm coming to you. I won't hurt you."

"Don't!"

"I have to, like I said. It's not safe out here."

"*You're* one of them."

He sighed. "No, I'm really not."

Ledger moved through the corn, doing it slow and making noise. So she heard, so she knew.

"Please...," she whimpered.

He found her in a small clearing. Baskerville sat watching her from ten feet away. The girl was a year or so older than he'd first thought. Maybe fourteen, but slim and undernourished. Her clothes were in rags and she had bruises on her face and arms. There were broken pieces of leaves and twigs in her filthy hair, and she sat huddled, shivering with exhaustion and terror. But there was fire in her eyes, though, and she clutched a sharp stone in one hand, ready to fight. Expecting to have to. Ledger knelt at the edge of the clearing.

"Listen to me," he said quietly, "I understand that you're terrified, and I know you don't know me from a can of paint, but I won't hurt you."

"That's what *they* said."

"And they lied. I bet a lot of people have lied to you. Your parents probably told you there were no monsters, but there are. The boogeyman is real and sometimes he's cold and dead and sometimes he's alive, like those freaks back there. But I'm not one of them."

She eyed him with enormous suspicion, the rock ready to strike.

Ledger crossed his legs and sat. He removed his knife from its sheath and tossed it lightly to land in front of her. "It's better than a rock."

The girl dropped the rock and snatched up the knife, raised it, held it ready to stab. Baskerville went *whuff,* but did not move.

"Where are you from, kid?" asked the ranger.

"I'm not a kid," she snapped.

"Okay. Sorry. Where are you from, *miss*?"

She said, "Richmond."

"Your family got out before they dropped the bombs?"

The girl said nothing, but after a moment she nodded.

"Are they still around? Your folks?"

The girl shook her head. A single bright tear fell down her dirty cheek.

"How?" he asked. "The walkers or…?"

She sniffed back her tears. "Them. The dead ones."

"Oh. I'm sorry."

"Another family took me in. We were together until…until…"

She stopped and Ledger didn't ask for details. They'd both heard enough horror stories. Retelling them only did harm.

"I was overseas when it started," he said. "On a job. I'm with—*was* with—the military, like I said. Things all went crazy while we were half a world away. By the time we got back everything was falling apart. I…I tried to get home, you know? My wife and our kid had gone to my uncle's place in Maryland. Nice big farm, lots of land, away from the cities." He shook his head.

After a long minute the girl asked, "What happened?"

He sighed again. "It took me too long to get home. You know how it is. The roads, the crowds, the walkers, the nukes. By the time I made it to my uncle's place there was nothing but burned fields and ashes where his house was."

"Your…your family…? Were they in the…you know?"

Ledger shook his head. "No. There were no bones. I looked. God help me I really looked. And the thing is, I don't even know if my wife made it to my uncle's place or not. Communication was lousy even in the first few days. I know she was *going* there, but that's all I know."

"What did you do?" The girl still held the knife, but no longer raised to strike. Instead she clutched it to her chest. Baskerville laid down and placed his big head on his front paws.

"I think I went a little crazy," said Ledger. "I looked everywhere I could, went to every refugee camp and rescue station. Spent months doing that. And then there was a while where I think I was out of my head."

Baskerville whined softly as if he understood.

"He helped me get through it all," said Ledger. "Big goof of a dog gave me a reason to keep moving, keep fighting, keep going."

The girl looked at the dog for a moment. If Ledger had wanted to he could have reached over and plucked the knife out of her hand, but he did not.

"His name's Baskerville? Like in the book?"

"Yup."

The girl nodded, and they sat for a moment. A breeze stirred the corn and starlings flew overhead.

"Lindsey," she said.

"What?" asked Ledger.

"My name's Lindsey. Lindsey Brewer-Munoz."

Ledger smiled. "Good to know you, Lindsey Brewer-Munoz."

"You're…Mr. Ledger?"

"Captain Joseph Edwin Ledger," he said. "My friends call me Joe."

She nodded but did not repeat his name.

"How long have you been alone?" he asked.

Her answer was a stubborn shake of the head. It wasn't information she wanted to share. Not yet. He accepted that, letting her set the rules.

"When did you meet those NKK lamebrains?"

Lindsey looked away and down. "This morning. Only a couple hours ago. I ran away and…" She shook her head again.

"They didn't mess with you?" he asked.

"No. They were…they were…"

She didn't finish the sentence and he didn't need to know what threats or promises the dead men had made.

"They're gone," he said.

Lindsey turned slowly and stared at him. She had very green eyes. "You killed all of them? All four?"

"We did," corrected Joe, nodding to Baskerville. "And I'm sorry if you saw any of it."

"Good," she said, and her pretty young face instantly became a mask of such utter hatred that Ledger almost recoiled. It saddened him, hurt him deeply to see so much contempt on a young woman's face. On any human face. It hurt worse to know that this girl would live with the knowledge of what almost happened to her, and have to bear the fear of the very real possibility of it happening in the future. Her innocence, or a chunk of it, had already been stolen from her. She would never again be able to believe that the world was not, at least in part, a truly vile place. And Ledger wanted very badly to put that genie back in the bottle, to seal it up, to make it not so, but the world was the world. Wishing for a better one wasn't going to change what had already happened.

He said, "I'm sorry."

The girl held onto the knife and the moment, ugly and raw, stretched and stretched.

Suddenly Baskerville leapt to his feet.

At the same moment Ledger heard the sounds coming from off to their left. The swish of cornstalks.

And the moans.

He shot to his feet, too. "Stay close," he ordered. There were more moans now. From their right. And more in front of them.

The dead were coming from all sides.

"Oh god," cried Lindsey and, still clutching the knife, she broke and ran into the cornfield, vanishing from sight.

~11~

Rachael Elle

Rachael and Pablo walked beneath a canopy of green trees. The road seemed to never end, though the signs for the River station were becoming more and more frequent, and newer looking the further she traveled, which Rachael took as a sign she was moving in the right direction. But she still hadn't seen any people, any survivors, which concerned her. It had been over a week since the last living person she'd run into, and she'd hoped the closer she got to some sort of sanctuary the more survivors she'd find.

Had the world slipped further into chaos? Was she the only one left out here, like a Twilight Zone episode gone horribly wrong?

Please let this be the right way. Please let there be people there, let this not have been completely in vain.

A sound rang out, deafening, startling Rachael in the silence.

A gunshot.

People. Her heart began hammering and hope—that lovely, dangerous thing—flared in her chest.

There were survivors somewhere nearby.

In trouble? Or hunting? Or…

Rachael urged Pablo forward, letting him take his lead but coaxing him into a canter and then a full gallop as she became more certain of the direction. The horse was fast and it raced along the blacktop. Rachael strained to hear above the sounds of his hooves.

The wind whipped through her hair and made her cloak billow out behind her.

Another gunshot.

Closer this time. Much closer. She was almost there.

She rounded a bend in the road at full speed, and *nearly slammed right into a mass of Orcs*.

Pablo reared, hooves flailing, kicking back the arms of the dead that turned to attack them, giving Rachael a split second to pull her sword, one hand clinging tight to the pommel of the saddle. She swung the blade, slicing through an Orc and kicking it back. There were more Orcs that she could easily count, most of them attacking what seemed to be an old broken down bus, its sides caked with old blood and dirt, fingers clawing against grimy metal, trying to get whatever was inside of there.

Was there anything inside of there? She couldn't hear any sounds, not over the sounds of the dead, but the gunshot had to come from somewhere.

Her horse bolted as an Orc attacked from their right, nearly unsaddling her as she clung tightly with her knees, keeping her grip on the sword, swinging it as best she could at the dead, but more focused on trying to stay on as clawlike hands tried to grab on to her legs or saddle.

Stay alive. She could hear Brett's voice in her mind, though if it was a memory or her imagination she wasn't sure.

"I'm not dying here," she growled to herself under her breath as Pablo turned sharply, ears flat against his head. She reined him in, trying to get him back under some semblance of control. He didn't want to be here, and she didn't want to either. It would be better to leave this place, leave the dead for whatever they were after.

She was turning him to go, to keep riding far away from this place, when she heard it. The terrified wail of a child.

Rachael's heart dropped. There were kids on the bus.

Every ounce of flight reflex was gone, every ounce of self-preservation. Now she had a mission, something she needed to do, someone to save. She might not be a superhero or the heroine of a book, but she was the only hero they had right now.

"I'm sorry, Pablo." The horse's ears were flat on his head, eyes panicked. "I know you want to run, but we have to do this. I know we can do this."

Most of the mass of dead was still distracted by the people inside the bus, their trapped prey, but Rachael was glad for that. A swarm of even five dead could overpower someone, and there were probably twenty or so, though it was hard to get an exact count. They were all slow, stained and tattered clothing falling off of bone and flesh. They all seemed a unified rust color as they moved, not individual people but a large mass of monsters.

This was life or death now, the big bad boss at the end of the level. She was staring it in the face, and there was no escape. She would have to fight.

"I am Arwen and Eowyn, I am Alanna and Arya." She yelled out loud to an unresponsive mass of the dead, raising her sword above her head as if she were inspiring an army to charge into battle, "I am Sif, I am Xena." She took a breath, trying to gather her courage. "I am Rachael, I am a warrior and I am not afraid."

Squeezing Pablo's sides, she urged him forward, charging down at an Orc that had turned to respond to her yelling. Her sword sang through the air, the crunch of splitting bone as the sword pierced the skull and the body collapsed. Her horse seemed to understand what she was thinking and kept to the edge, dancing out of the reach of the snapping grabbing hands that were now turning their attention to her instead of the bus.

As he ran, a handful of the Orcs turned to follow, giving Rachael the time to slice and stab, dropping their bodies and turning her attention to the next ones that came through.

There were five down now, but the horde kept coming.

Rachael was losing track, she felt like she had already killed more than a dozen, but there never seemed to be an end to this mass of bodies. She had no idea how many she had actually killed, all she knew was that she needed to keep going. Her arm hurt, and her hand was slippery from the sticky black blood of the dead. She clenched her fingers tighter around the hilt of the dagger. Any mistake meant her death. She knew that.

An Orc grabbed onto her leg, teeth attaching to her boot as she tried to kick them away, dragging her out of the saddle as it pulled her down. She yelled, whether from fear or surprise or as a war cry she wasn't sure, driving the dagger down through its skull with such force that she fell as the body crumpled, carrying her blade and her with it as another Orc latched its teeth onto Pablo, ripping a gash into his side as the horse let out something akin to a scream, more Orcs diving for his legs, teeth driving into the soft flesh they found there.

She hit the ground hard as Pablo fell, the air driving from her lungs as she rolled, trying to jump back up to her feet. The horde was split, half of the Orcs still continuing their assault on the bus, the others stumbling towards her, yellow teeth gnashing. One grabbed onto her forearm, teeth sinking into the thick leather. She swung her sword jerkily, ribs protesting, and she missed the skull, sinking her sword into the base of the neck. Wincing, she let go of the sword, using the hand to grab a dagger out of her belt and sinking that into the weak part of the skull at the top of the head of the Orc, which dropped hard.

Okay, this was bad. This was so very, very bad.

Pablo's panicked cries continued, but Rachael couldn't look at him, so instead her eyes fixed on the next body that lunged at her. Her eyes tracked the bodies, trying to figure out the best way to clear them without backing herself into a corner she couldn't get out of.

There wasn't time to try to retrieve her sword so instead she turned to face the next Orc in a half crouch, jumping to the side as it tried to lunge at her, turning in midair to drive the knife into the back of the head at the base of the skull. There were only three left coming, and she backed up a few steps, trying to judge which to take first. One came at her from the side and she dodged it, shoving its shoulder and using its stumble to grab onto the shirt and drive the blade between the eyes. Using a well-placed kick to the chest to knock the next one to the ground, she dispatched it with a quick stab. The last one's hands tried to grab hold of her, clumsy fingers attaching to a loop on her armor and pulling her towards its teeth.

With a cry she switched hands on the knife, driving it hard into the side of the Orc's forehead.

Her chest was heaving, ribs sending sharp warning pains as she moved. She ached everywhere already, but there was no time to wait.

Pablo had fallen silent, and Rachael didn't want to look. She couldn't look, she would have been able to handle it if she did. Squeezing her eyes shut for a moment, she swallowed down her emotions.

Heroes couldn't cry. Not when there were people to save.

Another gunshot rang out across the road, followed by the agonized screaming that Rachael had come to associate with death.

Her heart sunk, and, using her foot as leverage, she pulled the sword out of the Orc's neck from where it had lodged, ignoring the protests in her side. Sprinting forward, she sliced through the back of the head of an Orc that had turned to follow the screaming, and kept going. She couldn't see anything from this side of the bus, and she ducked around the back of the bus, hoping that most of the dead would be on the other end.

Slicing her sword through the side of the head of another Orc, she rushed towards the man that was laying at the foot of the door of the bus, still screaming as two Orcs dug their teeth and nails into him. The blood was everywhere. Rachael felt nauseous, but she swallowed it down, driving her dagger into the heads of the Orcs one by one, shoving their bodies to the side.

The man wouldn't stop screaming, clawing at the bites on his neck, and Rachael knew what she had to do.

"I'm sorry," she whispered, before driving the knife up through the side of his skull.

Then it was silent.

Rachael had the unnerving feeling tickling on the back of her neck that she was being watched.

~12~

Dez Fox

Dez had spent a lot of time hunting the forests of western Pennsylvania and northern Maryland. She understood the woods as well as any experienced hunter. She'd also hunted men in Afghanistan during the war. Being a soldier, a hunter and a cop had taught her a lot about how to read what the land wanted to share. In a police academy forensics class she'd also learned that contact always leaves a mark. Tracking, then, was looking for marks. Mankind itself made marks on the world—roads, buildings, cultivated fields, and more. These impositions on the land were mostly overgrown and eventually would fade, but that created a different kind of pattern, a different kind of trail. Where weeds and new growth grew it spoke to a lack of use, and in some places it was crystal clear to Dez that no foot—living or dead—had come this way in months. Elsewhere the weeds were bent and broken, or pushed aside. The passage of random passage suggested a single person using that route infrequently. Crushed foliage told a story of heavier and more frequent use.

Dez could read the stories of each. A careful living person, even one trying not to be seen and making maximum use of natural cover, still left tracks that showed they were in control of their bodies. The steps were more orderly, more evenly spaced. Dead feet tended to wander, to drag, to ignore cover and follow the path of least resistance. There was evidence of both kinds of travelers in the woods.

Twice she spotted zombies standing in the forests doing nothing. It was a phenomena she'd begun to realize was a thing. Unless drawn by scent, sight or sound, the dead would often slow to a stop and simply stand there. When the dead moved in packs the movement of the whole tended to draw the others, but Dez figured that even these groups would eventually slow down when the ones out front had nothing new to chase. It made a weird sense to her. After all, why would they just keep moving? Zombies were opportunistic hunters. They attacked and devoured life—animals, humans, birds—and they had already begun stripping areas of everything that could feed them. In the absence of prey, they stopped, no longer pulled by their senses.

That created a new kind of danger. The motionless zombies were like landmines and IEDs. They could be anywhere and because they remained so still and so quiet it was easy to walk right past one and accidentally trigger its appetite and aggression.

Dez paused in her search long enough to cut a green branch from a tree. She used a knife to strip the leaves and bark from it and to trim it down to a twenty-inch length with a sturdy Y at one end. She held that in her left hand and carried her blackjack in the other. That gave her a formidable set of tools for a technique she wished she could patent and sell. She'd be a millionaire with the first post-apocalypse must-have invention. Great for Christmas, perfect for stocking stuffers, she mused.

She had to use it less than two miles from the bus.

As she cut along an overgrown fire access road a solo zombie suddenly lurched toward her from the shade of an oak. One moment it was invisible, merely part of the landscape, and then next it snarled and lunged at her, gray fingers clawing at her shirt and hair.

Dez backpedaled to get her footing, set her weight on the balls of her feet, and as the creature shambled forward she used both weapons to slap its reaching arms down and then thrust the Y-stick hard against its throat. The mouth of the Y snugged in tight under the chin of that snapping mouth, and Dez quickly moved close and brought the blackjack down on the crown of the monster's head. The blackjack was made from a heavy pellet of lead wrapped in leather. The weapon's neck was flexible, which allowed for a lot of snapping speed. Handled one way and it would deliver a soft, penetrating blow that would render a criminal dazed or unconscious, often with a mild concussion. Used any other way it crushed bone and drove splinters through dura-matter and into the brain. There was a reason it had been outlawed by police forces across America. Just as there was a reason Dez Fox had taken it out of the box of weapons she'd kept in her trailer home when everything was falling apart. She'd nearly lost her job for using it once while busting up a biker gang brawl, now she was glad she hadn't thrown it away.

The blackjack whipped through the air and hit the zombie on the crown with enough force to send a shockwave up Dez's arm. She knew from hard, bad experience that it wasn't any trauma to the brain that stopped one of the dead. The blow had to do significant damage to the motor cortex or the brainstem. So, as the creature dropped to its knees, Dez used the Y-stick to set it for the killing blow. Another swing, another crunch, and then the zombie was a ragdoll. Dead for sure and forever.

She stepped aside and let it fall.

The creature had been a forest ranger once, she could see that from his pants and shoes and the few remaining tatters of shirt that clung to the destroyed body.

"I'm sorry," she murmured as she stepped away.

And she was sorry. Hard and brutal as she was—as she'd become—Dez Fox was not a monster. She mourned this nameless man, this victim of horror. As Billy Trout once told her, "There was a story in every single one of these poor sons of bitches."

A story. Sure, thought Dez as she moved off. A frigging tragedy.

Forty minutes later she found a dirt road that was overgrown but showed signs of frequent passage. Some of the wandering steps of the dead, but mostly human footprints. She squatted down to study them. There were at least seventeen different and distinct sets of prints along a stretch where rainwater had softened the ground. Several from big shoes that had to be men's, but there were smaller prints. Women's sneakers, or maybe from one or more teenage girls. She followed the smaller prints and it was soon apparent that a group composed of one adult male, two adult females, and a mix of children. A family, she wondered, or a group of survivors. Dez touched the edge of one print and the ground yielded, showing that it was moderately fresh. The last rain was a week and a half ago, and these prints had been made since then.

Dez's heart leaped in her chest. She knew that the odds of this being Billy Trout or even anyone from the busses was astronomical. You could sell a coincidence like that in a Lifetime TV schmaltz-fest of a movie.

But these were the prints of adults and kids. Living people.

Dez kept moving, following the tracks until they suddenly stopped. The tracks went a mile down the road and then there was nothing but blank dirt before her.

Except that wasn't what it was. Not really.

She dropped down onto hands and knees so she could study the dirt from a worm's eye level. Then she grunted and straightened, wiping soil from her palms. The road was not blank. No road ever is. The dirt, however, had been swept smooth. Dez moved to the shoulder of the road and prowled forward through the weeds, her eyes clicking back and forth between the shoulder and the smoothed dirt. She found what she was looking for nearly a hundred feet farther. It was a leafy branch that had been cut from a roadside tree, lying five feet off the road where it had been thrown. Dez picked it up, saw the traces of dirt that still clung to the leaves, and let it fall.

This was an old trick. Using those leaves like a broom to wipe out the signs of human passage. Old as time. But what concerned her was that it was poorly managed. Whoever had erased the footprints had only gone so far back and simply began at that point. They hadn't thought it through. Anyone with half a brain would do what she had just done...kept looking for when the footprints started again. It would have been far smarter to have the family walk off the road so that their prints vanished into the weeds, fallen leaves, and debris in the forest, and then, even if they had to return to the easier passage of the road later on, a tracker might have been thrown by the deception. Instead it was clumsy.

"Damn," she said, immediately concerned for this little family.

She quickened her pace, moving alongside the road until she found the point where the family had, indeed, come out of the forest.

Stupid.

It was stupid. No hunter or tracker would have been fooled long enough to simply give up. There was a logic to everything that happened in the woods. Everything made sense.

It was only human choice that made senseless decisions.

She followed the tracks all the way to the small side road that wound like a serpent's tail through fields of tobacco that had run wild with weeds.

The farmhouse was there.

The sight of it froze Dez's heart for a moment. It stood on a slight rise, its walls painted a smoky blue with shutters of a darker blue. A red barn, a tractor and harvester visible through the open doors. It looked at perfect and picturesque as something from a painting or a calendar. Or a dream.

Dez began running.

She did not intend to run. In was a rookie thing to do. Incautious and ill advised, but she did it anyway.

Because there was a curl of smoke coming from the chimney.

Because it looked like people were home.

Because it looked like the living still owned this small patch of the world.

And because the yard was full of zombies.

~13~

The Ranger and the Dog

The girl ran fast but not well. She was nimble enough but she wasn't skilled at flight through the woods. Not an overgrown forest like this. Catching her was going to be easy. Frustrating, mused Ledger as he set off, and actually a pain in the ass...but easy.

The hard part would be calming her down once he caught her again. That, and convincing her that he wasn't a rapist, murderer or general lowlife. He knew his looks were against him. Once upon a time he'd been what he called 'safe looking'. Blond hair, blue eyes, a winning smile, and a skin that took a surfer tan. But that was back when the world was the world. Now he was middle-aged, his skin was a roadmap of scars that marked battles on every continent and of every kind. He carried the marks of knife, bullet, fang and claw. No zombie bites, but that was probably the only type of physical harm he'd so far managed to dodge. He'd lived too much of his life out on the edge of darkness, out where bad things happen as a matter of course. Until this plague happened he'd been winning a lot of battles in the war of international politics and terrorism. In his moments of self-congratulation he'd taken some pride in the fact that he'd prevented madmen from burning it all down. He'd even stopped the release of a designer pathogen that might have done to the world what *Lucifer 113* actually accomplished. It was no comfort at all that this outbreak had taken place while he was off the local clock. He'd been overseas preventing a different kind of catastrophe. He had, in fact, prevented that disaster…only to turn around and discovered that despite all of his actions, sacrifice and best intentions the devil had slipped his leash. By the time he'd reached America it was all gone. There was nothing left of the country to save.

Hubris is a damned ugly thing, and perspective a terrible lesson to learn this late in life.

Now his world was his dog and whomever he could save.

Now his world was that poor damned girl.

And so he ran into the woods to convince her that she needed to be saved, and that he was the one she should trust.

Jesus wept, he thought as he followed Baskerville through the foliage.

~14~

Dez Fox

There were eight of them.

If they had been in a bunch, she might have tried it another way. She might have circled to slip in through the back door. She might have made some noise and tried to lead them away in a pack. She might even have risked using her precious bullets and dared the loud bark of the gun.

But they were spread out, facing the farmhouse from different points.

There was something wrong about that, and Dez should have noticed it. That was her second rookie mistake. That was the second thing she did that afternoon which should have warned her that weariness, desperation, fear and hope had begun to strip away her necessary caution.

Instead, she came running at the closest zombie, her Y-stick in one hand and blackjack in the other. It heard her too late and had only begun to turn when she slammed the weapon against the base of its skull. The blackjack shattered the bone and destroyed much of the brain stem. The zombie fell forward and lay there, twitching and flopping.

Dez jagged right, running toward the next, who had heard the commotion. It was forty feet from her and by the time she reached it, the creature was reaching for her. Dez used the Y-stick to stall it and the blackjack to kill it.

Then she raced toward the third, who had been standing by a hand-crank well. This one was a farm worker—big, heavy in the shoulders and arms, with a bull neck. He towered over Dez and when she rammed its throat with the Y-stick the creature's two-hundred and eighty pounds of mass did not simply jolt to a halt as the last one had done. One arm of the Y-stick cracked and folded back, too green to break off but too feeble to withstand that much mass in motion.

Dez yelped in fear and dodged grabbing hands that were the size of baseball mitts. She kicked the thing in the knee, trying to cripple it, but her balance was as bad as his angle and it was like kicking a tree stump. She fell hard on the ground and the broken stick went flying. She almost lost the blackjack and might have if that hand and arm hadn't been under her as she landed.

The zombie bent and clawed at her, and out of the corner of her wild eyes Dez could see other creatures closing in. She cried out as she rolled sideways and scrambled awkwardly to her feet. The big zombie lunged at her, but this time Dez was able to stay on her feet as she dodged. She slapped the reaching hands away and brought the blackjack down hard on the creature's forehead. Again and again, tearing dry skin, shattering bone, pulping the brain. She had to hit it six more times before she damaged the right part of the brain. Even then the thing tried to grab her as he fell. A limp left arm tripped her and she went down once more, panting, exhausted, her striking arm tingling with the shocks of each of her powerful blows.

It was then that Dez Fox realized all of the things she had been doing wrong.

Running in without thinking it through. Fighting badly, wasting energy and breath.

Three of the zombies were down, but that left five of them.

And something else occurred to Dez as the dead closed around her. The zombies had been standing in the field. They hadn't been clustered by the front door or windows. They hadn't been trying to get in. They hadn't been doing anything at all. Only standing there.

The way they do when there is no prey to draw them, to focus them.

She flicked a despairing glance at the house. The smoke still curled from the chimney, though.

Thin smoke. Faint. Fading. A dying fire in what she now realized was either a dead house, or one that had been abandoned.

Everything was wrong. The whole day shifted without a clutch and as each gear stripped Dez felt it like a punch to the heart.

She got to her feet one more time. The broken Y-stick was lost, but she had her blackjack and she had her gun. The five zombies were closing in, but they were not yet clutched like a fist around her.

"Kiss my ass," she told them.

Moving with equal parts caution and fury, she went after each of the zombies, one at a time. Using hard sweeps of her arm to parry worm-white grabbing fingers, using better timed and aimed kicks to break knees, using the blackjack with precision.

It took less than five minutes to kill them.

When it was done Dez staggered over to the well and collapsed against it, spent, bathed in sweat, gasping for air. She worked the hand-crank as fast as she could to pull up a bucket of water, then held it up to the light to make sure it wasn't polluted. It sparkled clear and sweet.

Thirsty as she was, Dez used all of the water to wash black blood from her hands and clothes. Six buckets worth, until she was soaked to the skin and shivering. Only then did she take some water for herself, and she drank as much as she could.

She stayed by the well until her heart, her breath and her tears all slowed.

All the time she watched the house. The smoke from the chimney was thinner, almost gone.

"Kiss my ass," she said again.

Dez pushed off from the stone well, snugged her blackjack into a back pocket, and drew her Glock.

And with that held in two trembling hands, she approached the quiet farmhouse.

~15~

Rachael Elle

Rachael could barely see the eyes watching her through the disgustingly clouded windows of the bus, but she could sense them on her. Wiping some of the blood on of her hands on the ground, she straightened up slowly, her eyes looking around to make sure there were no other Orcs ready to strike.

"I know you're in there, I'm not going to hurt you," she said softly, knowing they were listening as she sheathed her daggers and knives, holding her hands out peacefully.

There was no answer, though Rachael could hear the movement inside, and she cautiously pushed the partially open door of the bus.

What if this was a trap? The thought echoed through her mind, and part of her wanted to draw her dagger in case of an ambush.

But she definitely heard a kid before; it was a different scream than the sounds of a dying man. She only hoped whoever had a kid with them was a good person.

Taking a cautious breath, she stepped up into the bus, wondering who or what she'd find inside.

There were a handful of children clustered at the back as far away from her as they could. None of them looked old enough to have reached their double digits, though she was awful at guessing ages so she could be mistaken.

Their eyes peering over the tops of the worn seats of the bus were terrified, their dusty and dirty faces stained and damp with tears.

They were the eyes of children who had seen too much. They were the eyes of children who had grown up too fast.

Suddenly Rachael was incredibly conscious of what she must look like, with beat up leather and metal armor of her warrior costume, the splattered blood of monsters on her clothes, the blood of the man who had died protecting these children on her hands.

What had this world come to? What had this world made her into?

Say something.

"Hello…" Well, that was something… though definitely not helpful.

She tried again.

"Hi… I'm Rachael, and I'm here to help you."

Nothing. Silence, only broken by the occasional sniffle of a child holding back tears. None of the kids moved a muscle, their eyes still fixed on her, some in wonder, some in confusion, but all of them distinctly registering fear.

"I'm going to get you somewhere safe," Rachael added.

A few more sniffles, but no movement, no response.

If the gravity of the situation wasn't so serious, she might have laughed at how horribly this was going. It was like a scene from a bad horror parody. She needed to get them moving, she needed to get them somewhere safe. The gunshots would draw more Orcs, and she couldn't fight off a horde while trying to keep a bunch of scared kids safe.

Though of course they weren't going to go with her. To them, the bus was their temporary home, their place of safety; she could only imagine how long they'd been hiding in here. Probably since the world ended. And now she was a stranger, covered in blood and armed with a sword, which they just watched kill the only adult that was keeping them safe, telling them they needed to come with her.

She wasn't sure she would even trust her right now in their place, so why would they?

There needed to be a solution, she needed to get them somewhere safe. She wasn't going to leave them behind, not without any protection. She would never be able to live with herself if she didn't get them at least to a safe zone with adults and supplies.

"Please, I know you're scared, I know that you don't know me, but I want to help you. If you stay here the monsters will come back, and I can't stop them all."

A few of the kids glanced at the windows, the threats of monsters and nightmares enough to make them question what to do. But she was still a stranger, and the older kids eyed her with suspicion. They'd seen enough of this new world not to trust her.

Time for plan B.

"Can I tell you a secret?" she asked them quietly, and all of their eyes were on her. "Can I trust you?"

There was a slight nod from a few of the kids, and Rachael gave the most sincere and trustworthy smile she could.

"I'm actually from Themyscira. I'm an Amazon, just like Wonder Woman. Do you know who Wonder Woman is?" she asked the group, to a few more nods. "Well Wonder Woman is in New York trying to make sure everyone is safe, but she asked all of her Amazon sisters to come from Themyscira to help her. And she sent me to find all of you to bring you to safety. Why do you think I'm dressed like this? This is my magical armor, it protects me, just like her gauntlets do."

The children's eyes were on her in wonder, and she really hoped they were buying this. She was trying to make it as convincing as possible, and putting all of her heart and soul into it.

"Now I need to do my part, but I can't do it without all of you. Was there another grown up with you?"

"Miss Dez" one of the little ones in the back spoke up quietly. Okay, so there was another person, another adult. Maybe she could use that to get the kids to come with her.

"When did Miss Dez leave?" she asked, sitting down on the edge of one of the bus seats, leaning against the back of the seat as casually as she could, trying to look as comforting as possible.

"While ago, I dunno," a little girl mumbled.

"She said she'd be back by the time it got dark," another kid piped up, one of the older boys in the back.

So she had a decision to make. If this Dez was alive, if she was coming back, then Rachael didn't want to move the kids, not if she was expecting to find them still here and safe. She could only imagine the panic that could cause, how she'd feel if she was supposed to be meeting her group somewhere and they weren't there. How'd she feel if she went back to the hospital and they weren't there anymore.

She couldn't do that to someone, even if she'd never met this woman before. Especially not with children involved.

So they could wait it out until sunset; she didn't think it would be much longer before the sun went down, and she just hoped that no more Orcs would come their way. If she barricaded the door of the bus then they'd be safe enough here, at least until nightfall.

Then at nightfall they'd have to move.

"I'm going to stay here and make sure all of you are safe, okay?" Rachael asked, trying to keep her voice light. "I want to make sure Miss Dez gets back here to you tonight, and I don't want to leave all of you here alone. Is that okay if I stay with you"

Most of their hesitations around her had faded when she told them her big "secret," and they nodded. Of course they wanted a superhero around. She could protect them from the big scary monsters.

Well, she would do the best she could.

~16~

Dez Fox

Dez approached the house slowly, with caution, her shock and weariness falling away as her training and common sense came back online. She was badly rattled by how stupid she'd been, and she was glad Biel wasn't here to see it.

When she placed her foot on the bottom riser of the short set of steps to the porch it creaked. Just a little. Enough.

If there had been ears to hear.

Dez pointed the gun at the front door and then swung it slowly toward each of the two windows. Heavy shutters were in place, the slats down. No one could see out or in.

She took a breath and leaned on the step a little heavier, making the creak louder, more deliberate.

Waited.

Heard nothing but the wind across the tobacco leaves. Birds began to sing in the trees. A good sign, most of the time.

Dez took another breath, and this time used it to call out. "In the house."

Nothing.

"It's cool," she said. "I'm alone. I'm not here to raid or anything. Just looking for help." A pause. "I'm a cop."

As if that meant anything. She wasn't all that sure if it meant much before the world fell off its hinges, and a badge sure as shit carried no weight now. Not authority, anyway. Reassurance, maybe, and that's what she was hoping for.

Nothing.

She mounted the steps. They all creaked. So did the floorboards on the porch. The house was old, probably mid to late nineteenth century. It had seen a lot, felt a lot, and even after it was all falling apart the place had offered shelter to someone. Recently, too. She shifted her Glock to a one-hand grip and tried the door handle with the other. It turned and there was a faint click, then the door swung inward. The hinges, at least, had been oiled. Dez reclaimed her two-hand grip and followed the barrel of the automatic into the house.

As soon as he moved from vestibule to living room she knew that she wouldn't find anyone alive in there.

There was a breeze blowing through the downstairs and as she moved forward it became clear that the back door was open. She moved through the downstairs all the way to the kitchen, finding no one but seeing signs everywhere that told her this place had been occupied very recently. The fireplace held the coals of a dying fire, and a pot had been hung there filled with soup that had boiled over. Eight sleeping bags on the living room floor. Empty cans, stacked supplies, some weapons—baseball bats, an empty shotgun that had clearly been used as a club, an axe with a notched blade—but no people.

There was blood, though.

Red and black. Human and dead. Furniture was pushed out of place, plates were broken. There had been a fight here. But when Dez checked the back door it didn't show signs of having been forced. She retreated to the living room and studied the scene, looking at it as a crime scene, reading it. Two of the sleeping bags were stained with blood, and all of them were messy in a room that looked to be otherwise well-maintained. When she peered at one of the bags she saw two kinds of stains. The brown stains were old dried blood. Human blood. But spattered atop those were stains in which the white parasitic threadworms still wriggled. The adjoining sleeping bag was stained with blood that had not yet had time to turn brown. It was splashed red. She looked around and found the trashcan filled with old, stained bandages.

The scene made sense. It was a tragic story, but a familiar one. One of this party had been wounded and they'd done their best to patch the injuries, but either the wound was a bite, or the damage was so severe that it became fatal. In either case the wounded person had died in his or her sleep, then revived as a monster. It attacked the person sleeping in the next bag, and from there it was a slaughter. Badly handled, badly fought, and ultimately lost.

And yet…

She walked over and looked at the spilled blood on the floor. There were scuffs in it, the marks of sneakers. Mostly the balls of the feet, though, as if whoever wore those sneakers was running through the house and out the back door, leaving it open.

The dead do not run.

Dez stepped out onto the back porch and saw the bloody sneaker prints heading off into the woods. The scuffling footprints of the dead followed, and Dez had no way of knowing if the runner had escaped. Or had she been one of the zombies she'd killed to get in here? Some of them looked fresh, and Dez figured them to be owners of those other sleeping bags. And the big farmer had been the house's original owner.

Jesus.

She went back inside, closed and locked the kitchen door, and spent forty minutes prowling through the empty house. There were moldering corpses upstairs in the beds, which explained why the squatters hadn't settled up there. Each of the corpses had a bullet hole in their head and old bite marks on their withered flesh. Dez kept her mouth and heart hard as she went through closets and the attic. The place was a treasure trove of supplies. Blankets, boots, scarves and coats, tools, and more. And downstairs there were the supplies amassed by the squatters. Plenty of food. Too much for them to have carried, so Dez figured they'd raided the pantry here and maybe neighboring farms. There was enough food here to feed her busload of kids for a month. And the well-water was pure.

The building itself was sound, and she knew she could reinforce it and defend it. All she had to do now was go back and get the kids. Convincing them to leave the bus was either going to be a very easy or a very hard sell. Some were too terrified to leave; others were too terrified to stay.

She thought about it as she ate some Spam straight out of the can—having opened it with the key they conveniently attached to the bottom—and washed it down with a quart of fresh water.

Dez was just checking her gear for the trip back to the bus when she heard the scream. She raced onto the porch, gun up and out, and saw a teenage girl break from the shadows beneath the trees. Blond hair whipped behind her as she ran, and Dez looked for the pursuing dead. Saw none.

Instead she saw a monstrous dog come charging out of the woods, and behind it was a big and brutal looking man. The girl fled from them, screaming, terrified, making for the farmhouse. The range was too great for accuracy with a handgun, so Dez knelt, braced her elbows on the porch rail to steady her aim, sighted on the dog.

And fired.

The shot banged, loud and hollow in the air. The dog flinched but kept running. Dez fired again. And again.

Then, with a terrible cry of animal pain, the pursuing hound crashed forward and down, rolling over and over among the tobacco plants until it came to a stop. It lay there, panting and howling, its side pumping bright red blood.

Dez snapped off three more shots at the man, but he dove for cover.

The girl, startled by the shots, stopped in her tracks and looked wildly around. Dez rose up and waved frantically at her.

"Over here! Come on, I'll cover you! Run…*run!*"

The girl ran.

~17~

The Ranger and the Dog

Joe Ledger lay flat and tried to melt into the dirt as bullets punched through the air above him. The farmhouse was sixty yards away from him and he was certain whoever was shooting at him had a handgun. At that range a pistol is usually better thrown than fired, but this son of a bitch was dishearteningly good.

Shit.

Baskerville whimpered piteously, and that broke Ledger's heart. He loved dogs more than he liked people, and Baskerville was a friend. If the shooter had killed his dog, then Ledger was going to paint the walls with hair and blood. He drew his Sig Sauer and tried to aim through the weeds and wildly overgrown tobacco plants, but his view was almost completely blocked. To get better line-of-sight he'd have to move to higher ground, and that was likely to earn him a bullet in the brainpan.

Which is when he heard the shooter yell out.

"Over here! Come on, I'll cover you! Run...*run!*"

It was a woman's voice. Angry, scared. Desperate.

Joe laid his gun down, cupped his hands around his mouth and yelled as loud as he could. "Stop shooting," he roared. "I'm not trying to hurt the kid."

There was a pause that lasted two full seconds and then two quick shots that struck the small ridge of dirt behind which he lay.

Christ this woman could shoot.

Then there was a longer pause. Either the woman was swapping out her magazine or she was conserving her bullets. Only people in old, bad movies and video games had an unlimited number of rounds. In the real world when you ran out of ammunition you couldn't go to the store and buy more. And carrying a lot of bullets was problematic because they were heavy as hell.

It would be a very nice thing if this crazy woman had fired her gun dry.

After a full minute of silence, Ledger risked raising his head. He did it very fast and took a quick-look, then ducked back down and let his mind process what he'd seen in that fragment of a second. The farmhouse, the field, bunch of dead zoms, a well, and…

And nothing else.

No running girl, no woman.

Baskerville whimpered again.

"Screw it," muttered Ledger and he began crawling toward his dog. He kept his gun in one hand, though. If the woman wanted to turn an ambush into a war, then that was on her. Ledger wasn't a chauvinist. He'd blow a hole in anyone who wanted to kill him.

God help her if the dog died.

He crawled, teeth clenched, a furnace igniting in his chest.

~18~

Rachael Elle

A movement outside the window, barely visible through the grime on the glass, caught Rachael's attention, and she held up her hand to gesture to the children to stay quiet. The movement was too fast to be an Orc she thought, but it was hard to tell. Drawing one of her daggers, she crept silently back towards the front of the bus, crouching low, peering around the corner, waiting for whatever or whoever was out there to approach the door.

There was definitely someone out there, and Rachael was about 90% sure whoever was there… was alive. Now the question became was it someone that was looking to help them, or hurt them. Rachael had met enough people in this world so far to realize that it was about a fifty-fifty shot, and she didn't want to take that chance, not with kids at risk.

She could hear the person outside kicking a body of an Orc towards the back of the bus, and Rachael used their distraction to maneuver herself carefully down the steps of the bus, keeping herself close to the wall.

Whoever it was obviously didn't know that there were living people on the bus, or at least didn't know who was on the bus, so it couldn't be Miss Dez or anyone with the children out there. So it meant a stranger. A new player had entered the game, and Rachael didn't like new, unseen NPCs she knew nothing about.

If Brett knew all the stupid things I was doing today… she mused to herself, trying to keep her humor as a cover for her deep down terror. Taking a sharp intake of breath, she stepped out the door.

The first step out the door told her a number of different things.

One…the person outside was definitely alive, and her gut instinct was telling her that he definitely was not there to help them or anyone else he came across

Two…the person outside really wasn't expecting a superhero to come walking off of the school bus.

Three...she really needed to do a better job at analyzing a situation before just jumping out into a battle. That was going to get her killed.

The guy seemed startled to see her at first, though the nasty look on his face quickly melted into a neutral one, though still unsettling to look at to Rachael. He seemed like he was trying to wear a mask that didn't quite fit him, and she didn't like the vibe he was giving off.

Rachael was a big fan of gut instincts.

"Can I help you?" she asked, her dagger in her hand at her side, ready to strike if needed, but non-threatening.

"Survivors!" He feigned excitement, though Rachael's gut response didn't lessen any. "There's more of us! I've been looking for more survivors, looking for anyone. I've been on my own for so long…" He tried to look pitiful. "Do you have any food? Any water? There are more of you? How many are you?"

"Okay, that's more questions than I can answer at once!" She faked a smile and a laugh, trying to come across as non-threatening, naïve, trying to figure out what he wanted, why her gut told her not to trust him.

"Here, let me get you some water first," she started, turning her back a little, pretending to duck her head.

He took the bait, jumping at her with his knife out, trying to attack her. Rachael was ready, though, and she swung her dagger around to block his, before using his surprise to push him backwards with a strong shove.

They stared at each other for a moment, the girl in the leather warrior armor and the man with a nasty looking hunting knife in his hand and an even nastier look on his face, and Rachael cautiously adjusted the grip of her elven dagger which, compared to his, looked like a letter opener.

"Who the fuck are you?" the man snarled at her, and the sarcastic part of Rachael that came out when she was very afraid threatened to give him a stern Captain America-like comment about his language.

Not the time, Rachael, she chided herself, pulling her focus back on the man in front of her. "I could ask you the same thing, but I don't want to know. So how about you just walk away and go back where you came from."

The man lunged at her mid-sentence, swinging his knife around and slicing it dangerously close to her breastplate. Jumping backwards just in time, she nearly stumbled over an Orc's limp arm, catching herself on the side of the bus for balance before bringing her dagger up to block his second attack.

It had been a long time since Rachael had fought against someone who could fight back with a weapon, and suddenly she wished she was fighting against an Orc instead of a person. There was no way she was going to be able to beat a man with obvious experience in a knife fight. All of her fighting experience was Player vs Player LARP fighting, and foam weapons and fake damage points had far less at stake.

Using her free hand she pulled the second dagger out of its sheath on her belt, getting lower into a fighting stance. If she could block him with the one knife, maybe she could strike him before he got her. It was the only thought she could come up with, and she hoped it would work.

All she knew was that she needed to stop him. The little voice in the back of her head was telling her that she needed to keep him as far away from the children as possible.

He was fast, though, and she was barely able to keep up with blocking his attacks, let alone strike him with one of her own. Dancing away from one of his slices, she ducked quickly, using one knife to block his blade from hitting her, and swinging her other one down to slice across his side, before pulling a few steps back, trying to focus on a strategy. There had to be something.

The man with the knife was coming closer, focused on her with a terrifying furor in his eyes. He was pissed, and that was both good and bad. Bad that he now was going to be fighting with more anger at her drawing blood, even if just a small cut. But good, because angry people make mistakes, make stupid decisions. She'd learned that long ago in LARP.

He swung again and Rachael ducked, catching his incoming blade with her dagger and slicing her secondary dagger across his arm, this time drawing a deep gash. He cried out, dripping his dagger in pain, which Rachael kicked to the side quickly, her daggers still out in front of her, ready to strike.

She didn't want to strike an unarmed man, didn't want to kill anyone, but she would if he forced her to.

But he was pissed, spitting in anger as he backed up, clutching his bleeding arm. "Fuck you, bitch," he snarled, eyes burning her with an angry fire. "You better not be here when I get back with my friends, you better run fast, because if I find you, I'm going to love every moment of killing you. And it's not going to be fast or fun for you."

And then he was gone into the woods, and Rachael let her weapons drop to her sides, the threat still lingering in the air.

Oh, this was really not good.

~19~

Dez Fox

When Dez first yelled, the girl froze for a moment, caught in a moment of obvious doubt and confusion. The man and dog that chased her were one thing, and the farmhouse seemed to be a destination she thought might be safe. Or, safer, at least, than being caught by the blond-haired thug and his mutt. But Dez's voice was coming *from* the farmhouse and it was clearly a woman's voice.

It took the girl time to process that and make a decision. Maybe one full second.

And then like a startled deer she was running again. Moving fast and well on long legs. Dez fired four more shots at the spot where the big man had dropped. He heard him yelling something but couldn't hear him and didn't care what kind of bullshit he was trying to sell. The girl shot a terrified look over her shoulder, saw nothing, but ran as if there was a whole pack of killers on her tail. She blew past the well, ran up to the foot of the porch stairs and skidded to a stop, panting, face running with sweat, eyes wild.

"Get inside," Dez said. "I'll keep this dickhead entertained."

She emphasized the comment with another shot, but then her slide locked back. While Dez swapped it out for a fresh one—her last—the girl gave her a two-second up and down appraisal, looked over her shoulder once more and then ran up the steps and in through the open door.

Dez smiled and slapped the magazine into place and released the slide. The bastard out there in the weeds wouldn't know it was her last magazine. Besides, if one guy could get past her while she had a full magazine, a blackjack, a knife and a lot of female indignation, then she wasn't trying her best. Dez liked a good fight, especially when the payoff was kicking some guy's nuts up between his shoulder blades. That always felt good.

There was some movement out in the field near where the dog went down, but Dez had no clear shot. Nevertheless she knelt there, finger laid along the trigger guard, eyes moving slowly over the field.

Was the guy down, too? Had one of her rounds popped him?

Maybe. She hoped so, but she wasn't sure.

He hadn't returned fire, which probably meant he didn't have a gun or was low on bullets. She had a slightly elevated shooting position and had already proved that she was a good shot. Most people don't want to play that kind of game, especially these days.

A small scared voice spoke through the slats of the living room shutters.

"Is he gone?"

"No," said Dez.

A pause. "Is he dead?"

"We can hope."

Several long minutes passed and there was no movement at all in the field. Dez thought she heard the dog whining, but the wind was blowing past the house toward the field and she couldn't be sure. She straightened very slowly and carefully, weapon still trained on the field.

There was no movement and no shots fired in her direction.

"You have to go make sure," insisted the girl.

"No I damn well do not," Dez growled. "That's a great way to get a bullet in the brainpan. No thanks, honey. If that guy out there is setting a trap it's going to be for someone stupider than me."

"His name is Joe."

Dez cut a look at the shadowy form behind the shutters. "You know him? He one of your group?"

"Huh? Oh…no…I just met him. He was in a fight with some guys who…who tried to…"

She didn't finish, but Dez got the point.

The afternoon sun moved steadily toward the west and the shadows flowed out from the distant trees, seeming to flood the fields like black water. Dez moved to sit with her back to the living room wall so she could talk to the girl more easily while still watching the field. She was more than half convinced that the guy was dead. Her other half was less sure, because if she'd killed him then he should have reanimated by now. The fact that he hadn't left it all in a gray area. He could be dead with a bullet in the brain. He could be wounded and bleeding out. He could be hurt and waiting for nightfall, or for reinforcements. Or he could be unhurt and really pissed and simply waiting for his moment.

Once the sun was down it would be too risky to stay here on the porch, though. And defending a house was tough. Easy enough to do against the mindless dead; much tougher against a thinking person who really wants to get in.

As the shadows lengthened Dez thought about the food in there, and the other guns. Plus, she really needed to pee.

Twilight turned the fields to a featureless purple-black. There was no way Dez was going to get back to Biel and the kids tonight. The forests at night were a death trap in more ways than she could count.

So, Dez shimmied over to the door and pushed it open. It was dark inside, which was good. She'd warned Lindsey about lighting a fresh fire, and the one in the fireplace had long since burned out. Good.

She rose to a crouch and hurried inside, closed and bolted the door, and before she even stopped to go to the bathroom, Dez hurried through the house, floor by floor, to make sure all of the windows and doors were shut and shuttered. Then she found a bucket and relieved herself. A downstairs broom closet had been turned into an outhouse. Any port in a storm.

Then she called for Lindsey to join her in the kitchen. There was a mountain of trash in one corner, including many empty food and drink cans that were swarming with ants, roaches and other opportunistic insects. That kind of vermin no longer bothered Dez. The vermin outside were more important.

"Kid," she said, "we need to rig an alarm. Take some of these cans and stack a few in front of every window. If you can find silverware, then put a piece or two in the top can. If anyone comes in it'll make noise. Got it?"

Lindsey nodded and after only a moment's uncertain hesitation, began gathering cans. The girl impressed Dez by working fast and being smart in how and where she stacked the cans. When all of the cans had been used, Dez went around and inspected the work, using a candle for light. Whoever lived her was into big, chunky scented candles.

"Nice job," she told the girl.

"He can still get in," said Lindsey.

"Not without us knowing," said Dez. She patted the Glock on her hip and hefted a small-bore shotgun she'd found upstairs. The shells were filled with birdshot, but even a .20 gauge with a birding rounds would blow the junk off a rapist, and in the confines of a house there was no way for her to miss.

By the light of the scented candle, Dez and Lindsey opened two cans—Vienna sausage and kidney beans—and ate while they exchanged stories. Dez told her about the outbreak in Stebbins County, and how the massive super storm had slowed down the government's response. By the time the main cell of the storm had passed the plague had jumped the quarantine zone. The military tried to control the spread with the use of fuel-air bombs and a take-no-prisoners live fire response, but by then it was like trying to destroy an anthill with a pistol. The bombs did damage, but it only takes a couple of infected outside of the Q-zone to spread the infection again, and again, and again.

"So you have a whole bunch of school busses filled with kids?" asked Lindsey, eyes wide. "And they're okay?"

"I hope so," Dez told her. "One of the teachers is back there with them, and we reinforced the bus pretty well. They can hold out for now and I'll head back there at first light."

Lindsey looked immediately terrified.

"Hey," said Dez quickly, "don't sweat it. You can come with me. We'll put some supplies in a wheelbarrow and take it back to the kids. Or...maybe go grab the kids and bring them back here. That might be a better plan, come to think of it."

"*He's* out there," said Lindsey. "That guy Joe and his dog."

"Yeah, about that," said Dez, "you want to bring me up to speed here? What happened to your group and who's this Joe dickhead?"

Lindsey studied her plate for a while and fresh tears fell through the grime on her cheeks. "This wasn't my family," she began, and then told a story that had become familiar to anyone who had survived these last six months. Lindsey's family had been killed during the outbreak and she'd fled from one group to another, escaping as each new group was torn apart or died from diseases. These days even a simple infection could rage out of control. The group that settled in the farmhouse were a disparate band of refugees from all over the south and lower northern states. A fireman from Philadelphia, a West Virginian CPA, a mechanic and his wife from Kentucky. People running in every direction in hopes of finding a safe zone, and then dying because they made mistakes, got sick, got bit, got too weary to run, or gave up.

"We found this place, and it looked like the people who lived here had caught a break, you know? There was a National Guard rescue station not too far from here and the soldiers were keeping the forests clear. Or at least that's what we were told. We bunked down here and did our best to, you know, secure the place. But Mrs. Gillespie, the wife of the mechanic guy…she was pretty fat and had this heart thing. Angi-something."

"Angina?"

"Yeah. I guess she died last night." Lindsey shivered. "I can't believe it was only last night."

"Yeah. She died and woke up again?"

The girl nodded then got up, lit a small sterno fire in the sink where the light would show through the windows. She poured water into a pan and placed it on the flame. She explained how the rest of them woke up because of the screaming. Mrs. Gillespie had already bitten her husband and two others. They'd made the mistake of huddling together for warmth because the night was so cold. By the time everyone realized their mistakes it was too late.

Lindsey poured the hot water into cups, found teabags and handed one to Dez. It was some kind of sissy green tea crap that Dez wouldn't use to wash her books, but the tea ritual seemed to calm the kid, so she accepted it. They went into the living room and after Dez checked the windows and peered through the blinds into the field, then sat on a pair of overstuffed chairs set near the cold fireplace. Lindsey had her cup cradled in her palms and leaned over it, shaking her head. The bloody debris of the sleeping bags was all around them, evidence of horrors.

"What happened?" asked Dez. "After all this, I mean?"

"I ran," said Lindsey, and that tore a sob from her. Not from shame, because the girl, young as she was, already understood the necessary logic of survival. No, she wept from the weariness of having to survive when everyone else died and she had to start all over again. "I was trying to make it to the rescue station when I saw a bunch of guys cutting down some of the dead. I...I...was stupid. I didn't wait to see who they were. I was just so happy to see living people who seemed to be strong, you know? They were fighting the dead and winning. They were even laughing as they cut the zombies down. Like it was nothing to them. Like they weren't afraid of them, you know?"

"Yeah, honey," said Dez, stroking the girl's long hair, "I know."

"But they weren't what I thought," said Lindsey, and now there were ghosts moving behind her eyes. A different kind of fear. A kind that was older and crueler than the living dead. "A bunch of them took me to their camp and said that I'd be safe there. They said there were a lot of women and other kids there. They said..."

"Doesn't matter what they said," Dez told her. "They're assholes. You'll be smarter next time. And if I see them, I'll blow their dicks off and wear 'em as trophies."

It was meant as a joke, but Lindsey flinched back from those words. After a moment she said, "They're already dead."

"What?"

"Most of them."

"I don't understand," said Dez. "Did you kill them?"

"No," said a voice behind her, "*I* killed them."

Dez started to whirl, to grab her gun, to rise, but instantly froze as the cold barrel of a pistol was pressed against the nape of her neck. Lindsey screamed and backed away.

Joe Ledger pressed his Sig Sauer harder, forcing Dez to bend forward.

"You shot my dog," he said in a voice that was colder than anything Dez Fox had ever heard.

~20~

Rachael Elle

The kids were panicked again. They'd watched the man try to attack her, watched her kill him. She wished they didn't have to see that. They'd seen too much blood and violence already.

But so was the way of this world.

"But where's Miss Dez?" was the question of the hour, the question that the kids kept trying to ask. Rachael didn't have an answer.

Rachael didn't have a lot of answers anymore.

So instead she sat with all of the children, telling them fairytales she'd been told as a child, silly nothings that take the mind away from reality. The world needed a lot of distractions now, people needed something to take their mind off of what they were living.

This was what she needed to do. Save people, yes, but keep their minds off reality. She would reject this reality and replace it with her own.

Sounds like something she was used to doing, she mused to herself with a smile, and it would be worth it to see people smile again.

But she wasn't going to be able to do anything if she didn't make it out of here alive.

And right now there was no guarantee.

~21~

The Ranger and the Cop

"No!" screamed Lindsey and threw her cup of hot tea at Ledger.

He saw it coming half a second too late and roared in pain as the scalding liquid splashed his hand and neck and face. Dez exploded into movement, spinning, chopping up and back with her elbow, catching Ledger's wrist and knocking the pistol from his hand. The weapon went flying. Lindsey snatched up a heavy book and hurled it at Ledger, who ducked just as Dez came up off the chair, drove her shoulder into him and ran him backward. They crashed into the wall, knocking framed photographs off their nails. Dez tried to knee Ledger in the crotch and simultaneously head butt him.

He twisted and her head missed, but her knee caught his upper thigh. Not a full hit, but enough to send a wave of sick pain up through his groin and gut.

"Stop it!" he snarled, but Dez punched him in the face.

The damn woman knew how to hit. Ledger slammed back into the wall, but he rebounded with a two-handed shove that sent her staggering back. Lindsey grabbed Dez's teacup and hurled it at the ranger's face, but he ducked under it.

Just as Dez tried to kick him in the groin again. Her foot missed the intended target and instead hit Ledger in the chest as he ducked. She wore the steel-tipped shoes she'd worn as a cop, and it was felt like being shot. Ledger fell hard on his ass, then flung himself sideways to miss the vicious stamp that Dez launched to try and crush his kneecap.

"Get him!" screamed Lindsey, and she began plucking objects off the end tables to hurl. Empty coffee mugs, empty cans, a paperback, a box of shotgun shells. They rained down on Ledger as he rolled like a log away from Dez's next stamp, and the next.

Ledger rolled onto his back and kicked up to intercept Dez's next kick, jolted it to a stop in the air, then pivoted and swept her standing leg. She crashed to the floor. He scrambled to his feet, grabbed the corners of one of the overstuffed chairs and shoved it at Lindsey with all of his strength. It chunked into her and the girl went down with a yelp of pain. But Dez, on the floor, pulled out her blackjack and whipped it at Ledger. He danced backward but the heavy lead and leather caught him on the left heel hard enough to detonate white-hot pain through his foot and ankle. He staggered, and dropped, catching himself on his palms as Dez threw herself at him, trying for his head this time.

She almost had him.

He rolled sideways again, parrying her swing with one forearm and swinging a tight, hard palm-heel strike at her as she dropped onto him. His hand caught her right behind the ear and it rocked her. Hard. She crashed down onto the floorboards beside him, gasping and blinking and wincing.

Ledger got to his knees, grabbed her hair and pulled her head back as far as it would go, then whipped a rapid-release folding knife from its sheath inside his right front pants pocket, snapped the three-point-seven-five inch blade out, laid it against her windpipe and snarled at Lindsey, who was in the process of raising a heavy vase.

"Stop! Right goddamn now!"

She stopped.

Right goddamned then.

"Put the fucking vase down," he roared. "Do it."

Lindsey took a step back and let the vase fall. It shattered at her feet. She looked absolutely terrified. At that moment, Ledger didn't care.

"Put your hands in your front pockets. Deep as they'll go. Good. Now, go sit down," he told her. "No, not on the couch. On the floor over there, with your back to the wall and your legs straight out in front of you. Good. Stay there, kid. You move and this gets messy."

Lindsey sat exactly as ordered, her face white with terror.

Ledger bent close to Dez. "Listen to me," he said in a quieter but no less threatening tone. "Listen to me and understand. If I wanted you dead, you'd be dead. I could have killed you when I came in. Here's a news flash—I *don't* want you dead. I am Captain Joe Ledger. I was with the Department of Military Sciences before everything went to shit. I am one of the actual good guys. You, however, are a psycho bitch who shot my dog. The fact that you are still breathing is because you didn't kill my dog. He's hurt and he needs help. Tell me you understand?"

He had the woman's head pulled back too far for her to talk, so he eased the pressure by one half an inch. His knife didn't move.

"Yes…," she hissed.

"You're wearing a police uniform," said Ledger. "Or part of one. Are you a cop?"

"Yes."

"Where?"

"Stebbins County."

Ledger grunted. "That's where all this shit started."

"Yes."

"What's your name?"

He couldn't see her face very well, just her eyes as she looked up and back at him. Those eyes were filled with incredible hatred and fury. And shame, too, because she'd tried and failed to protect the girl. Ledger could sympathize, but he wasn't yet ready to let her go.

"Fox," she snapped. "Desdemona Fox."

Ledger said, "Wait…*what*? You're Dez Fox?"

He felt her stiffen, but it was Lindsey who spoke. "You *know* her?"

Ledger removed the knife, let go of her hair and stepped quickly back. Dez turned, fast as a snake, but he was well out of range.

"Everyone knows her," he said. "Everyone who watched the news when this shit started. The standoff at Stebbins Little School will have its own chapter in the history books…if anyone survives this, I mean. Dez Fox, JT Hammond, and Billy Trout holding off the National Guard who wanted to wipe the town off the map to try and stop the infection. Not that it would have worked because it was already outside the Q-zone, but…damn, you're really her. You're Dez Fox."

"So what?" said Dez as she got slowly to her feet. She rubbed her throat and seemed surprised not to find a drop of blood.

"Two things," said Ledger, "first, I had the blunt edge against your throat. You couldn't tell, but there it is. I just wanted to calm this crap down."

She glared at him.

"Second, you're supposed to be dead," he told her.

"Says who?" she demanded.

"Says Billy Trout. Or, that's what he thought last time I saw him."

Dez Fox took a step toward him, but then her legs buckled and she dropped to her knees, her eyes wide, mouth working, hands balled into fists. "Billy…?" she said in a tiny voice. "Billy? You *saw* him? You really saw him? Oh my god…is he alive?"

Ledger smiled. "Yeah," he said. "And so are a whole bunch of kids who all think you're dead."

Dez fell sideways and barely caught herself on one hand. She looked like she was going to pass out and she swayed, dizzy and gasping. "Wh-where?" she stammered. "Oh my Christ—*where are they*?"

Ledger opened his mouth to answer but his words were instantly drowned out by a long, terrible howl of animal pain from outside. Dez and Ledger raced over to the windows and stared out. Lindsey got up and joined them.

Outside, deep in the tobacco field but clearly defined by cold moonlight, figures were moving. They did not lumber like the ungainly dead. Instead they moved with the quick, furtive and deliberate movements of the living. Of hunters.

Of killers.

And they were closing in on the spot where Ledger had left Baskrville, drawn by the animal's terrible howls of pain.

~22~

Rachael Elle

Rachael sat in in the driver's seat, foot propped up on the dash, biting her lip, weighing her options. She did not want to be here much longer, but she knew the children were going to fight her about staying there as long as they could. The sun was almost down, there was no sign of this Dez woman, and then what? The men would probably be coming soon, and she couldn't risk any of them being there when they arrive. That would spell certain death for them, or worse, judging by the vibes she got from that man.

But alone in the woods? At night? In darkness, with scared, unarmed children with no means of defense? That would leave them open to attacks from animals, humans, and Orcs. That wasn't a good option either.

She needed to figure out a plan. The kids were resting wearily, some of the older ones watching her while the rest slept. They would be safe here as long as she didn't go too far out of sight.

"I'm going to go see if maybe Miss Dez is around here somewhere. I'm not going far, just up the road a little. If you need me, I'll be able to hear you," Rachael said to one of the older boys, and he nodded as she strapped her swords back into place and headed out of the bus.

She first stopped by the other side of the bus, dreading what she was going to see as she approached the body of her companion. She choked back bile and tears as she looked down at his body, but didn't let herself look long.

"I'm sorry," she whispered to him, reaching down to stroke his forelock one last time, before unhooking her packs she could reach from the saddle. She checked the supplies, which seemed a bit crushed but not damaged, and then reached to check for her cellphone. It wasn't in its usual pocket, and Rachael sighed, missing it, feeling it's loss.

And yet....

It was an artifact from the world before. That was not this world anymore. That was not her world anymore.

So she turned away, shouldering her bag and continuing down the road away from the bus, looking for any signs of people, good or bad, living or dead.

But there was nothing. The sun was low in the sky, casting a bloody haze over the horizon.

Appropriate, Rachael mused to herself. *Ominous.*

"A little obvious, though, don't you think?" she asked the sunset. It ignored her and continued to bleed colors across the horizon.

Suddenly the distant crack of a gunshot startled Rachael back into focus. She froze, listening to the echoes, trying to source the sound. It wasn't nearby. No. A few miles away at least, but it was there. She strained to listen for more. And they followed, the repetitive popping of distant gunfire.

It had to be the men coming for them. The panic rose in her heart.

She needed to move the group, get them to safety. They were her problem now; she needed to make sure they survived.

Be the hero they need.

It was now or never.

~23~

The Ranger and the Cop

Ledger ran across the room, scooped up his fallen gun, then kept moving through the house.

"Where are you going?" demanded Dez.

"Back door," he said as he ran. "Stay with the girl."

He opened the back door, checked the yard, and went out quickly and silently. There had been five men in the field and there had been the glint of metal in the moonlight. Guns or blades. Probably both.

Baskerville's howls filled the air, hiding what few sounds Ledger made. The dog sounded angry as well as hurt, and that was a good sign. If the poor bastard was simply dying there would be only the wail of despair that Ledger had heard too many times before from mortally wounded animals. But there was still fight in Baskerville's voice.

He heard men's laughter, though, and that was a bad sign. It meant that they weren't afraid of the dog.

Ledger ran low and fast. Once upon a time he'd been an army ranger, and then he'd been a cop in Baltimore, and for years and years after that he'd been the senior field agent for Echo Team. He'd led the best of the best into combat all over the world, facing all manner of terrors. He'd learned the habits of stealth from necessity. Haste not only made waste, it made corpses. Sometimes it was better to move slower in order to get all the way to the enemy's door without him knowing it. There would be time for speed soon enough.

He heard a man say, "Leave it. Stupid mutt's not worth a bullet."

The voice floated to him through the dark and it lit a match to the gasoline in Ledger's heart. He quickened his pace and brought his pistol up.

Five men painted silver by the moon. Black eyes and black mouths, and the black mouths of gun barrels. Were these men with the Nu Klux Klan, or just another pack of human predators hunting the wild? Ledger didn't know and at the moment he did not much care. The men were closing in around the depression in which Baskerville lay. One of them held a pitchfork, and as Ledger watched the man raised it to strike.

Ledger was thirty feet from them when he opened fire.

The first bullet took the man with the pitchfork in the chest and staggered him, but before the man could fall Ledger put two into a hulking figure beside him. The center-mass shots knocked a wet cough out of the bigger man's throat and he sat down hard on the ground.

Then everything went crazy.

The other three men began firing and trying to swing weapons and stab all at the same time. A small man with a big automatic began firing wildly and his first three rounds hit the wounded man with the pitchfork, blowing away jaw and teeth. Ledger ducked under the swing of a double-headed logging axe and then rammed the attacker backward into the line of fire. The axe man's body juddered as five rounds blew the blood and life out of him. Ledger whirled again and used his free hand to parry a slash with a hunting knife, then he buried the barrel of his buried under the knife-man's chin and blew off the top of his head.

That left the small gunman, who stood momentarily stunned as his comrade with the axe sagged down to the ground in a bloody sprawl. Ledger put three rounds into the gunman, two in the chest and one between his goggling eyes.

Then, suddenly, Desdemona Fox appeared out of the gloom, gun raised in both hands, and fired. Ledger pitched to one side, half aware that there was something behind him. A sixth man he hadn't seen. He landed, rolled and came up in a combat crouch, gun tracking a body that fell backward trailing blood from a shattered breastbone.

He swung his barrel back toward Dez to see that she was now pointing her weapon at him.

The moment froze.

A few yards away Baskerville whined in pain.

Ledger saw the black eye of Dez's Glock staring at him with unwinking intensity, and her own mad, wide eyes behind it.

He lowered his weapon, released the magazine, swapped in a new one, and turned away from her. Her gun was still pointed at him and he knew that he was taking a terrible risk.

"Make sure there's no one else," he said, as if they had been working together all along. "I have to see to my dog."

~24~

Rachael Elle

How do you motivate a bunch of scared kids to do anything? Rachael worked as a camp counselor once in high school, but that was different. This was life or death, but you couldn't say that to children. This was not her area of expertise.

But the time was now. She couldn't wait any longer.

Sitting down in the seat in front of a few of the older children, she addressed them seriously, looking them all in the eye.

"I need all of you to help me. We need to get everyone to a safe place, and I know one not too far away. But I need all of you to help me get everyone there."

"I'm scared," said one of the girls softly.

"I know you're scared," Rachael told her. "I get scared too. Being scared is what keeps you alive; it's what keeps you on your toes. You don't think that Batman gets scared sometimes? Wonder Woman? Captain America? Even Spider-man gets scared. But you know what they do?"

They looked at her silently, eyes wide.

"They face their fears. They look the bad guys right in the eyes, even when they're afraid, and they fight them. They help those who are smaller than them, who can't protect themselves. They stay good people. They fight for what is right."

She paused, looking between each of them.

"I know I'm asking a lot of you. But I need all of you to be brave. Do you think you can do that for me? Because I know everyone one of you has a superhero inside of you."

Rachael looked the girl that had spoken first. "Who's your favorite superhero?"

"Supergirl."

"I want you to pretend to be Supergirl. No, I want you to be her. You're big and strong and brave. You protect people in need. You defend the helpless. I need you now to each pick your favorite superhero, and I want you to be them. Close your eyes and choose one. Say their name out loud. Picture them in your head. *Be* them."

Each of the older children closed their eyes, focusing hard. Rachael heard a variety of names being said, from Spider-man to Thor (Rachael tried hard not to think about her Thor waiting back for her) to Black Widow to Batgirl. A good variety of heroes each of them idolized. She could see each of their faces lighting up as they pictured themselves as their heroes, a momentary blip of childhood happiness in a world that had forced them to grow up too fast.

"Do you have them all?" she asked after a few moments. They all nodded, opening their eyes. "Because all of you are heroes, and the moment that you step out of that bus, there are going to be monsters, and bad men, but superheroes will always triumph. I want you to remember that. You are all heroes."

She gave each of them one of the knives she'd been collecting, warning them to be careful with them, that they were only if they needed to use them. When she got to the final girl, her little Supergirl, she pulled one of her own daggers and handed it to her gently.

"This knife is very special. It was given to me by Wonder Woman herself, and I know that it's going to help you be very brave."

Standing again, she looked over the group of older kids.

"Now, we need to get everyone together. I want each of you to take the hand of one of the younger kids, because we need to stay together. I don't want anyone wandering off. As soon as we get to the safe house I'll make sure we go looking for Miss Dez. But until then, we need to be fast and quiet, okay?"

Peering out of the windows of the dark bus, she pushed the door open cautiously, glancing around for human or undead threats. It seemed clear for now, the full moon overhead casting a pale glow over the landscape. Behind her, each of her heroes were pairing off, taking care of one of the younger kids, explaining to them that they had to go, to be safe. Rachael's heart warmed, even though the fear she was hiding, hearing these children take care of each other like that. *Evil can't win if there's love in this world.*

Gesturing to the first hero and pointing down the road to a sign, she watched each of the kids cautiously, nervously checking around for any movement, from living or dead. But the air was still and calm, and she couldn't sense any close threats.

As the last pair exited the bus, she checked inside, making sure that there were no more children hiding. With it clear, she silently moved over to the children, taking the lead and gesturing for them to follow her.

The path that she had taken out of the woods was clear in the moonlight, and she turned down it cautiously, her heart pounding in her chest.

Woods at night were prime target for an ambush, and she could feel the tension and fear in the air from the children behind her. A twig cracked underfoot and one of the kids cried out in fear before the older child with him clasped a hand over his mouth.

But there were no sounds following, no moans or shuffling feet, and they continued on into the darkness, to what Rachael hoped would be safety.

~25~

The Ranger and the Cop

Joe Ledger knelt beside the big dog. Baskerville was barely conscious and whined piteously. Ledger shifted around to let moonlight spill on the animal as he gently probed for wounds. His heart was racing and he felt a terrible chill deep in his bones. Baskerville was a combat dog and a companion, that was true enough, but he was more than that to the ranger. He and the dog had been through everything together. Wars on foreign soil, battles with terrorists here in America, the crash of Ledger's helicopter once he'd returned to the States, the long and heartbreaking hunt for Ledger's family, and the endless battles since with both the living and the dead. Losing him now would inflict a deep wound and despite what he chose to show to the world, Ledger was not at all sure he could survive that kind of injury. Baskerville was the last living creature that he truly loved.

"Come on, boy," he said in a soft, soothing voice as his fingers probed in and around the pieces of leather armor, "it's all okay, everything's going to be fine."

He hated the thought that he might be lying.

From the way the dog had fallen Ledger expected to find a big, gaping wound. There was certainly a lot of blood. It was everywhere, black as oil in the blue-white moonlight.

Ledger heard Dez move closer but he didn't look up.

"Six of them," she said. "They're all down."

Baskerville yelped as Ledger's fingers moved up from his shoulder along the muscular neck to the dog's head. Then suddenly yellow light bathed the dog, turning the black blood to bright red, as Dez Fox aimed a small Mag-light down. Ledger cut her a microsecond of a look, nodded, and went back to examining his dog.

He found the wound, and once more his heart sank. The entire side of Baskerville's head was painted with blood.

"Oh, Christ," Ledger breathed.

Dez knelt beside him, holding the light at a better angle. "How bad is it?"

"I don't know. I need to get his helmet off." Ledger was as careful as he could be, but Baskerville whined and yelped as the ranger undid the buckles on the thick leather armor. He held the dog's head in one hand, lifting it to pull the iron-studded helmet off, then he dropped it and bent closer still to examine a long, bloody wound. Then Ledger frowned and reached for the helmet again, holding it in the flashlight's glow.

He suddenly barked out a harsh laugh.

"What's wrong?" demanded Dez.

"Look," he said, holding out the helmet. She took it from him and examined it. One section was torn and the heavy iron stud was pushed down through the leather. That part of the helmet was smeared with blood. Then Ledger lightly touched Baskerville's head in the spot corresponding to the damaged helmet. "The bullet hit the stud but it didn't penetrate."

"He's not dying?"

Ledger shook his head. "No, thank God. At least not from this. He has a pretty nasty scalp wound and probably the worst headache in canine history, but the skull isn't shattered."

"Concussion?" she asked uncertainly.

Ledger was silent for a moment. "No way to tell." He stroked the dog's neck and spoke to the animal. "You scared the crap out of me, you big goof. Luckily you got your granddad's hard head."

Baskerville whined again, but now his big tail whapped the ground.

"The stud was probably pressing down on a nerve," he said. "I think he'll be okay once he shakes it off, but we can't leave him out here."

As if to emphasize his words there was a faint moan from the black forest. More of the dead were out there. And maybe more of the living, too.

"Help me get him to the house," said Ledger.

"How much does he fucking weigh?" asked Dez, eyeing the animal.

"A lot." Ledger looked around. "Is there a wheelbarrow or something?"

"How the hell would I know?"

"You're here," he said. "Why wouldn't you know?"

"No…I got here right before you did. I have no idea what they have here."

"There's a wheelbarrow in the barn," said a voice behind them and they both spun, guns back in their hands. But it was only Lindsey, pale as a ghost, standing at the end of the flashlight's glow.

Ledger sagged and gave a rueful snort. "Christ, I'm getting old. I didn't even hear you."

"You could have gotten killed," snapped Dez.

Lindsey ignored her. "I saw the wheelbarrow. I think it's big enough." She looked down at Baskerville. "Will he be okay?"

Ledger saw the fragile smile on the girl's trembling mouth, and he nodded.

"Yeah," he said, and hoped it wasn't another lie.

The girl's gaze drifted around, alighting on each of the fallen, bloody men. She abruptly jerked back. "Oh, God!"

Ledger and Dez turned to see one of the killers tremble and then sit up. Another was beginning to twitch as well. Ledger began to rise, but Dez pushed him back down.

"I got this," she said as she picked up the big double-headed axe. She cut a look at Lindsey. "Don't look, honey."

But Lindsey did look, her eyes filling with strange lights as Dez brought the gleaming blade up and down, up and down, up and down. The field became unnaturally still until Baskerville broke the silence with a soft whimper.

"I'll get the wheelbarrow," said the girl.

"Not alone," said Dez.

Lindsey led Dez to the barn and they hurried back with a big Jescraft wheelbarrow of the kind called a Georgia buggy. Sturdy, with a big tray and thick wheels. It took all three of them to lift the whining, struggling, uncooperative dog into it. Dez collected the weapons from the dead men.

They did this all in silence and walked back to the farmhouse without a word, without a comment about the living or the dead.

Inside, Ledger and the others moved Baskerville onto one of the sleeping bags and placed a pillow under his head. They worked together to clean the wound and Ledger held the big dog's head while Dez used needle and thread to stitch it closed. Thirteen stitches. Baskerville shrieked at first and it was all Ledger could do to hold the animal still, but it was Lindsey who kept the dog from going completely wild. She knelt beside Ledger and began stroking his neck and shoulder, speaking slowly and softly in crooning sing-song voice. It calmed Baskerville by slow degrees, but there was a slightly disjointed quality in the girl's voice that chilled Ledger.

Kid's way out on the edge, he thought. *Holding on by her fingernails.*

He couldn't blame her. He was pretty ragged himself. And he wondered if anyone was—or could possibly be—sane anymore. He doubted it. Not in this world. Not anymore. Sanity seemed to have been consumed by the hungry dead along with security, faith and hope. He wasn't sure he wanted to hang a label on what was left. 'Survival' was too clinical a word for it, and he was afraid that the motivation they all had left was closer to 'delusional'.

When she was done sewing and the dog was resting, Dez turned to Ledger and poked him hard on the chest. "Tell me about Billy," she demanded.

He did. He and Baskerville had working their way from one National Guard rescue station to another, trying to find one that hadn't already been overrun. At each point, though, they found only evidence of disaster. One camp had high walls and stout locks, but everyone inside was already turned. In another they found only blood and a few corpses with head wounds. He found no survivors at all, and every day was a running battle against the zombies.

Then one morning while he and Baskerville were moving along a stretch of highway he saw smoke rising behind a distant stand of trees. They went to investigate and found four big yellow busses sitting dead on a side road, victims of the EMPs. A rough stockade had been built around the vehicles, though, made from branches torn down from the lush trees and tired together with vines, belts and strips of cloth. Sharpened branches were thrust outward from the dense walls of green and it made a formidable and intimidating barrier. However Ledger could see a dozen ways to get through it, over it or past it. It was the kind of protection that would be made by someone who had a good imagination, some common sense, but no real understanding of military tactics. Fair enough.

He called out to announce his approach and after quite a lot of time when nothing seemed to happen but during which Ledger figured he was being watched and assessed, a section of the wall was lifted out of place and a man stepped out. Like Ledger he was tall and blond, but he was younger and of a different physical type. And though the man showed some of the necessary hardening that any survivor in this world had to have, he was clearly not a soldier.

The man introduced himself as Billy Trout, a reporter for a cable news service up in Pennsylvania. Ledger, as it happened, knew the man's name. During the outbreak in Stebbins Trout had filed stories with the tagline, *"This is Billy Trout reporting live from the apocalypse."*

Ledger figured that Trout had been somewhat ironic at the start but that reality had caught up with the story. The man had, in fact, been reporting live from the apocalypse. It was one of the things no one ever wanted to be right about.

Trout told him about the floods, the storms, the traffic, the waves of zombies and the EMPs. He spoke about the kids they lost, and the other bus that had been overrun or lost in the madness. He spoke, with tears running down his face, about the woman who had saved them all. A fierce, cranky, gorgeous, aggravating, violent, wonderful woman named Dez Fox. He said that she was the love of his life and that if it wasn't for the job of keeping the kids safe, Trout doubted he would have wanted to go on living without her.

As Ledger told this story Dez sat in stunned silence, her own tears running in unbroken lines, fists balled. Lindsey huddled next to her, caught up in the story.

Ledger wrapped his account by saying that a band of seven National Guardsmen, along with nineteen refugees from the overrun camps, had appeared on the road. Ledger checked them out, vetting them for safety and sanity. Together they used better tools to cut down trees and turn the five busses into a real fort.

During their talks, Trout told Ledger something that rocked the ranger. He said that a small team of military contractors operating under the nickname 'the Boy Scouts', had helped Dez, Billy and the others escape the school. Ledger knew that team very well and he asked about the team leader, a former sniper named Samuel Imura. The look on Billy's face told Ledger what he didn't want to hear. Although Imura had helped to save all those kids, he was lost during a raid on a food distribution warehouse.

"You saw him fall?" demanded Ledger. "You saw Sam die?"

Billy Trout said, "I saw him fall, but…no, I didn't see them eat him. We, um, were spared that part of it."

Ledger grilled him on it, but that was all Billy knew. Sam Imura was missing, presumed dead. It was a hard and brutal fact, but it wasn't one Ledger was willing to buy outright. Sam had run with Ledger's Echo Team for years and had faced monsters before. He was a very hard man to kill. If the man had survived, he might have tried to make it all the way to California, where he had parents and a much younger brother, Tom, who was a police cadet. Billy could add nothing else of use, though.

The last two surviving members of the Boy Scouts, who Billy knew only as Boxer and Gypsy, had helped set up this camp but then moved on, searching for some branch of the military or government that was still functioning. Billy never saw them again.

Ledger stayed for a bit and then he, too, went on his way, looking for answers, for survivors, and for a purpose. He told all of this to Dez Fox.

Her response was to punch him in the chest. Very fast and very hard.

"You miserable cocksucker," she snarled. "You *left* Billy there?"

"First…ouch. Second, don't do that again," Ledger warned, rubbing a sore spot on his chest. "And…as for leaving Billy, sure, why not? He had all the muscle he needed to keep those kids safe. I've even sent a few families in his directions, some of them with a lot of supplies and some useful skills. Trout had it in mind to send raiding parties out to find wagons they could pull so they could take weapons and supplies with them."

"With them…where?"

"He told me that the plan was always to make it to Asheville, North Carolina," said Ledger. "That's where all the rumors say a community is forming. Maybe even a new government, if they can get their act together. Not really sure about that, but I'll probably wander down that way eventually. Not yet, though. I have some things I want to do out here first."

"Like what?" asked Lindsey.

Ledger shrugged. "Some of the guys from my old unit may be around. I've run into some stragglers who said they met a couple of fighters who might be people I know. The kind of people who would still be sucking air even with all this going on. Maybe you ran into them?" he asked. "Big surfer-looking guy everyone calls Bunny? Black guy with a goatee and an attitude named Top Sims? Top and Bunny have Baskerville's brother, Boggart, with them. And there's a woman out here, too. Tall brunette gal with a foreign accent who sometimes calls herself Violin? Any of that sound familiar?"

Lindsey and Dez shook their heads.

"Where was Billy when you saw him last?" asked Dez. She pawed the tears from her eyes. "Can you show me? Can you take me there?"

Ledger considered. "When I saw him he was six days walk from here."

"That close?" she murmured. "God."

"But that was weeks ago, Dez," said Ledger. "If he stuck to his plan then they're probably already on their way to Asheville."

"Maybe," said Dez, "but that many people, with carts and kids and all that…they'd have to leave a trail a blind moron could follow."

"Okay, fair enough."

Dez got up and walked over to the door and peered through the blinds at the night. Then she turned and told Ledger her part of the story. Everything from the point where she'd become separate until she'd left Biel at the bus to find a place to settle.

"Jesus Christ," said Ledger, getting quickly to his feet. "You left a bunch of kids in one of those busses?"

"It's okay," said Dez. "For the night, anyway. The kids know how to be quiet and we have corpses around the bus to keep them from smelling anyone inside."

Ledge shook his head. "Shit. That's not the problem. Didn't Lindsey tell you about the NKK dickheads?"

"NKK?"

"Nu Klux Klan," explained Ledger. "Those assholes we just danced with out there are probably part of their party. That's who grabbed Lindsey. I've been tracking a big party of them. I think they're going to try and take the Appomattox Rescue Station back from the biters and turn it into their fort, or something like that. They've been raiding survivor groups all through the area, taking women and kids, stealing supplies. They're worse than the frigging dead."

"Worse?" asked Lindsey. "How are they worse than things that want to eat you?"

He turned to her. "Because, little darlin' there are worse things than dying. Think about it. How would like to be *owned* by those assholes? How would you like to spend every day cooking and cleaning for them and every night getting raped by as many of them as wants you?"

"Stop it, Ledger," said Dez, putting a hard hand on his arm. "She's been through enough and she's scared enough already."

"No," said Ledger, "she's not. She's nowhere near scared enough if she thinks zombies are the worst thing out here."

They looked at each other for a long, tense moment. Ledger watched her eyes as she processed the implications.

She said, "It's a long way back to the bus."

"Okay," he said.

"It's dark out there."

"Yes it is," agreed Ledger.

She chewed her lip for a moment. "Which means that if the NKK jackasses are anywhere near the bus…"

"…then they won't see us coming," said Ledger.

"Wait," said Lindsey, alarmed, "you're not seriously going to do this."

"Kind of have to, sweetie," said Ledger.

"No you don't. Go in the morning, when it's safer."

"Safer for whom?" asked Ledger. "Right now they have numbers and all we have is surprise."

"Besides," said Dez, "we can't risk it. I'd never have left the kids behind if I knew these guys were out there. Never. Now I have to go back. I just hope to God it's not too late."

"Gets later every second," said Ledger. He glanced around. "Duct tape, electrical tape…anything like that?"

Lindsey ran to the kitchen and returned with a roll of gray duct tape. Ledger took out his rapid-release knife and began cutting strips out of a runner carpet. He wrapped them around his arms and legs and secured them with the tape, then helped Dez do the same.

"Carpet," she said, grunting. "Smart."

"Can't bite through it worth a damn," said Ledger. When he was well protected, he walked over to the weapons Dez had stacked on a chair, tore open a box of 9mm rounds and very quickly and professionally reloaded his magazines. He picked up the shotgun, shook his head, and handed it to Lindsey. "Keep this with you."

"I…I…"

"You're staying here," he said. "Lock the place up. Baskerville should be coming out of it pretty soon."

At the mention of his name the big dog opened his eyes and flopped his tail a few times. No whines now. His big, dark eyes were filled with dark magic. Ledger knelt by him and touched his forehead to the dog's, mindful of the injury. He spoke to Baskerville for several moments, his voice pitched too low for the others to hear. When he stood up, so did Baskerville. The dog looked wobbly, but a lot less than before.

"Give him some food and water, and stay alert," said Ledger. "Is there a basement or attic?"

"Both," said Lindsey, still clearly not liking the plan.

"Pick the one you think you can defend. If you have to, go there when we leave and wait it out. You don't have to protect the house, just yourself. Baskerville will help."

"Shouldn't she go with us?" asked Dez, then immediately shook her head. "No, honey, Joe's right. We'll be back as fast as we can. All of us."

She said this last to Ledger.

He grinned at her. It was not a nice grin, and he knew it. He knew the feel of that kind of smile on his face.

"All of us," he said.

Moments later they were a pair of shadowy phantoms who ran across the field beneath the moonlight and then vanished into the blackness beneath the trees.

~26~

Rachael Elle

The swarm came so suddenly Rachael almost didn't see them. She was having trouble judging the length of time it was taking for them to find the farm, though she didn't think it could be much further, when suddenly the movement caught the corner of her eyes, the large lumbering figures coming through the trees towards the back of the group.

Rachael reacted quickly, drawing her sword and dagger and racing back along the path.

"Run! Heroes, with me!" she said. Her heroes turned to look at what was coming. A few of them moved to follow her, pushing the small children into the arms of one of her other heroes who ushered the younger children down the path faster, holding his knife up and ready in case anything attacked them from the sides.

She instructed her heroes, keeping her sword out in front. "We need to keep moving forward, just keep them back if they get too close."

They were all moving quickly, just out of reach of the Orcs, and Rachael wanted to keep it that way. As long as they could reach the farmhouse in time, then they'd be safe. She didn't want to risk any of the children in close combat with the dead.

The trees were thinning, and the moonlight was shining through, and Rachael could see the farm through the edges of the trees. Her heart soared. They were almost there, they could make it.

"Run! Get to the farm," she yelled out to the children over her shoulder as she swung her sword through the head of one of the Orcs that moved faster than the rest, bracing her foot against its body to pull the blade out and kick the limp form away.

They were almost there. They were going to make it.

Pulling one of her heroes away from an Orc that lunged at it, she pushed all of them along the path, trying to keep the rear, to keep them from being overtaken by the dead.

There was a cry of fear from up the children far up ahead on the path, but it died out quickly, and Rachael hoped one of the heroes had resolved whatever the issue was.

She was the last one to burst through the edge of the woods, only to find the rest of the children standing, frozen in fear along the edge of the field.

"What are you—?" she started to ask, before looking up and across.

The farmhouse was up ahead, only a quick walk up the path and across the field. It looked dark and secure, comforting almost under the milky light of the moon.

So close.

What looked far less comforting were the dozen Orcs in the field before them that reacted to the cry of the children, and were now turning their way.

So close, and yet… so far

~27~

The Ranger and the Cop

Joe and Dez moved through the woods. He led the way and she followed, both of them letting their senses adjust to moonlight and darkness. There was a farm road, but it wound around too far south, so Ledger took them along a straight path and they found the highway in less than an hour.

There were a few of the dead in the woods, standing like silent trees until the scent of living flesh triggered them into movement. Ledger used the carpet gauntlet on his forearm to stall the biting mouths and his knife to puncture the top of the skull or brain stem of each zombie. He moved with a silent and deadly efficiency, not asking for help and not needing any.

"Christ," said Dez after Ledger killed another of the dead, "you're fast as shit."

"Fear is a wonderful incentive program," he said.

"You look like you've been doing that your whole life."

He paused and looked at her for a long moment, and he felt the weight of all his years and all those battles. "You have no idea," he told her.

She studied his eyes but did not ask questions.

They moved on.

Once they were on the main road they made better time but they were also more vulnerable. They compromised by running along the edge of the road that was not bathed in direct moonlight, letting themselves be invisible against the darkened trees. That saved their lives, because as they rounded a bend in the road five miles from the bus they nearly ran into a group of men.

Joe and Dez froze, hands on their guns.

A few hundred feet ahead of them were six men. Two walked in front, one with a flashlight and the other holding an old Vietnam-era military M-16. Two others trailed behind, both of them with shotguns. But the other two walked singly, one in front and one behind a line of eleven other figures. All female, ranging in age from late forties to early teens. Ragged, sobbing, terrified, and helpless, with their hands tied and ropes tied around their necks, connected each to the woman in front and behind.

Ledger heard Dez utter a low sound that was barely human. It was a primitive sound of bottomless animal hate. He glanced at her and then put his hand out to stop her from raising her pistol. She glared at him but he put a finger to his lips, shook his head, and then leaned close.

"There has to be a camp," he said very quietly. He did not whisper, because the sibilant 's' sounds carried. "We follow and we see."

Dez clearly didn't like it, but the men were going in the same direction they were. Toward the bus.

"They're dead men walking," was her reply. It wasn't a joke. Merely a promise.

"Yes," said Ledger in a voice every bit as cold and murderous as hers, "they damn well are."

Like ghosts, they followed.

The party of men and their prisoners kept to the main road. Every action they took made a statement: this road is ours. Everything was theirs. The women, the world. There was no doubt they were part of the larger NKK group. All of those men with all of their weapons and brutality. Of *course*, they'd believe that they had become the new apex predator in this broken world.

They had no idea at all of what else hunted in the dark.

And what followed them down that moonlit road.

~28~

Rachael Elle

Rachael's heart had dropped into her stomach, but she couldn't let the children see the fear on her face. The twelve or so Orcs were more than she could take on right now, not with all of the kids. And some of these Orcs looked fresh—faces mostly intact, no rotting, fresh blood glinting in the moonlight.

But she couldn't wait here, not with the small handful of Orcs coming up behind them. Instead she gestured the kids forward.

"We just need to run. Run fast! We're going to get to the farm, and then get onto the porch, and we'll get inside. They can't get us if we're inside. Heroes, get ready, fight if they come near you but don't go after them if you don't have to. Just get past them."

And before she could let her fear overcome her, she rushed forward, leading the group through the path of least resistance.

The zombies were slow, and fear kept the children moving quickly, but they were tired and their legs were short and heavy. Rachael stayed in the middle of the pack, cutting down any Orc that came too near to her sword, taking off hands, slicing at their heads, trying to keep the children safe. The first two, one smaller child and one of her heroes reached the steps first, climbing up onto the porch and hiding down behind the railing.

Driving her dagger down through the top of the head of one of the Orcs that came too close, she looked around as the next pair made it to the farm. Her eyes glanced back to the woods, where the small group of Orcs that had almost overtaken them in the woods was making their way into the field. That was bringing the number of Orcs coming their direction into the high teens, and Rachael didn't want to have to face them while worrying about the kids.

The group was almost to the steps, though, and the last few children were climbing up. They were almost to safety.

Not all the children.

Supergirl yelled out to her, pointing at one of the smallest boys who had separated himself from the group, darting away from the porch, down the path away from safety, crying as he fled in terror. Rachael's heart dropped, and she rushed after him without hesitation.

The boy tripped, screaming out as he fell down, hitting the ground hard. The nearest Orc was only two steps away from him, and Rachael was three. Throwing all of her body weight into it, she dove at the Orc, tackling him from the side and sending them both tumbling to the ground, but away from the boy.

Rachael's sword was knocked from her hand and fell to the ground as Rachael struggled to keep her skin away from the gnashing teeth. Bracing her arm against the Orc's neck, she drove her dagger through his eye socket.

But there was no time to rest, and she jumped to her feet as another Orc bared down on the boy. Grabbing her sword again, she knocked the Orc back with a squared kick to the chest, before using the Orc's lack of balance to slice down through his head.

One more now, coming at her from the side, and she sliced through the air with her dagger, which missed the sweet spot and bounced off the hard bone, knocking her off balance. The Orc rushed her, knocking her over, his teeth latching down onto her forearm, denting the leather bracer and pinching her skin. She cried out in pain, but used the angle to shove her knife through his temple.

Kicking him off, she didn't stop to check to her arm for any broken skin. Instead, shoving her dagger back into her scabbard, she rushed back to the little boy, scooping him onto her hip with one arm, wincing a little at the weight.

It was harder to run now, but she moved as quickly as she could, dodging the oncoming Orcs, swiping her sword left and right, severing necks and dropping bodies as they crossed her path. She was fighting with a furor, a need to save these children, and nothing was going to stand in her way.

The porch was only a few more steps away, and she rushed up them, dropping the boy gently into one of the other children's care and doing a quick headcount. They were all there. There were still a handful of the dead in the field, close enough to the house to be a threat, and, checking to make sure that the kids stayed in place, she stepped into the path again, driving her heavy sword through bones and heads, dropping the last few of the fresh Orcs.

They made it. Safety.

Sheathing her sword, she turned to step up towards the door, but was greeted by the loud snarling growl of the huge dog stepping out of the dark doorway.

So close.

~29~

The Ranger and the Cop

After half an hour, Dez gripped Ledger carpet-covered sleeve to stop him.

"They're headed straight for the bus," she said, panic bursting in her voice.

"Shit," he said, realizing she was right.

"How do they know about it?" Dez demanded. "No one knew we were there."

"Maybe they don't," said Ledger. "I ran into some of these clowns near here. They had a camper in the woods. That's where they took Lindsey. I chased her through the forest and came to the farmhouse. This road would go right to that campsite, and it's the easiest route. These guys must have used a forest path or some farm road to maybe try and catch some stragglers from Appomattox. They'd have stuck to the woods for their raid, but to take prisoners back to their camp is easier if they used this road, especially at night."

"But they're going to go right to the bus."

"They probably don't even know it's there."

"How would *you* know?"

"Because these guys have been working the woods west of you, staying off the main roads to avoid National Guard patrols. It's your good luck that they didn't find you sooner and, sorry to say, it's also good luck the Guard didn't find you and bring you in to the rescue station. Being out here probably saved your lives."

It was a small, cold consolation and Ledger could see it on her face. "We have to do something. They're going to walk right up to the bus. Maybe some of them already have."

Ledger thought about all those kids and felt a coldness in his heart. "I know," he said, "and we have to be ready for that possibility. But consider this, Dez, these assholes are out here rounding up prisoners. They're not going to kill those kids. They'll want to add them to their catch and take them back."

"Only women and girls," she fired back. "There are boys back there. They'll just up and kill them."

"Maybe not."

"Why the hell not?" she demanded.

He looked at her. "Don't be naïve."

Her face, already pale in the bad light, went whiter still. "God."

"How much farther?" he asked, then had to jab her in the shoulder to get her to focus. "Hey! How much farther to the bus?"

She blinked and then looked around. "Three miles, tops."

"Okay," he said quickly, "new plan. You keep following them. I'm going to see if I can circle around and get in front of them. The bus is our target. If there's anyone else there—more of *them*, I mean—then you and I will regroup and make a new plan. Don't look for me—I'll find you."

"And if it's just these six?"

He shrugged. "Then it's going to suck to be them. But listen, don't go Billy the Kid on me, okay? You follow and wait and then we hit them on my go-order, *capiche?*"

She clearly didn't like it, but Dez nodded. As he began to move off she caught his wrist. "Ledger," she said, "we're going to get my kids back. No matter what it takes. No matter what we have to do. You understand me?"

"Yes, ma'am," he said and sketched a salute.

"Ledger—?"

"What?"

"Call me ma'am again and I'll kneecap you."

He grinned and moved off into the woods.

It was rougher terrain, but that did not matter. The group of men could only go as fast as their weakest and smallest prisoner. He had no such restrictions. Within minutes he'd pulled parallel to the group and then raced on ahead. He stayed in the woods, dodging vines and two zombies he didn't bother to stop and kill. The ground sloped upward and he ran up, trying to ignore the protests of old scar tissue and middle-aged knees. Instead he accepted the pain and ate it, fed on it, let it fuel the anger that drive him on. He tried not to think about what horror might have come for his wife and child while he was away trying to save the world from the wrong doomsday weapon. Had someone come to help them? Had they fallen to the dead? Or had it been men like these who had arrived when no one else would come?

That was another kind of pain that threw gasoline on the fires of his hate.

Ten minutes later he found the bus.

It sat on dead tires and all around it there were bodies.

None of them were alive.

~30~

Rachael Elle

The snarling dog bore down on Rachael, and she drew her knife slowly, trying to keep the kids behind her. She didn't want to hurt the animal, but she only had one knife and the dog had a mouth full of dangerous weapons. She'd never been on this side of a dog attack, never quite witnessed how many teeth a dog that size could have, but she knew how much damage an angry dog could do, to her, to the kids. And after everything, she wasn't going to let any of the kids get hurt.

"No, Baskerville—*don't.*"

A young girl's voice rang out from the darkness behind the snarling dog. It wasn't one of the heroes, though. Rachael's eyes darted up to the doorway as the dog stepped back, his dark eyes still fixed on her, still giving a low growl, but teeth no longer bared.

"You got bit," the girl said from the darkness. "I saw you."

Rachael glanced down at her arm, before holding her hands up, dagger still in one of them. Then she raised her arm. "It didn't break the skin. See?"

"Prove it," said the voice and there was a metallic click. Rachael knew the sound of a shotgun hammer being cocked back. "Show me."

Rachael fumbled with the buckle on the bracer for a moment before sliding it off, then she raised her bare arm to show the bruised but unbroken skin. "I'm not infected. None of us are…but there still some of those *things* out here. It's just me and some kids. Please...can we come in?"

"No. I don't know you."

One of the little ones called out, "Is Miss Dez here? Rachael said Miss Dez would be here...."

The little girl stood with her arms wrapped around the boy that Rachael had saved.

There was a scuff of a footstep and then a young woman stepped out of the shadows and into the moonlight. She held a heavy shotgun with the black barrels trained on Rachael's chest, however her eyes flicked toward the kids. The dog stood with her and Rachael could see a horrible wound on its head and the line of fresh stitches. The dog looked mean and maybe a little crazy.

The young woman frowned. "You know Dez?"

"I don't," Rachael admitted. "But these are her kids. She's been protecting them and she went looking for supplies or a new place to hole up. She was supposed to come back and get them, but she never did. I found them in a bus out on the highway. There were monsters everywhere...and some bad men, too. I'd seen this place and thought I'd bring them here so they'd be safe while I went to look for her."

Rachael glanced over her shoulder, before looking back to the girl. Uncertainty was carved into her young features.

"Look," said Rachael, "we can't stay out here. It's not safe. You have the gun and the dog. You can even take my knife, just let us in."

The girl considered for a moment, before lowering the shotgun slightly. Baskerville stepped down to sniff at Rachael and then at a couple of the kids. He'd stopped growling when the girl lowered her weapon.

In the fields behind them one of the Orcs moaned. Far away another seemed to answer its plaintive, endlessly hungry call. The girl nodded to herself. Then she stepped to one side and jerked her head toward the front door.

"Get in," she said, "but don't do anything stupid."

"Thanks," Rachael told her and began gently but quickly pushing the kids up the stairs. When they were all inside, she paused and glanced back over the field, over the shadowed mounds of bodies in the moonlight.

We made it, she thought. *We'll be safe here.*

Then she spotted a figure standing at the edge of the field, almost lost in the shadows of the forest. The girl with the shotgun followed her gaze.

"It's one of the zombies," said the girl.

The figure walked a few paces forward and moonlight bathed his face. Rachael saw dark eyes and a wide, white smile. Hair stood up all along Baskerville's spine and once more he uttered a low, deadly growl, however this time it was directed to the shadowy figure. Then the man turned and, without haste, walked into the utter blackness under the trees.

Rachael watched him go. Then she turned to the girl to tell her that it wasn't an Orc out there, but it wasn't necessary. The girl looked like someone had punched her in the gut. No, worse.

"It's *them,*" whispered the girl in a voice that was full of sickness.

"We need to talk," said Rachael.

The girl nodded and her face was a ghastly white. "Not out here."

She went in and the big dog followed. Rachael lingered a moment longer, looking at the featureless blackness of the trees.

Okay, she thought, *this is really, really bad.*

~31~

The Ranger and the Cop

Ledger drew his gun and moved down the hill.

The camp Dez had built around the bus was ruined. There was blood everywhere—splashed on the side of the bus, spattered inside, and streaked along the ground. Bodies lay in ungainly sprawls, but Ledger could not find bullet wounds or shell casings. The wounds he did find confused him. They weren't the normal stab or slash wounds, nor were they the deep clefts left by an axe-blade. No, these were very long wounds, the kind a sword might make. From the angle, depth and length of the cuts, ledger guessed the weapon hadn't been a Japanese katana, which left injuries more like scalpels. A cavalry sword? Or something stolen from a museum, perhaps. That wasn't out of the question. He'd been planning on looting a museum for older and sturdier weapons and maybe some real armor.

Whoever had used the sword was a little sloppy but had some moves. He saw boot marks from small feet. A teenage boy with a narrow foot or a woman. That didn't square with Dez's intel. The adult she'd left in charge, Mr. Biel, would have been too big and—according to Dez—not much of a fighter. And none of the kids were supposed to be old enough to do this kind of damage.

So, who was the swordsman. Correction, he thought, swords*woman*.

"Curiouser and couriouser," he murmured. The corpses had head wounds, but there were smears to suggest that at least one of the dead had reanimated and walked off. There were no small bodies, and he thanked God for that. If God was up there and listening.

As best he could by the pale moonlight he tried to read the scene and it soon became clear that there were several overlapping stories here. Based on the orientation of footprints—particularly of which sets were more recent and overlapped others—the truth began to emerge. The teenager or woman—and he was moderately sure now that it was a woman—had led the kids away from the bus after the fight. However there was a second group of prints that seemed to almost obliterate the marks of the swordswoman's group. All of these footprints were male. It was a large party of men, and they'd come to the bus, poked around for a while, and then left. However they went in exactly the same direction as the woman and the kids. Following them.

Or hunting them.

More of the NKK? The sinking feeling in Ledger's gut told him that his guess was right. If there had been better light he might have been able to tell how much time had passed between when the woman took the kids and when the men began to follow. Best case scenario was half a day. Men could move faster through the woods than a bunch of kids, even if they had to follow the trail at night.

Ledger heard a sound and paused to listen. It was the rude laughter of the men leading their captives along the road. Ledger was already tired of them, of their existence. And although he'd just met Dez Fox and had never met any of the kids, they belonged to the Stebbins County refugees. He'd liked Billy Trout and liked the things the man had said about Dez. She was a little harder to like in person, but he reckoned that he wasn't seeing her under the most convivial circumstances. Fair enough.

Ledger checked his weapon, looked around for the best vantage point, and then stepped into shadows. He had no doubt at all that Dez would be following the men, or that she would be ready. His concern was that she would not freak out when it was clear the bus was empty. Nothing to do about that now but try to ride the wave once it started and hope for the best.

He waited through five endless minutes, and then he heard a male voice ring out in sudden surprise. "Hey! Look at that shit!"

The man with the flashlight and his partner with the M-16 came running up the road. Ledger heard the rifleman yell, "Jose, Nucks, stay back, keep an eye on those bitches. Barney, Turk, get your asses up here."

Ledger waited until the four guards—the two from the front and the two working the rear of the sad caravan began stalking forward, all of them with guns, all of them alert to danger.

And all of them looking the wrong way.

Ledger hoped Dez Fox was ready, because he damn well was. He stepped out of the shadows, closing in at an oblique angle, behind the range of the rearmost man's peripheral vision. He moved without a sound and made it all the way to the closest of the four. The man, a bruiser with huge hands clamped on a double barrel twelve gauge, never saw Ledger coming. One minute he was working his way forward with his friends and then he was dead.

Ledger shot him in the back of the head from three feet away, then turned to fire two rounds at the other man in the back, and then four rounds at the first two.

Pop-pop.

Pop-pop.

Pop-pop.

Pop-pop.

Eight shots. Eight muzzle flashes brighter than the moonlight. Four men falling.

It hadn't been a fight. Ledger hadn't wanted a fight. Not a fair one. Never a fair one with men like these.

He spun in time to see more muzzle flashes in the darkness. There were screams, high and shrill and filled with terror as the women saw the fire from the guns, heard the shots, but did not yet understand. All they could know is that death and horror had once more reached out to them. Helpless, bound, humiliated and afraid, all that was left for them to do was scream.

And so they screamed.

Suddenly a voice rose, louder than the thunder of the guns. A woman. Dez.

"Shut. The. Fuck. Up!"

She bellowed it with all of the leather-throated volume of a drill instructor. The sound of her voice, and the power promised by it, smashed through the screams with more shocking force than a slap to each screaming mouth. The women flinched back, stunned to silence, all turning to stare at the woman who had appeared out of the night as if conjured by dark magic.

Dez lowered her smoking gun. The two men who had been guarding the prisoners were down, their heads pulped by hollow-point rounds.

"Officer Fox," said Ledger, being formal in order to make a statement. To suggest that some kind of old-world order still existed. "All the hostiles are down."

Dez glanced at him, then nodded. "Secure the perimeter. I'll release the prisoners."

He was pleased that Dez had understood and was quick enough to roll with the drama. He had put her in charge of the moment, and she took that role and ran with it. A woman in charge, a man taking her order. It was a useful fiction in the moment, and he could see the panic ebb ever so slightly among the prisoners.

Ledger faded back and gave Dez a moment to cut the first woman free, then watched with approval as she handed her knife to the woman. It gave the freed prisoner a task and it gave her power. *She* would free her fellow prisoners, and it set a precedent that as each one was freed she turned to help with the person in captivity next to her. Dez was doing it exactly right. This wasn't stuff they taught in the military or in the police. It was the kind of thing learned through experience and compassion out here in the storm lands. It was a kind of benign manipulation that turned a helpless prisoner into a member of a winning team.

"Ledger," called Dez, "report."

He trotted over. The women shied back from him, and pulled the children close. Assuming a role of strength and protection even in their fear.

In quick words but a deferential tone, Ledger told her that the bus was empty, there were no indications that any of the kids had been hurt, and that they had been led away by an armed woman. He paused and told her than a party of men had come along sometime later and appeared to be following. This dragged some sick cries from the women, but Dez kept her cool.

She looked around for the oldest and calmest-looking of the women. "What's your name?"

"Shannon Byrd," said the woman.

"Okay, Shannon, here's the deal. Captain Ledger and I are going to find my kids. We're going to leave right now. You and the others can take the guns from the dog meat over there on the road and stay here until we come back…or you can all come with us. You get to make the call, Shannon. This isn't a democracy."

Shannon studied her for a moment, then looked at the others. As she did so she idly touched the rope burns on her throat and fingered the edges of her torn blouse. There were bruises in the shape of a man's grasping hand on her upper arm. She walked over to one of the dead men, bent, picked up his shotgun, hefted its weight in her hand, paused for a moment, spit on the corpse, and then walked back to Dez.

"We're going with you."

The other women milled around for a moment, and the kids stared in shock and uncertainty, then a teenage girl who had a split lip and a black eye went and got the other shotgun. She cracked it open, checked the rounds, knelt and picked the dead man's pockets for extra shells, stuffed them in the pockets of her jeans, and rejoined the group.

"I used to hunt wild pig," she said in a thick southern accent. "I'm okay to hunt some more of 'em."

That did it. The other women and some of the kids took guns, knives, ammunition, and water. Dez and Ledger gave them the world's shortest course in gun safety, and then they turned toward the trail of footprints leading into the woods.

"This isn't going to be easy," said Dez.

"Nothing is easy anymore," said Shannon.

"Nothin' was ever easy," said the southern girl.

They headed into the woods.

Hunting.

~32~

Rachael Elle and Lindsey

"We need to get the kids somewhere safe," Rachael insisted as she followed the girl through the living room, dining room and into the kitchen. She buckled her bracer back on as she walked. The kids—heroes and little ones—had settled around the big kitchen table. Most sitting, some standing, all of them looking around at their new surroundings in silence. There was almost a sense of wonder in them, as if they'd forgotten what it was like to be anywhere but inside a bloodstained bus.

"They're safe here," the girl said, setting the shotgun down on the table.

"No, they're not. Look…let's start with who's who, okay?" Rachael asked. "I'll go first. I'm Rachael. I'm from Pennsylvania. I'm a long way from home, but I'm trying to find people to bring them to safety. Your name is…."

"Lindsey," the girl finally responded.

"Okay, Lindsey. I'd say 'nice to meet you', but that would be kind of weird."

"Tell me about it," Lindsey muttered.

"There are some really bad men after us," said Rachael, "and I think that was one of them out there, so we need to get the kids somewhere safe. Is there an attic or a basement? Somewhere they can hide?"

Lindsey nodded. "There's a basement and the door's really solid. Someone put a crossbar on it, you know, *after,* and they reinforced the wood with some kind of metal. Stainless steel, I think. There's lots of stuff down there but as long as they stay quiet they'll be able to hide."

"Mind showing me?"

Lindsey nodded and opened a door that was built into the wall so that it looked like the front of a pantry. It was hard to tell if that was something done before the dead rose, or after. Probably after, Rachael decided. To hide it from scavengers. She wondered what happened to the clever people who did that, and who reinforced the door so heavily from the other side. After all those precautions, what had tripped them up? What was the mistake that killed them?

She wanted to ask Lindsey, but doubted the girl knew. And maybe that wasn't the right conversation to have in front of the kids.

The basement was large and very solid, with a poured concrete floor, wooden rafters, and boxes of canned food. There was a big stack of furniture pads in one corner, more than enough for everyone to have a bed and something to cover themselves. The pads were old, covered with cobwebs and spider eggs, but who cared? Rachael tapped Supergirl on the shoulder and drew her to one side.

"Okay, I'm going to go check the rest of the house with Lindsey," she said. "You're in charge down here. I need you to make some smart choices. Everyone gets food and picks a spot to sleep. You and the other heroes make sure they all stay calm, understand?"

The girl nodded, eyes wide with fear but her chin was firm. *Being a hero,* thought Rachael. *Nice.*

"Now," she said, lowering her voice, "if anything happens upstairs I want you to close the door and bar it from the inside. Once you do that no one will know you're here. But you have to be absolutely quiet. Not a sound from anyone. Promise?"

"I promise," said the young hero.

Rachael held her fist out for a bump, smiled, and turned to the group of kids. "Okay, troops, we need to wait for Miss Dez. She's going to come back soon but until then you need to stay completely silent down here. I know all of you can do that! Wonder Woman, Black Widow and all the other heroes would be so proud of you. Whatever you hear upstairs, stay here and stay quiet."

The kids nodded, their eyes huge and haunted. Rachael followed Lindsey back upstairs, praying to herself that this would work.

~33~

The Ranger and the Cop

It was a nightmare trip through the woods.

Ledger could feel it and he was a trained Special Operator. Dez Fox had been a combat soldier in Afghanistan and was an experienced cop, but he knew she was feeling it, too. The women and children who moved through the black forest with them were refugees of an ongoing horror. He hoped that their worst memories were behind them and not waiting to be experienced.

The moon was moving behind the far hills and it dragged its generous light with it, yielding the woods to armies of shadow. It would have been difficult enough if the only dangers waiting for them were rabbit holes, vines, and deadfalls.

If only.

Ledger had Dez's Mag-lite and picked out their trail. The group of men had not been gentle with the forest, instead choosing to smash obstacles out of their way as often as possible. That, Ledger knew, had to have been noisy because the passage of those men had pulled behind it a wake of hungry dead. Drawn to noise, movement, lights, and the smell of human flesh, the zombies had come from all over the forest and were trying to catch those men—and the party of children that went through here first.

Ledger covered his light and stopped his party fifty feet back from a loose knot of shambling dead.

"We have to go around," said Dez.

"We can't. We'll lose their trail and lose too damn much time."

Dez pointed with her Glock. "We don't know how many of them there are."

"No, but the wind's blowing this way. They won't know we're coming up on them and we can take them out one at a time. These things don't learn from what happens from their buddies. Killing them is rinse and repeat."

"It's not that easy, Captain Macho."

"Of course it isn't." He holstered his pistol, handed her back the flashlight, drew his rapid-release knife and a heavier Ka-Bar. "Here's the plan. You keep the civilians together and keep them moving. I'm going to see if I can clean up our trail."

"Why you and not me?"

He smiled. "You know the kids," he said. "The women trust you. Lindsey trusts you. You're thirty years younger than me and that makes me the most expendable of the two of us."

"But—."

"And, no offense meant, Dez, you're a cop and I'm what I am."

"Which is—?"

"A killer." Ledger could hear the bleak sadness in his own voice, and he left her without another word, moving quickly along the path.

~34~

Dez Fox and the Refugees

Dez watched, squinting through the gloom, not risking the flashlight to see what Ledger was doing. All she could make out was a confusion of dark forms moving within the greater wall of shadows ahead. Soft sounds drifted back, but they were indistinct. The other women and kids crowded around her, asking hushed questions, seeking comfort. It made Dez feel weird. Back in Stebbins County, despite wearing a uniform and badge, she was hardly the pillar of the community. Known for her drinking, sleeping around, off-duty brawling, on-duty brutalizing of child molesters and wife beaters, and being generally regarded as a redneck hick cop. No one had ever held her out as a role model or a leader.

And then the world ended.

During the outbreak she'd stayed alive and on her feet while other people fell. Even her partner, JT Hammond, a seasoned cop and the closest thing to real family Dez had, was bitten. He'd died a hero's death, but he'd still died. It left Dez in charge of the kids who had gone to Stebbins Little School because that was the town emergency shelter. The parents and teachers who'd taken them there, along with most of the county's children, had died. Only a few hundred kids and a dozen or so adults were left. All of them deferred to Dez, drawn to her strength more powerfully than they were repelled by her pre-outbreak reputation.

For the last months she'd protected the kids at the bus. Now she had a bunch of women who had been brutalized by the living, by the kinds of men Dez had always despised. Instead of playing nursemaid or team leader or whatever the hell she was supposed to be, Dez wanted to be ranging ahead to find the NKK thugs and see how many of them she could dismantle. Maybe she'd go crazy and make a bandolier of nutsacks. That might be fun. Might be a good way to go all the way nuts.

Except…

Billy Trout was alive. *Alive.* The other kids she'd saved from Stebbins were alive. And the kids from her bus were still alive. They hadn't found any small bodies along this path.

She forced her hands to stop shaking and hoisted a convincing smile of confidence onto her mouth as she calmed the women. She assured them that everyone was fine, it was all cool, and that Ledger was following *her* orders to clear the road. The women, desperate for something to believe, clung to her words as if they were gospel.

Then, much sooner than she expected, Ledger came back, moving quickly but without reckless haste. He waved Dez over for a quick private chat.

"I took out a few of the deadheads," he said, "but there weren't as many as I thought. Stragglers, mostly. I was going to keep going, but I spotted the hunting party."

"Jesus. Did they have my kids?"

"No," said Ledger, "and that means we caught a break. No, make that two breaks."

"What do you mean? Since when was lady luck giving us anything but a bad handjob?"

He grinned. "Stealing that," he said. "But, to answer the question, I think whoever's with the kids is smart and it's pretty obvious she knows she's being followed. There were a couple of times along the way here that I thought she tried to hide her trail, and up ahead the NKK guys are trying to decide which of three separate trails to follow. The gal with the sword pulled a fast one."

"I guess this is a 'you go girl' moment, but how's that help us. *We* don't know which trail she took, do we?"

"I think maybe we do. One trail heads off southwest and I think it's supposed to look like the kids are circling back to the bus. The second trail heads due northeast towards the Appomattox rescue station."

"That's been overrun."

"Sure, but I think sword gal wants whoever's following to think she doesn't know that. Right now that trail looks best and it follows the path of least resistance."

"Oh. You said there was a third track, though."

"Yup. And even though it's not much of a trail to follow, I think it's what the sword gal took."

"Why are you so sure? Are you a Cherokee scout or something?"

"No, and not a boy scout either, toots," said Ledger. "I guess I 'get' devious people, and the third track is devious."

"Devious how?"

"It looks like one person went that way, and the prints are the same shoes as sword gal. But they're too deep."

"So…?"

"So, I think she had the kids walk that way in single file, making sure they each stepped in the other's footprints. And then she walked over that so it looks like only one set of prints went that way. If you don't know much about tracking, it just looks like a clear track left by a single person."

Dez nodded, appreciating it. "That's pretty badass. I want to meet this chick."

"Me, too. I'd like to buy her a beer. Maybe a couple."

"Keep it in your pants, Blondie."

He laughed. "Seriously, just a beer. I have a wife."

Dez avoided his eyes for a moment. Ledger had made the statement with total certainty, and as far as Dez reckoned that kind of statement was irrational. Maybe scary. *Don't go getting weird on me now,* she thought.

Ledger did not notice her reaction. "Here's the real prize in the Cracker-Jack box, Dez. The trail the sword gal took…? You go that way and you walk right up to the farm."

"Which farm…?" she began, then stopped. "Shit. Those assholes are going straight to the kids and Lindsey."

"Nope," said Ledger. "They sent some scouts down the other trails. I'll bet they'll find something on one of them. If sword gal's as smart as she seems there'll be something *to* find."

"Even so..."

"Even so," said Ledger, "we need to split up. You can cut off this path and hit the fire access road that cuts across the farm road. If you leave now you might get to the farm before the kids. It'll help if they see you."

"Why split up? What are you going to do?"

"I'll catch up." Ledger glanced back the way he'd just come. "I want to have a little fun first."

And with that he was gone again.

Dez Fox stared at the empty woods into which he'd just vanished. Who *was* this guy? She had always loved the tall, tanned, blonde types. Guys who looked like they might have a Viking gene lurking around in their DNA. Billy had that, even though he was the least physical guy she'd ever met. Some of the guys she'd bang when she was mad at Billy were like that. Most of them were roughhouse bikers who she turned into revenge fucks when Billy walked out on her. He did that a lot. Or used to when there was a world.

But Ledger, even though he was a lot older than her, was a classic example of the type. That he was powerful, experienced and confident was evident. That he was a good man was clear, too. Maybe a bit more of a boy scout than she usually liked. Dez preferred her men to be crazier than she was, and that was saying something.

He was a good guy, but he wasn't necessarily a nice guy. And he was sexy. Like Chris Hemsworth if he was fifty-something and hadn't been eaten by zombies.

Dez felt a strange and unwanted attraction to him, though wanting to bed him and wanting to hit him upside the head with a tire iron were running neck in neck.

Then, as if superimposed over the thought of Ledger was a smaller, thinner, less capable, less heroic, less crazy, more rational and normal man. Billy Trout. Dez seldom felt guilty for what her thoughts did and what her passions wanted, but at that moment the ache that pulsed in the broken places of her heart were not for Joe Ledger. They were for Billy Trout.

"Nothin's ever easy," she growled, echoing the words of the southern girl with the shotgun. She set her jaw and turned around to gather her refugees.

~35~

Rachael Elle and Lindsey

Rachael and Lindsey swapped shorthand versions of their stories as they hurried from room to room to make sure the house was buttoned up against what they both knew was coming.

"'Nu Klux Klan'?" asked Rachael, laughing despite the tension. "Are you serious?"

"Yes," said Lindsey, who wasn't smiling.

"That is the stupidest thing I've ever heard and I used to watch *Real Wives of New Jersey*."

"Stupid or not," Lindsey said coldly, "they're going to come in here and…and…"

Rachael crossed to her and took the young woman by the shoulders, shaking her slightly and then holding her steady. "If they try, we'll kill them," she said, and she was surprised by the vicious coldness in her own voice. "We have guns and blades, and we have a fortress."

Baskerville *whuffed* loudly as if wanting to be included in her inventory.

"Right, and we have a furry four-legged tank."

The dog wagged his tail. He seemed to understand and appreciate her description.

"We don't know how many of them there are," protested Lindsey.

"And they don't know what kind of raw, unfiltered hell they'd be stepping into if they try to break in here."

Lindsey looked at her. "You're only a pretend hero, you know. That costume and all…it's not real."

Rachael shrugged. "What's 'real' anyway? The world ended and there are zombies out there. Tell me what's 'real'."

Lindsey said nothing.

"I've killed Orcs and I've killed bad guys. I used to work in a bank, for Christ's sake. I used to be a nerd girl. Now I fight monsters, and here's the funny part…I *win*. I'm still alive, and so are my people. So are those kids. You want to stand there and tell me that isn't real?"

Lindsey began to say something, the stopped and shook her head.

Baskerville suddenly growled and an instant later they knew why. Outside, on the porch, there was a creak. The kind that only sounds like what it is. A heavy foot stepping onto an old board.

"Oh, god," breathed Lindsey.

"Gun," snapped Rachael. "Check the kitchen door. Keep quiet."

The girl ran to grab the shotgun she'd left on the kitchen table. The dog trotted behind her, ears back, head low, nails clicking on the floorboards.

Rachael ran into the living room and crouched down next to the front door, her back pressed against the wall, sword and dagger in her gloved hand. Despite her brave words her heart pounded like thunder.

~36~

The Ranger

Ledger wished he had Baskerville with him. The dog could track a frigging white ghost in a snowstorm. And he was the best friend to have in any kind of fight.

"Stupid mutt," he grumbled under his breath. "Why don't you have the good sense not to stand in front of a bullet? Big dummy."

He prayed that Baskerville's wound wasn't serious. Losing the dog would crush him.

Somewhere out in the world was Baskerville's littermate, Boggart. When Ledger last saw him, the other dog was with Top and Bunny, the other two veteran special operators he'd served with for many years. Finding them was very important to him. With them, he could start building a real team of rangers who might make a serious difference in this world. Hell, if he had Top and Bunny with him—and a healthy Baskerville and Boggart—these NKK idiots would be dead meat already. Be nice if Sam Imura was with them, too. If Sam was still alive. Sure, the bad guys had the numbers, but Ledger and his team had faced steeper odds before. They'd walked through the Valley of the Shadow and stepped over the bones of their enemies. Time and time again.

As he moved to intercept the NKK hunters, he had to work on his emotional reaction. These men offended him on a level that ran all the way down to his soul. Years ago, when Ledger was a young teenager, he and his girlfriend, Helen, had been attacked by a group of older teens. Those boys had stomped Ledger nearly to death and while he lay there, broken and bleeding, he saw the things they did to Helen. It destroyed them both. They physically survived the assault, but healing tissue and knitting bones did not mean they, as people, had survived. Years later, after several failed suicide attempts, Helen took her own life and it was Ledger who found her. He had been studying martial arts since the attack and had grown up big, tough and vicious, but none of those skills could help him save the girl who had stepped off the edge of the world and let the big dark swallow her.

The NKK hunters were no different from those boys. They were users, takers, destroyers of hearts and souls. They believed that they had a right to anything they took by force. No law applied to them, and the world's infrastructure had collapsed as if in homage to their dark desires. The world bared its throat to them.

That's how they saw it, but Ledger saw it differently. If no laws applied to them, then no laws protected them either. No laws, no restrictions, no mercy. They were hunters of a certain kind, and he was a completely different hunter.

He was glad Dez Fox, the women and those children were not here to see what was going to happen.

~37~

Dez Fox and the Refugees

The women and kids were scared but they were visibly changing from helpless victims to a group of armed survivors. What had begun when they first took the weapons from their dead captors was continuing as Dez led them through the woods. The simple fact of finding the fire access road where Dez promised it would be strengthened them further.

For her part, Dez wanted to kick herself for not exploring the area around the bus more thoroughly. The farm where Lindsey waited for them had been there all along. Sure, the family who owned it and the refugees who had holed up there all died, but maybe they wouldn't have if Dez had been with them. Maybe, she knew, was a terrible word. It was thorn in the skin. Maybe if she'd found the farmhouse months ago Biel would be live and the kids would be better nourished and…well, *saner.* Maybe she'd have met Ledger sooner and maybe he would have been able to lead her to Billy.

Maybe, maybe, maybe.

The moon was down now but there were no clouds and there were stars by the billion.

There were also zombies on the road.

Not many, but enough. Eight or nine of them, spaced out, looking lost but turning toward the sound and smell of the living coming toward them.

"If Ledger can do it," Dez muttered, and then ran ahead of the group, attacking the zombies before they could attack her charges. She smashed aside their white hands with a carpet-coated left forearm and smashed skull bones with her blackjack.

Rinse and repeat.

That thought made her smile.

Then someone was beside her. It was the teenage girl with the shotgun. As Dez was clubbing a dead National Guardsman to the ground, the girl took a stance, tucked the stock of the shotgun into her shoulder, and fired.

"No!" yelled Dez, but her voice was blasted away as the twelve-gauge roared. Ten feet away a zombie crumbled to the ground, the top of its head blown away.

"Got 'im," said the girl with pride even as she fished for a fresh shell. Dez ripped the gun out of her hand and nearly hit the stupid kid with the blackjack.

"What's wrong with *you*?" demanded the girl, trying to grab the gun back.

Before Dez could answer they heard something that froze them all to silence.

It wasn't the moans of the dead still on the road, or even the ones now drawn to them from the surrounding woods.

It was a voice. Male. And close.

"It's them. They're over there," he yelled.

It was not Ledger's voice.

Dez drew her pistol as the refugees swirled around her.

"*Run!*" she roared.

~38~

Rachael Elle and Lindsey

Outside, the footsteps were muffled, and it was hard to tell exactly how many men were on the porch. Rachael didn't like that, but she didn't want to risk peering through the shutters or blinds. There could be two or there could be fifty. This wasn't a fair fight, even with what they hoped would be an element of surprise.

The first footsteps stopped outside the door, and she held her breath. The doorknob shook a little, but the lock held, and Rachael braced herself for them to break down the door. The seconds dragged on, but the crash of the door never came. Confused, Rachael stood cautiously, back still against the wall, but listening for any sounds. The footsteps hadn't started again, but she couldn't tell where anyone was anymore.

Suddenly the window in the kitchen shattered, and Rachael heard Lindsey yell and her shotgun fire loudly. That seemed to be the invitation the men outside were waiting for. The slam of boot against door startled Rachael, but she reacted quickly as the door flew open, swinging her sword quickly and catching the first man through the door with surprise as her blade lodged in his neck. Pulling it back, she let his body fall to the floor as the man behind him yelled out with surprise, firing his gun uselessly, the bullet striking the wall on the other side of the room.

She waited for the next person to come through, but another crash from the kitchen distracted her. This time the door, she was sure of, and another shotgun blast.

In the moment she was distracted, several men had come into the room, and Rachael rushed them from behind, gashing one man across his shoulder, ducking as he swung around at her cursing, before swinging and slicing her sword into his leg. He collapsed, and then turned her attention to the next man, knocking his gun out of his hand with her dagger and slicing across his chest with the blade.

The third man had a knife, and she feigned an attack with her dagger, which he went to block, before swiping the other way with her sword, hitting him hard in the head, downing him with a scream and a shower of blood.

She heard Lindsey shout, and another crash in the kitchen, and what sounded like falling furniture.

Slamming the door shut, she pushed one of the chairs in front of it to barricade it, before running into the kitchen to see if Lindsey needed her help. There seemed to be more men in the kitchen, though most of them were on the floor bleeding thanks to Baskerville, whose muzzle was soaked in blood. The dog leapt at a man coming through the back door, and Rachael stabbed down hard into the neck of one who lunged at Lindsey on the floor.

Shoving his body to the side, Rachael held out her hand to help Lindsey up.

Before either of them could say anything, another crash came this time from the living room. Looking at each other, they both ran together to the room, Lindsey in the lead with the shotgun.

Glass and wooden shutter pieces littered the floor, and a number of the men were climbing in through the window. Lindsey didn't hesitate, priming the shotgun and pulling the trigger. As she reloaded, Rachael rushed forward, dragging one of the men that was climbing through out of the window and stabbing her dagger into his chest before pushing him to the side to swing with her sword.

Would this ever end? There seemed to be a non-stop stream of men coming through, and Rachael knew they wouldn't be able to take them all on themselves.

~39~

The Ranger

There are times and circumstances where a smaller force is more dangerous than a larger one. Skirmishers, snipers, and Special Operators have always known this. They use mobility and the absence of the time delays caused by chain-of-command decisions to act with autonomy and without hesitation. In the right conditions and with the right planning they can come out of nowhere, strike and vanish. Terrorists tried to use this tactic but while they were often effective, they had no escape plan. Joe Ledger was many things but suicidal was not one of them.

What he was, however, was vicious, cold and skillful.

He crept up on the hunting party and stalked them, counting their numbers, identifying the members of that group who seemed to understand what they were doing, and those whose presence could be exploited to become liabilities. He looked for the leaders and the fighters. Several of them appeared to understand something of woodcraft, which was not good. But they walked with the arrogance of power, expecting to be more dangerous than anything they encountered. That was very useful.

At one point the party split to follow another pair of trails, and again Ledger assumed they were both false trails set down by the woman with the sword. Whoever she was, the woman was really sneaky. Ledger liked sneaky. About half the men followed one trail and the other half kept following the same set of prints. There were thirty men in the party Ledger followed. A small army. They were all armed, but not every man had a gun. More than half had axes or improvised pole-weapons. One man carried a sledgehammer, which was dangerous but impractical.

Lacking any sound suppressors, Ledger holstered his gun and drew his knives instead. He kept the rapid release folding knife in his right because that required speed and dexterity and he was mostly right-handed. The heavier Ka-Bar was in his left, and though it was not his dominant hand, SpecOps fighters are trained to be lethal with every limb.

He moved ahead of the pack and then flattened out beside the trunk of a big maple. Absolutely still. The blades he held were blackened to a matte finish. The group passed fifteen feet to his right, following the lead of a man who seemed to understand how to track. Three of the men held flashlights and everyone was staring at whatever was illuminated by the beams. Ledger did not look at the light, not wanting to spoil his night-vision. As the group moved down the trail, Ledger fell into step with the man bringing up the rear.

"We'll get them," he said to the man, and it took the guy a couple of seconds to realize that he didn't know his new companion.

"I—," began the man, but Ledger clamped a hand over his mouth and cut his throat. He pushed the dying man against a tree to keep him from crashing to the ground.

One down.

He took the man's flashlight and moved to take his place, shining the light forward at the men in front. If they turned, all they'd see is a silhouette behind a bright light.

The men were not walking in formation, and occasionally one would lag back, or even deliberately stop to let the rearguard catch up.

Ledger liked that.

Two down.

Three.

Four.

Somewhere behind him the dead men would be undergoing a process of transformation as they bled out. The pathogens and parasites of *Lucifer 113* would be staging a hostile takeover of the motor cortex, the cranial nerves, the respiration and other functions, discarding what wasn't necessary, acquiring what was. In less than a minute each of those dead men would rise and then see the bobbing lights, hear the chatter of men talking, smell the meat.

Good.

One of the men loudly announced that he had to take a leak. He stopped, unzipped, and died without even knowing death was upon him.

Five down.

Then six. And seven.

It was the eighth man who turned at the wrong time, maybe to say something, and saw a stranger with a wicked grin and a bloody knife. The man got half of a scream out. He died, but the scream was enough.

Then everyone was screaming and yelling.

And firing.

Joe Ledger was gone before the hunters began firing, and almost at once they were firing at the wrong thing, in the wrong direction. Ledger went deep into the brush, cut left and circled around before coming back at the group from the front. He spotted the tracker, who stood next to the brute with the sledgehammer. The tracker had a pistol in his hand and he was firing wide of the group, aiming at God knew what. With all the lead flying the leaves and branches were dancing and popping, making it look like the woods were filled with attackers.

Ledger sheathed his Ka-Bar and folding knife, drew his pistol, and ran at the tracker. He fired two rounds into the man's back, then parked a single round in the side of the sledgehammer man's neck. He kept firing, taking six more men and then he was gone again just as the hunters realized that not all of the gunfire was theirs. They turned, their yells rising to shrieks of fury and panic. And they did the one thing they probably thought was the smartest move, but it was the single stupidest thing they could do. It was a hit and run specialist's dream reaction.

They spread out to try and find him.

They didn't know who was out there or what he looked like. Or even how many attackers they were facing. Instead of forming a defensive group, they offered themselves up to the demon in the forest.

And Ledger began hunting them.

One after another after another.

~40~

Dez Fox and the Refugees

"Run," screamed Dez again, shoving the women and children forward. The man who'd yelled was not yet in sight but he sounded close. A hundred yards? A little more? Too damn close in any case.

The southern girl had her shotgun back and had reloaded it. She was white-faced with the horror of the consequences of having fired that shot.

"I'm sorry," she said, and kept saying it. Dez wanted to punch her.

"Shut up and *move*."

They began walking backward, both of them pointing guns toward the darkness at the other end of the road. Nothing seemed to move down there, and there were no more shouts.

"Maybe they…," began the girl but then there was a single sharp *crack* that split the air. The girl coughed once, then she abruptly sat down in the road. The shotgun clattered to the blacktop. The girl looked up at Dez and opened her mouth as if to offer another apology, but all that came out was a torrent of dark blood. The girl's eyes rolled high and he fell backward.

Dez stared at her for a moment.

"There!" came the shout. A different male voice.

Dez whirled, saw figures emerging from the shadows alongside the road. Four men.

Six.

More.

"Christ," cried Dez, and she fired four shots and then turned, not knowing if she hit anything. Gunfire tore the night apart and something buzzed past her ear with the angry urgency of a wasp. Dez ducked and jagged right, then ran into the woods alongside the road. She'd been shot at before, and she knew that when you know you had a near miss it's not time to celebrate your luck—it's a wake-up call that your store of luck is running low. She didn't push it. Instead, she ran.

Guns *pokked* and banged in the night and she heard the whine of rounds and the dull crunch of bullets hitting trees or skipping along the blacktop.

How far was the farmhouse?

It had to be close. She caught up with the women and barked at them to leave the road and follow her. Together they dove into the woods, cutting at an angle to try and pick up the farm road.

Something moved in front of them and one of the women screamed in absolute terror and agony as a dark shape grabbed her. Dez struck the thing with her blackjack, crushing its forehead, but as it fell back it took a mouthful of bleeding skin. Blood pumped from a torn artery in the woman's throat and she tried to stem the flow with palsied fingers. Dez stared at her, into her eyes.

And shot her.

The other women gasped and drew back, horrified, sickened. But then they turned and kept running. This was the world. This was how the world was. Appalled at what she had just done, Dez turned and followed.

Men shouted behind them and Dez could hear them crashing into the woods. They fired randomly but there was no way they could see to aim. It was a chase now. A race.

The woods thinned abruptly and the women and kids ran into a wooden rail, rebounded, fell down, crying out in pain. One woman reeled back clutching a broken wrist, but Dez grabbed her by the hair, forced her to bend and shoved her between the slats. The road was right there.

"Left," she cried as she half shoved, half carried the injured woman. "Go, go!"

They hit the hard-packed dirt and ran in a pack. Dez let go of the woman with the broken arm and faded back, shoving and slapping at the others to make sure they all kept moving. Then she saw the first of the men reach the rail. In the darkness they crashed into it, too, and in the moment of stalled impact, Dez took aim and fired. Even in that darkness the men were easy targets. She didn't need to kill, she needed to stop them. She aimed center mass and emptied an entire magazine into them. Their howls of pain and fear filled the night. Dez ran, swapping out the magazines as she went, slapping her last one into place. That gave her ten bullets. There were at least two-dozen men behind her, and maybe more. No telling how many she'd killed or wounded. The rest would be coming. A hail of bullets tried to find her in the dark.

She cut off the road and ran through the tall weeds on the verge, then dodged between a stand of maples to enter the corner of the big farm field. The house was there and she could see the shapes of darkened figures pelting through the tobacco plants toward it. The front door opened and light spilled out. The fool kid had not thought to douse her candle before opening the door. That light was a beacon, it was the brightest thing in the world right then, and it drew every single eye toward it.

The living, and the dead.

But then Dez realized, with a sick lurch of her heart, that the figure in the doorway wasn't Lindsey. And it wasn't someone coming out of the house. It was a man, and he was going in. Other men clustered around the place and only then could she hear the sounds of gunfire and screaming. Coming from the house.

But worst of all, threaded through those sounds were other noises.

The howl of a dog.

And the high-pitched, terrified screams of children.

~41~

Rachael Elle and Lindsey

The front door burst inward again, half torn from its hinges by a powerful kick. The chairs Rachael had used to brace it went flying, and a huge man filled the entrance. He had monstrous shoulders and wild hair and in his hands was a scythe he must have taken from the barn. To Rachael he looked like a mad killer from one of those old slasher films. The kind of relentless killer who hunted for teenagers having sweaty sex and then killed them in brutal ways.

The man spotted Lindsey, who had come running into the living room for more shells. "*Bitch*!" he roared and charged at her.

Maybe he didn't see Rachael, or maybe he didn't think she was real. A woman dressed in armor carrying a sword. Or, more likely, his mind had snapped and plunged into a place so dark that nothing mattered, not even his own safety. He raised the scythe and swung it with a feral growl. Lindsey dropped flat on the floor and the blade missed her by two inches. But then Rachael was there. She swung her sword in a smaller, tighter arc, the blade shearing through denim and filthy skin and muscle. Rachael was savvy enough not to try to cut through the leg. Bone was so much harder to cut than movies made it seem. It caught and snapped blades.

She pierced flesh and the speed of her slash left a slender red line on his trouser leg that seemed like nothing at all until the man turned toward her—and then the wound parted in a red scream. Blood geysered out. Rachael dodged away, light as a dancer and swung the blade again. This time she aimed higher and this time the blade bite through bone, but it was the more slender and vulnerable bones of the big man's wrist. The scythe flew away with one hand still clutching it. Rachael's third cut was through the flesh of his throat.

She kicked him sideways so that he fell across the threshold as a second man leaped inside, a butcher's cleaver in his hand.

Her blade was longer, faster and she already moving.

Behind her Lindsey finished loading the gun and ran back to the kitchen. Down the hall there was the sound of a piercing shriek buried beneath the savage growl of a brutish dog.

And outside…

The night was filled with gunfire and shouts.

~42~

The Ranger

Ledger ghosted the hunters, making them pay for their arrogance, making them afraid of the dark and of what was in it. They had been so powerful for so long, comforted by the conceit born of victories over others, now they were learning the realities of the food chain. When there was a lot of gunfire shattering the night, he contributed his own, often slipping between hunters and killing one and then yelling as if he was one of the surprised hunters. In the dark, in all that confusion, the hunters could not tell that he wasn't one of them, and he killed them for their lack of awareness.

Then he melted into the woods when he felt his luck was running thin, but even then he growled at the two men closest to him to come on, to follow, and they followed because when panic rules the moment the startled tend to take their cues from anyone who seems to know what's what.

He led the men twenty feet down a deer path, and then he killed them, too.

Of the thirty men who had followed this trail, half of them were dead or dying. Ledger went silent and moved away from the confusion, circling back to the path that would take him to the farm road.

Behind him the men fired, and screamed, and did not understand anything about what had happened. As Ledger faded away he heard fresh screams and knew that the confusion he'd left behind was grinding on itself. Men shooting their companions in the dark. And things that had once been part of that group of living rising as the hungry dead.

Ledger grinned as he ran.

~43~

Rachael and Lindsey

Screams filled the house. Three men lay on the floor clutching at savage wounds ripped into them by the dog that, either despite or because of his wounds, had gone into a killing frenzy. As they forced their way through windows, Baskerville grabbed them, tore at them, and left them crippled and shrieking on the floor.

Lindsey had thrown the shotgun down because the barrels were too hot to touch and now held a bolt-action hunting rifle in her hands. Firing clumsily but unable to miss because there were men at every window.

In the living room, Rachael was hacking at men who crowded each other to get inside. One man opened up with a handgun, and Rachael had to run into the dining room to survive. She grabbed the corner of the big table and with a grunt of effort turned it over, spilling weapons and boxes of shells. Gunfire hit the big oak but few of them punched through. As much as she was loathe to do it, Rachael dropped her sword and picked up a small-frame automatic, checked that it was loaded, crouched down at one corner of the table and reached around to fire blindly. She'd read about 'target-rich environments' in novels. That was when it was almost impossible to miss because there were so many hostiles. She fired her gun dry, hearing screams. She swapped out the magazine. She'd been to gun ranges and knew how to use a pistol, but she didn't like them. She was a swordswoman. But this wasn't a time for preferences. All that mattered was surviving.

She fired and fired and fired.

~44~

Dez Fox

Dez raced across the farm field, not bothering to run serpentine or take cover. There were figures everywhere and everyone she saw seemed to be caught up in a frenzy of bloody violence. It was like running through hell itself.

Men dressed as hunters wrestled with pale-faced corpses dressed as soldiers or farmers. One of the refugee women had a man down and was stabbing him over and over and over while a nine year old girl tried to pull her back from whatever brink she'd climbed out onto. Zombies lay dead, and dead hunters were twitching their back to unlife. Dez fired her last bullets, killing six men. She had no idea if they were zombies or NKK hunters. They fell and her slide locked back. A zombie lunged at her and Dez's pistol went flying. She jammed the carpet armor into its mouth, drew her blackjack and beat the thing's head into a ruin.

Then a hand clamped on her shoulder and she was spun toward a pair of living men. Hunters who leered at her and—despite everything that was happening around them—began tearing at her clothes.

As if she was there for the taking.

As if she was helpless.

The blackjack whipped through the night, shattered finger bones, deconstructing faces, smashing into eyes, breaking, dehumanizing. Destroying. As the fell she bent and searched for weapons. Found a revolver with four rounds left. She ran toward the house and found targets for each round.

Then she brained a zombie with the butt of the gun and lost the weapon as the creature collapsed against the side of the well.

"The house!" someone yelled, and Dez saw one of the refugee women pushing children up onto the porch. But the picture was wrong. Men rushed at them, grabbing the kids, pulling them away from her. One of the men swung something at the woman and she fell with the kind of abrupt looseness that spoke of a broken neck. Dez tore across the field to the gravel turnaround in front of the house. There were three men trying to drag the kids away. She hit one from behind, crushing his skull, feeling the bones give beneath the heavy leather-wrapped lead. As the man staggered she shoved him toward another of the men, and he had not yet seen her. He turned sharply, crying out in surprise as the dead weight collapsed against him. Dez ignored him as he fell and closed on the third man—the one who had killed the refugee woman. He held a heavy length of black pipe wrapped in electricians tape. The end glistened.

Dez did not pause to challenge or threaten. She attacked, driving right at the man as he raised his pipe to strike. She went in low and fast and slapped the blackjack across his right kneecap. The degree of pain it inflicted must have felt like a gunshot and it instantly became the whole of his world. His pipe fell as he reached for his shattered kneecap with both hands.

The blackjack did terrible things to him.

Dez turned away, her face spattered with blood, snatched up the pipe and stepped over to the third man, who was still trying to climb out from under the improbably heavy slackness of his dead friend. He froze, looking up at the pipe as it whistled down at him. There was one split second of sad resignation on his face, and then he didn't have a face.

Dez ran to the kids, who were quivering with terror. They were the three youngest from the group of refugees.

"Stay close," she told them, and climbed the steps to the house. She needed to get to the other guns. There were too many of the hunters to fight with only a blackjack and a piece of pipe.

A voice rang out behind her. "That bitch just killed Marty."

Dez turned to see two of the hunters rushing in, both of them armed with baseball bats. Dez turned and ran from them, her shoes slipping on the bloody porch stairs. There was a man in the doorway, but he was looking the wrong way, so Dez smashed in the back of his skull and shoulder-shoved him inside.

And damn near got shot.

As the man fell a bullet chunked into the doorframe inches from Dez's ear. She dove sideways and as she fell saw that the living room was heaped with corpses and with badly wounded. All men. The only person on her feet was a woman who looked like she stepped out a movie about Vikings. Leather and fur and armor, but she held a gun in her hand and the barrel was tracking toward Dez's face.

"No!" cried Dez, but the woman swung the gun back toward the doorway and fired six shots. Dez turned to see the two men who'd chased her reeling backward.

Dez was up in a flash and ran up and over the bodies, falling, slipping, and finally crawling toward the crazy woman with the gun. She herded the refugee women and girls with her.

"Get behind the table," she roared, and they obeyed without question, flooding around the heavy oak barricade. They could all see the Viking woman with the gun, but she was female and so were they. The attackers were all male, and that drew a deep and recognizable line in the sand for all of them.

"Dez Fox?" demanded the Viking woman as she reloaded.

"Yeah, but who the fuck are you?"

Instead of answering, the woman tossed the gun to her, bent and picked up a sword. The refugee women had their weapons, though all of their guns were empty. Even an empty gun is still a metal club, though, and they clutched these as they huddled behind the barricade. Dez joined them, liking the solidity of the oak table.

There were screams—a girl's—from the kitchen, and the deep-chested growl of a big dog. The Viking woman flashed Dez a wicked grin and yelled, "For Asgard!"

Then she ran into the kitchen. The next screams Dez heard were all male.

Dez gaped for a moment longer. "This is fucking nuts," she said.

And then more men came pouring into the house.

~45~

The Ranger

Joe followed the sounds of gunfire all the way to the farm. He ran as fast as he could, wishing he hadn't used so much of his ammunition. Would he get there in time?

Would it matter if he did?

The NKK had the numbers, and if they took hostages…what then?

He broke from the forest and plunged into the tobacco field.

The house was under siege. There seemed to be an army swarming around it. Too many to fight.

But as Ledger closed in he realized that more than half of those men were no longer alive. Freshly killed hunters staggered through the overgrown plants and dirt, attacking anything with a pulse. There were at least a dozen fights in progress as the zombies fell upon their former friends. But that left several living hunters. Too many?

He saw a corpse just beginning to rise and its dead hand still clutched an assault rifle. A Sig SG 550 with a bulky box magazine. Ledger had lost a lot of his faith in the kindness of whomever was on call in heaven, but right then he would have knelt and kissed the Pope's ring. He kicked the zombie in the head, pinned it to the ground with a knee and tore the rifle from its twitching fingers. He brained it with the stock, then slapped pockets until he came up with a second magazine. As he shoved the magazine into his pocket he assessed the scene, calculating the odds and doing dangerous math in his head. His best chance of survival was to turn around and go. He had a family to find, friends to find. This wasn't his war.

"Fuck it," he said, "and fuck you."

Ledger began running toward the house.

~46~

In Hell

Dez Fox fired at a man wearing a John Deere cap exactly like the one she'd worn when she went out drinking back home. Seeing it reminded her of too many things, so she put a bullet through it. The man fell but his finger jerked the trigger of the huge single-barrel ten-gauge shotgun he carried. The buckshot sprayed the room and two pellets caught Dez—one in the shoulder and one in the cheek. She staggered, pain exploding and blood pouring from the wounds. One of the refugee women sat down with her back to the wall, a dozen spots on her face and throat suddenly blossoming with red. Her eyes rolled up and she fell over. Two other women rushed to try and stanch the wounds, and Dez had no idea if they were already too late.

Another man raised a Ruger Blackhawk at her, but he suddenly shrieked and twisted around as one of his dead friends on the floor bit deeply into his calf.

There were a dozen corpses crowning the living room and a few had been dropped with head wounds. The others were writhing and moaning as new life ignited in their brains and new hungers awoke in their souls.

The four living men who were trying to get to Dez and the refugees. The men were all armed with axes, clubs and knives and they screamed and began smashing at the newly reanimated dead. The room became a slaughterhouse. Blood shot from torn arteries;

howls of rage and agony filled the air. Dez began scrabbling on the floor for fresh rounds. Finding some, not finding enough.

"Oh…fuck me," she breathed.

Lindsey struggled to reload her gun, but her hands were streaked with blood and sweat and the weapon slipped from her grasp and landed on the chest of a dead man. She bent for it, but then the dead man's eyes snapped open and his eyes clicked toward her. She saw the exact moment when they changed from the vacant eyes of the true dead to the predatory eyes of a monster.

She tried to yank her hand free, but the creature had a solid grip and was stronger than her. It pulled her hand toward its mouth, which was working as if already chewing on her.

"Watch!" yelled a voice and Lindsey looked up as Rachael stamped a booted foot down on the zombie's face and then swung her sword in a glittering arc. Lindsey fell back with the dead hand still clamped around her. She yelped and swatted at it until the slack fingers fell away and it lay like some grotesque spider on the kitchen floor.

Rachael grabbed Lindsey and hauled her unceremoniously to her feet and shoved her toward the corner by the stove. Heavy iron pots were stacked on the drain board, including a cast-iron frying pan. She hoped the kid would get the idea, but didn't have time to watch. Men were still trying to fight their way in through the shattered door and the kitchen windows.

So many of them.

It confused her. They'd seen how many of their own had died in this siege and yet they kept coming. The cost was so high. Were they lost in some kind of battle madness or group hysteria? Was it a lust for revenge for their fallen friends? Or were they just insane?

She swung and stabbed with her sword, but with each blow her shoulder and arm muscles were screaming at her. Even hardened by six months of combat against the dead, she knew she wasn't able to keep fighting for much longer. Her wrist throbbed from the impact shock of each blow, and the smell of blood was making her sick. Her heart was beating wildly in her chest and each exhalation felt like a blast of heated air from a furnace.

Joe Ledger rushed the house, coming up at an angle that would let him see the front and one side. Six men were fighting a knot of zombies. Ledger hosed them with the assault rifle from fifteen feet away. The living went down and the zombies dove onto them, biting the bleeding flesh. Ledger left them to their grisly meal. Those monsters could be dealt with later and for the moment they were useful to him.

He saw another of the dead staggering toward the slaughter, but Ledger spun him around, grabbed him by the hair and back of the belt and ran him toward a hunter who was slapping a fresh magazine into his gun on the porch steps.

"Here," said Ledger as he flung the zombie against the man. They went down in a wild tangle of teeth, scrabbling fingers, blood and howls.

Ledger caught the man's gun before it could land in the dirt. With the assault rifle in his left, he ran up onto the porch with his new pistol leading the way. The three men on the porch turned to see their comrade wrestling with a zombie and a stranger rushing at them.

They died.

The last of them fell backward into the living room, and Ledger stepped on his chest as he entered the house.

He saw Dez Fox behind a dining room table and everything around her was an orgy of murder. The dead outnumbered the living and they were tearing the hunters apart. Soon there would only be zombies in here. Sixteen at least.

Ledger paused for one moment, doing more calculations about how many rounds he had left between pistol and assault rifle. Every single shot would have to count.

A zombie crawled toward him and tried to bit his shin. Ledger whipped his leg up and brought his heel down in a devastating axe kick. He couldn't hear the snap of bones beneath the general din, but from the wall the monster fell Ledger was certain that he wouldn't need to use a bullet on that one.

He raised his gun and fired.

Fired.

Fired.

Dez Fox was seldom happy to see most people. She liked kids and dogs. She liked banging men. But she wasn't really a people person.

That said, when Captain Joe Ledger stepped through the door, a gun in each hand, she would have married him on the spot. Or banged him. Or whatever. He was nobody's idea of a white knight and she was ten million miles away from being a damsel in distress. She'd have cut the balls off of anyone who even suggested that. But Ledger was a fellow cop, a fellow soldier, and he was here. Not to rescue her, but to help her save her kids.

Behind her the refugee women and girls huddled in a quavering mass, all of them pushed to the edge of total hysteria.

As soon as he opened up on the crowd of hunters and zombies, the mass of struggling bodies seemed to turn, to focus their awareness—however fractured—on him. That gave Dez time to find the box of nine-millimeter rounds and cram some into a magazine. No time for a full count, though. She slapped it in place and began firing.

Baskerville raised his muzzle from the dead hunter and sniffed the air. It was thick with the smells of blood, piss, gun smoke, and sweat, but there—deep inside the olio of scents—was something else. A scent he knew like none other. The scent of his pack leader.

He threw his head back and let loose with a howl of terrible red joy.

A man grabbed for Lindsey, missed her arm and caught the shoulder of her blouse. He yanked hard just as she lunged backward, and the whole front of the shirt tore away. The bra she wore beneath was soiled and spattered with blood, old and new. The man actually leered at her and started to say something. She grabbed the skillet off the stove and swung it with all of her fear, strength, anger and disgust across his face. He spun away from her, spewing teeth and dropped at once to his knees. Lindsey hit him again, this time on the back of the head. He pitched forward at once and began twitching like a trout on the floor.

Rachael was fighting two men, both of them armed with knives. One had a big Buck hunting knife and the other had a bread knife. She had a sword and dagger.

She wanted to say something, to drop one of those cool lines that heroes in movies always managed to come up with in the heat of the moment.

This wasn't a movie. This was her life, so she saved her breath for fighting.

The slide locked back on Ledger pistol and so he jammed the empty gun into the throat of a hunter, crushing the windpipe and hyoid bone. The man clawed at his throat as if he could somehow force it to breathe, but that option was no longer his and he fell with a look of profound defeat on his face.

Ledger took the SG 550 in both hands, set the selector switch to single shot, put the stock to his shoulder, braced his feet and began firing. One head shot after another.

Bang.

Bang

Bang.

Each shot was a crack of thunder in the room. Anyone who tried to charge him, living or dead, died. Either from one of his heavy 5.56×45mm NATO rounds or the bullets Dez Fox fired. Caught between two superb killers with automatic weapons the hunters and the zombies all fell.

Down.

Down.

Down.

The last man tried to make a break for it, running over the bodies of his friends toward the smashed in window. Ledger stepped into his path and slammed him across the face with the stock of the assault rifle. The man went staggering back, spun, looking for another way out. He saw Dez point a gun at him. The man tried to speak, but his jaw was broken and only blood and a mewling mumble of words came from his mouth. He raised his hands in a pleading gesture. Begging for mercy where none existed.

Dez Fox shot him in the face.

Lindsey swung the skillet at the hands reaching in through the window, breaking bones. There were no howls of pain though...only moans of unassuageable hunger.

She kept smashing though, the skillet heavy in her bloody hands. It was the only weapon she had left.

One of the two attackers was down, but the other was giving Rachael a real right. He was quick and although she had the longer reach with her sword, he moved like a cat, parrying, evading, dancing out of the way. As they fought he kept up a patter of ugly words, using them with as much skill as the knife he carried.

"You're pretty good with that thing," he said, laughing, "but that won't matter none. And you're just making it worse for yourself, darlin'. Ol' Teddy's going to teach you some manners, yes ma'am. I'm going to enjoy teaching you the facts of life. Oh hell yes. And you look like you'd enjoy it, too. You got a rack on you and I—."

And Baskerville slammed into him from the side.

Rachael stood there, her arms sagging to her sides, her weapons feeling like hundred pound weights, chest heaving and sweat pouring down her face and throat. She watched the dog and the man. The dog and what it did to the man. The dog and what quickly stopped being a man. It was a dreadful way to die, but her heart was a stone.

She looked around the kitchen.

Lindsey was hammering at dead hands with a skillet. Baskerville was tearing at something that no longer even screamed. Everything and everyone else was dead.

Dead.

She stood in a lake of blood.

This is the world, she thought. *Just this.*

Death and pain, the rapacious malevolence of the living, the ending hunger of the dead. This is what the world has become. This and nothing more.

"God...," she murmured. She did not even feel the tears that ran like molten silver down her cheeks.

Then she looked down at the floor and saw that some of the old floorboards were warped from age. Blood seeped down between them and fresh horror rose in her mind as she imagined the slow rainfall of red droplets falling into the basement.

It was only then that she could hear the muffled screams. Not of pain, but of horror. The children.

Good god, the children.

She took a deep breath and raised her sword and dagger, and staggered with leaden feet over to the window to help Lindsey. To fight. To *end* this.

But as she reached Lindsey to push her out of the way, a voice rang out behind her.

"Move!"

Rachael and Lindsey both turned to see Dez Fox come striding into the kitchen. A small group of women and children—all strangers to Rachael—crowded behind her. Dez pushed between Rachael and Lindsey, raised her pistol at the dead...and fired. There were other shots—the heavier bark of an assault rifle—from outside and more of the dead fell away. The guns roared and roared. And then stopped.

Everything seemed to stop.

The whole world juddered down to stillness.

Rachael listened to the night. She heard nothing. No new shots, no means, no cries of anger or pain.

Nothing.

Baskerville suddenly went running into the dining room, through the living room and outside, yelping and barking. Not in distress.

In joy.

A moment later the dog came back inside and with him was a tall man with graying blond hair, a tanned face lined with age and scars, carrying an assault rifle. Captain Ledger. The one Lindsey had told him about. The man looked down around at the carnage. Then he dropped the weapon onto the chest of the man Baskerville had just killed. He smiled, a faint and sad smile that showed his age.

"It's over," he said.

And Lindsey began to cry.

~47~

Dez Fox

Dez Fox went down into the cellar and her kids swarmed around her, pulling her down the last few steps, hugging her, kissing her, clinging to her despite the blood and dirt on her clothes. She dropped to her knees and wept with them. The last of the women survivors went with her and together they shared in the thing that exists when all of the violence and bloodshed and horror has passed.

Life.

~48~

The Farmhouse

It took days to bury all the dead.

It was grisly work. Backbreaking and heartbreaking. The bodies of the refugee women and children who'd been killed were given markers. It was the wrong time of year for flowers, but Ledger had no doubt there would be some in the spring.

The corpses of the NKK men were buried in a gulley and covered over with wheelbarrows filled with dirt. The only marker was when Baskerville raised a leg and pissed all over it. Dez saw that and laughed until she cried.

While the women were burying the dead, Ledger spent most of his time in the forests. Hunting. Twice Dez went with him. They'd worked in grim silence and never once talked about the things they did out there. All that mattered was that they could tell the refugees, without lying, that none of the NKK men would be coming back. Not one. Not as living attackers or dead biters.

It would have been nice to be able to say that all threats had been dealt with, but Ledger was tired of lies.

The nights at the farmhouse were long. There were tears and there were stories. One of the women died two days later. She was the one who'd taken some of the buckshot in the throat. Dez made sure she wouldn't rise again and they all stood with her when the woman was buried alongside the others. No one had a prayer to say except Rachael, who recited something in Elvish. Ledger cut a look at

Dez, and she raised her eyebrows as if to say 'it's better than anything I have'.

It was nearly a week before Rachael told them she had to leave. The whole group walked her out to the road and Lindsey handed her a sheet of paper with everyone's name on it. Rachael looked at it and then turned away to hide the tears that sprang into her eyes.

She walked alone down the road and everyone stood and watched until she was out of sight.

~49~

Rachael Elle

Rachael couldn't find the words in her head to express how grateful she was to see the hospital ahead as they left the woods, excited to be back with her friends, and nervous that something had happened to them, all at the same time.

As the approached the large gate, she saw Matt, one of her Avengers Tower survivors, guarding it, broadsword in hand, and her heart soared. He called out to her in excitement, and she heard the sound of the gate being unbolted.

She smiled at the women who traveled with her.

"This is home. At least, for now. It's safe here. There's a lot of us here. We're going to build a future."

She expected Matt to be the first one out to great them, but it wasn't him that rushed out to her. Instead her eyes focused on blonde hair and red cloak, broad shoulders and big muscles, the image of a true superhero, and her heart rushed as a smile came to her face.

Brett ran towards her, his smile matching her own, but he stopped as he approached, his eyes taking in every inch of her, as if he didn't believe she was real. It had been nearly a month since she'd been gone, and so much had happened

She had changed so much. She'd become nearly a different person. She had a mission now, a goal, something she needed to do. It wasn't just about saving people and bringing them together. It was about making this world, and the hand they were dealt, worth living, for everyone.

She could only imagine what she looked like, but she knew now what she was. She didn't need to pretend to be a superhero, she didn't need to play make believe.

And she knew that Brett could see it too. She didn't need to make believe she was a hero anymore.

Because she was one.

~50~

The Ranger and the Cop

Joe and Dez organized the survivors into work teams. They fortified the house, repairing damage from the attack and reinforcing every door and window. Stronger shutters were constructed with wood stripped from the barn. The women began digging a trench around the house and the kids spent their days sharpening sticks to line the bottom of the trench. Dez and two of the refugee women went hunting—for food this time. They brought back two deer and a half dozen rabbits. But the next day one of the girls went out and set snares to catch rabbits. She returned with six live ones. Two male and four females. Everyone approved. Maybe they'd be able to find some chickens and cows, too. Anything was possible. And that was something Ledger saw—the dawning of belief, of hope for survival and maybe even a future.

Seeing that chipped away some of the black ice that clung to his heart. And it rekindled some of his own optimism. The next morning—he was pretty sure it was a Saturday, not that such things really mattered anymore—he told Dez that he was leaving the next day. She protested, they argued, crockery was thrown. But in the end he played the best card he had. Billy Trout and the other busses. Dez couldn't take all those kids and the women on a hunt for Billy. It was a better job for one person and a dog.

They ate a last meal, a big breakfast, and there were a lot of hugs and tearful goodbyes. As if Ledger had been part of this community, this *family*, for years. Lindsey gave him a list of names, too. Ledger folded it carefully and put it in his pocket. It was something he knew he would want to read again. Maybe often.

Then it was time to go. Ledger clicked his tongue for Baskerville and the dog sprang to his feet, but once they were on the porch, the big hound seemed to stall. The animal looked around at the faces of all the kids and at the women who had fought alongside him. His big tail swished back and forth.

He got a lot of hugs and even some kisses, too.

"Come on, you big goof," growled Ledger. "You're a shameless damn flirt."

Joe got a lot of kisses and hugs, too. It made him happy and it broke his heart. That these powerful women and these beautiful kids should embrace him and kiss his cheeks as if he wasn't a monster and a killer. It was proof the world was absolutely goddamn insane.

Lindsey stood by the door, kids all around her, and there were tears in her eyes. Ledger kissed her on the forehead. Then he and Dez and Baskerville walked out to the road and stood for a moment watching the clouds move across the sky.

Dez fished something out of her pocket. A note sealed in an envelope. She looked deeply embarrassed and then handed it to Ledger. The envelope was pink and the name 'Billy' was scrawled across it.

"Don't say a goddamn word, Joe," she warned. "It was the only stationary I could find."

It was very, very pink. He laughed.

"I will kneecap you," she said, "hand to God."

But she laughed, too. It was a strange sound, rare in the world these days. They both seemed to realize it at the same time and their laughter faded. Still, they smiled at each other. Dez cleared her throat and nodded to the note. "You'll give it to him?"

"If he's still where I left him, yes I will."

"What if he's not there?" she asked.

He shrugged. "Guess I go looking for him."

"You don't have to," she said.

Ledger looked around at the big, empty world. "What else have I got to do?" he asked. It was meant as a joke, but Dez looked as if it was the saddest thing she'd ever heard.

"I'll find him," Ledger said.

She studied him, then nodded. "Yeah, I know you will."

He bent to kiss her cheek, and Dez Fox suddenly grabbed him and pulled him to her in a fierce embrace. She kissed him with a startling and intense heat, and then shoved him back.

"What…what…?" he said, unable to form a cohesive question.

Dez gave him a wicked grin. "That's so you don't walk away from this thinking you got nothing out of it."

He shook his head. "You sure Billy Trout didn't just seize the moment and run away *from* you?"

"Seriously, one round through the kneecap," she said, laying her hand on the butt of her pistol. He mimed zipping his mouth shut.

They stood for one moment longer, two warriors who were now connected on a level they could not express in words but which each of them completely understood.

"Goodbye, Desdemona Fox," he said.

"Goodbye, Captain Ledger," she said.

Baskerville *whuffed* quietly, and then the big man clicked his tongue again and turned away. He never looked back at the old farmhouse.

Not once.

-The End-

Rachael Lavin is a Cosplayer, LARPer, and all around Nerd. An art degree stuck in a banking job, Rachael rejects this reality and replaces it with her own. When she's not writing, she can be found hunched over her sewing machine, taking pictures, or running around the woods with foam swords. She is a graduate of the Experimental Writing for Teens program created by Jonathan Maberry. She currently lives in Doylestown, PA with her fluffy white demon dog and 200 pairs of shoes.

Jonathan Maberry is a NY Times bestselling novelist, five-time Bram Stoker Award winner, and comic book writer. He writes the Joe Ledger thrillers, the Rot & Ruin series, the Nightsiders series, the Dead of Night series, as well as standalone novels in multiple genres. His comic book works include, among others, *CAPTAIN AMERICA, BAD BLOOD, ROT & RUIN, V-WARS,* and others. He is the editor of many anthologies including THE X-FILES, SCARY OUT THERE, OUT OF TUNE, and V-WARS. His books EXTINCTION MACHINE and V-WARS are in development for TV, and ROT & RUIN is in development as a series of feature films. A board game version of V-WARS was released in early 2016. He is the founder of the Writers Coffeehouse, and the co-founder of The Liars Club. Prior to becoming a full-time novelist, Jonathan spent twenty-five years as a magazine feature writer, martial arts instructor and playwright. He was a featured expert on the History Channel documentary, *Zombies: A Living History* and a regular expert on the TV series, *True Monsters.* Jonathan lives in Del Mar, California with his wife, Sara Jo. www.jonathanmaberry.com

If they have to call Joe Ledger
It's already hit the fan
JOE LEDGER: SPECIAL OPS
BONUS FEATURES•CHARACTER PROFILES
Behind the scenes
of the Department of Military Sciences
Joe Ledger Short Stories
Two Original Brand New Stories
JOIN THE HUNT!
WWW.JOURNALSTONE.COM

CPSIA information can be obtained at www.ICGtesting.com
Printed in the USA
LVOW07s2010070416

482624LV00004B/235/P

Flesh and Fire

JournalStone's DoubleDown Series, Book VIII

By
Lucas Mangum

JournalStone
San Francisco

JOURNALSTONE
YOUR LINK TO ARTISTIC TALENT

JournalStone books may be ordered through booksellers or by contacting:

JournalStone
www.journalstone.com

ISBN: 978-1-942712-91-6 *(sc)*
ISBN: 978-1-942712-92-3 *(ebook)*

Library of Congress Control Number: **2016933401**

Printed in the United States of America
JournalStone rev. date: April 22, 2016

Cover Art and Design: Robert Grom
Author Photo: Jim Julian
Photo Credits: Woman in Forest © lekcej/shutterstock, Fire circle © lassedesignen/shuttstock

Edited by: *Aaron J. French*

For Tim. 1985-2007

Acknowledgments

It's been said that no one achieves anything on their own. That claim is especially true of first novels, so I'd like to thank the following people: my wife, Jean, because living with a writer is hard and she's been a trooper; Jonathan Maberry for believing in me, encouraging me, and being an all-around righteous dude; and Christopher Payne at Journalstone for accepting my little story about Hell and transcendence. A huge thanks is also owed to anyone who helped get this manuscript into its current form, namely: crime author Dennis Tafoya; thriller author Jon McGoran; my brother, Vincent Mangum; Patrick Galloway; filmmaker and critic, Scout Tafoya; and screenwriter Joe Augustyn. From the bottom of my heart, thanks to all of the above listed, as well as anyone who bought me a drink, talked writing, or kept me company over the last four years. You know who you are, friends, and if you look hard enough, you may see pieces of yourselves in the story you are about to read.

Flesh and Fire

~1~

~Chloe~

If this is dying, Chloe thought, *I'd like to do it again sometime.*

The brightest light she'd ever seen washed over her, burning brilliant whitish yellow. Blinding, but soft, it reminded her of the sun, finally showing its brilliant face after weeks of rain and starless nights. It brought warmth, security, and a deep sense of euphoria, better than the greatest high, more intense than her strongest orgasm.

Moments ago, she'd been in her room, sinking into the bed below, as if it were a cloud. Her vision blurred and her surroundings fell further away. She gave each of them one final glimpse, pausing the longest on the Yamaha DX7 keyboard, upon which she played all of her music, and the photograph of her and Todd smiling drunkenly as they held each other in the parking lot of the Black Horse Pub.

As she slipped away, she only regretted not being able to tell him goodbye. Maybe even apologize. She settled for humming the melody to "Blissfully Damaged," a song he'd written for her. Maybe doing so would, through some kind of clairvoyance, allow her to commune with him in her final moments.

The poison killing her now had also destroyed their relationship. She'd been clean for a while, but it hadn't lasted. Once he'd seen he couldn't help her, he'd run away. She didn't blame him. He didn't really know everything. He didn't know about the dreams, or the monster that pursued her in them, or how she sometimes even saw and

heard the monster when she was awake. She'd never told him and because of this he just saw her as an addict, no matter how much he'd loved her.

Now she'd never be able to tell him.

Now she was dying.

And she accepted it.

Embraced it.

~Les~

Les's fingers trembled as he reached for the phone. He mentally talked himself through dialing the number scrawled on the crumpled Post-It. As he cranked each digit he opened and closed the fist of his free hand. When the phone started to ring he cleared his throat, which was raw from hours of crying. His pulse thudded in his ears.

Another ring.

He clenched his fist but nothing stopped the pounding of his blood, the trembling in his limbs, or the looming threat of more tears.

A click.

"Yeah."

Les froze at the sound of Todd's familiar greeting. What the hell was he supposed to say? The man on the other line had loved his daughter, but the relationship had ended months ago. How much would it matter that Chloe was dead? All he knew for sure was that he wouldn't tell Todd what he had seen when he found her.

"Hello?" Todd said, with a touch of annoyance.

"Todd, it's Les."

"Les! What's up?"

Les bit his lip and grabbed a handful of stringy hair with his free hand.

"Les?"

"I..." He leaned on the counter in hopes that the presence of something solid would stabilize him. "It's Chloe."

Todd didn't respond. For a moment Les thought the call had been disconnected, but when he listened he heard faint breathing just below the hiss of the phone line.

"An overdose?"

Les closed his eyes and saw his daughter splayed across the bed, her dark hair in the clutches of… Of what? He tried to wipe the image from his mind.

"Yes, an overdose."

And that's what the police and paramedics knew it as. After all, the bag of heroin had been found on the bed beside her. The syringe still hung from inside her elbow, the needle embedded in her soft flesh.

"Fuck, man, I'm sorry," Todd said.

"Yeah." Even with his eyes open, he saw her dead gaze staring up at him.

"I just… Jesus… Are you okay?"

"I guess I have to be, right?"

The two men hung on the line, saying nothing. Something had to be said. Chloe deserved better.

"I thought you might want to know."

"Thank you." Another pause. "Do you need anything?"

A hell of a question; Les couldn't even begin to answer it properly. Chloe was dead. He wanted to believe her pain had reached its end, but his gut told him otherwise. Though he couldn't say for certain what awaited her after death, he feared damnation, especially for a lost junkie soul like hers.

Instead of telling Todd all of this, he swallowed to fight back more tears and asked if Todd wanted to know the funeral arrangements.

"Yeah, yeah, sure." On the last word Todd's voice cracked and Les thought that in the next moment they'd both break down. They'd do it without shame because they were old friends, because they both loved her.

Instead Todd cleared his throat. "Listen, Les, I… I better go."

"Of course. I just thought you should know. That's all."

"Thanks. Take care, Les. You call if you need anything."

"Will do," Les said, knowing he would not.

~Anna~

Anna watched Todd from the doorway of his study. His face in the lamplight had gone ghostly pale since hanging up the phone. He sat with his shoulders crunched against his neck. One hand tapped on the desk, making a hollow, rhythmic drumming that echoed through the hallway. She didn't like the way he looked or that tapping, not one

bit. He seemed far away, like maybe he'd left his body and the tapping was just some remaining nervous twitch.

"Babe?" she said, using caution.

The tapping slowed, but did not cease. It became more dissonant, unsteady. She liked that sound even less.

"Babe." She tried to add firmness to her tone without losing the sense of concern. It wasn't as easy as she hoped. To her she just sounded annoyed.

He jerked in his seat to face her and she saw redness in his eyes.

"Are you okay?" she asked.

He looked down at his nervously drumming fingers, then back at her. He offered a smile that was gone as quickly as it appeared.

"Fine."

"Who was that on the phone?"

He frowned, looking at the phone as if noticing the object for the first time. He opened his mouth. Thankfully, he stopped tapping and she almost let him be. Not one to eavesdrop, she hadn't heard the conversation, but his demeanor in the moments since had troubled her deeply.

She knew their relationship was off to a rocky start. Their fathers had set them up. She knew about Chloe, the girl who used to play shows with him at the Black Horse, and that he'd been seeing her most of the summer. But that September, Todd had shown a real desire to commit. He'd taken a higher paying position within the bank and asked Anna to move in with him. This was their first apartment, a modest one-bedroom in the wooded suburbia of Havertown. They could afford a bigger place with Todd's bank manager salary, but she'd insisted on saving as much as possible so they could have a *real* home in which to raise a family someday. She feared that this phone call, whoever it had been, could erase all of their progress.

"Who was it?" she asked again.

Todd shook his head. "It was no one. Just a friend."

"Todd…"

"Chloe died." The words came out of his mouth as if her prying had loosed something within him.

"Oh my God, are you okay?" She crossed the room and made to embrace him, but he closed his arms against his chest and turned away.

"I don't know. I guess I saw it coming, but…"

She knelt down in front of him. "That's silly. There's no way you could've..."

"She was always in trouble, like there was something after her."

"Was she using drugs?"

"Yes, but..."

She placed her hands on his shoulders and made him face her. "Were you?"

"What are you, my mother?"

She backed away and crossed her arms. "That's not fair."

"I know it's not. To answer your question: no, I wasn't. I was always trying to get her to quit, but her problems just seemed so much... *bigger* than her addiction. I don't know what I'm saying. It was a deep relationship, but there was so much I didn't know about her. There's so much I'll never know about her now."

Heat flared in her cheeks. That hurt. Not that he admitted the depth of his and Chloe's relationship, but his disappointment that he would never know his ex-lover's secrets. Anna wondered if he still loved Chloe. She took a breath, counted to ten. She reminded herself that her jealousy could be addressed later.

"Do you want me to leave you alone?"

He rose to his feet. "I... think I'll go for a walk."

He picked up the black case holding his guitar and slung it over his shoulder. He hadn't played since they'd moved in. Seeing him hold the instrument gave her a brief flash of hope. While she had never expressed it to him fully, she didn't want to see him give up his hobby just to please her or his father or whoever. She just wanted him to be himself.

She moved aside. "Okay, just let me know if you need anything."

He passed her and went into the living room. At the front door he glanced over his shoulder and gave her a weak smile. She had to give him points for trying.

Then he was gone.

~Les~

It wasn't that Les didn't believe in ghosts. To say that meant that he didn't believe his eyes. Or what he'd heard. Or what he knew.

The night he found his daughter dead, he'd come home from a ten-year high school reunion at Master's Catering. His white cooking apron sat crumpled on the passenger seat of his Malibu and the car reeked of fried scallops.

Up until he came home, it'd been a good evening. A mild breeze in the air gave the night a comfortable chill. He had gotten up that morning—something he had learned to appreciate. In spite of the dying trees and the looming winter, things never seemed livelier.

He pulled into his garage and killed the engine. The quiet night amplified the grind of the rusty gears as he closed the garage door. Once confined, the mustiness of the garage felt more oppressive. With an urgency that he didn't so much think about as felt, he rushed into the house.

The living room was silent, except for soft music coming from upstairs. Chloe. He'd seen lights in her bedroom window when he'd pulled up. It was odd she was home. She'd been out much of the time since she and Todd had broken up. He'd hardly seen her since and had worried she was using again even though the times he'd asked her, she would smile, hug him, and tell him, "no."

His worry for her increased each day. The same way fathers usually worried about their children, he would sometimes think. Other times he suspected that maybe he worried because she was special and being special meant sometimes you faced greater challenges, more powerful adversaries.

Like addiction.

Was it just addiction?

It had to be, right?

Thinking of all this compelled him to take the stairs two at a time, not giving a damn about the hip he had injured overseas, or his high blood pressure. He knew, like parents sometimes just know, that something was wrong. Either it was the quiet in the house, the way his every movement echoed like voices in a crypt, or the fact that as soon as he'd come inside the joy he'd felt in the October air had fallen away—but he knew.

He rounded the first flight, then the second, and stumbled into the hallway, barely slowing his pace. The door to her room hung ajar. He said her name. He knocked. He said her name again, this time with more force, doing nothing to mask the alarm in his voice.

"I'm coming in."

He pushed the door open and saw it kneeling over her on the mattress.

Its skin was the color of charcoal. Tendrils of flame wrapped around the figure's gaunt limbs and rose from its hunched back. Through the flames, he made out the lean definition of the shape's musculature, the imprints of its ribcage, the tendons sticking out behind its knees. The figure was man-shaped, but Les doubted it was human.

Despite the fire, the room was cold. Like a meat freezer. The chill cut through Les's shirt and raised gooseflesh upon his chest and arms. It made his balls shrivel between his legs, and his shoulders shudder.

It held her hair and face in its fiery grasp. Her dead eyes stared up at Les. He screamed her name and reached out, but couldn't move forward. His feet planted, his legs locked into place. Bad hip flaring, his teeth gritting against the pain.

The fiery shape turned and looked at Les with eyes that burned a brighter red than the flames consuming its body. An expression of anguish held its face. Les had lived down the street from a kid, Allen Wentworth, who'd always been in trouble for hurting the neighborhood pets. Once, Les had seen Allen strangling a cat in the woods, the cat's claws digging into Allen's forearms as the boy throttled the animal. The figure's eyes reminded Les of Allen's that day. Full of suffering, as if it regretted its actions, but couldn't stop itself.

Then it disappeared. Its eyes, the fire, the chill. Everything. No evidence of the charcoal-skinned creature remained. The drapes hung unscathed. The sheets crumpled beneath Chloe were clean. Her body remained, though she was gone too. She lay sprawled across her bed. Lifeless eyes staring. Syringe hanging from the inside of her elbow.

He had read deeply about the occult and considered himself a believer in the supernatural, yet he felt he couldn't have seen what he thought he'd seen. What would a demon want with his daughter? How could it have left no trace behind? Could he have hallucinated it?

Les touched his daughter's face and wished he could use something from his books to bring her back, but he knew from past experience that it took a special type of person to properly utilize those spells, and he had no such ability. Instead, he remained at her bedside, before calling the authorities so they could come and take her away forever.

~Chloe~

She knew only the light and a euphoric sense of floating. She hadn't expected this; she hadn't expected anything. No undeserved reward, no cruel and unusual punishment. Only sleep. Whatever this was, this was better. As she glided through the sea of bright warmth, a soothing swish, like the gentle splash of waves on a beach, accompanied every movement. The place had a smell, too, sweet and strong. Like Mother, she thought, without understanding how she knew.

Natalia, her father's only true love, had cast a shadow over their lives. She'd died while giving birth to Chloe, and existed only in photographs and Les's stories. A mythic figure. Unreal in her legacy and tragic in her absence. Thinking of her brought a wave of sadness that broke through Chloe's ecstasy, like a wind chill on an otherwise warm day. The next thing she knew, she was falling into darkness.

In the inky surroundings, the cries of countless others assaulted her ears. Some of them human, some animal, she could only interpret them as full of agony and fear. Underneath, a dry, gritty sound. Bone against bone, a chorus of grinding teeth.

Her heart hammered like a machine gun. No longer dying, desperation took hold.

As she fell hands clutched at her from out of the darkness and she screamed. They tore at her clothes and kneaded her skin, pulling her out of the chasm and moaning like diseased animals. She saw only glimpses of the rotting, scaly things as they tore her black dress to shreds.

She twisted and kicked in their clutches, preferring to fall than to be groped. She clawed through a forest of bulbous hands. Something primal was awake within her, a violent will to live as old as the universe itself. Rather than pull away from the creatures and back into the pit, she dove into the tangle of limbs and reptilian bodies. She bit and scratched. She drove forward until she fell again. This time she tumbled down a spiraling wet shaft. She reached the bottom, wounded and bleeding, not yet broken, happy to stand on solid ground.

Dirty crimson light illuminated her surroundings. Pointed rocks grew from above and below. Somewhere nearby, waves crashed against land. Behind her, wailing and gnashing of teeth. The rocks along the wall jutted out like gnarled tree branches. Gray rags hung on them, along with something like hair. Some of them moved. She realized then what they were as the skeletal limbs reached for her.

"Help me," one rotting mouth said, "please…"

Sobs fell from her mouth as she backed away, her cries echoing in the massive cavern. She turned and ran toward the sound of the waves but in front of her, she heard more bellows of pain. She stopped and looked around. Water splashed upon the shore, blood red in the dirty light. The dome of the cavern gave way to a sky full of swirling fire and black smoke. Panic surged through her, beginning in her heart and spreading like wildfire on a dry field throughout her body until a scream burst from her lips, joining the chorus of terrified, suffering voices. Like them, she had nowhere to go.

A lean, shadowy figure emerged from the blood-red ocean and put his face into the light. Deep angry scars marked his cheeks and brow. His eyes burned with something like rapture. She knew him. He was the monster of her dreams, her rapist and lover, her imaginary friend, her angel and demon, but this was no dream. Every precise detail overwhelmed her senses: the wet jagged earth digging into her feet; the stenches of burning hair and rotted meat filling the air. She had entered a new reality and he had brought her here. She thought of how she had felt guided tonight, by something outside of herself to buy the heroin, to shoot enough to overdose, and she understood.

Samael approached her, reached out his hand like he was blessing a martyr, and she knew she was destined for pain.

~Todd~

The guitar felt heavy as Todd pulled it out of the back of his car. He hadn't played since breaking up with Chloe and now, holding it under the moonlight while pulled over on Potter Way, the full weight of Les's news crushed down upon him and he wailed. His cries tore from his chest and carried across the empty field. The secluded farmhouse in the distance stood silent. The night birds and insects kept up their incessant chirps and whines. The world moved on, unaffected by his anguish.

After their first show at the Black Horse Pub, he and Chloe had stopped here on Potter Way. The energy of performing a song together, the patterns she traced on the inside of his thigh, and her teeth nibbling his neck made him unable to postpone his passion for her. Anyone looking closely enough from the main highway could have seen them, but that was part of the thrill.

They kissed hungrily. He fumbled at the straps of her dress from across the car's center console. She climbed away from him, cast a devious smile and went out the passenger door. He pursued her farther down the dirt road. Every few seconds, she glanced over her shoulder at him. She stopped in the middle of the tall grassy field, turned to face him, and let her dress fall to the ground. Her skin glowed softly in the moonlight. Bluish light accentuated the swell of her breasts and smooth angles of her hips. Black shadow concealed the mystery between her legs. He ran to her, shaking off his clothes.

The heat of her embrace enveloped him in the summer night air. He collapsed on top of her and slipped inside of her oily warmth. It almost ended before it began. He shut his eyes and buried his face against her neck. They jockeyed to find the perfect rhythm, giggling like children. When they synced together, he felt as if they were not just in harmony with each other, but with everything from the smallest blades of grass in the field to the moon shining upon them.

It ended with her on top of him, her head and shoulders thrust back, hair suspended behind her, breasts heaving. They lay naked in the grass afterwards, her breath slowing, his legs tingling.

Now, recalling the memory brought bitter tears. He felt none of the closeness with nature that he had felt that night. Instead, a deep gulf surrounded him, separating him from everything, and that seclusion brought a longing that hurt him physically as much as emotionally. His hands hung suspended over his guitar, unable to form a chord and strike it. The effort of moving beyond this moment felt impossible, like a force held his body in place, condemning him to experience this pain over and over.

He mouthed her name and it came out in a cracked whisper. The last time he'd seen her, he'd ended their relationship. He thought of his words to Anna, *There's so much I'll never know about her*. The longing ran deeper than wanting to know more about Chloe. He lived with Anna now. They had a date planned for their wedding. As that day approached, he felt that it held a deathlike finality. His old self, the guitar-playing free spirit, had little time left before the beast of true adulthood swallowed it. He'd laid awake nights, thinking of breaking off the engagement and running back to Chloe, because in spite of her damage, Chloe felt like more of a kindred spirit to him than Anna. Maybe taking her back would have proven disastrous, but he feared a life without her. He feared a life without passion.

Todd reached up the neck of the guitar to its tuners and twisted one knob and plucked the associated string. In one of Les's books, there had been a passage about a special way to tune instruments to make the notes resonate within the spirit world. He wasn't sure if he believed in any of that, but he liked the idea and had even written a few songs in the secret tuning. A vain hope that he could contact Chloe by playing a song rose within him. At least he could tell her goodbye and that he was sorry for leaving her. As he fine-tuned the D-string, he saw a glowing figure standing in the middle of the field.

It shined white with hints of green and formed the shape of a man. The shape moved forward, gliding over the blades of grass and illuminating the night. Todd set his guitar down and stared at the approaching specter. He tried to move back inside the car, but his feet locked into place. The rippling outline of the figure held him hypnotized as it came closer. A smell like creamy lavender drifted across the field and created an instant sense of euphoria, like Todd was standing in a dream. The shape drew closer, the smell stronger, the glow brighter.

Inside the light, he saw his reflection. The figure reached a shimmering hand forward and pressed it against Todd's chest. The touch burned for a moment, before the spirit disintegrated into the night, and Todd knew he was marked.

~2~

~Todd~

Todd's eyes snapped open. He touched the empty spot on the bed beside him, sighed and squeezed the satin top sheet. Where the hell was Anna?

He sat up and groaned, feeling aches in his bones that he could've sworn hadn't been there a week ago. He got out of bed and checked his phone for a message from Anna. She'd been working late, but had she come home at all? He dialed her number, expecting nothing. After five rings, her voicemail picked up to tell him his expectations weren't unreasonable.

He would've called the police if this hadn't become somewhat normal for her lately. She'd been working a lot, well into the night. Since she worked in Philadelphia, which was a long commute, sometimes she got a hotel. Usually she called.

"Hey, where the hell are you?" he asked after the tone. "You said you'd let me know if you weren't coming home."

He hung up, slumped his shoulders and sighed. He tossed his phone down on the bed and staggered to the bathroom, stopping to grab the pressed suit that hung on the door.

Fuck. He remembered feeling like he wouldn't have been caught dead wearing a suit.

In the bathroom mirror he shaved away the growth on his face from the past day and examined himself. Most of his hair had gone gray, even though his driver's license still said it was brown. Laugh lines creased the corners of his mouth and eyes. He was old.

Fifty-two, to be exact. He remembered not being sure if he'd make it to fifty-two and living too much in the moment to give a damn. His father had died last year, at seventy-seven. Twenty-five years away from fifty-two. Didn't seem so long at all now and that scared him. Too much of his life felt unresolved for death to loom so near in the future. Could he get his life together in another twenty-five years? What if he died sooner than that? How much would be left unfinished?

In his twenties, during those rare times when he did think about getting older, he certainly never saw himself *here* at fifty-two. With how much he and Anna worked and how little they saw each other, he had a hard time identifying as a married man. His son, Dale, had run off to join the Marine Corps and they no longer spoke. His daughter, Katie, still lived at home as she worked her way through nursing school, but it was only a matter of time before she left. He'd miss her.

Sometimes he thought about getting out of the house himself, perhaps even starting over completely.

While more stable than his family life, his job left much to be desired. He spent eight hours a day in a cubicle, the sort of thing he once swore he'd never do. He supposed it had gotten him far, by someone's standards, his father's, perhaps. An acre of land. A Cadillac. A big, three-story house with two-hundred thousand left on the mortgage. A newly remodeled kitchen that he wasn't sure he could pay off if his marriage fell apart. A son that refused to talk to him. A daughter too sweet for her own good.

On the way to the kitchen, he saw that the door to his studio hung ajar. He stopped and stared into the crack, catching glimpses of the items inside. Forgetting that he had to be at work soon, he pushed the door all the way open.

The stacks of old notebooks, the in-home studio equipment, and the black Gibson that hung on his wall brought a wave of nostalgia. Stickers from local bands that hadn't existed for decades covered the guitar. Todd sighed. He hadn't entered that room in years.

"Dad?"

He closed the door quickly, as if ashamed of the room's contents, then turned and saw Katie standing in the foyer. She wore a too-short denim skirt and a bright yellow top. Open toed shoes revealed toenails painted bright pink. She smiled and it lit her entire face. It was summertime and she embodied the joy that it brought younger people.

Since she was in school and summer still held some significance for her. For Todd, it just meant the days got longer and hotter.

"Want some breakfast?" she asked.

He caught the aromas of bacon and coffee. He checked his watch to make sure he had sufficient time to enjoy the food. He smiled at his daughter, nodded, and followed her into the kitchen. She moved with a spring in her step, seeming to dance as she walked. He couldn't remember the last time he'd had such energy.

"What are you so happy about at six thirty in the morning?"

"Can't I be excited to cook my dad breakfast? I haven't seen you in a while."

Todd tried to recall the last time he'd sat down to a meal with his family and couldn't.

"Besides, I had a long and crazy night, and I'm running on my second wind."

He sat down at the granite island in the center of the kitchen. "You didn't sleep?"

Katie giggled. "Nope. Summer's officially here. No more finals, no more early classes. I'm looking forward to three months of enjoying myself."

"Well, if pulling all-nighters is your idea of enjoying yourself...Did you see your Mom?"

"I actually just got home."

Jesus. He cringed against the idea of her being up all night doing God knew what. Funny; he'd probably done much of the same things she was experiencing now, but it was different for him to know she behaved this way. She was his *daughter*. He'd been wild at her age. The thought didn't come with as much regret or disdain as he expected.

Katie cracked an egg and let it fall into the frying pan. She looked over her shoulder.

"Did you not see her last night?"

"She said she was working late, but she wasn't here when I woke up this morning."

Katie cocked an eyebrow. "How long's that been going on?"

"What do you mean?" He played dumb. No sense in letting Katie in on their marital problems, at least not until they directly affected her. *If* there were marital problems. She'd probably just forgotten to call. She'd get his voicemail and apologize. Then they could talk their issues out.

"Never mind, I guess." She turned back to the pan, pushing the eggs around with the spatula. "Anyway, my friends and I were driving around listening to your album. You really used to rock."

Used to.

Todd sipped his coffee and remembered the door to his studio hanging open, the glimpse of his past he'd allowed himself. "Thanks. I think."

"No, really, we all enjoyed it. Jake always thought you were kind of a square, but he's changed his opinion of you."

"Who's Jake and why does he think I'm a square?"

Katie set a mug of steaming black coffee down in front of him. "You met Jake a few months ago one night when he picked me up. Anyway, you're always wearing suits and stuff. He didn't mean anything by it."

Todd recalled dressing in front of the mirror this morning and thinking how much he'd transformed over the years. He couldn't get offended if someone from his daughter's generation thought he was a square. Had he met his future self at her age, he would've thought the same thing.

Katie put a plate with eggs, bacon, and strawberries in front of him.

"Looks good."

"It wasn't difficult to make, honest."

She crossed the kitchen and fished into her purse. She pulled out a CD case with an image of a much younger Todd on the front holding a guitar, the same instrument that hung in his study. She set it down next to him.

"It's like looking in a mirror isn't it?" Katie said.

"Not quite."

"Do you want me to put it back? I didn't get a chance to last night."

She started to pull it away, but Todd reached out and pinned the case to the surface. He remembered writing the eight songs that made up the entirety of the album with the confidence that they would resonate with everyone who heard them. He remembered recording them during his first year of marriage with a certain desperation and hope that they wouldn't disappear forever, that someone, somewhere would hear them, that they would outlive him. In a strange way, having his daughter hear and enjoy them made it feel like they had.

That he'd started to record them the day after Chloe died hit him like a punch in the gut.

"Are you okay?"

"Yeah. Food's a little spicy, that's all. Spicy, but good."

"Just like Mom used to make." She sat down across from him. "So what's really going on between you two?"

"I'm sure everything's fine, Katie."

He said it without believing it and it hurt to lie to her.

"If you say so," she said. "I just worry, Dad."

"If I'm not worried, you shouldn't be. I think work's been keeping her really busy." More bullshit, but what else could he say?

Katie tensed her jaw. Her eyes burned with a determination to know more. She opened her mouth, and then closed it. She sighed. "If you say so..."

He gave her hand a light squeeze. "I say so. You know, I think I'm going to take this CD to work today. Maybe I'll give it a listen, see if these songs hold up."

She took her hand away and smiled. "You may surprise yourself."

"Not all surprises are pleasant."

~Chloe~

Thirty years, a blink in eternity.

Thirty years that felt like thirty thousand had passed.

Thirty years she had suffered in that horrible place.

Thirty years ago, she had died and learned that true death, an eternal sleep, a peaceful rest, didn't exist.

The familiar voice and chord progression of the song "Blissfully Damaged" rose among the sounds of suffering as she knelt in the muck of Samael's chamber. The demon that had helped her die stood over her as her mutilated flesh healed and grew back over her bones. Over the past thirty years this destruction of her body had become a ritual. Samael tore her apart and put her back together, unmaking and re-making her every day.

The notes of the song paralyzed him and awoke in her a long-buried will to escape. She ran towards the sound through eruptions of flame and the grasping claws of the damned, the notes getting louder with every step. The music projected from a yawning chasm that had

opened in the ground. She closed her eyes, jumped in, and landed in these woods.

Behind her a fiery tear in space closed up. The chirping of birds, the scurrying of squirrels, and the gentle rustling of leaves replaced the song. The smells of ashes and burning hair faded with every moment, replaced by damp and lively smells of mud and foliage. She saw that she wore a short black dress, identical to the one she'd worn the day she died. In the other world, she'd always been naked and vulnerable.

Thinking of the place from which she'd escaped sprung her into action. Without knowing where to go, the frantic need not to get caught carried her forward. She didn't know how much more pain Samael could inflict upon her, but she was confident that if he caught her, he'd think of something.

Fog parted below Chloe's bare feet as they struck the forest floor. She brushed aside low-hanging branches and strived not to slow her pace. Her leg muscles burned as she ran. Her heart rate quickened. Wind whipped against her face, blowing back her hair and stinging her eyes. She hadn't felt with the senses of this body since dying, and she'd been dead nearly a decade longer than she'd been alive. All these new sensations held meanings for her. The crunch of dry leaves under her feet meant freedom. A breath of cool morning air meant she was alive again, truly alive. Maybe now there was hope.

Downhill momentum carried her to the shoulder of a road. The cool pavement beneath her feet brought calm. She stopped to risk a look back and listened. If Samael was after her, he wasn't too close behind.

Slight vibrations in the ground and the hum of a motor heralded an oncoming car. With it she caught ear of the familiar song that had reached her in that other world. She stood on the side of the road and awaited the right moment.

~Todd~

Todd sang along with his younger voice as it carried through his Cadillac's sound system. Much out of practice, he'd even forgotten some of the words and how to hit certain notes, but it felt good anyway. Like his twenty-two-year-old self still lived somewhere inside his middle-aged body.

The route to work cut through heavily wooded hills, farmland, and at one glorious moment overlooked the valley that cased the serene Willow Lake. Though an unbearably tedious job awaited him at the end, these forty minutes, with the gorgeous scenery and the rolling rhythm of movement brought peace to his thoughts. Hearing his own music today brought an even more special vibe to his commute.

The realization that the songs still held up brought the best feelings and the music gave way to images. A crowded bar full of people that he looked upon from the stage. Bright spotlights and neon signs. The images awakened something within him. Singing to these songs, remembering the stories they told, brought clarity to dreams that he forgot upon waking and phantom smells that pulled him into depths of melancholy.

Todd pressed the gas pedal to the floor and watched the speedometer climb. His car glided over the asphalt, carried by energy not of this world. The music pounded the atmosphere. His young, strong voice soared through it. His words told of the tragedy at the forefront of his heart back when he'd recorded them. Now the words stung and exhilarated him.

He remembered Chloe. Though he'd written some of the songs before meeting her, they seemed to serve as prophecies for the fate that would befall her. They'd loved each other, but he had left her. He'd thought it for the best, or at least he'd heard it enough times to believe it. After trying normal life for a while, moving in with Anna and giving up music to focus on his banking job, he changed his mind. He'd intended to go back to Chloe before tragedy had claimed her.

He could feel her in his arms now, smell her, taste her. Drifting farther away, he remembered her greeting him with a kiss as he got off the stage, and sang louder. Something like a weight belt tightened across his diaphragm. Back then those words brought purpose, like he stood out from the rest of the herd, like he mattered.

Todd relived everything now as he sang.

He whipped the car around a corner and almost lost control. He tightened his hands on the wheel and steadied the vehicle. His mind cleared and the cold present replaced the vibrant moving pictures of the past. He glanced around, making sure no police had witnessed his reckless driving as his tires screeched in protest. Only the woods that lined the road had observed his transgression. At his speed, one of those trees could do him a lot of damage.

The hill declined, which meant he was closer to work. Havertown Community Bank's corporate headquarters operated in the town below. He drove closer to the gray heart of reality, but the melodies of each song pulled him away again.

He almost missed the black-clad figure stumbling into the middle of the road. He slammed on the brakes, but was going too fast. As his tires screeched he saw the doe-eyed look of terror on the face of a young, dark-haired girl. For an instant, he thought he knew her. Fading between reality and memory had blurred his awareness. He was, however, sure he was going to end her life if he didn't react quickly. He cut his steering wheel to the right, his foot still pressed down on the brake pedal, and went off the road. His car dipped into a grassy ditch at the edge of the woods. His body jerked. He raised his hands as fast as he could, but his face connected with the steering wheel.

Silvery stars exploded in front of his eyes. For a moment, he thought they might be spotlights, blinding him as he tried to look at faces in a crowd. But he wasn't in a club; he was in his car. The gray steering wheel with the Cadillac logo sat kissing distance from his face. His raspy voice crooned about fiery crashes fusing two lovers together, the need for that magnitude of passion, and a quickly approaching doom.

How fitting.

He turned the music off and pulled on his door handle with a trembling hand. With his pulse pounding between his temples, he tried to maneuver his way out of the vehicle. Too rattled to muster a lot of strength, it took two efforts to get the door open.

Once out, he made an inventory of himself and confirmed that he was in one piece. His car he wasn't so sure about. A large crack split the driver's side headlight, and it shined no light. Fog swirled around the hood. At least he hoped it was fog, and not smoke.

Thankfully, his car rested in a shallow ditch. Upon closer examination, he saw that other than the headlight, the front of the car had only a few dents and scratches, and his tires still held their air.

Back by the road, the girl in black wandered toward him and he realized exactly who she was.

* * *

He first met her at an after party for one of his gigs. Her father Les cooked at Master's Catering and had organized this, along with many other parties. Someone worked the door and the parties always turned a profit. Like most nights, on the night he met Chloe more people attended the after party than the actual gig. A diverse group of people packed the dance floor. Younger rock and roll kids decked out in denim jackets covered in patches. Well-dressed older guys and their dates, trying hard to recapture a youth that had long passed them by.

The hall smelled of spilled liquor and air freshener. A couple that had just snuck into the bathroom snuck their way back into the hall. Todd watched them try to play it cool as they shuffled back to the dance floor, amazed that on other nights of the week the hall hosted serious parties for serious people. The debauchery that sometimes transpired on nights like this made it hard to believe that anybody serious ever set foot in here. Once two young punks beat the shit out of a middle-aged dude who'd slammed down enough shots to think it smart to start a fight with the two younger, stronger partiers. Pretty funny to think that the next day the hall had hosted some kind of business card exchange. The staff probably had all kinds of crazy stories. Todd knew Les did.

He considered Les a good friend. Though much older, Les always spoke to him as though they were equals, very different from the "daddy knows best" manner of Todd Sr. Les enjoyed Todd's music and because of his job at the catering hall, he knew a lot of people and almost always brought a crowd to Todd's shows.

Les clapped him on the shoulder, and he almost spilled his drink. Les said something in slurred speech and Todd spun around on his stool to face his much drunker counterpart.

Les's gray-streaked hair hung in a shoulder-length mess, but he stood tall in the dim lights like a rock star, in good shape despite his lifelong love affair with booze. Todd hoped then to be that cool when he reached Les's age, was absolutely sure he would be.

"What's up, man?"

"Someone I want you to meet." Les jutted his thumb to his right. "This is my daughter Chloe. She's home from college for the summer."

Todd stopped the drink at his lips. The young woman's dark hair fell in perfect ringlets across smooth, milky shoulders. Even in the dim light of the hall, her wide, dark chocolate eyes glistened. A black dress came to the middle of her thighs and showed him her statuesque legs.

Despite the booze in his system, the sight of her gave him a moment of perfect clarity.

"She's a musician like you."

Todd left the bar, but not before getting her a drink.

Les smiled, not seeming to mind that Todd had ordered his daughter a drink. Les had always respected him. If anyone could buy his daughter a drink, Todd could. If Les had planned it as a setup, he wasn't subtle about it. He left the scene as soon as Todd and Chloe held each other's attention.

Todd fumbled for words as he handed the gorgeous woman a drink. He and Anna were dating, but no mention of serious commitment had passed between them. The field lay open before him.

"So you're a musician?"

"Yeah, I play keyboards." She considered the drink in her hand, held it down at waist-level. "I'm not classically trained or anything, but I pick things up pretty fast. Mostly write my own stuff."

"That's really cool. More than cool. My songs could use some keyboards."

"Yeah, I'd be up for jamming." She smiled, shy and restrained, but beautiful in spite of that. Maybe even because of that. "I'm home for the summer. Maybe even longer. School's not going so well." Her eyes shifted.

Todd gave a dry laugh. "I know the feeling. I barely graduated last year."

"Hey, at least you finished, man. What'd you major in?"

Todd rolled his eyes. "Finance. Thrilling, huh?"

"I never would've pegged you for that."

"Oh, trust me. It's very much a back-up plan. I'm taking my music as far as it will take me."

"That's good. I don't think I'd be alive if it wasn't for music. No matter how bad shit gets, I'm usually okay as long as I can play."

"I know what you mean." He did. He had spent many nights alone in his room, strumming chords into his headphones, the door locked against the rest of the house. Whenever he had a fight with his father or Anna, playing took him away to a special place. Somewhere between oblivion and rapture.

She put her unfinished drink down and asked if he wanted to come outside and smoke with her. He agreed and they made their way through dancing people and out the double doors. He noted the way

she moved, in free sweeping motions as if she swam through the air in front of her, delicate and pure.

Outside, he bummed a cigarette from her and she lit it for him. They smoked in silence. He tried not to be creepy as he just watched. Her hand as she brought the cigarette to her small mouth moved with beautiful elegance. He kept quiet, afraid to ruin what could be a perfect moment.

Nearby, a group of kids in leather stood in a circle smoking and passing a flask around. Crickets gave the surrounding woods symphonic life and muffled the music from inside. An owl hooted every few moments in no particular pattern. The others finished their cigarettes and went back inside.

"I should've gotten us more drinks," he said.

"Maybe." A long pause. "I'm not really supposed to drink."

"Oh?"

Chloe flicked some ashes off of the cigarette and watched them drift down to the pavement. "I'm an addict."

Todd tried to play it cool because in spite of her confession he liked her, her mystery, the fact she liked what he liked, and that she was the daughter of a good friend.

Against his will, nervous laughter escaped him. "What do you like?"

She sized him up to gauge how he'd respond. She took a drag from her cigarette and looked away. "Heroin."

That almost stopped the conversation. The drummer in one of his previous bands had been a heroin addict. His dependence on the drug led to his departure from the band and he'd died of an overdose, isolated from Todd and the others he'd called his friends.

Chloe sensed the awkward silence and apologized immediately. Todd looked her up and down, stopping at her dark eyes. They captivated him, hypnotized him. Instead of turning him away, her damage made him want her more. Underneath her fragility, he saw untapped light and beauty begging for release. When he stared into her eyes, he saw the opportunity to save a life, to smooth out her rough edges, and create something perfect.

He moved in to kiss her and she pulled away. She laughed a little.

"I just told you I'm addicted to heroin. If that's not a sign that I'm trouble, I don't know what is."

"Maybe I like a challenge," he said and tried again.

She held up a hand to his lips. "Look, you seem like a really nice guy. You don't want any part of me. Believe me."

"Look, it's behind you right? You're sober now." He looked at the drink in her hand. "Well, sort of. But look, if you're trying to make things better for yourself, you'll probably want someone to support you."

"And that's you?"

"Maybe it's me. Maybe it isn't. How about this: I won't kiss you tonight, but I'll give you my number. You said you'd be up for jamming. We can start there and see where it goes."

She dropped her gaze. When she returned it, she was smiling that shy, restrained smile. "All right, we'll see where it goes."

A couple of weeks later, he brought her on stage at one of his shows.

"Everyone, say 'hi' to Chloe," he said as she took her place behind her Yamaha DX7. "She's gonna help me sing this next one."

They'd written the song together in the days leading up to the show. It was called, "The Lie," and its lyrics had come from a discussion they'd had about marriage and kids. *This could be so great: you can be my best friend; they can carry on our legacy. But it can't be obligation, baby, no. We can't be like the others, oh no.* Todd sang the first verse and she harmonized him during the chorus. *Inner fires reduced to embers in a backyard grill if we should fall into this lie. I love you more than the stars in the sky, but don't let us fall into the lie.*

* * *

As he saw her now, on the side of Route 32, in the flesh, these recollections hit him like a high speed train. Staring into her dark, desperate eyes opened a door within him, one that had been locked for decades, like the door to his studio, but even more secret, more forgotten.

Her being here was impossible. Les's voice as he called to deliver the news of her death repeated in Todd's mind. He remembered feeling like Les's voice had been full of emotion that could burst forth at any moment.

Just as impossible, she looked not a day older than when he'd last seen her. The same raven hair fell in thick ringlets across her silky, pale shoulders. The petite body still possessed the same tight definition.

He didn't believe in the supernatural. As a young man, he considered himself open to the possibility, even trying different churches, studying various religions, and listening to Les talk for hours about the occult, but these interests died in the place of a lonely routine limited to his bedroom, his office cubicle, the road to work, and his dinner table.

Because of this lack of belief, the sight of his thirty-years-dead ex-girlfriend standing before him sent him into numbed hysteria. He couldn't speak. He could hardly move. All he could do was gasp and stare. He took several steps back and braced himself against the cool skin of his car.

"You remember me." Not a question.

Even her voice was the same. Its soft, lively tone resonated through him.

"How...?" he sputtered.

"I have no time to explain." She walked toward him and he tensed up. A frightened yelp escaped his lips. Death overshadowed her presence, challenged everything he knew, and part of him tried to reason that this was a dream. She looked over at his Cadillac. "Is your car okay?"

His lips moved, but no words came out. He nodded.

"We need to put some miles behind us."

Todd shook his head, a nugget of rationality returning. "What? No... I..."

"Todd, please," she said. The pleading tone of her voice snapped him out of it. Her eyes were soft.

"I can call for help."

But he already knew that he wouldn't make it to work today. Sanity, responsibility, and all that he convinced himself had mattered over the last thirty years now seemed less significant. He remembered the song he'd written for her, about how she'd come into his life black-haired, and blissfully damaged.

"Chloe, how are you here? I just don't believe..."

"I will explain everything." Once an elderly woman had slipped and fell outside his bank. His co-worker had been a woman named Kristin who had stayed with the victim until the EMTs arrived. She'd talked to the old woman in a level, purposeful voice. Todd had known then that Kristin had meant to keep the woman calm and he recognized the same tone in Chloe's voice now.

"We just have to get in the car first, okay?" she said.

A whooshing sound came from within the woods, reminding him of a bonfire doused in lighter fluid.

Panic entered her voice. "Right now, I need you to get me out of here."

Beyond the hill, a red orange cloud filled the sky, like a volcano had erupted. Agony-filled screams came from inside, and another sound, like stone grinding against stone, the single most horrible thing he'd ever heard. It brought to mind a verse he barely remembered from his childhood youth group Bible studies. Something about wailing and gnashing of teeth. An icy chill crawled from the base of his spine to the back of his skull and he shuddered.

"Okay," he said.

They rushed toward his car. He did everything he could not to look at the fire, or her. Both were sure to make him insane. He flung his door open, slid into the driver's seat, and reversed the car out of the ditch.

~Anna~

"Shit."

Anna hung up after listening to Todd's message. Part of her hoped he was at work already, but another part wanted him to confront her. A conversation about the state of their marriage and what actions they should take was a long time coming.

Keith wrapped an arm around her shoulders. He buried his face into her neck, sniffed her, touched his lips to her skin. The kisses made her feel young and pretty again. *Desired*. She rolled over to face him, returned his affections.

Keith was nearly ten years her junior, divorced and childless, damaged goods for all intents and purposes, yet always quick to assure her that he wasn't seeing anyone else. He'd started at Marcus and Marcus over a year and a half ago and his attitude and work ethic had immediately drawn her to him. He flirted, but never in a way that made her uncomfortable, and rarely dropped his professional demeanor around the office. When he cornered her at the company's July Fourth party, after several drinks, she hadn't resisted. She returned his kiss and thus began their affair, almost a year and still going strong.

She cursed again. "I knew I should've called him."

He wrestled the phone out of her hand. "It'll be fine.

She stared hard at his boyish features. He knew about Todd and her children, but it frustrated her when he pretended not to care. Of course he did. For all the devotion to a bachelor's lifestyle, a deep part of him wanted to commit. He talked of his ex-wife often, and Anna got the idea that he was lonely. She made it pretty clear when their affair started that she wouldn't leave her husband, but knew in her heart of hearts that one day Keith would ask her if she would.

"Are we still on for this weekend?" he asked.

"Yep."

She smiled and tried to hide her racing thoughts. Whatever she would say to him if he asked for a commitment from her would require practice. She suspected he'd ask her about it this weekend.

"Good. I'd hate to spend the weekend in the mountains alone."

"I'm sure you wouldn't have trouble finding a date." She winked at him and got out of bed.

The room around her was a classic bachelor pad. A too-large television sat on a stand filled with workout DVDs and dumb action movies. Empty beer bottles covered the furniture, and books by guys like Tucker Max and Neil Strauss lined a shelf fashioned to look like a boat standing on end. In a lot of ways, it seemed he never really grew up. She sometimes found his success at work difficult to believe when he spent such a large portion of his spare time drinking craft beer and seducing her.

She closed the door behind her and turned on the shower, undressing and stepping under the hot water to wash away the sins of the night before. She shut her eyes, recalling Keith touching her as if she were a delicate thing, and then ravaging her when she asked for it. Could she remember the last time Todd had touched her the same way? Maybe on one of their birthdays, but even then it had felt obligatory, passionless. When he told her he loved her, it sounded scripted. She wondered if it sounded as mechanical to him when she said it.

As she finished the shower and toweled off, her naked body confronted her in the steamy mirror. She grimaced upon viewing the parts of her that hung where she'd previously been tight. Around her eyes and mouth, the years left their cruel marks and only further examination brought satisfaction. Her green eyes still held vibrant color. The curves of her chest and ass were impressive for a woman her age. She

offered a smile to the twin in the mirror, hung the towel on the door, and exited the bathroom.

"Should've stayed longer," Keith said when she came back into the room. "I was thinking about joining you."

She blew him a kiss. He caught it with his right hand.

"You should've spent less time thinking and more time acting."

As the words came from her mouth, they cemented to her reason for the affair. It made her bad and being bad was more exciting than being who she was the rest of the time.

~Todd~

Todd and Anna drifted apart the more time he spent with Chloe. Anna wanted someone to marry and have children with right away. She wanted everything in its place and possessed specific ideas about where everything belonged. More and more he felt that Anna loved him for the mask he wore at his day job. She never came to his shows to support him or the after parties to spend time with him. Anna and Todd's fathers worked together and had set up their first date like an arranged marriage.

With Chloe he could live in the moment, and have companionship without being truly tied down. Passion, spontaneity, and little expectations filled their time together. She always attended his shows and never suggested that music was just a hobby, because to her it meant just as much as it did to him. It was a means of survival.

In the time they were together, she also stayed clean.

But one day he came home to an eerily silent apartment. The television played a car dealership commercial, the volume all the way down, the muted images the only signs of life. He called her name, then stepped into his front room. She did not respond.

She'd moved in a few weeks prior, and since then she had greeted him regularly with a kiss and asked what their plans for the night were. What open mic were they going to enter? What band were they going to see? Would they just stay and play their instruments in the intimacy of his apartment, singing to each other softly?

He shut the door, expecting that to draw her attention. He stood in the front room and waited, listened. She didn't come walking down the hallway. No one greeted him from one of the other rooms. He called her name again and stepped further into the apartment.

A haunted atmosphere lingered about the place. Even though only a few weeks had passed, he'd grown so accustomed to having her around. Her absence seemed fundamentally wrong somehow. He checked the kitchen and saw the sink immaculately clean. The refrigerator hummed indifferently.

He looked in his study, a small half-bedroom where his guitar and amp stood proudly beside Chloe's keyboard. Recording equipment littered the floor and a few notebooks sat stacked neatly in the corner. He had purposely chosen not to furnish the room, so he'd have more space to play in it. He hoped to find her there, perhaps recording with headphones on, but he didn't.

At the end of the hallway, the bedroom door hung open a crack. Sunlight from the large window leaked through. Staring into the light he thought the worst: that she may have left him. Even though the bliss of their companionship was unwavering, the fear that it would one day dissolve always lay not so deeply underneath it. Part of it came from the extreme nature of their passion; the other part of it came from his father's staunch disapproval over her. But her addiction made up the strongest component of his fear.

He reminded himself that she'd beaten it. They'd beaten it together.

He gave one last sidelong glance into the studio where they made such beautiful music together and continued down the hallway. The bathroom was dark and empty. He tapped once on the bedroom door and pushed it open. As the door swung in, he heard a stifled sob.

She was sitting on the edge of the bed, her sleeve pulled up and her dark wavy hair falling down to obscure her actions. He didn't need to see to know. Their eyes met, but only for a moment before she looked away. Her face flushed with shameful red and she fell back onto the mattress. Todd saw the needle.

"What the fuck, Chloe!" It was more of an angry objection than a question.

She tried to sit up to face him, but fell back in a heap. He sat beside her, threw the syringe across the room, and took hold of her shoulders.

"Goddamn it. Don't do this."

Her half-closed eyes and slurred speech made him even more upset. What she said upset him further. "You don't understand. You don't understand."

She said it over and over, and he felt mocked.

When she sobered up, he drove her back to Les's.

"I'm sorry," she whispered when they pulled up in front of the house.

"Look," he cut her off. "I just need to think right now."

She respected his request and left his car without a word.

Instead of going home that night, he went to visit his parents. He mumbled a greeting to his father, who watched TV in the living room, and found his mother sitting in a wicker chair on the back porch, reading a Danielle Steel novel.

"Hey, Mom. Mind if I sit?"

She set the book down in her lap. "No, go ahead. What's up?"

He mulled over whether or not he should tell her everything. Chloe's relapse felt like a personal defeat, and he hated to admit such a loss. His mother had always been more understanding than his father though. Maybe she'd have some sound advice.

"Chloe relapsed tonight."

His mother gave him a sympathetic smile. Before she could give her advice his father pushed the back door open and stepped out onto the porch.

"What's going on?" his father said.

"Nothing, just talking to Mom right now."

Todd Sr. narrowed his eyes. "Is everything okay?"

"Can we talk about it later, Dad?"

"It's about Chloe, isn't it? I knew she was trouble."

"Honey!" Todd's mother said.

"Whatever happened with you and Anna?" he asked. "She was a nice, normal girl."

Todd had expected him to say all of those things.

"I don't need this right now, Dad. I just need to think."

"What you need to do is leave that piece of trash."

Todd's mother put her hands up. "Honey, things aren't always that simple."

"Oh, I'm sorry, do you want our son hanging around with some junkie?"

"No, not exactly, but..."

"Then it is that simple. Jesus, you always act like real problems are too complicated for me."

"You know what?" Todd said. "I should've known coming here was a bad idea."

Todd stormed out as his parents argued amongst themselves and drove to the nearest bar to drown the fire of his rage with whiskey and beer.

The next morning, while in the grip of a vengeful hangover, he called Chloe.

"Hey, it's me."

"Hey," she said. "It's nice to hear your voice. I didn't expect it."

"Yeah, about that..." A tear fell from his eye as he gripped the phone. "I'm sorry. I guess I just thought you'd get clean and that would be it. No bumps in the road, no falling off the wagon. I guess I wasn't being realistic."

"I can't blame you for getting mad, but you're right. Expecting this to be simple isn't realistic."

He swallowed. "Listen, you can come back, if you want. We'll get through it."

"I'd like that," she said.

~Samael~

The fire retreated. Like that old story of the burning bush, the flames never consumed anything. When snuffed out, the fire left no trace that it had ever been there. The cries of the eternally damned went with it. Samael stood in the woods alone, the sweet music of pain replaced with the chirping of insects and the wind hissing through the trees.

Lush lively foliage, adorned with red and yellow flowers surrounded him. A snake sunned itself on a nearby rock. Frogs croaked in a bubbling spring. A bird flew from tree to tree, carrying a worm in its mouth, presumably to feed its young. The signs of life had resumed moments after the burst of flame died down, and reminded him how much he hated this place.

Flesh and fire shadowed his earliest memories. His mother's exposed breasts scourged by lacerations, her wrists bound together above her head, as flames engulfed the kindling piled at her feet. He remembered little of his father, just blood and dead staring eyes. He presumed that his father had been killed prior to his mother's execution. Perhaps he'd died defending her. Samael never knew and never desired to find out. After six hundred years, he could still hear his mother's screams as her flesh blackened and sizzled. He remembered

little else about her, except that he felt tremendous sadness at her death. All his searches above and below proved fruitless. He only knew her through loss, through pain.

Men in holy robes carrying swords mandated that his family die. After the execution of his parents a family of affluent Catholics had adopted him. Baptized immediately, they had rechristened him Andres Cotillo. He had grown up under their care, studying their religion. He had marveled at the Bible and its passages of violent prophecy, and memorized prayers without ever feeling the meanings behind the words. Every thought of the Church had brought the pain, the visions of his mother's final agonizing moments.

His new family's home had been a gothic mansion erected on skeletal stone frames with vast expanses of glass and doors between pointed arches. As a young boy he would run through the expansive hallways, relishing the hollow sounds of his feet striking the marble, loving the feel of the air rushing through his lungs. While his new family had stressed prayer, concentration on the Gospel stories, and the lives of the saints, he had preferred sensation. Intense moments of physicality had brought the elation he had been told to expect from spiritual discipline. Soon he had even come to love the tears, the pain, the loss.

But that was a long time ago. The sensations of this place were shallow, insignificant to the pleasures and pains of the world below.

Most would consider the place he'd come from to be Hell, but for him it was home. He'd been there long enough to have made himself more than comfortable. He fed on suffering. For a man of his tastes, that other world was like a sprawling, endless smorgasbord, but his favorite dish had escaped, and he intended to make her pay dearly for it. It was more than that, wasn't it? It hurt having her gone. Agony filled every moment he spent apart from her.

He pushed his way through the woods, sensing that she'd been there. A burn swept across the map of his body, danced over every scar, and made his loins stir. He closed his eyes and focused.

He moved forward a few paces and the warmth faded. He stepped right and the sensation became even fainter. The itchiness from the sunlight returned to his skin. At the flare of pain he sucked in a seething breath. He stepped to his left and the burn became pleasant again. He was walking in her footsteps, ascending the same hill she had only moments before, each step filled with fire. At the top of the

hill, he opened his eyes. A paved road stretched below. He grinned. He closed his eyes again, forgetting that he was back in an earthly vessel. Focusing on which direction she'd gone, he made his way to the bottom of the hill and waited by the side of the road.

~Bradley~

For Bradley Farnsworth, this morning marked the end of another shitty shift at Omega Suppliers where he worked as a night watchman. He'd left home in a rush that evening and grabbed one of Maggie's bodice-rippers from the bookshelf instead of one of the crime paperbacks he enjoyed. With writing too laughable for him to even use the content as spank material, he'd given up a few pages in and spent the rest of the night staring at the security feeds and squeezing a stress ball.

Now free, he burned down Route 32 behind the wheel of his blood red Chevy Camaro. The rumble of the V8 engine surged through his body and brought with it a feeling of immense power. He bought the car as a present to himself after his honorable discharge from the Coast Guard. Maggie joked that he loved the car more than her. When behind the wheel with the pedal pressed all the way to the floor and the blacktop disappearing beneath the hood at an alarming rate, he suspected that might be true.

The Black Veil Brides tore through his speakers with their brand of grandiose heavy metal and Bradley pounded his fist against the steering wheel in time to the beat, occasionally singing along. He knew he wasn't much of a singer, but in the loins of the Camaro, he was a rock star. No doubt about it. As he grooved to the music and zipped the car around each curvaceous bend, the night's stress seemed to fall away. A case of Molson waited for him at home and maybe he could coax Maggie into a morning fuck before she left for her shift at Kohl's.

Trees flew by in his periphery. The road bent and arched. The engine of the Camaro roared with furious life. Bradley's hands clenched around the wheel, his palms slick with sweat, his shoulders tight with tension. The sun peaked above the horizon, illuminating the sights around him.

Beyond the next turn, a naked man stood right in the middle of the road.

~Samael~

By the time Samael heard the car and felt its vibrations beneath him, his patience had worn thin. His desires for Chloe burned his nerve endings as she drew farther and farther away from him. More than anger, a piercing agony skewered his spirit. He felt desperation at losing her, as he'd lost her before. Back when she'd been called Clare.

Clare lived alone in a hut on the edge of a small village. A widow, her husband succumbed to plague the previous year. She had no children. When Samael found her, she was outside tending a small garden. He fell at her feet, too weak to do anything else.

She reached down and touched him with a tenderness that he'd never known. She spoke to him in the most soothing voice and without quite understanding why, he wept, soaking the earth below with his tears.

Clare took him inside, fed him bread and some meat. After he ate, he rested. She let him stay without as much as hinting that he should move on, her manner as tender as her touch.

On his third night there, she called him into her quarters. When she pressed her naked body against his, he found that she'd lost none of her tenderness. They made the sort of love he never knew existed. A human love. There was only pain in knowing it would end, that their embrace would break. They exchanged no harsh words, nor did they subject each other to hurt. It was tenderness as he'd never experienced it.

He stayed with her until the day they were killed.

Now as the vehicle approached, a grin spread across Samael's face. The chase would be resumed, but a more immediate gratification of his urges awaited. He stalked out onto the road and watched as a red car whipped around the corner at incredible speed. Its brakes screeched as it swerved to avoid him.

Samael watched in awe as it slid out of control and into the opposite lane. Its red body demanded attention, burning like a bright fire in the middle of the road. He felt the sudden urge to feel its curves and angles beneath the caress of his fingertips. He imagined its heat, its rumbling engine, purring at his command. Up close this machine's majesty inspired awe unlike anything from his time on Earth or the

place from which he'd come. Such wonder had escaped him for so long, but feeling it now elated him.

He'd get that bitch, and after her punishment, she'd never even think about running away again.

The car jolted to a stop and the owner got out, throwing his arms into the air.

"What are you? Fucking crazy?"

Samael smiled, the horror he would inflict upon this man crossing his thoughts like an elaborate play, Grand Guignol blood flowing like a waterfall over the edge of the stage.

"You just walked out into the middle of the highway! You have any idea how fast I was going?"

The man pressed his lips together and scowled when Samael said nothing in return.

"What's your problem anyway?"

Samael smiled wider. As he did, his eyes burned and he saw the world through a red orange filter. The man's angry expression instantly became one of fear.

"What the...?"

"...hell. Exactly."

Samael's arm stretched forward, the skin and bones extending beyond its normal length. The man barely had an opportunity to avoid Samael's fist as it thrust into his chest. Upon impact, the breastbone shattered and the organs in the vicinity ruptured. He reached in deep and tiny slits opened in his palm. Worms crawled through the slits and spread through the car owner's chest cavity, greedily devouring his insides. The man's dying gasps would have been horrible had anyone else listened, but to Samael, they rang out like notes in the most beautiful song.

The car owner's body dropped to the pavement as Samael's hand retracted. Touching the man so deeply, he'd learned the man's name was Bradley Farnsworth. Twenty-nine years old. Survived by a wife and two children. Worked as a night watchman at a nearby warehouse. His father, a vacuum salesman.

Normally, Samael enjoyed learning the stories his victims' bodies told with their dying breaths. He liked the memories that weren't his, songs he'd never heard, lovers he'd never taken. They made him stronger, made his blood rush and set the fire in his belly to maximum heat. But he didn't have time to relish them now. He sifted through

Bradley's most treasured memories and most embarrassing failures and deepest fears until he found what he needed. When finished, he knew how to drive Bradley's car.

Samael ran his hand across the vehicle's red, metal skin before entering. The leather seat cooled his bare flesh as he hunkered down. He pressed his foot down on the pedal and the engine revved, sending pleasant tremors through his body that brought ecstasy and power. He now understood why humans worshipped these vehicles. Why they lost themselves behind the wheel, drove recklessly and died in them.

He thrust into gear, eager to taste that freedom, and slammed on the gas pedal. As he split the open highway and focused on his target, he realized he had a hard-on.

~Todd~

"I died. I'm sure my father told you."

Todd veered off of the main highway and onto another road, not wanting to drive into Havertown behind the wheel of a perfectly drivable car with a strange girl in the passenger seat. He'd already called Shay, his boss's secretary and told her he'd been in an accident and wouldn't make it to work. She'd responded with that mix of concern and suspicion she expressed whenever anyone called in sick.

Todd processed what Chloe said and thought again of the phone call he'd received from Les thirty years ago. The unspoken tension between them. The grief he'd known was there.

"I know. Sorry I didn't come to the funeral." The sentence felt weird coming out, but what the hell else could he say?

"I don't blame you."

The music played at a whisper, overwhelmed by the hum from the road below.

"So, you died. How are you here?"

The calm in his voice surprised him. His instincts screamed at the insanity of it all. Perhaps his need for answers held him together.

"Do you have a cigarette?"

It took a moment to register what she asked. "I gave those up years ago. I'm sorry."

"Shit."

She slouched in her seat and looked out the window at the trees as they passed. Her bare feet rested on the dashboard and she folded

her hands against her mouth. Her eyes betrayed the presence of deep dark thoughts.

"Most people think death is the worst possible thing that can happen to someone. I never felt that way. Sometimes I thought it would be quite nice, maybe even a release. I romanticized it. In an immature way, I thought it would let me stay young forever. You remember? We talked about this."

Todd wanted to correct her. Death was the worst thing for anyone to face. Just this morning, thoughts of his looming death had brought a feeling of anxiety.

"I don't know if I still agree with that. I mean, getting old isn't ideal, but to glamorize death is taking things a little far. My life isn't perfect, but I certainly don't want to die."

He thought about that a moment, the sum of the parts that made up his life. Anna's absence. Dale's estrangement. Katie's hopeless devotion. Maybe it went beyond imperfection. Maybe death *was* the only thing that could set it right.

"You shouldn't." Her eyes reminded him of people interviewed after a traumatic event. Wherever she'd been for the last thirty years had left her broken. "Everyone thinks death is the end, and that they should accept it. They have no idea. No amount of suffering can compare to what awaits beyond this world."

"You were in Hell?"

"You say it like there's an alternative."

He tried to process what Chloe said and his thoughts clashed with each other. Through most of his life, he believed there were only two possibilities for what came after death. He didn't think about it often, but he figured that either atheists were right, and that once dead, people fell asleep forever, or that religions were right, and the good went to Heaven while the bad went to Hell. Was there really only Hell, or was that just all Chloe knew? Was she paying for sins she committed during life? Nothing she'd done could have been that bad. If her claim proved correct, then everyone he knew who'd died (his parents, several friends and coworkers, Anna's father) all suffered in some cruel afterlife. One day he would suffer. His children too.

"This can't be possible. That can't be all there is."

"It might not be, I mean, I escaped didn't I? From what I understand, and I don't understand everything, there are several doorways

between your world and that one. Hundreds, maybe. Maybe even other worlds."

Todd shook his head, not wanting to believe any of it. Everything she said challenged his worldview. He considered himself a realist, someone who believed in what he saw and experienced. Chloe in flesh that should've decomposed long ago, tore open the veil that covered his eyes and showed him a new reality.

"How did you get out?"

"I don't know. I heard music. This music, I think." She turned a knob on the dashboard and the music grew louder. He had almost forgotten his album on the car stereo. His thoughts since picking up Chloe had provided his head with enough noise. Now his singing voice ruled the car again. He looked from her to the system. The seconds on the track's running time ticked forward.

"I don't understand."

"I don't either. I was there, in the middle of that nightmare, and I heard you. Through everything, I heard you. It was like you were calling me back. So I ran to your music, toward the sound of your voice like they were the only things that mattered."

He wanted to pull over, but her sense of urgency spooked him enough to think stopping would be a bad idea. She retreated into her own thoughts, while he looked at the road ahead and mused that it seemed to stretch on forever.

He asked her what dying had been like.

"Dying was a lot like being high, or getting off." She laughed dryly. "Maybe I felt that way because I was overdosing. I'm not sure. You do see a light at first. It's blinding. You tingle all over, feel more alive in that moment than you ever could imagine. If you're not afraid, and that's a big if, it's actually the greatest feeling in the world. In some ways, exactly how I imagined it would be, until I started to fall."

The whole time she spoke, he sat still, not even breathing. When she finished his phone rang, nearly jolting him out of his seat. Anna.

"Jesus," he said, looking at the phone. "This is crazy."

He showed her the lit faceplate.

"Your wife?"

He nodded.

"Answer it if you have to."

He looked from her to his phone and back to the road. A spectacular view of distant mountains loomed ahead. Between the road and

the mountains lay a deep valley with some homes, a lake, and sprawling acres of forest. A large white cross stood on one of the mountains and Todd wondered about the relevance of such symbols in the face of what Chloe had told him.

He sighed, acknowledging the crossroads that faced him. Ringring. Thirty years of marriage to Anna meant he owed her an explanation, even if only partly true. Ringring. On the other hand, her absence lately really bugged him. Ringring. He didn't know if there was a legitimate reason for her unavailability. Ringring. Or if she was cheating.

His phone stopped ringing and he put it down. He could help Chloe today, then come home and try to repair the rift between him and Anna.

"What do you need me to do?" he asked.

"My father, is he still alive?"

"I think so. I don't know."

"If he is, we need to see him. He'll know where to start."

~Chloe~

The prospect of seeing her father again made her eyes prickle with the promise of tears. The last time she had seen him, he had been on his way to work, dressed in an apron and his black slip-resistant shoes, and holding his keys in his hand. He had asked what she had planned for the evening. "Not sure," she'd said. "Might go see friends, or I might stay home and listen to music." He had asked her if she was okay and she had known he had meant to ask if she was sober. As she had given him all the reassurances that she was fine, she did her best not to think about the twenty-bag of dope waiting for her in the drawer to her nightstand. That had been the night she'd died.

Her father's apartment stood in a complex called Blue Bell Springs, a development of box-shaped brick buildings in the suburb Millville. Designed to look like a small neighborhood the complex was divided into sections named after trees: Holly Court; Willow Court.

"Kind of a downgrade from his old place," Todd said as they got out of the car.

"He probably lives alone and doesn't need the extra space."

"You think?"

"He never remarried after Mom died." She led the way into her father's section. "I got the idea he never stopped loving her. I used to catch him sometimes, looking through old photos and drinking a bottle of bourbon. I doubt that it's changed. If anything, I bet he spends his nights looking through photos of me."

She stopped walking as a sob squeezed out from between her lips. She wanted to believe her father could move on and live life despite the fact that she and her mother hadn't, but she knew the wish was in vain. He'd always been emotional, attached, devoted; a good man.

"Hey." Todd put a hand on her shoulder. "It's gonna be okay. We're gonna figure this out. I don't know how, but we have to."

She nodded. Todd was a lot like her father in that way, which was why she'd fallen in love with him so many years ago.

They found the right apartment and went to the door. Todd had looked up her father's address on his cell phone, which was fascinating in its own right. Even more fascinating was that the phone was able to navigate their route to the apartments. It blew her mind because there hadn't even been cell phones when she'd been alive.

How Todd had aged impressed her less. In his early twenties, lean muscles armored his wiry frame and thick, wild hair topped his head. She guessed he'd put on a pound for every year she'd been away, and he'd lost most of his hair. He stood beside her a soft shell of his once vital soul. She worried about him. Regardless of what they learned when they visited her father, she didn't anticipate an easy journey and worried he wouldn't survive the ordeals ahead. She examined his face to see what remained of the man he'd once been. Something had to be there. How else had he found the power to call her from the fire? Otherwise they were doomed. She settled on his eyes, twin blue-green kaleidoscopes that carried a faint trace of the fire he'd once possessed. He caught her looking.

"What?"

"You've changed," she said.

He raised his eyebrows. "Is that good or bad?"

"I don't know. It's change."

Something between a croak and a laugh came out of him.

"It's surreal being back."

"You're telling me." He pointed up at the brick structure that housed her father's apartment. "Do you think he can help us figure this out?"

"If anyone can do it, he can." Saying that centered her a little.

"Nervous?"

"He's gonna freak when he sees me."

The spark in Todd's eyes got brighter. "Well, if I didn't have a heart attack, I'm sure he'll be fine. He's always been a trooper."

"I hope you're right."

Her finger danced around the rectangular door bell.

"Maybe you better."

"He may be just as shocked to see me. We haven't spoken since you died."

Sadness jabbed her in the chest when he said that. She'd hoped that after her death Todd and her father would have become friends again.

"I think you should go first."

Todd stepped forward and stared at the ground as he reached for the doorbell. This was going to be as difficult for him as it would be for her. He depressed the doorbell and it emitted a tinny buzz.

They waited. A full minute passed before the door locks clicked open. The sounds set her pulse into a frenzy. Though confident that her father could help them, it didn't change the fact that seeing him again scared her. Before she had time to walk away and rethink her decision, the door swung open with a light groan.

He stood on the other side, leaning on a black and silver cane. His hair still fell to his shoulders, now white and stringy. Pinkish puffs of skin clouded the outside of his eyes. Though always skinny, he'd lost a lot of weight and exuded a frailty that she hated. He frowned at Todd.

"Something I can do for you, son?" Then his eyes shifted to her and his mouth fell open. He took a step back. A tear trickled out from one eye, slid down his nose and fell on the concrete step. He said her name once, under his breath. He pressed his hand against his chest. "Dear God."

Todd held up his hands. "It's okay, Les. We can explain everything."

"Explain? You can't be fucking serious." All the color had drained from his face. The way he clutched at his chest made Todd worry that he would have a heart attack right there.

"Dad," Chloe said and reached out to touch him and he stumbled backwards. "It's okay. It's really me. I need your help."

He looked from her to Todd, holding his cane out like a weapon. Chloe stepped forward, her hands outspread in a defensive gesture. "Please, Dad."

"Don't come any closer."

"Les, it's really her."

"That doesn't make me feel any better, son. And who the hell are you?"

"It's me, Todd. Please let us in. She needs our help."

"No way."

Chloe took another step toward him. "Dad, I escaped Hell. The last thirty years have been a fucking nightmare. I know you blame yourself for not being able to help me, but it's not your fault. Right now, though, you have the chance to help me. Please, I don't know where else to turn."

He bit his lip and nodded, but fresh tears fell from his eyes. He sucked in a lungful of air. "My sweet girl, is it really you?"

~Todd~

"Are you sure neither of you want a drink?" Les called from the kitchen. Tremors filled his voice.

Todd couldn't think of anything he wanted more. The events of the day had swept him up like a treacherous wind and dropped him in the middle of something deep and unexplainable. Being with Les and Chloe again, in spite of how much he and Les had aged and how long it had been since Chloe's death, felt like he'd entered a time warp to the past, a past he'd buried with an overabundance of work and a family coming apart at the seams. Tension moved into his nerves and tightened around the back of his neck. He could only imagine how the old man felt. Les had watched his daughter die, and now she was here, alive, in a body that hadn't aged a day. Todd could use a drink, and certainly couldn't fault Les for having one.

Todd looked at Chloe and she shook her head.

"No thank you," Todd said. "We're fine."

Yeah, right, he thought. Pretty fucking far from fine.

The thud of Les's cane on the wood floor jolted Todd out of his thoughts. Les entered the living room, spun the chair at the desk around and lowered himself into it. He laid the cane across his knees and folded his hands around a glass filled with a generous serving of

bourbon. The color had not returned to his face, though his eyes had reddened from the tears.

"It's good to see you again. Both of you." The ghost of a smile played at the corners of his mouth. "But I don't know what to say. I've known for most of my life that the supernatural exists, but God, seeing you here alive…"

"It's good to see you, too, Dad, but we don't have much time."

"Why?" Les asked. "What is it?"

"When I died, it was peaceful at first, the only time I truly felt free."

Color came back to Les's cheeks. He looked angry. He said, "When I found you there was something in the room with you."

"It was him… Samael. He was waiting for me when I fell into that other place." She looked down at her hands. "The truth is I knew him. I feel like I've always known him and now he's after me."

"Who is he?" Todd asked.

She shook her head. "He said he knew me from a long time ago. He called me Clare. When I was below he used to show me things from his memories."

"He wasn't a demon?" Les asked.

"No, he was human. At least he used to be. Maybe he's a demon now, after six hundred years in Hell, after the..." She paused. "His parents were killed in some kind of inquisition when he was very young and a rich family took him in. Though devoutly Catholic, his adopted mother was quite... depraved. As he turned to step down from the altar the day of his Confirmation, he saw the lust in her eyes, her teeth grazing her bottom lip. He was just a boy then, but on the verge of manhood and old enough to understand what she wanted, what *he* wanted.

"Their first night alone, she used a leather strap on his chest and belly. With her fingernails, she raked his back; with her teeth, she gnawed his shoulders. The sex followed, but only after the pain, which she delivered and demanded in return. Through his encounters with her, he learned how to use pain as a source of power, as a gateway to pleasure.

"It went on for years until his adopted father caught them together, and Samael fled into the night. He wandered the countryside for untold time. Starved and weary from his travels, he stumbled into this Clare woman's village.

"He showed her to me and I can see why he thinks I'm her. I look like her. They loved each other and for that period of his life, however short it was, he knew what it was like to live like a human being, to love."

Les knocked back some of his bourbon. "He told you all of this?"

Todd looked from Les to Chloe. He leaned forward, completely enthralled by her story, believing it, despite how crazy it all sounded.

"No, he showed me." Terror flared in her eyes and she looked away. "The people of her village didn't like that he stayed with her. He was an outsider and they were sleeping together out of wedlock. Finally, their affair caused enough trouble to incite the authorities to do something about it.

"They refused to repent and were killed, maybe even by the same people who killed his parents. He became the monster he is today in exchange for being reunited with his love. I guess that's who he thinks I am. And maybe I am her, I just don't know anymore. I've been down there so long everything just kind of runs together."

Todd felt a spike of jealousy. "What'd he do to you?"

Les trembled. His hands squeezed the cane in his lap.

"When I was a child, I used to dream about him. He entered my room and I'd leave my body behind. At first it was nice. He used to entertain me with magic tricks, most of them involved fire, but he always assured me there was nothing to be afraid of. I believed him because he seemed so friendly.

"He told me that I wasn't who I thought I was. My real name was Clare. I dismissed it all because I thought I was dreaming."

"Sometimes you mentioned him, but I thought the same thing. Either you were dreaming or you had an imaginary friend. I should've known."

"You couldn't have. I was just a little girl."

"Exactly why I should've protected you."

"There's nothing you could've done, Dad." Les bit his lip. "Anyway, for a while, he stopped coming. I forgot about him."

She choked on the last word, seemed to consider for a long time what she would say next. Todd dangled in suspense.

"When he came to me again, I was nearly thirteen years old. I remember it so clearly. That day in school, a classmate and I put on a presentation about the story of Persephone and Hades. I'd been so fascinated by that story."

She paused again. The terror in her expression increased. Todd could see that she almost didn't want to tell this part of the story.

"That night he came up from the floor. I thought I was dreaming, like before, right up until the moment he..." The terror dispersed from her eyes and her face tightened with anger. Lively red washed her pale cheeks. "He raped me that night. The next morning I had my first period."

"Jesus," Todd said and put his face into his hands.

"He came to me many times throughout my teenage years. Sometimes I saw him in broad daylight, following me down the street, watching me in a crowd."

Todd took her hand. "Why didn't you tell me?"

"I stopped seeing him when we met. That's part of why I called you when you gave me your number. I thought maybe there was something special. Maybe something about our bond would hold him off. When he started appearing again, what could I say? You wouldn't have believed me. It was crazy."

Todd pointed at Les. "Your father would've."

"She had no way of knowing that." Les gritted his teeth. "I don't know if I could've helped her anyway. All the things I've learned, fucking useless. All it did was make me realize just how futile our lives are. There are forces outside that can come in and do with us as they please. Rape our daughters. Turn us into monsters. I'm so sorry, but I don't think telling me then would've made any difference."

"We might not be completely helpless," she said. "I escaped when I heard Todd's music this morning. I don't know how, but it opened a door and I was able to escape through it."

Something shifted in Les's expression. "'Such strains as would have won the ear/Of Pluto, to have quite set free/His half-regained Eurydice.'"

"What the hell is that supposed to mean?" Todd said.

"It's Milton, a reference to the story of Orpheus and Eurydice. A part of you, a very deep part, still loves Chloe. That old passion combined with the power of music, played in the right tuning with the right amount of soul can do incredible things."

Todd said nothing.

"Do you remember the way I told you to tune your guitar? It came from an old book I used to have, and it was supposed to give your songs a special power."

"The power to raise the dead?"

"Among other things. I truthfully never thought it would work." He smiled and got to his feet, rising with incredible energy for his age. "Her being here proves otherwise."

He limped to one of the several bookshelves in the room and reached for one of the texts. He held it out in front of him with the cover towards Todd and Chloe. A symbol drawn in charcoal decorated the center. Around it were other smaller symbols—stars, animals, and shapes—spiraling into the central image.

"Have either of you seen this symbol before?"

Todd leaned forward, examining its angles and points. "No."

Chloe bit her lip and nodded.

Todd took the book in his hands. "What is it?"

"It's everything," Les said, as if the very statement overwhelmed him.

~Anna~

The steering column of Anna's Infinity protested as she pulled into her neighborhood, as if it, too, was afraid of what waited at home. She reminded herself that Todd was at work. She could at least put off the confrontation until later tonight. In the best case scenario she wouldn't have to deal with it until after the weekend. After she sorted out matters with Keith.

She examined the rows of opulent homes that lined the street with their sprawling lush grass, expensive cars parked like oversized trophies in the driveways, and manicured trees that shaded the sidewalks. A dog leapt with canine exuberance as a teenaged boy threw a Frisbee in one yard. A brightly colored Playskool swing hung from a tree branch in another.

When they had first purchased the home she and Todd had stood outside the house with Holden Stillwell, the fast-talking realtor with the cartoonish smile. She'd been seven months pregnant with Katie then, her belly swollen like a beach ball. Todd had held her hand and looked at her like she was the most beautiful woman in the world. Dale, smack dab in the middle of his terrible twos had been very vocal, often interrupting Holden and making the realtor stumble.

She hadn't thought of that day in years, but now she remembered it like it was yesterday. Their excitement. Their idealism. That romance

had faded over time, but she couldn't pinpoint one deciding event that had killed it. There were numerous things she was tempted to attribute it to: the death of Todd's father, her miscarriage of their third child, Dale leaving to join the Marines in a fit of rage; but the truth was that the spark in their relationship just dwindled.

She thought of the night Todd had gotten the news that his former girlfriend (what had her name been? Clare? Zoe?) died and wondered if his heart had ever been in their marriage. They both worked a lot and spent little time with each other. He often seemed obsessed with his job, as if he was working to distract himself from some ache, some longing. Perhaps she seemed the same way to him. Once both kids had been old enough for school, she started her career at Marcus and Marcus and worked her way up to where she was today. One of the top performers, she made almost as much as Todd did at the bank. For all of their other shortcomings, they'd never had to worry about money.

She parked her car in the driveway, behind Katie's black Corolla. She looked through the windshield at her house. The sun shone in the sky behind it and the home's boxy, angular shape cast a long shadow upon her. She opened the glove box and contemplated the pack of cigarettes hidden within.

"No." She closed it, took a stabilizing breath and stepped out of the car.

~Todd~

Les's words repeated in Todd's mind. The cruel Hell from which Chloe had escaped was believable in the face of her dread. The fact that she was here, too, had become easier to accept. She was either really here or he was having a really long, strange, and realistic dream. Harder to accept was Les's assertion that Todd still loved her and how that love, along with his music, had been enough to raise her from the dead. How was that even possible? Then again, his criteria for what was and wasn't possible had changed a lot in the last few hours. *Did* he still love her? They'd been together so long ago. In the time since, she'd died and he'd raised a family. Still, the question remained. He would've given anything to know what was going through her mind. Did her father's statement disturb her as much as it disturbed him? She hadn't taken her eyes off of the symbol.

“I was given this book by a friend in the Navy,” Les said. “No one knows exactly how many are in existence, though he suspected that there were very few. When he heard about Natalia, your mother, Chloe, he said the book might help me with the pain.”

He took a sip of bourbon and grimaced bitterly.

“I thought he meant that it would help me contact her, possibly bring her back, but I was wrong. What it did was help me see just how large the world is, that maybe she’s out there… somewhere.”

Todd looked from the book to Chloe to Les. “Wait, but why were my songs able to raise her from the dead? You're a musician, why couldn't you do it?”

"I tried. Believe me." Les's face darkened, making shadows in his eyes. "Maybe there's something about you. Did anything ever happen to you that you couldn't explain?"

"Shit, Les, life is fucking inexplicable sometimes," Todd said, but he thought back to the night Chloe died, to the glowing figure who had touched him out by Potter Way. He remembered it the way he remembered dreams, and some days, he wasn't sure if it had even happened, but he remembered feeling marked by the experience. He nodded. "Yeah, the night Chloe died, I was visited by...I guess it was some kind of spirit."

"Perhaps that gave you the power to wield the magic your songs possessed," Les said.

"If that's true, why didn't I bring Chloe back before? I wrote those songs years ago."

“I wish I knew how to answer that."

"Well, what does that book say?" Todd asked.

"Just that music, played in the right key, with the right amount of emotion can shift the cosmos, reconcile God to man, raise the dead. I suppose that today, for whatever reason, the timing was right."

"What does it say about keeping me safe?" Chloe asked.

Les handed the book to Chloe and she put it on her lap and traced the symbol with her fingertips. Les took a gulp of bourbon. "There are passages about bringing spirits home so they can finally be at rest. I think what it means is that Chloe has to go home."

She looked up from the book. “I don’t understand.”

Todd tensed. He didn’t understand either, any of this.

“Here’s what I know.” Les drained his glass with a grimace. For a moment, Todd thought that would be it, that Les finishing his drink

was a way to say that there was no way of knowing anything. It was a scary prospect. Finally, mercifully, Les said, "Hauntings are believed to be ghosts that haven't moved on because of some trauma that keeps them trapped in a certain place. In some cases that's true. In others, the haunting is when a ghost returns home, someplace familiar, someplace where its happiest memories are replayed. The home becomes a personal paradise for the inhabiting spirit, as if the spirit has found a way to hang onto life."

Todd's nerves begin to settle. Though outlandish and far-fetched, it at least carried some positivity with it.

"But where's home?" she asked, handing the book back.

Les met her eyes. The darkness in his face never left. Instead, the shadows grew longer, deeper. "I don't know, but you will. You just have to make it there first. After that, you'll be safe. Samael won't be able to get to you there."

Todd broke eye contact and turned to Chloe. Her leg jittered urgently. "We should go."

She nodded in agreement. They went to the door and Chloe embraced her father.

"I love you," she said. "I missed you so much."

"I love you, too, my sweet girl. No matter where you go, don't ever forget that."

"I won't, Daddy." She planted a kiss on his cheek.

Todd held his hand out to Les after Chloe opened the front door.

Les took it. "Nice to see you again, old man."

"You, too, gramps." They shook like old friends, keeping their eyes on each other, transmitting so much emotion and calling up years' worth of memories with just one brief contact and few words. They broke and Todd caught up with Chloe outside. When the door closed behind him, there was a terrible sense of finality to it.

~Anna~

Anna pushed open the front door and entered her home. As she crossed the foyer and went to the stairs, she noticed how quiet the house was. She guessed Katie was asleep. Otherwise, there'd likely be music on the stereo. *Good.*

She crept past her daughter's bedroom and stepped into hers. She pulled clothes off of hangers in her walk-in closet, careful to select the

proper outfits and deciding on two nice dresses, a casual outfit, and a silky robe. In the middle of draping the clothes over her side of the bed, she stopped to notice Todd's side, unmade and still holding the indentation of his body. The sheets on her side were neatly tucked in. Before her conscience could act up, she threw the rest of the clothes on the bed and dragged her overnight bag out of the closet.

As she unzipped the bag and flipped it open, the image of Todd's side of the bed returned to flood her mind's eye. A moment of honesty washed over her and she wondered how such a wedge had come between them. They'd loved each other once, hadn't they? She thought about how they'd met, the first awkward date set up by their parents, and the sudden rush to marry that had been welcome but had come unexpectedly.

Things moved at the speed of life after that. Both of them worked a lot. Between that they'd somehow managed to raise two children. When she thought about it, they'd never really taken the time to talk about what each of them needed, what their goals as a couple were. The truth was that she had liked the brash musician who stubbornly pursued his artistic dreams without worrying too much about the future. The man he grew into, overworked, with little rigid aspirations for himself and his children wasn't a bad man, but he was boring, too much like her, as if he was trying to remake himself in her image. And they never talked about it.

Too late to do anything now, she thought and started to pile the clothes into her overnight bag.

Footsteps shuffled out of Katie's room. She took a breath and held it, as if doing so would prevent her being detected. The footsteps got closer until they approached her bedroom door. Anna shut her eyes and tensed as the door opened and in popped Katie's head.

"Hi, Mom."

Anna opened her eyes. Katie was fully dressed and Anna got the crazy notion that her daughter had been waiting for her to come home. Katie looked past her, at the suitcase on the floor and frowned.

"Are you going somewhere?" she said, her voice razor sharp.

Heat rushed into Anna's cheeks. The lie came out almost involuntarily: "A business trip…"

"Cut the shit, Mom. Dad said you didn't even come home last night."

"He what?" The temperature of the heat in her cheeks rose dramatically.

Katie raised an eyebrow.

"Listen, honey, I don't know why your father is letting you in on our business, but..."

"Seriously, Mom?" Katie gave her mother a look that said they were two adults having a conversation, that this wasn't a talk between a mother and her little girl where one was in a position above the other. Here, in this moment, they were equals.

Anna wished that Katie would be that little girl again. Things had been a lot easier back then. She could just be a mother, not worry about the growing rift between her and her husband, or have to keep any secrets. Motherhood was a challenge, but a manageable one. This was manageable, too, but there was much more at risk. Could it end with anything other than heartache? She forced herself to loosen up and turned on her saleswoman persona. A little P.R. would do the trick, at least for now.

"Katie, I understand this is all a little strange, but I assure you things are fine. Your father and I have both been working really hard. I'm sure you can appreciate that, with your workload from school. I'm hoping to put away enough so I can retire earlier than originally planned, so I've taken on a lot of extra work. Sometimes I stay late at the office. Sometimes I have to go away. That's all. There's nothing going on that you need to concern yourself with. Okay, honey?"

She knew that was going to bite her if the truth ever did come out, but damned if she wasn't somewhat impressed with herself.

Katie nodded once. "If you say so..."

Anna did something then that sealed the deal and thus made the guilt swell larger within her. She reached out and hugged her daughter, tightly, reassuringly, and closed her eyes against the regret.

"Thanks for understanding, sweetie. Your father and I love you very much."

When Katie left the room, Anna breathed a heavy sigh, but felt no relief. She looked from the stuffed suitcase to the door Katie had just walked through.

Just get through the weekend. After that... what?

After that what?

~Samael~

The roaring of the rapidly turning engine was the perfect companion to Samael's frantic inner workings as he pulled into the town called Millville. Sensing that she was close, fire worked in his nerve endings. Hot blood rushed through his veins, making every capillary feel as if it could burst at any minute. The pursuit was nearing an end. As he grew closer to her location, he could almost taste her flesh on his tongue.

According to the sign, the town's population was over forty-seven thousand. These thousands were totally unaware of the events unfolding. Insects, oblivious to anything beyond the doomed corner of the universe they occupied. Too weak to explore anything else; too dependent on tomorrow to *really* live. As he drove into the heart of the town, he fantasized about pulling them from their homes, stretching their thresholds of pain and fear, making them forget about tomorrow and experience every agonizing moment of the present. But their faces all became Chloe's. It would be all too easy to lose focus with the temptation of raining down new carnage, devouring the darkest secrets of new souls, showing these people the only type of love he understood, but *she* belonged to him and *she'd* run away. That was more important than playing with new toys, because he couldn't live without her.

The sense of her proximity grew stronger and more rapidly. He checked to see if he'd increased speed, then realized that he hadn't. No, he wasn't just coming for her. She was coming toward him. He surveyed the road ahead, checked the sides of the street. Nothing. He drove on, her presence coming ever closer. With his left hand, he grabbed hold of his swollen genitals and tried to assuage the tension. He couldn't afford to lose focus.

The car came down the road in the opposite lane. Sunlight reflected off of its slick black body, blinding him, but he knew she was in the car. He could feel her. His need for her throbbed and the coming release flashed before his eyes. First the violence, then the sex, and afterwards… Serenity: enveloping, sweet, tragically temporary.

Only through this destruction could he feel anything. It brought the closest thing to love that he could experience. He bore this burden because of the covenant he'd made. The day he fell into the underworld's dank, ashen caverns he wandered out into Hades' always decaying landscape, broken and grieving the loss of Clare. All around

him, bodies writhed in various positions of pain. Rotting, skeletal hands reached for him so that he may join their damned ranks.

He met someone that day, a creature made of bone and magma, its hard body swathed in fleshy robes upon which organs hung from hooks and nails. The creature regarded him with red eyes that smoked like embers and spoke in a voice like the collective hum of a thousand wasps.

"Like everyone else here, there is something you desire," the beast said, pointing a twisted, smoldering finger at Samael. "Unlike the others, you have something that *I* desire. You have deep rage in your soul that could be very useful to me. If you do as I ask, you will see your love again. She'll be reborn of fire and her mother shall be consumed in it. This is how you will know her. All you have to do is let me make use of your talents."

Now, as the black car passed beside him he saw her, his dark angel, his slave, his lover. Another man sat in the car with her, some poor bastard that had agreed to help. Samael wondered if the fool knew exactly what he was getting into. The odds weren't good, and neither were the odds that the poor fool would live to talk about it. At least not in this world. Samael toyed with the idea of bringing the man with him and Chloe to the other world. Chain him up and force him to gather up the pieces of Chloe after every mutilation. Perhaps that would be fitting for the infidel who dared to come near what didn't belong to him.

As they passed, Samael stared right at them, and they drove on, not noticing. The tires of Farnsworth's red machine screeched as Samael jerked the steering wheel around and continued his pursuit.

~Todd~

The sign for Millville grew smaller in the rearview of Todd's Cadillac. His mind and heart raced, vying for the winning spot. Their meeting with Les had been so unlike a reunion with an old friend. He still had tons of questions, but another part of him didn't want to know. Maybe he'd had enough revelation for one day. Maybe he'd be better off after he took her home and she left his life for good.

He looked her up and down, wondered if he really meant that. Back when they were kids, he'd loved her unequivocally, would've done anything for her. He'd run away when shit got bad, but even

then, he knew he was taking the coward's way out. The truth was that he'd loved her too much and the possibility that he couldn't save her had torn him to pieces. Could it be the same love now that made him want to let her go? If he saved her this time, would he truly be free of her?

He stopped at a lonesome intersection in the middle of grassy farmland, looked both ways and turned left, back toward the highway. The sun made a golden halo around Chloe. She caught his stare and granted him a smile. At first, he couldn't understand how she could smile under their circumstances, but then its warmth melted him, made him feel a little more at ease. He relaxed his hands on the wheel and looked back at the road ahead.

A quick glance in the rearview mirror showed a red sports car gaining behind them. He ignored it, directed his attention back to the road. At the end of the fields on either side, walls of trees bathed the road in shadow. Todd kept his foot on the gas, driving for the black ahead. He drove without music. Only the hum of the engine kept the silence at bay. He stared into the darkness, hypnotized, letting the focus on the road ahead drown out his doubts and anxieties. The highway below seemed to carry them forward. If he couldn't have heard the tires rolling over the asphalt so clearly, he would've sworn they were gliding through the air. He flexed his hands on the wheel, listened to the hum, recalled the route to Chloe's old hometown.

A loud crash reverberated in his ears and control slipped from his hands. In less than a second, his car went from being a sanctuary to being a death trap. The steering wheel slid from between his fingers and the car swerved to the right. He vomited up a slew of curses. Chloe screamed beside him.

He snatched the wheel and steadied the car, but the anxiety didn't subside. A glance in the rearview mirror showed the same red car from before, this time right on his ass and coming closer.

"Oh, God, it's him!"

Todd took her word for it. He slammed the accelerator. The engine's hum became a groan as the speedometer needle climbed. Before he could gain a lead, the red car rammed them again. Todd held on as the car swerved back towards the side of the road. Countless tree trunks waited, hungry for a meal of flesh and metal. In the nick of time, he got back on the road, veered into the opposite lane, then back into place.

He gritted his teeth. "Fuck! Goddamn it!"

"Jesus, he's coming up beside us!"

One look into his side mirror confirmed her warning. The car's black grill filled the glass. He pressed the pedal to the floor, tried to push it farther. The engine growled in protest. The speedometer climbed higher, but the red car came right up beside them. The driver looked across at them, grinning like a madman. Then Todd saw the damnedest thing he'd seen all day: the man's eyes ignited with orange red fire, turning his face into the mask of a demon. The sight of their pursuer's true face forced Todd's body to seize. He released the gas pedal, hoping to outmaneuver the other car. Not a second after they started to slow the red car sideswiped them, sending Todd's Cadillac off the road towards an obstacle course of trees and rocks.

* * *

For the second time that day, Todd sat dazed behind the wheel of his car. Silver specks exploded before his eyes and adrenaline stampeded through his veins. Somehow he was still alive. The front bumper of his Cadillac had collided with a stump of a long ago fallen tree, deploying the airbags and filling the atmosphere with the screech of tearing metal. The coppery taste of blood played on his tongue as he reached across the center console and felt Chloe's form beneath his hand. Soft and warm, she trembled with the aftershock of impact. Apparently the undead weren't immune to trauma. He opened his eyes and turned to look at her.

"You okay?"

She regained composure and frantically jiggled the seatbelt. "We have to get out of here."

He cast a nervous glance back towards the road, elevated from where his car sat disabled. Trees shaded the air around them, choking the sunlight. He turned the key in the ignition, got no response from the car.

"Todd, come on!" She already had her door open.

He let go of his key and grabbed the driver's side door handle. As he maneuvered, he saw the gaunt, naked body of the red car's driver reflected in his side view mirror. *Samael.*

The pursuer moved in confident strides. A knowing smirk spread across his face, as if the man knew that he'd won, that the hunt had

been too easy for him. A competitive animal awakened inside Todd, choosing fight over flight. He pushed his door open and got out of the car. He set his sights on the man, clenched his jaw and his fists, prepared to fight.

"No, Todd, don't!"

The man, the demon, came closer. The cocky smirk grew bigger, its mockery all too clear. Todd couldn't remember the last time he'd been in a fight. It'd probably been at least before high school. He'd grown out of fighting earlier than most kids he grew up with, but now, the urge to knock the smile off the face of Chloe's pursuer burned within him. The man seemed to be looking forward to the confrontation, curling and uncurling his fingers, hunching forward as if ready to charge. Chloe's voice continued to plead, to protest. Todd barely heard her.

The man came forward and his eyes caught fire and reminded Todd that he was facing down something otherworldly. At the sight of those eyes, the urge to fight shrank. Todd's shoulders slumped. He backed off and turned away from the fiery eyes, unable to look at them anymore without feeling insignificant and weak. Finally hearing Chloe's cries, he picked up his pace.

Samael maintained an arrogant speed. Above the noise in his head, and his and Chloe's frantic running, Todd heard the slow crunch of the man's footfalls on the forest floor. It was a hopeless situation; that was the only thing of which Todd could be sure. The woods stretched for miles. They had no car. The man in pursuit was no man. A demon, maybe. Or something worse.

A voice cried out behind him. At first he thought it was the demon, but it sounded too human, too vulnerable. Todd looked over his shoulder, saw another figure standing behind the man with the fiery eyes. The figure stood at the side of the road, hunched over and gripping a shotgun. In the sunlight that lit the edge of the woods, he recognized the features of Les.

"Dad!" Chloe cried out.

The monster of a man's smirk became a full-on grin and he turned towards Les. "So… You're her old father."

Les kept his eyes on the man, showing none of the fear Todd felt. The man took two steps, then Les leveled the shotgun and fired. The shot tore through the air like the voice of an angered god. The exit wound exploded out of the man's back, showering red chunks of flesh

onto the forest floor. The man fell clutching at the air, then at the wound in his chest, and then lay still. Apparently even demons couldn't stand up to a twelve gauge.

Chloe took Todd's hand and pulled him towards the road. His leg muscles tightened in protest as he started to run again. Samael's empty eyes stared up at a ceiling of branches and leaves. Blood soaked the ground beneath his body. Demon or not, he was clearly dead.

Regardless of that seemingly obvious fact, Todd made an effort to move farther away as he passed the body. Chloe seemed to have the same idea and made no move to resist his pull. Les held his position at the edge of the road, his lips curled into a sneer, his eyes filled with a focus that made him look much more vital than he had back at the apartment. He kept the shotgun aimed, ready for anything.

They reached the side of the road, and Todd squeezed Les's shoulder.

"Thanks for the assist, old man."

"Anytime, young shithead." Something Les used to playfully call Todd back when they were friends. Les looked at his daughter and gestured with his shotgun. "He's not dead, is he?"

Chloe shook her head. Todd looked at where the man lay in a bloody heap, found it hard to believe, but remembered this was a different world with different rules than the one he knew.

Les cocked the shotgun.

"My car's still running. You two get in it, and get the hell out of here."

Todd put his hand back on Les's shoulder. "No way, you're coming with us."

"Dad..."

"Not this time, kids."

She stepped in front of the shotgun barrel, spreading her palms. "It doesn't have to be like this."

"Yeah, it does. You and Todd get out of here, and let me handle this flaming pile of hellshit."

"I won't let you."

Behind her, the dead man stirred. The dried leaves crinkled under him as blasphemous life returned to his body. He raised one hand and closed his fist around the air.

"Come on, Dad, he's coming back."

"Move out of the way, Chloe."

The dead man raised another hand, clenched another fist.

"Dad…"

"Todd, take her out of here."

Todd froze, the correct choice unclear. Each end would have tragic consequences. He didn't relish the idea of letting Les sacrifice himself. They had history, and if it hadn't been for Les he wouldn't have even met Chloe. On the other hand, if he and Chloe didn't leave now, he'd surely be killed and Chloe would be taken back to the underworld. He could try to persuade Les to come with them, but time was running out and Les appeared to be set on standing his ground.

Samael sat up, the wound in his chest now almost entirely healed, the muscles and scarred flesh restored.

"I'm not going with you," Les said. "This is your only chance. Now you go before he gets up."

Todd took Chloe by the elbow, hating the fear that filled him, hating that Les had to die to make their escape easier. He tugged at Chloe's arm and at first she remained glued to her spot in front of the shotgun barrel. The man rose to a crouch. Todd pulled on her again, this time more roughly. She cast a look at her pursuer, almost at a full stance, and she complied, giving her father one last look, and running towards the idling car on the shoulder of the road.

~Les~

Les stared into the demon's eyes and saw the madness that burned within them. The bullet hole had been reduced to one of many white scars that dotted and crisscrossed the demon's torso. He no longer moved like someone who'd been shot. Instead he moved with raw anger, hooking his hands into claws, tightening his muscles so that they popped out on his arms and neck. His mouth was frozen in an animalistic snarl. His irises burned like twin match heads held up in the shade of the forest.

Les heard Todd and Chloe drive away behind him. Knowing they were safe brought some relief. He aimed the shotgun between the beast's flame-filled eyes, just above the bridge of the nose. As he squeezed the trigger, the demon ducked and charged.

Before Les could react, the gun was pulled from his hands and fingers closed around his throat. His perspective shifted within a matter of seconds as he was lifted off his feet and into the air. The demon

threw the shotgun into the forest. Les's air passage closed off and wooziness set in, making the woods behind the demon appear hazy. He tried to kick free, driving his toes toward his assailant's abdomen, but he was held out too far and couldn't reach. He squirmed. He tried to pry the fingers from his throat. The iron grip wouldn't unclamp. Les coughed as the hand choked him out. Unconsciousness closed in, a swallowing cloud of inky blackness that would suffocate his life force. *Fine, let it. I've done all that I can…*

He was gone, but only for a moment.

Impact brought him back from the void as his body was driven into the ground below. He felt one shoulder blade disintegrate and a tremor of pain ravage the rest of his body. His blinking eyes stared up at the sky. Blood filled his mouth and he coughed it out onto his chin.

The face of the demon came into view, twisted features and teeth filed into points. In the burning eyes, he saw rage and none of the regret he'd detected when he'd first seen the demon standing over Chloe's bed. Samael's expression told Les that this wouldn't be quick and painless.

Samael lifted him high into the air and threw him down to the forest floor. More parts of him broke when he landed and he cried out in agony. The demon was upon him within moments, pulling up his beaten body and jacking him up against a tree. The pain was terrible, but at least he knew that the longer he endured it, the closer Chloe would get to safety.

He pulled a rosary out of his pocket and jammed one end of the cross into the demon's ribs. The demon let out a howl of surprise and let Les fall back to the ground. There was a sickening sound as the demon pulled the religious jewelry out of his flesh. The cross sizzled in his hand until he tossed it away. It didn't buy Les as much time as he would've liked, but it was something.

The demon made a grab for him, but Les was waiting with a jagged stone in his one good hand. The pointed end of the rock connected with the demon's temple and drew blood. Les knew this wasn't a conflict he would win, but he intended to give this monster the fight of its life.

A kick brought Les back to the ground with the wind knocked out of him. The demon straddled him. Les was immobile, beaten to the point where there was no fight left. Fatigue hampered his attempts at crawling away. He coughed more blood onto his chin. His one arm

was totally useless. He tried to focus on Chloe and Todd, the hope that they'd escape Samael and get to safety. It worked at first, giving him something else to hope for, even if all hope was gone.

When Samael reached into him and began to work, there was only pain.

~3~

~Samael~

It was the perfect place to wait for her. Swimming in the murky waters of the underworld, Samael let the bloodthirsty sirens peel the flesh from his bones. It always grew back, only to be flayed again. He came to this sea to be tortured, whenever the act of inflicting pain grew monotonous. When he needed a break from the norm, something new, coming to this place rejuvenated him.

He wanted to be at his peak when she arrived.

He opened his eyes as she fell from the sky, broken, bleeding, and afraid.

Her spirit body glowed in the darkness, and upon her skin, Samael could see her book of life. Every step, breath, sin, and every meaningful relationship swirled and danced across her skin like an animate work of art. He'd waited for this day as long as he could, then had forced her hand and brought her here. Like him she'd spent her life wanting to know and feel so much more than her limited experience allowed. They differed in that she was a victim. His victim.

Now that she was here, she didn't have to be a victim. Things could maybe be as they were before. He could love her and she could grow to love him.

He took her trembling naked figure into his arms. He could see that Chloe's faith was one of finality. She'd believed most of her life that death would be the end and that she'd sleep forever. Her shock as Samael held her was similar to that of the faithful when they came

here, those of the conviction that death would bring them peace and heavenly reward.

She looked up at him with pleading eyes, begging him not to hurt her, to let her go. He tried to find the words to explain himself. He tried to find a way to show his love, but found that he'd forgotten how. He punched into her chest cavity and stole her heart. Even in the underworld, it pumped with hot life. He closed his fingers around it, feeling her essence travel into him, letting his essence invade her.

Disbelief kept her from struggling free. Despite all she'd seen, she still waited for sleep to come. His hold on the deepest part of her confirmed that it wouldn't. He held her heart out in front of her eyes for her to see, showing her love as he now understood it: possession, total ownership. He tossed her heart aside and pinned her to the ground. As he entered her again, first sexually, then digging his fingers into the sides of her face and burying his teeth in her neck, he read her thoughts. They consisted mostly of one repeated phrase, a question:

Why can't I just die?

***

Samael licked his lips as he recalled the sweet memory. He left behind the mangled corpse of her father and the smoking wreck of the black car, crawled inside Farnsworth's vehicle and revved the engine. Pleased with his handiwork he accelerated, prepared to reclaim what was his.

Remembering the first time he touched her brought the memories and secrets that he had stolen from her. He saw places she'd been and people she'd known. His thoughts drifted to a town called Red Grove, the house where she'd grown up, the streets she'd walked, the places she'd eaten, drank, and fucked. He mined Les's memories, too, and heard the so recent instructions for her to go home.

When she got there, he would be waiting.

~Chloe~

The car pulled off at an exit that said Red Grove, Population: 34,581. When the trees broke, they came upon a street lined with houses. Occasional renovated homes stood taller and more lavish than the others, but for the most part a lot of the dwellings looked the same

as they had when Chloe had lived here. Few stores were still open, the rest abandoned behind whitewashed windows and "For Lease" signs. A large brick church dwarfed all of the structures. Saint Justin's. She'd only been there a few times, for christenings of her cousins. Her father had always maintained that the spiritual world was too large and wonderful to be confined to a church. Thinking of him got her choked up. The final image of him, shotgun in his hands, eyes possessing the age-old instinct to protect his daughter, brought a gush of tears.

"You okay?" Todd asked. It was the first time he'd said anything since they'd driven off in her father's car. He stared ahead at the road, but seemed to be looking inward, trying to process everything that had happened.

"What the fuck do you think?"

He pressed his lips together. "Yeah."

"I guess I just wanted this to be different. I didn't want anyone to get killed. Certainly not Dad."

"I never thought I'd see him again. I hate to see him go so quickly."

"With Samael, I doubt it was over quickly."

She swallowed. The thought of her father being assaulted by Samael was the worst thing she could imagine. Samael inflicted pain with an artist's passion and a surgeon's precision. She only hoped that all the years her father spent studying the occult had helped him find a passage away from the agony, that he'd be spared the fires of the underworld.

Todd tightened his hands on the wheel as they passed by the church. "Do you think this will work?"

She scaled the steeple with her tear-stung eyes. Over the crucifix white clouds moved across the sky, gently indifferent to her plight.

"God, I hope so."

"God…" He said it like the word tasted bitter to him, like the idea that such a being existed in this new, altered worldview was the most distasteful thing imaginable. He bit his lip and looked like he was about to say something, but was afraid to speak. He'd had this tick for as long as she'd known him. He had done it a lot towards the end, when confronting her about drug use, when she had started to slip away.

She looked back toward the exit, thankful not to see anyone behind them. She knew that Samael was undoubtedly still after her, and felt bitter relief knowing that her father had bought her some time.

Todd drove silently, but his eyes shifted back and forth in quiet desperation. She put down her window to let some air into the car. The scent of pine trees was strong, clean, of this world. She hoped it would ground him and keep him focused on the task at hand. He let out a bleak sigh as he pulled the car into the parking lot of the Black Horse Pub.

She sniffed and wiped at her eyes. "What about you? Are you okay?"

He put the car in park and shut off the engine. He took his time responding to her.

"Let's just get through this."

She looked up at the wood-carved sign for the bar. The face of a black horse accompanied the stenciled name. Its wide yellow eyes, once wild and vibrant, were now faded and split.

What would getting through this entail? If her father's advice had been wrong somehow, then he'd died for nothing. That would be worse for her than a thousand hells.

~Warren~

Warren Glaze's father had given Warren the money to open The Black Horse Pub back in 1979 after Warren's career as a salesman failed. He had hoped to open a place to get a beer, listen to good music and meet people. After thirty-five hard years, Warren liked to think that he'd made a successful run at it. There were some regulars, some people who came and went, and for the most part there was little trouble. People who moved on either died, relocated, or got sober. Sometimes they came back, because they either passed through town or fell off the wagon.

The dead never came back, of course.

That was silly.

At least that's what he would've said before the night a ghost walked through the door and sat down in front of him.

Warren never considered himself a religious or superstitious man. Proud to call himself a realist, he believed in what he could see, touch, smell, hear, and feel. A cold craft beer sliding down his throat. A

crunchy blues guitar riff. Cigarette smoke swirling through the air (he missed smoking desperately; he'd quit after it'd been outlawed indoors). His fingers petting his wife Trish's curves. Concrete stuff.

The ghost walked in with an older man that Warren sort of recognized. He wondered first who the man was. When he saw the ghost beside the man, he tripped over his feet. He stopped himself short of crashing into the shelves and knocking bottles of liquor to the tile floor.

It was a slow night, but Nelson Sharpe sat at the bar drinking and noticed Warren's stumble.

"Shit, War! Watch your step. You ain't as young as you used to be."

Warren glanced around. A group of men in the pool hall continued to play, keeping to themselves, while Nelson watched him with mixed concern and humor. He did a double take at the couple walking through the door.

The ghost was a young, dark-haired beauty. She wore a small black dress. He remembered her because she'd been a huge presence in the Black Horse during its formative years. She and her boyfriend, Todd, had played a handful of memorable shows that summer. Was the man with her now Todd? No, no way. And no way was this woman who he thought she was. That was just crazy. She had to be a daughter or something.

Nelson tapped on the bar. "You all right, War?"

Nelson followed Warren's gaze.

"Relax, stud, looks like she's spoken for. Although, she clearly likes them old."

"Can it, Nelson."

The ghost crossed the bar with her man. Though a pretty young thing, something stretched her features into a mask of panic. Her dark eyes surveyed the room with intense urgency. Her teeth pressed hard into her bottom lip. Warren couldn't take his eyes off of her. Nelson laughed dryly.

"Not polite to stare, old man."

The ghost seemed to hear. She turned to lock eyes with Warren. She *was* a ghost. He couldn't mistake her features. The man walked ahead of her and blocked Warren's view, it brought him out of his hypnotic state, but left him feeling confused.

The man sat down at the bar and the ghost sat beside him. Warren looked back and forth between the two. His mouth opened and closed,

unable to find words. He glanced over at the stage, empty tonight, but full of memories. Many of them involved this ghost before him and—yes, the man sitting beside her. But why had Todd aged and she hadn't?

Because she's a ghost, stupid. That's why.

He gulped.

"What can I get you two?" It came out in a small, fragile voice and at first he feared he'd have to repeat himself to contend with the music playing on the jukebox.

"Warren," said Todd, "it's been a long time."

"Todd… Jesus, man! Is that really you?"

"It's me. I know how I look."

Warren managed a laugh. "I didn't age so well myself."

He made himself look at the ghost.

"Who's this?"

"Come on," she said, a rich voice that evoked the first time they'd met. Todd had introduced them before a show. She'd come up to sing. Together Todd and this ghost had captivated the audience. They were local rock stars. "Don't you recognize me?"

He shook his head. "I recognize you, but it's *impossible*. You can't be *you*."

"Hey, War, you gonna introduce me to your friends?"

He flashed Nelson a look.

"What? Did I say something?"

"Can we talk?" Todd asked.

Warren nodded. "Sure. Hey, Nelson, I'm gonna run to the back. No helping yourself. And don't let those jokers in the billiard hall try anything funny."

"Aye aye, boss man. I'll stand guard."

Warren motioned for Todd and the ghost to follow him and stiffly walked to the kitchen. Audrey, a college student working the summer away at his bar, was back there playing on her smart phone. He would have admonished her, but it was a slow night. He told her to leave them alone and watch the front.

"Make sure Nelson behaves himself."

She nodded and left the kitchen. When they were alone, Warren collapsed against the wash basin. He spread his palms out and took a breath.

"Okay, what the hell?"

"I've been thinking the same thing." Todd turned to Chloe. "Do you… feel anything?"

She shook her head, her lips pressed together in a grimace.

"What does that mean? Feel anything?" Warren had started to sweat. He tried to remember if he'd taken his blood pressure medicine that morning.

"We thought…" Todd started and seemed to think about what he'd say next.

"We thought maybe I could be at peace here."

"I don't follow."

"She's a wandering spirit…"

"I gathered that much, I guess."

"…and it's said that spirits like hers can be put to rest if they… come home."

"This is home to you?" Warren started to laugh. "My shitty dive of a bar is home?"

"We had some great times here," Chloe said.

Todd nodded in agreement, but looked sick. Like he was the undead one.

"You had some good times here and you want to what, haunt my bar?"

They stood silently. Chloe looked down at her hands.

His disbelief gave way to genuinely romantic thoughts of the times when she'd been there. He remembered how she sang, her voice ethereal and throaty. When she died, he'd read about it in the paper. A long shift at the Black Horse had caused him to miss the funeral, but he'd been to the grave. For the first few years, he left flowers, tulips of various colors. These days he hardly thought of her, but she'd had an impact on him. It hurt to know that her soul had never been at peace all these years.

"How do you know if a place is... right?"

She shrugged.

"You just know that this place isn't?"

She shook her head.

"Hell, what are you gonna do then?"

"I guess I'll have to try somewhere else."

She moved to embrace him and he froze. When he found that her arms were warm and not like dead flesh at all, he returned the hug. He

saw them out. They said very little to each other. When they left, he told Nelson and Audrey that they were just some old friends.

He never saw Chloe or Todd again, except when he dreamed.

He never told anyone about the day he saw her ghost until the day he died.

~Todd~

They parked along Potter Way, where they'd made love after their first live performance together, where Todd remembered being touched by something otherworldly. Thick, lively trees lined the dirt-covered road. Around their stumps empty beer bottles glistened in the sunlight, surrounded by stomped out cigarette butts and discarded food wrappers. Todd remembered the path being less dirty back then, but maybe his nostalgia romanticized it.

What would happen if this were the right place? Would she vanish into thin air? Drop dead? Burst into flames? He got out of the car and watched her stride out into the road and glance around. A temperate breeze blew through the leaves, creating a sound like shuffling papers. The wind carried with it the dirty sweet aroma of fertilizer. Her bare feet struck the gravelly path at a tentative rhythm. She probably knew just as little about what would happen next than he did.

She faced him, her dark eyes wide and expectant. Back towards the road, a truck's engine hummed, muffled by distance. A gnat buzzed around Todd's face and tried to kamikaze into his eye. He blinked against it and swatted it away. He and Chloe stood nearly ten paces apart as if waiting for each other to draw a gun.

He sighed. "Nothing?"

His single-worded question struck a nerve and her expression changed from anticipatory to panicky. Even from where he stood, he could see the anxiety tightening her face. Worse case scenarios projected themselves from her widening eyes, her twitching lips, her jaw that locked and loosened. She turned toward the field and ran.

Like the night they'd first made love, she ran through the trees lining the road and into the green grass, casting beckoning glances at him over her shoulder. His legs locked into place as he watched her sprint into the sprawling meadow. He remembered the night so clearly, despite not thinking of it for some time. The way her dress had

fallen to earth in one smooth motion. The way the moonlight bathed her pale figure in bluish twilight.

"Come on," she said, calling to him now, as she had then with the promise of lovemaking.

He pushed his way through the trees and out into the field. The day had drifted away from them and the late-afternoon sun beat down from the western sky, making his skin impossibly hot under his work shirt. Still he strode through the grass, trying to catch up to her. She moved without grace, every step now uncertain, fearful.

"Chloe, what are you doing?"

She ignored him, showed no sign of slowing. He thought she'd long passed the spot where they'd been together, but it was hard to tell. The passage of time rendered his memory unreliable. The old barn that had once stood at the one end of the field was no longer there, bulldozed and replaced by nothing but prickly patches of weeds.

"Wait!"

She kept her pace, lurching frantically ahead. When she stopped and spun to face him, he was out of breath. He put his hand to his chest and felt his heart protesting beneath the breastbone. He continued to approach her, slowing his pace, gulping down precious air. He halted in front of her.

"What are you doing?"

She thrust her hands forward, grabbed the sides of his head, and kissed him. The force as she threw herself at him nearly knocked him on his ass. He steadied himself with his arms as her mouth worked on his. His heart beat harder. He tried to pull away, thinking of Anna, thinking that the woman kissing him had been dead.

She bit down on his lip and pulled her face away.

"Love me, *please.*"

"What, Chloe, no..."

She silenced him with another kiss. This time, with his mouth mid-protest, she slipped her tongue inside. The smoky sweet taste brought forth a storm within him, a storm that carried him backwards in time to the moment they'd first come to this field with her warm arms enveloping him in the summer wind.

He returned the kiss, moved to embrace her. She slumped to the ground, dragging him with her. Once upon the earth, she reached between them. Her fingers brushed his growing hardness as she started to lift her dress.

"Please." Desperation filled her voice.

Logic came between him and his desire. This was wrong. She was undead. He was married. His marriage was falling apart, but this certainly wasn't going to make things better. He couldn't believe he was even considering this.

He pushed off of her. "I can't."

Her face hardened. "Why the fuck not?"

He sat down beside her, looked off into the distance at her father's car parked on Potter Way. They'd come farther than he thought. Its midnight blue paint job glimmered in the distance.

"I just can't."

They sat in silence. Another car passed on the main road. Then another. Up above a large bird of prey circled the sky.

Chloe crossed her arms tightly across her midsection. "I just thought, maybe we could recreate the moment. Maybe that would help me somehow."

"Did you really think that would work?"

"I don't know. You have any other ideas?"

He wracked his brain, tried to ignore the persisting hardness in his pants. The carnal side of him most certainly did want her, and another part of him felt maybe if his music had called her back, loving her now was only right. However, the idea of doing it scared him. She had been dead for thirty years; she couldn't still be human. Even if he didn't worry that having sex with her would further complicate his relationship with Anna, he couldn't get past the fact that he was a little afraid of her.

He said, "What about your old house? Why haven't we tried there yet?"

"I don't know, Todd. It's not exactly the happiest place. I…died there, remember?"

He sat up straighter. "Yeah, but it was home, right? I mean, how long did you live there?"

"For most of my life, but…"

"So it'd be familiar, right?"

"After thirty years, the only thing that's familiar to me is Hell."

He fumbled for something else to say. His rejection had undoubtedly hurt her and he wanted to move beyond that as quickly as possible. She stared defiantly at him. Her dark eyes held a bright intensity

that made him want her, despite how wrong it was. He looked away unable to stand her gaze another moment.

"Your house, it's worth a try."

"So was this."

"Chloe, I just can't. I told you I'd get you to safety and I'm going to do that. But we can't be…together. I'm a different person now."

The words coming out of his mouth sounded scripted and lifeless, the way he sounded whenever he told Anna that he loved her or the way he sounded delivering a sales pitch to a potential client. He hated himself in this moment, more than any other moment in his life.

"Fine." She got up and stomped back towards the car.

~Anna~

Keith stood leaning against his driver's side door, hands tucked into the pockets of his blue jeans, staring ahead like he was posing for a fashion magazine. She parked parallel to him in the lot of Marcus and Marcus and he greeted her with a smile. Even facing away from the sunlight, his whitened teeth glistened.

Unease stirred in her belly as she admired him from the safety of her car. Her confrontation with Katie hung fresh in her mind. Her daughter was tough and Anna had to give her credit. Their exchange had left Anna shaken and ridden with guilt for lying. Going behind her family's backs was one thing. Telling lies to her daughter's face was another. She flexed her hands on the wheel, took a stabilizing breath, and got out.

Keith greeted her with a hug. As she broke the embrace, he pulled her in for a kiss. In his passionate reverence her unease grew stronger. When their lips separated, he held her out at arm's length and looked into her eyes.

"You okay?"

She nodded a bit more quickly than she wanted to, afraid it may look like she was overcompensating. He scanned her face.

"Are you sure?"

Damn him for knowing.

"Yes, Keith. I'm fine." She kissed him again for reassurance. She kept it controlled, touching her tongue to his with gentle precision, squeezing him softly. It was important to show him that she was totally at peace with their transgression. She wanted to let go and enjoy

their first time going away together. The unease lingered, but she vowed to take the 'fake it 'til you make it' approach. She reiterated, as much for herself as for him, "I'm fine."

He stroked her cheek and flashed his million dollar smile. "Okay, I believe you."

"I'm just excited to get going, you know?"

His demeanor brightened, all concern whisked away by enthusiasm. "That makes two of us. Come on!"

He led her around to the other side of his car and opened the door for her. She grinned at him as she settled into the passenger seat. A danceable beat coupled with a dirty guitar on the car's stereo system. The song reminded her of the indie rock that Katie listened to and her thoughts shifted again to their confrontation.

Cut the shit, Mom, Katie had said. She remembered the words and came face to face with the reality that if the truth ever came out, her daughter may end up hating her.

Stop it!

As they pulled away, she rolled the window down and let the wind blow against her face and through her hair. She imagined her reservations blowing away with it, carried into the oblivion of the late-afternoon sky.

~Katie~

Neither Anna nor Keith noticed the black Corolla parked at the opposite end of the lot. The aggressive music of the New Bomb Turks assaulted Katie's sound system and her thoughts raced along to the music. She contemplated following them, though she knew she wouldn't have to in order to know what was going on. She'd seen the kisses.

She killed the music and threw her head back. "Fuck."

The cramped car and the sprawling parking lot suddenly felt very lonely. She stared into the rearview, acknowledged to herself that her family was royally fucked up, but admitting it didn't make the fact any easier to swallow. Instead it fed her neediness, made her feel suddenly cold and vulnerable in spite of the warm day. She crossed her arms and curled her knees up to her chest. She remained that way for a full minute, then gave a grim sigh and dug into her purse for her cell phone. She dialed Jake's number and prayed he'd answer.

~Chloe~

While in front of her old house, memories played like a fast-moving film reel through Chloe's head. She recalled moments like parking her bike on the cement driveway as her father called her in for dinner, sitting on her back deck with her girlfriends watching the sunset, and swimming in the backyard pool. Though still out of reach, they seemed closer now than when she'd been in the world below. A ghost of hope rose within her, but it drowned under a wave of sadness. First, because her freedom had come at the sacrifice of her father. Now, something else she hadn't expected. She and Todd, reunited ever so briefly, would also have to part ways.

"If this works I guess you can go back to your life and forget about me."

He opened his mouth to respond, but no sound came. His eyes examined every inch of her, as if wanting to capture a permanent image. She touched his face, fully expecting the rejection he'd shown in the field. Instead he reached up and held her hand there. Their eyes met and embraced. She froze, knowing all too well that whatever she did next would forever alter the course of her existence. A crazy part of her wanted to stay. She didn't care that she'd always be looking over her shoulder, so long as she could be here, in this real world where people lived, laughed, suffered, recovered, and loved.

"God, I've missed you… this… everything," she said.

"You can't stay, can you?"

She hadn't expected him to say that. They hadn't spoken since the encounter in the field and she thought maybe he was upset with her for trying to seduce him. Now it seemed he regretted rejecting her. She thought about trying again, but knew there was little time.

"I have to go."

He stared ahead, zoning out into the distance, and nodded absently.

She'd have given anything to know what he was thinking.

"What about the people who live there now?"

She looked towards the house. The lawn was well-kept, a set of glistening wind chimes dangled beside the front door, and inside the kitchen window several appliances were set up. Someone definitely lived here.

"You gonna haunt them?"

She shrugged. "I guess so."

He laughed, but it was lifeless.

"Wait out here for a bit, in case it, you know, doesn't work."

"Yeah."

"Thanks for all you've done today. I don't know if I could've gotten out of this without you."

"Don't celebrate yet. We have to make sure it's right first."

She nodded, took his hand, and squeezed it. She kissed him, this time without the urgency she'd shown in the field. Instead it was a light touch, a show of friendly gratitude.

He watched as she pulled away, pushed the car door open, and climbed out of her seat and out of his life again.

The pavement stung Chloe's feet and she winced. She focused on the house ahead and reminded herself that the pain would only be temporary. For being a passage to something as wonderful as freedom from oppression, rest for the weary, the front door looked rather plain. It was just over six and a half feet tall, off-white, and decorated by three square windows across the top. Her heart palpitated as she walked toward it.

This *had* to work.

She crossed the yard tentatively. If this did work, thirty years of suffering would come to an end. Thirty years? It dawned on her that her suffering had endured for much longer. It had dominated both her mortal and immortal lives. Part of it, she knew, was her doing, but what about the rest of it? The pain had started here. It had started at home. Maybe even before that.

A chill raced up her spine as she thought of Samael's insistence that she wasn't who she thought she was. That she was someone that had been promised to him long ago. If that were true, would she ever be free?

Her bare feet curled and she squeezed clumps of grass between her toes. She shut her eyes. A tear rolled down across her face. She took a breath and moved forward. The brass doorknob turned in her grip. There was a click of its latch, followed by a subtle creak of its hinges as she pushed it open.

Samael stood in the entryway, waiting for her. Fresh blood dripped from his hands and she looked past him to see two crumpled corpses, a man and woman. Their bodies were twisted in macabre

poses and their chests were open, leaking viscera and blood onto the hardwood floor. Samael licked his lips.

~Anna~

Anna watched the front of Keith's car swallow up the road ahead. Bass notes vibrated through the interior. She felt them in her chest and nervously twirled her fingers in her lap, only half aware she was doing it. Occasionally Keith sang a line of the song and squeezed her knee. Cold air blew from the vents, raising gooseflesh on her arms.

"Do you ever worry about this?" She asked it without taking her eyes off the winding road.

He turned down the stereo and the throbbing bass became a muffled knock. "What do you mean?"

"What we're doing. Do you ever have second thoughts about it?"

"I worry about how long it can last sometimes. You've got your family and I have ... well, nothing really holds me back."

"I guess that's why you're so attractive to me."

For a stretch, neither of them spoke. Keith turned and slowed down when necessary. The music remained muted, lightly bumping against the speakers, whispering through the air. She and Todd used to drive around like this, but with no destination in sight, just moments passing by. Looking back, she wondered how many of those moments she'd ruined by telling him to slow down or watch a car changing lanes or insisting they find *something* to do. She didn't know how to relax back then; she wasn't sure she even knew how to now.

"Something's on your mind, I take it?" Keith asked.

"Tell me something, Keith. Tell me about your ex. When did you know that the marriage was beyond redemption?"

He sucked in a deep breath. "Where did that come from?"

"Just humor me, okay?"

"Sure." He stayed silent, his jaw pinched tightly closed. His eyes were on the road, but they'd narrowed and a frown wrinkled his otherwise smooth features. "The hell of it, Anna, was that I didn't know. I never knew anything was wrong until she was ready to leave."

"Come on, really? You didn't have the faintest clue?"

"What about you? When did you think your marriage was unredeemable?"

She gasped. "I never said it was."

"Then what the hell are we doing? Why would you do this if you thought there was something left to save?"

Each word of his question pierced her like a series of darts. How do you respond to that? He'd basically just called her out on her bullshit. Bullshit that she'd done her best to ignore for the extent of their nearly yearlong affair. Occasionally it had come bubbling to the surface, but she felt like overall she'd done a good job of repressing her misgivings. Today though, her confrontation with Katie and now Keith's pointed questions had dragged everything out into the open. It was all she could do to not cry.

"I'm sorry," he said. "We're just having fun, right?"

She dug her nails into the palms of her hands. "Do you love me?"

Now it was his turn to be caught off guard. He looked like she'd slapped him. She watched intently, waiting for him to answer. His mouth moved, but no words came, it looked like he was chewing on what he would say, getting an impression of how it would taste.

He looked at her, his eyes expressive, and she knew how he'd answer before he got the words out. When he affirmed what she already knew, she looked away from him, back at the black, empty road. She took almost a full minute to digest what he had said.

"Stop the car."

"What? Why?"

She thought about the implications of his confession and the possibility that maybe she loved him too. She must love him if she'd spent the last year risking her marriage and her family. The whole thing was goddamned crazy. Now, no matter what path she took, someone would get hurt. Maybe the best thing to do was go home and think about it, really think about it.

She remembered the night Todd came to her door near the end of that summer where he'd drifted away into the affections of some girl named Chloe. She listened from the top of the stairs as her father greeted him as if no time had passed at all, asked about Todd's father, and offered a drink. Todd took a seat on the couch and she waited for him to get settled before she came down to see him.

When he embraced her that night, he said he was glad to see her. She remembered feeling he meant it. Something in his features betrayed a willing vulnerability, that he was open to trying.

After having a drink with her father, they drove off to a movie. *Poltergeist*. She'd been tense the whole time, like she was now, until finally she asked him where he'd been.

"Really," she'd said.

When he had hesitated, she asked him if there'd been someone else even though she had known there had been, because their fathers had been close and her father had always relayed what he had felt was relevant information.

Todd had lit a cigarette, delaying his response even more. Finally, "There was, but it's over now. I didn't do it to hurt you."

"Who was she?"

"Does it matter?"

She had taken one of his cigarettes and lit it. "No, I guess not."

"I mean it though. It's over."

"What about us? What do you really want out of this?"

He had seemed to think hard about this. Expecting a plethora of answers or maybe even one cosmos-shifting one, she had tried to stay open to whatever he would say.

"To be loved, I guess. To be important."

She had put her hand on his. "I can love you."

He looked from her hand to her face. A sense of security had settled over the atmosphere and she felt the tension loosening its grip.

After that night, things had happened quickly. In a month's time, he had proposed, and they'd been married that spring. By the next summer, she was pregnant with Dale.

Todd *had* loved her. Maybe he still did. She took Keith's hand and squeezed, more of a consoling gesture than one of romantic affection.

"Just, please, Keith. I need you to take me home."

He took a deep breath. "Sure."

~Katie~

Katie studied the remaining pink sunlight that shined through the canopy of trees above. A cloud of marijuana smoke billowed up beside her and Jake handed off the joint, which she took gratefully. She held the sweet smoke in her mouth, closed her eyes, and savored it. Jake

always got good stuff. She coughed it out and opened her eyes to watch it ascend.

Her body tingled and a wave of relaxation settled over her. It was nice to be away from home. More so, it was nice to be with Jake. They'd met two semesters ago at some party her classmates had talked her into attending. She had noticed that he'd looked like he wanted to be there even less than she did, so she struck up a conversation. They liked the same music and he had a sense of humor so they became fast friends. He was fun by nature and gentle when she needed him to be so they became eventual lovers. He drank a little too much, but he was a dreamer that always looked ahead to a better future, and he was a great listener.

"I fucking hate my family," she said.

He took a hit from the joint, exhaled, and sipped from a bottle of beer. "Your mom acting out again?"

"It's way worse." She told him about the confrontation, the younger man she didn't recognize in the parking lot of Marcus and Marcus, the kisses, how her mom and this man left together.

He coughed. "Holy shit, you followed her?"

"Jake..."

"I'm sorry. Just... wow."

She wished they'd waited to smoke until after she told him everything. They were having too good a time and she didn't want to ruin it, but then she reminded herself that the main reason she had invited him out was to talk. She just hoped he wasn't too stoned.

"So yeah, I don't know. It's really upsetting, and it's not just her. My dad acts like nothing's happening. Like everything is right with the world. How can he not know something weird is going on?"

Jake propped himself up on his elbow and focused on her. He put out the joint on the hood of his car and flicked its ashen remains into the dirt road. She continued.

"Could be denial, I guess. I just hate seeing him so oblivious and her being so... so..."

He waited for her to finish the sentence.

"...so shameless."

He nodded. "I can't imagine what they're going through. I swear people lose their minds at their age."

He was speaking from experience. A week after turning fifty, Jake's father had quit his job, divorced Jake's mother, and left her everything but his Pontiac, which he used to drive down south to find a permanent new home. Jake hadn't spoken to him in three years.

"I'm sure it's not easy on you, but I'm sure the last thing your mom wants to do is hurt you, and your dad's not a dumb guy. He's probably playing dumb because he thinks that will protect you or some shit."

She reached down and took another beer from the cooler. "You're probably right."

"Whatever your mom's going through is probably giving her tunnel vision. Maybe as shitty as this is, it'll help you grow and stand on your own."

"What? You don't think I can stand on my own?"

He put up a defensive hand. "That's not what I said. I think you're perfectly capable. Separating yourself from your parents and their bullshit issues may be a good opportunity to show yourself just how capable you actually are."

"You are so high," she said with a laugh.

"So are you." He kissed her.

She returned the kiss, but quickly pulled away. "I'm concerned for them though. I can't just pretend nothing's happening."

Jake shrugged. "Maybe you should confront your mom."

"You think so?"

He finished his beer and took another. "And your dad, too. Fuck it. Let them know how much their stupid drama is affecting you."

She nodded, feeling empowered for a moment. "I wonder if I could really do it."

"Sure you could."

She returned her attention to the pink sunlight glowing between the leaves. The idea of calling her mom out was both terrifying and exciting.

"I think my dad needs a hug more than anything else. He always seems so lost, like he's adrift somewhere far away and his body's been left behind."

"That's it? He's off the hook."

"Well…"

"So you are mad at him, too, right?"

She thought for a moment, then nodded.

"Then I wouldn't let him off easy, I mean, if you plan on confronting them at all. You can always just let it go."

She looked away from the sky and down at her hands. "You know I can't do that."

"Then you know what you have to do."

She nodded.

He took her chin in his hand. "Now how about we finish that kiss?"

~Chloe~

Chloe was too petrified to react as Samael stepped through the door frame, flashing his jagged teeth, his hands clenching and unclenching. Those teeth had bitten into her many times before. Those hands had ravaged her on more occasions than she could count.

"Welcome home," he said, his voice barely above a whisper.

Hearing the malicious intent in his words, she snapped out of her trance and turned to run. He fell upon her, snaking an arm around her throat and forcing her face into the dirt. He squeezed and she felt her air supply closing off as his hot flesh pressed against hers. He laughed as he strangled her, so sure of himself.

A car door slammed and a voice cried out.

"Hey!"

Samael released her, pushing her back to the ground and getting to his feet. She raised her head and saw Todd standing outside his car in a fighting stance. She got to her knees.

"No, Todd, don't..."

A slap to the side of the head from Samael silenced her.

As she fell, she heard herself repeating that last word:

Don't.

Don't.

Don't.

~Todd~

Todd watched Chloe pitch to the ground. Samael came for him at a speed he didn't believe possible. He had no time to outmaneuver the

attack. Samael reached for Todd's hair and snatched a fistful of it. Suspended into the air, his scalp caught fire with excruciating pain. He sounded alien to himself as he screamed a shrill, childlike cry.

Everything that had happened, from Chloe's reemergence to helping her get here, to their long history together, seemed so unimportant now. Only survival mattered. He kicked and struggled, but Samael didn't let go.

Todd looked down into the demon's face and saw eyes ablaze with angry fire. The skin on Samael's other hand took on a ghostly pigment. Inside the translucent flesh, white worms writhed and twisted. Todd tried to pull free as the ethereal hand touched his chest.

Intense chills spread through his core.

"Well, I hope she's been worth it," Samael said.

Memories of his life with Chloe, long before she died, played through his mind and he knew Samael was sharing these memories. From touching him, this beast was able to explore Todd's soul, his thoughts, and his deepest, darkest recollections. They shared a perverse sort of intimacy. Within seconds, Samael learned everything about Todd. Samael tore these memories from him with the greed of a man near starvation tearing into a package of food. It was as if Todd's life flashed before his eyes, but each image was ripped away rather than peacefully transitioning from one memory to another.

"You've known her a long time," Samael acknowledged. "You've *loved* her a long time, but this is fate, and you have no right to interfere."

Samael threw him across the street and he crashed into the trunk of a car with a metallic thud awakening new pains in his body. The car's spoiler dug into his ribcage, taking the wind out of him. His hands crossed his midsection as he fought to catch his breath before Samael approached.

Chloe's subjugator moved slowly now, confident as the sky darkened above him. Todd tried to rise and almost fell forward, but Samael took him by the hair again. The pain in his scalp intensified as Samael lifted him off of his feet. He felt the roots of his hair tearing free, unable to support his weight. He braced for the end, but knew deep down that no expectation could prepare him. This monster intended to take Todd to Hell.

His heart slammed in his chest, protesting the cruelty of the moment, perhaps intending to force its way out and flee to a safer place.

Todd expected his life to flash before his eyes once again, but all he knew was immediate terror and pain. Samael pulled back his ethereal fist, undoubtedly intending to punch right through Todd's heart.

The release came. He flew away from Samael in an instant. He felt no pain. He fell forever.

That's okay, he thought. *How long did you think you could keep this up anyway?*

* * *

Todd awoke to a sting on his cheek. A dark-haired angel hovered over him in the night sky, her face haloed by silver light. She was saying something, but he couldn't hear her. He wondered if Chloe had been wrong about the hereafter, if he was now in Heaven.

He spoke her name and his lucidity returned. There wasn't an angel hovering over him. It was her, and she was yelling at him to get up. He recalled the pain in his cheek. Had she slapped him?

"Come on, Todd. We have to go."

He shook the last of the haziness from his head and let her help him into a sitting position. She looked off to the left and he followed her gaze. Samael lay in a bloody heap. Les's car was nearby, the hood baring a large dent and splotches of blood.

Chloe took his hands in both of hers. "We have to go."

There was commotion behind him, a few frantic voices and some doors opening. He looked back at Samael and saw the man starting to stir.

"No fucking way."

"Let's go!" Chloe pulled him up. "Now!"

Todd limped his way to the car, his muscles and bones aching in countless places, and wondered how much more abuse his body could take. Chloe rounded the vehicle ahead of him and slid into the driver's seat. Someone hollered for them to stop.

"I'll drive. Come on."

Instead of arguing, Todd let himself into the passenger side and crumpled into the seat. Chloe put the car in drive. The tires squealed as she floored the accelerator and he jerked back against the seat.

"Buckle up," she said.

"Can you give a dead girl a ticket?" The ridiculousness of his words made him realize how disoriented he was.

"No, but I can put you through the windshield. Buckle up!"

He obeyed and looked ahead. "Fuck."

Samael stood in front of them, shaking the pain out of his limbs. Chloe kept the gas pedal pressed down. Samael raised his head and gritted his teeth. He bent his knees, prepared to jump.

Chloe hit him head on and he tumbled over the top of the car. Samael's naked flesh struck the pavement behind them with a wet slap. Chloe swerved out into the next street. Brakes squealed and a horn honked. Todd rubbed his aching head and stared at the blood trickling down the windshield. The madness of the moment came at him from all sides. The car's engine roared angrily as Chloe accelerated.

"God… Holy fucking shit!"

Chloe made another turn and then another. Without her saying it, Todd knew that her primary goal was to get lost.

* * *

Todd braced himself against the dashboard to stop himself from shaking, but the effort only made things worse. Nearly twenty minutes had passed since Chloe drove them out of Red Grove and back onto the highway. Not a word passed between them, but the inside of the car was tense in the bombed out aftermath of their confrontation with Samael. Night had fallen and the air surrounding them was black as crude oil. Every time he tried to catch his breath, he saw himself suspended in the air by Samael, the ghostly fist reared back to strike, his life on the threshold of its end.

"J-Jesus, I can't stop sh-shaking."

Chloe pulled over and slammed on the brakes.

"What are you doing?"

She didn't respond. She kept her hands locked tightly on the steering wheel and drew in a sharp gasp. Todd leaned back and tried to catch his own breath.

"I can't believe it." He curled his hands into tight fists, held them together and released them. His normal breathing still hadn't returned, but he no longer felt like he was going to have a heart attack. "I don't think I've ever been… so close to death before."

He looked at Chloe for acknowledgment. She pressed her head against the steering wheel. Her dark hair fell in front of her face and made it impossible to read.

"What is it?"

She stayed silent. As he struggled to get his breath back to normal, the moments crawled by.

"Chloe?" He heard desperation in his voice.

She raised her head. Fresh tears had sprung from her eyes and glistened in the dashboard lights.

"You have to let me go. You can't keep risking your life for me. You have something to live for. Me, all I know how to do is run, and no matter how far I go, how fast, he'll find me. I can't make you a part of this."

Each word hit Todd like a punch to the gut. None of them were meant to knock him out. They were crueler than that, even if she didn't intend them to be. They pummeled him into submission, stretched his threshold for pain, but never delivered a knockout blow. Instead he was forced to remain lucid while he endured the sharpness of her words. They reminded him of a conversation they'd had after her third relapse. It was the time they decided to part ways for good. He hadn't caught her in a lie or found her in her room plunging a needle into her arm.

They'd been on their way to a gig at the Black Horse in the dead center of summer. His car windows had been down, letting the warm air inside. His guitar and her keyboard equipment had shared a space in the back seat with a folded up blanket, a pillow, a notebook, and a copy of Stephen King's *Night Shift*, as well as empty coffee cups and crumpled packages that had once held food. He'd had The Cure playing on the stereo, filling the car with energetic gloom.

As he'd driven, it had seemed like a perfect night, but for the fact that he'd been able to tell something had been bothering her. Her answers had come out in few words. She had hardly been able to look at him. Whenever he asked if she was okay, she had smiled and told him "yes," but her eyes had betrayed a deep sadness. Though he'd known she was lying, he hadn't wanted to pry. They had to put on a show and he hadn't wanted anything to stop them from doing what they did best.

Nothing had. They played their set, one of the best sets during their run as the Black Horse's house band. Their energy on the stage

had spread throughout the bar and everyone had danced and clapped. As they played, he had even forgotten that something may have been wrong. For all he knew, it could've been his own anxiety.

Outside the bar they had loaded the last of their equipment into his back seat. She put a hand on his arm and said his name. He had turned to her, seen moisture in her eyes and had known what she'd say before she said it.

"It happened again. I'm sorry."

He'd leaned back against the car, stared up into the night sky and felt his energy from the show sucked out of him. He tried to compose himself. He'd known she was struggling with something he'd never understand, but that hadn't stop him from feeling hurt and betrayed. He'd remembered the last two times it happened, and her promises that it wouldn't happen again.

"Chloe..."

She'd tried to hold his hand, but he pulled away from her.

"Todd, listen," she'd said. "I'm really sorry, but I'm trying. I'm trying so goddamn hard, but it's just not working. I'm... it's like something's after me... that nothing I do will stop it. It always catches up."

He'd wondered then what she meant by that, but now, in the present, he knew she'd always meant Samael.

After her confession and subsequent plea for forgiveness, he'd ended it for good. He said he couldn't keep doing this, and until she came back from the dead, he never spoken to her again. He'd left because he was scared he wouldn't be able to help her, and it had felt better to abandon her.

Now, after she asked him to do the same, he remembered the conversation well. He looked her up and down. She met his eyes. Her expression was hard, as if maybe she expected him to take her advice and she was bracing for the hit. Years had passed since that night and looking back, he felt like maybe he'd been scared the entire time.

"Earlier today, I would've agreed with you in a heartbeat. I mean, I have you in the car with me, which should, by all accounts, be impossible. This is just... we just came from the town we grew up in. We used to drive those streets all the time. We used to take our instruments to get them fixed over at Lynd's. I used to play shows at the Black Horse Pub and you'd get on stage and sing with me. I haven't thought about any of this shit for years."

"Were you trying to forget?"

"I guess I was. And today, today has felt like a dream and I can almost convince myself that it is, except you're here. This is really fucking happening." He ran a nervous hand across his head. "I can't forget. I can't let go."

"But you must. It's okay if you agree with me. It's okay if you're even sorry I came back."

"That's the thing, Chloe. That's what's driving me nuts." Another dry laugh. "I thought I had the life I wanted. I gave you up for this life and now it's falling apart. Not a little, but a lot. I almost never see my wife; I'm pretty sure she's having an affair. One of my kids won't even talk to me and the youngest is stuck in the middle of all this." He looked away, as if ashamed of all he was telling her. "In spite of the danger we're in, in spite of the fact that I've almost died three fucking times today, I'm so glad to see you alive."

"Alive?" She smiled and he couldn't believe that she was doing it. "I thought about you until the day I died. I tried to focus on you sometimes, in that other world, but the pain was usually too much for me to think about anything else."

He looked down at his hands. "I'm sorry, Chloe."

"It's not your fault."

"But maybe if I'd stayed with you…"

She put a finger to his lips. "None of that matters now. What matters is what we can do to make it better. That's all."

"You're right." He kissed the tips of her fingers. "And now, I'll do anything. I swear it. I won't leave you"

~Chloe~

His eyes had determination in them that reminded Chloe of the young man she'd fallen in love with so long ago. She touched his face and he flinched, but he relaxed the more she stroked his cheek. She loved the feel of his skin under her fingers. It reminded her of the old days. The skin was older, and he had changed so much, but the fact that he'd trusted her and taken her this far showed that he possessed

at least some of the fire she'd admired in him. She leaned forward and kissed him.

At first he pulled his head away and shut his lips, but she persisted until his mouth came to meet hers. She slipped her tongue inside. He seized handfuls of her hair and pulled her tighter against him. He smelled like a mix between coffee, Old Spice and frantic desperation. Their lips parted for a brief moment and he whispered her name. They kissed again. A sea of emotion flooded the moment, and she allowed herself to get lost in it, to fall beneath its intense and troubled waves. His mouth worked on her vigorously and her lips buzzed with electric pleasure.

Dread sank in. This moment would end and that was worse than Samael's pursuit and all the fires of Hell. They had to be closer than this.

She broke the embrace, but only temporarily, unbuckled her seat belt and climbed over the center console. She settled her knees alongside each of his hips and brought her hands down to his belt buckle.

"Chloe, don't," he said, but his hardness told her otherwise. She shut up his protests with another kiss.

She worked him out of his pants and touched him. He was hot with desire and he responded to her touch with a soft whimper. As she lifted her dress, she held her sex above his. He tensed.

"Relax," she said, and buried her mouth into the soft flesh of his neck. "I just want to be as close to you as possible. I've missed you so much."

She slid him inside her with ease and shut her eyes, feeling the intense connection, the familiarity of it. They'd made love like this many times before, pulled over to the side of the road, so taken with passion that they couldn't wait until they got home. As he moved inside her, as she rolled her hips against him, it was as if they were young again. Her dark hair swung back and forth between them. He groped her hips as if needing the constant reminder that she was actually there.

Her left knee knocked against the passenger side door. Being confined together like this made it perfect. It was as if they were in a small room that belonged only to them and when they were in it, attached to each other this way, they were safe from everything. She wanted it to last forever, but knew it couldn't.

He squeezed her tightly and cried out as he came. She collapsed against him. The aroma of passion filled the car's interior. As they held each other, she thought of how she never expected to make love again, or even feel love again. But she felt it now and it was as if the feeling had never gone away, that it had only been lying dormant all these years waiting to be awakened by contacting the one she loved once again. A crazy part of her wanted to stay. She didn't care that she'd always be looking over her shoulder, so long as she could be here with Todd.

"God, I've missed you," she whispered into his neck.

He nodded and she knew it meant he'd missed her too.

"You still have to let me go."

"No. No fucking way."

Chloe flinched at his surge of emotion. They remained connected. He stopped softening.

"You can't just come back into my life and expect me to pretend you're still dead."

"What about Anna?"

He blinked and seemed to lose focus for a moment. He regained it just as quickly. "I can't do anything until I know you're safe."

She shook her head. "We're all damned, Todd. I told you about Hell."

"You can't know for sure that's all there is. There has to be another way."

"Sure there is. I run forever, and I won't put you through that."

"I couldn't live with myself if I left you. I already let you die once."

"Todd, I..."

"Why didn't staying in your house work?"

"I..." She bit her lip.

"How did he find you there?"

"I don't know. I guess it's like I said; it was never truly home for me. I always knew that I belonged somewhere else."

"Where have you ever felt at home?"

"What do you mean?"

"If you could be anywhere in the world right now, where would it be?"

"Right here. Right now." She kissed him and tightened her sex around his. "What are you thinking?"

"I'm thinking… what if you went somewhere else that you'd been in your mortal life, somewhere you were happy. Do you think you could be safe there?"

"I don't know. It's…"

"Worth a shot, don't you think?"

She crawled off of him and nodded.

"Any ideas?"

The silence that hung between them was more than a pregnant pause; it was a pause in its third trimester, swollen so that it could burst at any given time and give birth to crying, bloody, but hopeful, possibilities. An idea came to her. She settled back into the driver's seat, put the car back in drive and made a U-turn.

"I know just the place."

~Samael~

Samael awoke. The jarring pain in his limbs and torso had been reduced to a series of dull throbs. Something wailed in the distance. Sirens, coming closer. He opened his eyes. Several people were standing around him.

One of them, a middle-aged man wearing a bandana in his hair, gasped. "Holy shit, he's fucking awake."

Some of the others grumbled amongst themselves. Samael glared at the man and started to sit up.

"Hey, don't move, Mister. You don't know if anything's broken."

Samael ignored him and got up to his knees. He locked eyes with the bandana man. "Everything in me is broken."

He got to his feet. Several of the onlookers gasped. One lady spat a string of obscenities. He started to walk away.

"Come back here, you need a doctor," someone said.

Samael continued walking. He heard the sirens approaching, but as his mobility returned, his strength wasn't far behind. He'd get to Farnsworth's car before those vehicles arrived to take him away. The temptation to stay behind and wreak havoc on the people who'd been standing over him as he'd lain unconscious was strong, but the urge to pursue was much stronger. What little pain remained turned to rage. Every time she escaped him, every bit of punishment she inflicted on him would make it that much worse for her when he caught her.

Opening the door to Farnsworth's car, he thought back to when he touched Todd. They'd shared something then, an intimacy greater than any lover could ever hope to achieve, greater than any killer could wrench out of his victim. Samael had felt this intimacy before, with many before Todd. With a touch, he could reach into someone's deepest self, know their stories, hear their most hidden thoughts, and know the people who've meant the most to them.

As Samael had touched Todd, he had seen a home in an unremarkable, but quaint neighborhood. Behind the door, a tall young woman with almond hair styled in bangs that fell to the side had stood in the foyer. She was beautiful in that young and energetic sort of way. From Todd's thoughts, Samael had known that she was Todd's daughter.

Up the staircase and into a large bedroom, he had seen another woman. Her dirty blond hair fell across her shoulders in subtle waves. A deep sadness had haunted her blue eyes, like she'd spent much time staring into some black, unforgiving abyss. Like Todd, she was old enough to know, to really know, she was going to die and that she had more years behind her than she did ahead of her. Despite this, or maybe even because of this, Samael desired her. At another time, he would've maybe even fallen for her, back when he was alive, back when he was human.

He mined the memories he'd gleaned from Todd to see how he could find this house and these two women. The most important thing he gained from reaching inside Todd was that the bastard was still very much attached to this world. Samael expected that if he hung the pieces of this world that meant the most to Todd in the balance…

He grinned. The pain disappeared. His confidence returned.

~Katie~

Katie was curled up on the sofa with Jake watching *Ancient Aliens* when she heard the front door open. The high from the marijuana had mostly worn off and now she just felt sleepy. With her hand locked with Jake's and her head on his shoulder, neither of them spoke but said so much. It was her idea of contentment. She didn't think about

marriage much. Her studies consumed most of her time, but moments like this, where time seemed to stand blessedly still, when she and Jake could forgo all deadlines and agendas and just *be*, the idea of spending the rest of her life with someone, Jake specifically, seemed like the most wonderful thing in the world.

She had her reservations, sure. Seeing how her parents' marriage had spiraled into a relationship of non-communication and shameless dishonesty made her wonder if committing to someone was even worth it. Was it always bound to come undone? Had the era of true love gone by?

The door closed and soft footsteps that she recognized as her mother's reminded her that she had a conversation ahead of her. As a bag of luggage dropped to the floor, Katie sat up and looked behind her.

Anna walked into the living room, her eyes red as if she'd been crying and her shoulders slumped in despair. The hair that had been so well-manicured earlier was now a tangled mess.

"Mom?"

"Hi, Katie… Jake. How are you guys?"

Jake stood up, surprising Katie. "Good. I'm actually about to get going. I gotta get up early."

He leaned down and kissed Katie on the cheek. "Want to walk me out?"

Katie looked from him to her mother. Anna forced a smile.

She and Jake left the living room after exchanging goodbyes with Anna. At the door, Jake faced her.

"I want to leave you guys alone. You've got a lot to talk about."

"What do I say?"

"Just like we said." He silenced her anxieties with a kiss and a hug that made her feel secure, but once he shut the door and she rejoined her mother in the living room her courage melted away. They stared at each other, the fallout of their earlier confrontation still weighing heavily on them both.

"Do you want a drink?" Anna asked.

Katie opened her mouth to reply, then closed it and nodded. She couldn't recall ever having a drink with her mother. Now the idea seemed to cement something for her. They were both adults now, about to have a truly grown-up conversation.

Once the wine was poured, they sat across from each other at the kitchen island. Katie tried several times to start, but the words didn't come. She forgot all the practicing she'd done with Jake and even felt regret for being so harsh with her mother earlier. She sank deeper into herself, practically seeing the mental and emotional walls that rose around her.

"Katie." Her mother's voice came out scratchy and weak.

"Yes, Mom?"

"Where's your father?"

"I... dunno."

For a moment, Anna looked like she was going to cry again. "I have to tell you something."

Katie almost said, "me too," but decided to let her mother talk.

Anna finished half of the glass of merlot in one gulp. She wasn't much of a drinker. Katie could count the amount of times her mother had had a drink in the past five years pretty easily. Most of them were on birthdays. Katie guessed the bottle was there to make things easier.

"Oh, Katie, I'm so sorry."

"Mom..."

"No, I am, I... your father and I..."

Katie looked at the wear and tear on her mother's face. She wondered how long her mother had been crying. From the looks of it, she'd been crying for hours. From the suitcase she'd dropped in the hallway, Katie figured that whatever trip she'd planned to go on with the other man had been cut short. Maybe her mother had broken it off with him. Maybe there was something left of their family.

She took Anna's hand and squeezed. "Look, whatever happened is over and done with. You're my mother and I love you no matter what." She gulped, finding it hard to speak. While her words were true, she was still deeply hurt and felt like not expressing that was letting her mother get off too easily. On the other hand, the woman before her, the woman that, for better or worse, had raised her into who she was today, looked now as if she needed nothing more than a friend.

"I appreciate that, Katie." She looked around, suddenly seeming frantic. "Has your father come home at all?"

"No." Katie looked behind her mother at the digital clock on the stove. It was almost eleven in the evening. She released her mother's hand and felt whatever relaxation was left over from the marijuana

she'd smoked that day siphoned out of her. Where the hell was *he* now?

"Christ, I guess now I know what I put him through."

Katie flashed Anna a look, no longer feeling that sense of compassion. "Why'd you do it?"

Anna slammed the rest of the wine and refilled her glass. Katie hadn't touched hers.

"I was selfish." Anna sniffed. "I had needs and your father wasn't available. He never was. He was always so wrapped up in work."

Katie pounded a hand against the island. "Yeah, he was trying to support us."

"And I wasn't? We both worked very hard. I guess I'm partially to blame. Neither of us made any time for each other, but he was just so…" She wiped her eyes, and relaxed her shoulders. "Either way, I was wrong. He was always so distant, even early on but I guess I let him be that way."

Katie mulled it over. She hated to admit her mother was right. Her father had been distant. She felt like maybe it went beyond just being immersed in work. He'd always had a look in his eyes as if he were focused on something far away. His distance deepened severely after his father had died. After that, even work seemed to be of little interest to him.

"Katie, it's all over now. I'm ready to come home and work things out. There still has to be something left to repair, right?"

"Hey, we're family. Family's always worth fixing."

Anna smiled and it looked genuine, brightening her face and making her look ten years younger. "You're sweet. You always were."

"Maybe we should call Dad, see where he is."

Anna nodded.

"This weekend we should all do something," Katie said. "Maybe we can all go out to dinner on Saturday and Skype Dale together when we get home."

"I'd like that. Hopefully your father and Dale will too." Her face darkened. "I guess this all depends on what happens when we call your father."

Katie got to her feet. "I'll do it. You relax."

Katie crossed the kitchen and dug into her purse. She came up empty handed. "Shit. I left my phone upstairs."

"You can use the landline."

Katie nodded and shuffled from the kitchen to the living room where the nearest phone hung on the wall. She took the phone off of its cradle and turned to face one of the large bay windows that overlooked the back yard.

Before she could dial a single digit, she screamed.

~Chloe~

Chloe turned on the windshield wipers and stared ahead, hypnotized by the filthy rain that washed off the hood of the car. One of the wipers made a squeaking sound as it dragged itself across the glass. She had taken them on a back road in the hope that the more loops and detours she made, the harder it would be for Samael to pinpoint her exact location. At the very least she hoped that it would buy her enough time to find her way home.

Since Todd had asked her about a place that had really felt like home, she tried to recreate memories from that time and place: sitting on the carpeted floor of the bare apartment with Todd, eating Lo Mein; the way they frantically kissed each other as if not doing so would kill them; and making sweet music with her DX7, his Gibson, and the sounds of their voices. She wanted to close her eyes and let the memories lull her into perfect, eternal sleep. Let them become dreams that would never end.

Shadows filled the car. The squeak of the windshield wiper cut through the monotonous drone of the engine and the light drizzle of rain. She thought about making love on the side of the road, their bodies entwined in a dance of flesh and fire, and smiled. She tried not to think about his face as Samael held him by the hair, holding him in limbo between life and death. She hummed the melody of "Blissfully Damaged," and willed the nightmarish image away.

"Are you sure this is where you want to go?" Todd asked.

"Yes. When I was with you there, it was so…"

"Perfect."

"Yes."

"What about towards the end? When you were relapsing?"

"It won't be about that when I go back. All I'll think about is you. That will be how I remember that place."

Todd's expression hardened. The rain started to fall in sheets. Somewhere in the distance, lightning slashed a brilliant wound across the dark sky.

"After this, if it works, I'll never see you again."

She let his words sink in. Part of her wanted to ask him to come with her, to cross over into the next world, wherever *that* was. In spite of the uncertainty, it still sounded nice. They could maybe even have things the way they were, before she died and sunk into the chasm and Samael's vile embrace. Could she really ask him to do that? It would be entirely selfish. Even though he was dissatisfied with the world, she felt that he might still be too tied to it to let go completely. But he had taken her this far. That showed promise.

"You'd have to give up everything you have. Everything you are." She could've sworn that the rain started to fall faster, the drops growing fatter, as she spoke. "Could you do that?"

He turned his eyes to the road and didn't speak up again for a long time.

~Anna~

The glass of the back door shattered and a naked man stepped into the living room. Glistening shards covered the floor and crunched beneath his feet, though he didn't seem to notice. If anything, he seemed to enjoy it. His mouth stretched into a maniacal grin.

Anna watched as Katie tried to run down the hallway. The man moved with incredible speed and caught her by her hair. Anna screamed as her daughter was thrown to the ground. The naked man turned to Anna. He was lean, but imposing, his extremities made up of ropey muscles and nasty scars. His penis grew hard between his legs. She looked him up and down, hot panic surging through her.

"My dear, you are even more beautiful in person," he said. Anna couldn't place his accent, but it struck her as very old, and she shrank against his words.

"Who are you?" she shrieked, trembling, inching backwards.

He took a methodical step toward her. The thing that stood out the most to Anna as she backed away was the look in the man's eyes. Within them was an animal presence, filled with anguish and burning lust. Spiritual pain afflicted him, but he seemed to derive a great deal of pleasure from it. His tongue ran across the pointed tips of his teeth.

Every breath came out a hiss. He took his time, knowing that no matter where she ran, he'd catch up. In some deep, horrible place within her heart, Anna knew this too. His knees bent as he prepared to lunge forward. Anna braced, trying to plan an escape route as quickly as she could.

Before he could spring, Katie wrapped her arms around his shins. He attempted to wiggle free, but she maintained her grip, closing her hands around each of her forearms. Exertion came alive in her face. She grunted against the man's movements.

Anna looked from Katie to the man to the pathway through the dining room. The front door was in sight, a single light in the foyer illuminating it like a beacon. She looked back at Katie and their eyes met for one frightful moment.

"Mom, *run!*"

Anna's legs froze in place. She felt drunk and panicky all at once. *The damn wine!* "Katie…"

"Go!"

Anna turned and headed for the dining room. She pushed her way around the table, shoved a chair out of her path. She entered the foyer and nearly tripped over the edge of her suitcase. She stopped in front of the door. All of her maternal instincts told her that this was wrong. She couldn't let her daughter make a sacrifice for her sake. She should be protecting Katie, not the other way around. Her hand fumbled with the doorknob as the indecision tore at her. Then something crashed and Katie screamed. Anna turned and looked back at the kitchen. Another crash. This time no one screamed.

"Katie?" The tremble in her voice rendered the name incoherent.

The naked man staggered out of the kitchen and locked onto her with hateful eyes. Katie was nowhere.

Before Anna could react, he descended upon her. A sting in her cheek corresponded with a hard smack and she fell back against the front door. Blood collected in her mouth and a tooth fell loose. When she opened her eyes, her vision was blurry, a smeared picture. The naked man stood over her, his fists clenched, his penis fully erect. She had a horrible notion that he meant to shove the member in her mouth and choke her with it. She squirmed in revulsion and moaned her protest. Even though she had read that there could be a sexual component to violent behavior, she had a hard time imagining how all this carnage could be arousing to anyone.

He reached down and grabbed her around the throat. His face came to meet hers and he seemed to regard her with a sort of reverence.

"Sweet woman, you remind me of my mother."

His tongue shot from his mouth. As he brought his face closer to hers, something awoke within her that she never thought she possessed. While she considered herself a brave woman when it came to closing business deals, giving presentations, and never backing down when she believed she was right, the sight of her attacker's slimy tongue and sharpened teeth closing in on her mouth awakened a different nerve. She transformed into an animal with a need to survive.

The inner beast awoke with a howl of rage and she grabbed the man by his testicles. He yelped in pain and instantly removed his hands from her throat. Anna dug her nails in and twisted, never silencing her primal howl. He flailed his arms around and tried to pull free.

She gritted her teeth. "You like pain, you *bitch!*"

Anna pressed herself up into a standing position, but made sure to keep a firm grip on his balls. Tears filled her eyes. She forced him back as liquid power scorched through her veins. Letting out the beast inside felt honest, empowering. She resolved to pull his testicles off and he kept screaming. She pressed against him, yanking his scrotum upwards in her tight fist. Words of hate and violence flew from her lips. Even in her heightened state, they surprised her. She continued to squeeze and pull as hot blood poured over her knuckles.

Impossibly the man's screaming turned to laughter. The pain went out of it. When his eyes met hers, she saw pure mad joy. He loved every minute of this and the sight of that masochism caused her to loosen her grip for a moment. He pushed her back against the door.

"Come on," he said. "Is that the best you can do to hurt me? I've felt hell's fires upon my skin. Everything you've given me fails to excite."

She released his balls and brought her hands up, raking her nails across his face. Flecks of blood and skin tore loose under her claws, but he never stopped coming for her. He snaked a hand forward, through her offense and took a fistful of her hair. He yanked her to the side, twisting her neck so that she faced the ceiling of the foyer. The hanging lamp burned in her vision in the last few moments before her attacker raised his other fist and bludgeoned her into unconsciousness.

~Chloe~

The skyline glistened in the darkness like a thousand beacons in the inky night. The highway groaned beneath the car as if they rode on the back of some great beast. Rain still fell in jerky bouts, but the storm had all but passed. Behind them lightning filled the clouds with pale flashes. Sanctuary was still a ways away, but much closer than it had been. Chloe could feel it in her blood. Soon she would sleep.

She hoped.

"Man, I really missed seeing this skyline at night," Todd said.

"It's pretty."

"Yeah, I don't leave the suburbs much these days. I hope the old place is still there."

Her heart dropped. She hadn't thought of that.

He took her leg and squeezed. "I'm sure it still is. Those old buildings usually stick around forever, even if no one figures out what to do with them."

"I hope you're right." She breathed. He had to be.

Behind them, in the distance, another burst of lightning covered the sky in a white sheet. Below them the highway groaned.

~Katie~

Katie awoke to pain. Every extremity throbbed, but she felt the biggest hurt in her head. As far as she could tell, she was in the back seat of a car. From the tightness in her wrists and ankles, she ascertained that she was bound. The smell of leather mixed with blood filled her nostrils. She was dizzy and wondered how long she'd been out. At this time, she only knew these sensations. Memories of how she'd gotten here came with great difficulty. She tried to remember where she'd last been. She recalled sitting out in the woods, on top of Jake's car, smoking pot and discussing her family. Her mother… A pang of sadness… Her heartbeat quickened. She glanced around.

Her mother sat on the seat beside her. Similarly bound, she stared ahead, her eyes haunted and full of tears. A closer look showed Katie that her face was bruised. She turned her head and saw another face in the rearview mirror. The face's scarred features brought the memories rushing back and Katie sobbed.

Anna jolted at the sound of her daughter's cries. She took Katie's hands in hers. She told Katie to be quiet, that everything was going to be okay. Even as Katie heard it, she knew her mother was lying. Stories like this never ended well. You heard about it all the time on the news, men kidnapping women. They never get found. Not until it's too late.

"What do you want?" Katie screamed. "Why are you doing this?"

The man in the driver's seat ignored her. He started to sing. She didn't recognize the melody, but it sounded old. It was in an eerie minor key and it made her think of death. Katie kept screaming.

"Katie, honey," Anna said softly, "screaming won't do us any good."

Katie fell silent, but her fears hummed loudly inside her mind. This man had to be on drugs or just plain crazy to punch through their back door and walk across that glass. And he was full of hate. She could tell that just from looking at him, the way he moved, the ghostly stare of his cold eyes. She knew how this would end, but she wanted to know why. She wasn't ready for this. Her life would be stolen from her before she had a chance to do anything with it. The least her killer could do was tell her why. But he didn't. Instead, he continued humming that deathlike melody, staring ahead at the dark road, only occasionally looking back at her and her mother in the rearview mirror.

He's not human. The thought came from nowhere, but it had such certainty to it. She considered herself rational. While she didn't rule out spirituality, she always saw it as a positive thing. Evil, to her, was a creation of humanity. But now, facing evil, she rationalized that it had to be otherworldly because the idea that a human being could be so cold, so full of violence was just too horrible to comprehend.

She squeezed her mother's hands. A sob escaped her lips.

"I'm sorry," Anna said. "It wasn't supposed to be this way. I wanted better for us."

She collapsed against her mother's shoulder and closed her eyes. She lacked the vanity to hope that she and her mother would be saved. Instead she prayed this would be over quickly.

~Todd~

The buildings lining the streets of the warehouse district stood mostly empty and in various states of dilapidation. The yellow glow of the street lights revealed a bunch of broken windows and crumbling

bricks, rusted bay doors closed forever, words spray painted in bubble letters, and patches of grass growing out of cracks in the pavement.

Thirty years as a suburbanite had made Todd fear streets like these. He couldn't help thinking that at any moment, him and Chloe would be tailed by a suspicious car or jumped at one of the intersections. The assailants wouldn't be beings from a spiritual world. They'd be thugs looking to pocket Todd's valuables and have their way with Chloe. Yet so long ago, Todd held none of these fears when he traveled these streets. Long ago, he'd called this place home.

Chloe cut the wheel to the right and drove down a dimly lit alley. An old station wagon with four flat tires was parked along the curb. Movie posters that had mostly peeled away covered one building's wall. A crumbling shell of a building that might have been a church stood on the corner, its brick remains scarred with ashen fire damage. A chain link fence stood loosely around the ruins. The end of the street forced them to turn left. Beyond the turn, a development of brightly lit apartments lined the streets.

Todd marveled at the scene before him. "It's weird to be coming home. Really weird. I can't believe how much I've missed all of this."

"Yeah, you totally sold out."

Todd's laughter immediately broke the tension that held him. Her joke reminded him of something she would have said in happier times. He put his hand on her leg and squeezed. Her flesh was cool under his fingers, soft. When she pulled up to his old apartment building on the right he released her and put his hands on his knees. He sucked in a deep breath and asked her if she was afraid.

"I am." She looked across him at the stairs leading up to the front door. "I don't know what will be waiting for me when I open that door. I mean, I have my hopes, but there's really no telling. I may just drop dead. Maybe I'll become a disembodied ghost. Or maybe I'll just fall right back to Hell. There's always that."

Something that felt like an icy set of fingers tickled their way down Todd's spine. "Maybe I should go with you."

"I can't ask you to do that."

"What if I told you that I wanted to?"

"Would you really want to give up your life? What about the people you love?"

He looked away from her. "I love you."

"I'm not the only person in your life, Todd. You still have a good twenty, thirty years left in you."

He stuck his fingers in his mouth and wished they were a cigarette. He stared up the concrete wall of the building. He thought about hiding behind that wall and having his memory erased, about aging backwards and being twenty-two again, and about the choices he'd made in life, how he'd abandoned Chloe to her addiction and left her for dead.

"If I could start all over again, I would've made a different choice," he said between biting his fingernails. "I would've stayed with you."

"I know. If I could do it all over again, I wouldn't have chased you away."

"Chloe, no..."

"It's okay. I could've told you more, maybe found a way to *show* you. We've both done things we regret." She took his hand out of his mouth and held it in her lap. "Listen, none of that shit matters anymore. What matters is what we do from here on out. You've done so much for me since I found you again. I'll always love you, whether you come with me tonight or not."

Overhead a helicopter's rotors made a steady *whup-whup-whup* sound. As it crossed just above their car, its propellers reached a peak volume and synced with Todd's pulse. As the maddening sound of the helicopter's flight faded into the distance, his anxiety remained. The time to make a decision had come.

"Let me at least walk you to the door."

She killed the engine. They left the car and met outside. Under their feet the pavement was wet. The sounds of cars speeding down the distant highway broke the silence of the night. The helicopter's sounds fell to a whisper as it flew into the distance. Warmth overwhelmed the night air. Somewhere ahead, a bat flapped its rubbery wings. As he looked at the building's dark windows, he wondered if anyone lived there. If so, would they know if she shared the apartment with them?

They ascended the concrete stairs and came to the front door. Todd pulled on the handle, but it didn't give. He turned to her, hoping she'd be able to open the door. She pressed her lips together and took Todd's hand. His fingers tingled in her gentle grasp. She caressed the top of his hand and took his grip off the door handle. Closing her eyes

she turned the knob. The door came unlatched and opened a crack. She smiled up at Todd and even amidst the dirty light from the street lamp, it was radiant.

Before she swung the door open and went in, she laced her hands behind Todd's neck and her dark chocolate eyes held his. She brought her lips up to kiss him. When their mouths met Todd shut his eyes and let himself get lost in her sweetness. He tried not to think about the next moment, in which she would leave him forever. And forever, he knew it would be. She took her lips from his and he brought his face forward, hoping to get one last morsel of her.

"Thank you for helping me get here."

"I guess this is 'goodbye?'"

Her gaze shifted to the crack of the open door for a moment before she refocused on him.

"That's up to you. You have to decide if walking through that door with me will be what delivers you."

He thought about it. If he left he'd leave behind a good job that had paid for the five bedroom house and the education of his two children. And they were wonderful children. Katie had a bright future if she focused on the things that mattered and lived with passion. If he left he'd never see her again, and any chance of reconciling with Dale also would be gone. He couldn't deny his love for Anna, but more and more he was unsure of what kind of love it was. As he stood there looking from the car to Chloe, he couldn't help thinking that all of these things may have been attachments that have been pulling him away from his true self, his *essence*.

Images of sitting across the living room of his apartment with Chloe, him cradling his guitar, she leaning over her synthesizer, played through his head like a beautiful film. They were always so in sync, when they played music, when they made love, when they spoke. With Anna there had always been a strain, even in the beginning, and a dissonance that grew as the years went by.

"I don't have any other choice. I need to go with you."

She smiled. "You do have a choice. That's what makes it so much more wonderful."

He nodded in agreement.

"Are you sure this is what you want to do?"

A large moth with colorful wings caught his eye as it danced in the porch light behind her. Its approach was tentative, as if it was attracted to the glow but feared being engulfed in flames. The moth hung in the air as if on a string, an unseen puppeteer dangling it in the air and bouncing it up and down. Even as it hesitated, it moved forward a little more, inexorably attracted to the luminosity in spite of any danger. It would reach the light, Todd thought, and he would go in with Chloe. He wasn't sure what would happen when he went through that door with her, but he knew it would be okay. He and the moth, in spite of anxieties and uncertainty, shared that common optimism about their respective destinations.

In the window beside the light the reflection of a shadowy figure approached from the street below. Todd's gaze shifted to the path of the moth and saw that it had caught itself in a spider web strategically spun around the light. The crafty spider approached its prey with rapid urgency. Todd looked back to the reflection in the window below the light. Before he could say or do anything, he heard Chloe scream.

He spun and followed her line of sight to the street. Samael stood on the sidewalk. At his feet two women knelt. One of them was young, auburn-haired, in her late teens. The other was older, blond and still beautiful. Even under the deceptive shadows of the city street, Todd recognized them.

~Chloe~

The night before she died, Chloe dreamed she was running through the woods outside her father's house. In the dream the trees stood taller, bare branches scraping the night sky like the fingernails of an angry lover. They surrounded her house, blocking the street and her neighbors' homes. The night sky was starless but a strange red glow backlit the clouds and throbbed in time with claps of thunder.

No matter where Chloe ran, no matter how fast, the trees prevented her escape. Every attempt to reach her house resulted in failure. She'd get just in front of the back deck, then end up back in the woods, the house gone from sight.

As the dream went on, she would realize that she had been here many nights before. These dreams were always the same: oppressive, hopeless, and filled with an overwhelming feeling of being devoured

from within by something older than God. Upon this realization, she knew that *he* was here, that man of fire, the one who had chased her all her life.

The realization that this was a dream did nothing to comfort her. Instead, it awakened something between panic and resignation. If he had chased her for this long, and every night she had safely awakened, this had to be the night her luck ran out. You can only outrun fate for so long.

The woods caught fire, surrounding her in a circle of orange-red flames that got closer and closer. She looked around for a way through them, but no exit presented itself. From the fire he came and he embraced her in his burning arms.

~Todd~

"Anna! Katie!" Anna strained to raise her head. She only got it up a few inches. Deep purple bruises covered her face. "What the fuck did you do to them?"

"Have a look for yourself." Samael grabbed Katie by her dark hair and jerked her head up. A bloody gash gleamed on her cheek.

Chloe pushed her way in front of Todd. "Leave them out of this!"

Samael threw Katie to the ground and stepped forward. Paralyzing fear seized Todd as Samael's eyes burned.

"I've come back for you and since you won't come willingly, I've chosen to use other means. If you walk through that door, either of you, they die."

Todd's guts shriveled inside of him. Before, the choice of running off with Chloe was a distant thing. Leaving his life behind had no immediacy. Though it would hurt Anna and Katie, he knew they would pull themselves together and get on with life. Just moments ago, he had been ready to pursue his own salvation and leave the attachments of this life behind. Now, the consequences stared him in the eyes.

"Come back to me and I'll let them go."

Tears streamed from Chloe's eyes. She looked utterly vulnerable and it hurt Todd to see her that way. She brought her hand out to meet his. Their fingertips touched lightly. For a moment time seemed to stop, then she drew her hand away. The frailty left her features.

"I'm sorry, Todd. I can't."

"What?"

Chloe turned to stare down Samael. "How do I know that you'll let them go if I go with you?"

"Chloe, no, there has to be another way."

"You don't know anything," said Samael. "But have no doubt that if you don't come with me, they *will* both die."

Todd watched Chloe as she stood at the head of the stairs, statuesque and doing all she could to hide her fear. His thoughts were chaotic. He saw no good way for this to end. A truck drove by in the distance, its engine roaring like a great beast.

"I'll go with you."

Todd reached for her. "No!"

Chloe clutched his body to hers. For a beautiful moment, Todd thought they would be inseparable. He tried to forget where he was, to focus only on the warmth of her as she pressed against him. He tried not to think about letting her go in the next minute.

"I'm sorry," she whispered in his ear. "This is just where I belong."

"No! There has to be another way. Just go inside. The door's *open*."

"He'll just kill your family in front of you if I do that. I can't have that on my conscience."

He had nothing to say, because he knew that he couldn't sway her. She broke her hold on him and started to push away. He gave up the fight and let her slip from his arms. His heart jackhammered against his sternum as he watched her descend the stairs. Over her shoulder, he saw Samael grin, the joy the demon derived from Todd's misery evident. That smug expression sent Todd into a fit of rage.

"No!" He lunged down the stairs. "You son of a bitch, you leave them the fuck out of this!"

He pushed past Chloe who tried to call him off. He barely heard her. He raised his fists like a barroom brawler and charged. The demon held his ground. Todd jabbed forward with his right hand, hoping to land a shot in Samael's mouth. He'd seen the guy get up from a lot and was pretty sure that this was a losing battle, but *fuck it*. Better to go down swinging than to stand by while a monster used your loved ones as pawns.

Samael effortlessly dodged Todd's assault and countered with a backhand slap. The blow took Todd to the ground. Samael stepped on the back of Todd's neck and applied pressure. Pieces of gravel dug into Todd's cheek and teeth as he tasted the scummy pavement. Blood

mixed with grime as his nose gave way under pressure. Samael could kill him easily. A swift drive of the heel to the back of his skull would do the trick, but killing him fast was not likely part of Samael's plan.

"Samael, stop! You let all of them go or you don't get me. Is that clear?"

"You're in no position to bargain with me, slave!"

Todd tried to push himself up. His face was being crushed. Samael had him firmly pinned.

"If you kill him, I'll run back up these stairs. Now get off of him or you'll never see me again."

Some of the pressure gave. Even though Todd didn't want to die, he still couldn't make peace with Chloe giving herself up. He protested against the pavement with a choked cry.

Chloe said, "I mean it. Let… them… go."

Samael's heel lingered. For a moment, Todd imagined the foot coming down to mash his head and Samael catching Chloe before she made her way through the door. That was entirely possible and would erode the nobility of anyone's sacrifice.

Samael removed his foot.

"Now, get away from them."

Samael stepped away. Todd tried to get up and look at what was happening around him, but blood and tears filled his eyes. Chloe approached and stopped at Samael's side. Todd wiped his eyes and saw Samael looking down at him. Chloe was looking away. Samael bent so that Todd could smell the fire on his breath.

"Take your family and go. Your part in this story ends tonight."

Part of Todd wanted to get up and fight back, but he had no spirit left.

Samael put an arm around Chloe's shoulders. She tried to shrink away, but he pulled her to him. His eyes narrowed at Todd.

"Go now, before I decide not to hold up my end of the bargain."

Todd got to his feet, then wiped his face on his shirt. He stood frozen in place. Another thought of lunging at Samael crossed his mind, but the futility of such an attack had already been proved. The conflict would end in Todd's death and probably everyone else's too. He went to Katie and avoided looking at Chloe.

Katie's hands hung limp in her lap as she knelt on the pavement. Quiet sobs fell from her lips. Seeing her in this state hurt, especially when he took into account this was partially his fault. Samael never

would've come for his family if he hadn't run away with Chloe. He bent and put his arm under Katie's shoulders and lifted her off the ground. She was dead weight in his arms at first, then eventually she shuffled her feet as he led her to the back seat of his car. She wept as she buckled in.

"Dad… what's happening…?"

Not so much unwilling to answer as unable, he shut the door. He turned back to Samael, Chloe and Anna. All three watched him. Chloe's expression was broken and full of shame while Anna looked at him with a mix between contempt and disbelief. Samael's smugness hadn't faded in the least. Todd walked toward the trio, moving his feet in short, uncertain strides. When he got to Anna, he stole a look up at Chloe. Fear had crept into her expression now and Todd guessed that the reality of her decision had dawned on her. He bent to take Anna's arm. She looked up at him, her gaze toxic up close.

"What have you done?" she asked.

Saying nothing, he offered his hand. Despite her obvious anger, she took it and let him help her up. The walk back to the car this time seemed much longer than before, like the longest walk of his life. Numbness overtook him as he helped Anna into the passenger seat.

As he drove away, he couldn't breathe. He couldn't look back.

But, *God,* he wanted to.

His breath didn't return until Chloe's screams died under the drone of the car's motor.

* * *

Todd lay on his back, his eyes wide open. Except for the gentle hum of the ceiling fan's motor, dark silence filled the bedroom. Anna faced the wall. All she'd said since coming home was that she just wanted to lie down.

They'd spent the day in the hospital, getting their wounds looked at. The doctors all said that neither he, Anna nor Katie were seriously injured. All day, Todd kept thinking that was a lie. All three of them were deeply hurt, but in places the doctors could never see with their instruments and X-rays. Todd knew as he lay on top of the blanket, the cool breeze of the fan providing little comfort, that their wounds would leave permanent, profound scars.

Few words were exchanged between Todd and his family throughout the day. Katie had shot him several sympathetic looks as the hours went on, but there was nothing else from her. There was even less from Anna. He'd done most of the talking, telling the doctors and the police that they were attacked. No, he didn't know their attacker. No, nothing had been stolen. Yes, he'd be willing to look at a lineup. He didn't voice that he knew it would do no good. Samael was long gone. Anna and Katie seemed to know that somehow, too. He made no mention of Chloe. It disgusted him how good he was at lying.

He turned over and focused on the back of Anna's neck. Her dirty blond hair lay splayed across the white pillow. She smelled like her strawberry shampoo. They'd showered separately; she'd spent nearly an hour in there while Todd waited for her to come to bed. Now, despite her silence, he knew she was awake from the restless way she breathed. He said her name once.

"Don't," she replied.

Todd returned to his back. His eyes had adjusted well to the darkness. The ceiling was a chilling shade of gray and offered him no answers. Looking within only yielded emptiness. He didn't sleep for a long time.

~4~

~Chloe~

Cold mud slid down Chloe's skin as she crouched in the filth that covered the floor of Samael's cave. Her flesh crawled with the lingering feel of the previous violation. Samael took a handful of her hair and raised her head to make eye contact with him. The motion was almost tender, but because it was done with his hand, it exuded menace. He stared at her with eyes not full of fire, but ashen soullessness.

"Clare, my sweet Clare, have you learned your lesson?"

"I'm *not* her. Stop..."

He tightened his grip on her hair and tilted her head back. Above her on the ceiling, gutted bodies of the damned bled and shat down upon the floor. They should have been dead, all of them, but they wailed in their immortal suffering.

"You are who I say you are, whore. I've died for you. I've tortured and killed for you. You are mine."

She watched the suffering above her, fastened by their ankles in the stone ceiling. They writhed and howled, sounding like wounded animals. Thirty years in Hell and she never got used to seeing them. She supposed she never would.

"Tell me you're mine. I've fought for you and won."

"You'll believe that whether I tell you or not."

He pulled harder on her scalp and took her by the throat with his other hand.

"Tell me or..."

"You'll kill me? I think we've gone far past that."

He dug his fingernails into the soft skin of her neck. The five fresh wounds stung and trickled warm trails of blood down her exposed breasts.

"There's no escape. You can't tell me that you haven't learned that already."

"I escaped before. He'll call to me again. Or I'll find another way."

"Sweet Clare." He ran his tongue across her face, licking the filth from her cheek and sucking the tears from her eyes.

"That's not my name. Clare is dead."

He pushed her into the muck below. Shit and spoiled meat filled her mouth and nose, and she came up coughing.

He straddled her. "Say you belong to me. I need to hear it."

"Fuck what you need." She cringed fearing another onslaught of physical violence, but instead he grinned.

"Remember when I used to leave you alone down here, sometimes for days or weeks at a time? Soon enough, you remembered you belonged to me. You called to me. You let me call you Clare, told me you loved me, because as horrible as you say I am, nothing is worse than being in Hell alone."

She crawled backwards away from him.

"This is your last chance. Swear you're mine or I'll leave you down here again."

"Go to Hell."

"I'm afraid there's no deeper Hell than this. Enjoy your isolation, slave. Call to me when you're ready to mind your manners."

"You know how to show a girl a good time, don't you?"

He turned away and walked off into the darkness. Above her, the damned wailed and gnashed their teeth.

~Todd~

He woke, alone and in pain. Tight knots bulged in his neck muscles. Opening and closing his mouth came with great effort. He sat up slowly, afraid any sudden movement would break him. He felt like he had run a marathon where at the end the spectators got up and beat the shit out of him.

Something rustled in his closet.

"Anna?"

No response.

He staggered to his feet. Dizziness overtook him and he almost collapsed back to the bed. He put his hands out to steady himself and took a deep breath that brought a stab of pain to his ribs.

More moving came from the closet. He crossed the bedroom, slid the closet door open and walked in. Anna knelt stuffing clothes inside a suitcase. He should have seen this coming. He almost said nothing at all.

"I guess I can't blame you," he said.

She turned to look up at him. Redness filled her eyes. Her lips were twisted in a disdainful expression. Her hair was up, but in a mess. Todd sighed, trying to find the words to comfort her.

"I'm not mad at you." He knew she was lying, but he let her. "We need to stop kidding ourselves. This hasn't worked for a long time."

Todd watched her shove a pair of stockings in the zipper compartment.

"I had an affair. I guess I'm still having one."

The pain that struck him felt more obligatory than genuine. The events of the previous day had numbed him. "Who is it?"

She looked away, buried her gaze in the contents of her suitcase. He watched her teeth sink into her lip. Fresh tears filled her eyes. She said one name: Keith. Todd had met him a few times, at parties put on by her company. Keith was at least ten years younger than her. He didn't bother asking how long it had been going on, but she told him anyway: over a year. He nodded slowly, taking it all in.

"I started because… I don't know, you stopped being the man I married." A cliché, but she was right. "You were so hopeful and full of life when you were younger. You had your music, your dreams. Then you just started to remind me of my father and your father."

"I thought that was what you wanted, someone more stable. Someone…"

She shook her head. "Just stop. It's too late to try to fix this. I've moved on. It looks like you tried to. I don't know who that girl or that *man* was… What were you a part of?"

"If it's too late, what's the point in explaining? You wouldn't believe it anyway."

For a moment, her mouth opened like she meant to protest. Then she shook her head. "I guess you're right."

"Yeah."

He sat down on the bed and watched her pack. He kept his hands folded in his lap and expected every article of clothing placed in her suitcases to gouge him emotionally, but instead he felt nothing, which was worse somehow. She continued as if he wasn't there. When she finished, he helped her take the bags downstairs.

"Did you already speak to Katie?" he asked.

"Yes, while you were sleeping. She's not happy with me."

"What about Dale? Have you called him?"

"I'll do it later."

"He'll probably tell you it's about time."

Her face twisted into a grimace.

Their feet made a hollow sound on the hardwood steps. He glanced at his studio in his periphery. The door was closed. He wondered if he'd ever open it again.

"I'm going to my mother's first. I don't know what I'll do after that."

Todd opened the front door and let her out. He followed, dragging his feet. The hot sun beat against the top of his head. One of his neighbors, Mr. Morris from across the street, watered plants and stared at them as they walked. Todd bared his teeth and said, "Why don't you mind your fucking business?"

Mr. Morris dropped his gaze and continued to water.

Anna frowned at Todd. "At least I know this matters to you on some level."

"Of course it does. Everything matters. I'll miss you and I'm really..."

"Please don't apologize. It doesn't sound good coming from you."

After the car was loaded, they stood awkwardly in front of each other saying nothing. She shrugged and reached out to hug him. He returned the stiff embrace. She broke away, slid into her car, and slammed the door. He watched as she drove away.

* * *

Todd limped back inside and shut the door against the sweltering day. Anna had driven away rather quietly. No squealing tires, no angry moan of the engine. It was like she had already shut herself down from the emotions between them. And why shouldn't she? he thought. She owed him nothing.

He looked around. "Katie, you home?"

The full minute of silence that followed told him no, she was not. Her car parked in the driveway meant nothing. She could've been out with friends or that boy, Jake, or whatever his name was, the one who thought Todd was a square.

He stomped back up the stairs, needing to feel the firmness below him, needing to hear each step he took. He entered his bedroom and examined the bed where his and Anna's outlines still made impressions in the sheets. He sighed and turned to the walk-in closet. It lacked a good portion of Anna's clothes. Some still remained, but he doubted she'd be back for them. Viewing the empty spaces they'd left, something like a cold hand tightened around his heart. Looking at the expensive suits that now hung alone, he got the crazy urge to tear them from their hangers, pile them in the back yard, and set them on fire. He knew it was crazy, and he didn't care.

He entered the bathroom where the towel from Anna's prolonged shower still sat in a crumpled mess on the tile floor. Her toothbrush and other toiletries were gone. This was for real.

He looked at himself in the mirror. A day's growth gave his face a prickly darkness. Red cracks filled the whites of his eyes. His features sagged under stress and a lack of sleep. He looked like he'd aged ten years in the last forty-eight hours. As he examined himself, a spirit of loathing crept into his thoughts. He hated the face that looked back at him more than anything. Even self-pity was more than that face deserved.

He lashed out. A cry of rage tore from his lungs and he threw his fist into the glass. Spider web cracks split the mirror and blood smeared at the point of impact. He screamed and punched again, ignoring the pain in his hand, knowing only the desire to destroy his image, to shatter it forever so that it could never return.

~Chloe~

Chloe couldn't tell how long she'd been alone down here. The smells of death and shit made her woozy. The mouth of the cave had closed behind Samael and she had no way of escaping. Above her, the damned cried out in agony.

The creature of bone and magma levitated towards her. Vestments of ragged flesh dangled from his arms. Wounds on his torso pulsed and oozed with fiery blood.

"Has he left you here all alone?" the creature said in a buzzing voice.

Chloe had seen him before, in the memories Samael shared, but in person his presence was even viler. He reeked of decay and burning hair. His black tongue rolled over dying crustaceans that clawed at the inside of his mouth.

"You know who I am, I see." His expression became something like a smile. "Then you know that I can get you out of here."

She shook her head.

"Oh, I can, dear Chloe. That's your real name, right? He thinks you're his long lost love and maybe that's my fault, but you're not. You're you, or at least you think you are. Are we ever who we think we are?"

Chloe spat at him. "Is that what you came down here to do? Play games?"

He buzzed in response. "My dear, I told you what I came here to do. I came to set you free. All you have to do is ask."

So, it would be a game after all. "In exchange for what?"

The beast crossed ropey arms across his broad chest. He regarded her with eyes that switched back and forth from insect to reptilian.

"Now, why do you assume that I want something in return? Can't I just offer you something out of the goodness of my heart?"

"Because you're the devil, right? That's what you do, make deals?"

"Devil's a strong word, especially when you use such an official-sounding article ahead of it. The living tend to think there's some kind of hierarchy down here, but I'm surprised you, with your thirty years of experience, see this place as anything but the chaotic wasteland that it is."

"But you do make deals, don't you? You don't have the goodness in your heart to offer anything out of."

"Well-played," the beast said. "I suppose I'll get down to business then."

Chloe straightened, more interested than she wanted to be. It had been a hard day and maybe, if what he wanted was reasonable, she'd consider it.

"I want Todd."

She shrunk back. "What? No."

The beast cocked its bulbous head. "No?"

"Absolutely not."

"And why 'absolutely not?'"

She backed away from him. "No deal."

"You love him? Is that it?" The beast made more of that wasp-like buzzing, but higher pitched and more frenetic. Was he annoyed? "Did you ever stop to think, Chloe, dear, that you wouldn't be here if it wasn't for him."

"That's bullshit."

"Is it? Maybe this time around you gave yourself up willingly, but would you have even had to if he hadn't left you to die back when you two were kids? Think about it. If he would've been more of a man, we could've avoided this whole mess altogether. You know that's true."

"Who cares? He made a mistake."

"Are you really that noble, love, that you would let his mistake condemn you forever?" He came towards her, floating over the filth. She tried to cringe backwards, but hit a fleshy wall. He pressed a dripping, meaty hand upon her shoulder. "Think about it. Just say the words and you can finally be at rest."

He drew out the word 'rest' and said it without the accompanying buzz. For the duration of the word, he almost sounded human. Hearing it spoken in such a way brought strange, unexpected comfort. His touch warmed her against the cold filth in which she stood.

"He left you. Make him pay and have your freedom."

She touched the beast's hand. The suffering cried above her and she imagined what it'd be like to never hear them again. She pictured existence without Samael's cruelty. She believed it would be much like the warm light and euphoria that had greeted her in the first moments after her initial death. Or maybe she'd be on earth, wandering, but without the threat of Samael's pursuit. Either way, it beat her current situation.

But she couldn't betray Todd. She'd never seen his abandonment of her as a betrayal. It had always been about the claim Samael had made on her. She thought about the devil's words, how Samael mistaking her for Clare had been his fault.

"You're wondering how I caused Samael to believe you are his lost love?"

"Yes."

"Do you know who your mother was?"

"You know that I don't."

Again, that almost-smile spread across the beast's features, revealing the dying crustaceans squirming in his mouth. Some fell out and plopped into the soupy filth below.

"I needed him. Souls like him are integral to existence here. Only one thing keeps this great machine moving and that's pain. I told him he'd see his love again, that she'd be born of fire, so long as he keeps feeding the machine."

"Who was my mother?"

"She was a spiritual being. Something like what you'd think of as an angel. She traveled the world for centuries, healing people and inspiring spiritual movements. Having children was never something she was meant to do, so your birth destroyed her body."

"Is she still alive somewhere? Maybe down here?"

His eyes flashed a deeper shade of red. "Enough questions. Do you want your freedom or not?"

"I won't give you Todd."

He held up a hand. "Then..."

"I'll give you Samael."

"What do you mean? I already have him."

"Hardly. He's too busy chasing me when he should be doing work for you."

The beast said nothing, but the sound of buzzing wasps filled his chest.

"Chasing me to the surface and causing all kinds of chaos above can't be what you had in mind when you gave him his deal."

The red eyes narrowed as the creature examined Chloe. The buzzing rose in volume as if whatever was causing it would burst from the devil's chest. He said, "I won't just give you your freedom. You have to earn it."

She cringed. Of course there'd be a catch. She'd have to blow this devil or have sex with him or worse, she thought.

Reading her mind, the devil laughed. "Oh, don't worry. I've no carnal interest in you."

"What then?"

"When Todd calls you back, you must go to him. Samael will follow, I'm sure." The devil reached underneath a fold of skin and pulled

out a tuning fork. "If you can beat him, use this to call me and I'll take him back to Hell."

She took the tuning fork in her hand. "How do I know Todd will call me back?"

"He will. He never could exist without you."

"So, what do I do now?"

This time, when the devil smiled, it looked genuine. He said, "You wait."

~Todd~

The black iron gate of Red Grove Cemetery hung open. Todd drove his repaired Cadillac between the two marble columns and onto the gravel road that wove through the field of headstones. He passed a couple of mourners at one grave, standing under umbrellas. Gray clouds threatened a summer storm and made this an all too fitting day to visit an old graveyard.

The tires groaned against the gravel below as the car stopped. He got out and glanced around. The gray clouds moved across the sky with a sense of urgency. He didn't bother to get his umbrella out of the back seat. He left his car behind and wandered out among the headstones.

Though not one hundred percent sure where her grave was, he had a general idea. He vaguely remembered from the last time he'd visited it, several years ago. He walked down the nearest row. After spending two days alone in an empty house, hardly moving except to wrap up his wounded hand, it felt nice to be on his feet again.

Down one row, then another, he watched the names as he passed each marker. He recognized none of them, despite once living in this town. The more time that passed, the quicker he moved. A raindrop kissed the top of his head as he turned down another row. By the time he found her, a light drizzle had begun to fall. He dropped to his knees and traced the curves and lines of her chiseled name. He braced a hand against the top of the headstone and squeezed. He shut his eyes. Instead of words, a dry croak slipped from his lips. He took a deep breath, rolled his shoulders back and tried to begin again.

"Chloe." Hearing her name broke his heart, even though he thought it impossible for his heart to break any further. "Chloe, I'm so

fucking sorry. I don't know where you are now, but I hope you're not suffering... I hope somehow..."

He knew it was dead hope. He'd last left her in the arms of a monster that claimed to love her but would surely drag her back to Hell. Maybe Samael did love her in some twisted way. In fact, Todd was pretty sure he did, but it was a monster's love, the love of someone incapable of loving in a nondestructive way.

The rain picked up and the drops fattened. In blatant disregard for the summertime, the precipitation fell in ice cold sheets.

"I don't know what to do anymore, Chloe. My life... everything since the day I left you thirty years ago has been full of failure and regret. I've lived a falsely and I had a way out and I couldn't leave. You can say that none of this is my fault, but I'll always think that it is. Had I never left you back then, it never would've had to come down to a choice between saving you and protecting my family. If I'd just protected you back then, I wouldn't have fucked everything up."

Tears flowed as he uttered the last sentence. The rain fell with them, now a steady downpour. His clothes soaked through, stuck to his skin.

"I don't know what to do anymore. How can I live on knowing what I know? Knowing that you're suffering? Knowing that my family is broken? Knowing that the world beyond is fire and chaos? What am I supposed to do?"

He pressed his head against the cold wet stone. Shivers wracked his body in the icy rain. A brief fear crossed his mind that he'd catch pneumonia and die, but was quickly eased when he realized that he wasn't sure if he even cared about dying. Whether he died or lived, all was lost.

He hugged his arms to his chest and opened his eyes. The rain fell in rivulets down the marble face of the headstone. The carved letters of her name bled water. The ground below him turned to mud. He knew she wouldn't feel the rain where she was, but knew it'd probably be better if she could.

As he studied the patterns, a hand fell on his shoulder.

"Get out of the rain, son, you're gonna catch your death out here."

He looked over his shoulder and saw the man that loomed over him. Stringy long hair fell across square shoulders. When he'd last seen the face, it had been much older and twisted in a determined expres-

sion, a fighting spirit afire in its eyes. Now the face held a restful serenity and seemed much younger, but he still recognized it. Todd got to his feet and backed away, hardly believing his eyes despite all he'd learned about the fine lines between life and death.

"Les."

The old man gave him a single nod and regarded him with deep, staring eyes that couldn't possibly belong to a dead man.

* * *

Todd sat with Les inside the Cadillac. In spite of the fact that it was the dead of summer, Todd ran the heater to dry his clothes. Seeing the ghost of Chloe's father inspired a curiosity that made him want to live, at least a bit longer.

"Don't pretend you don't know why I'm here."

"Chloe."

Les nodded. Sheets of rain splashed against the windshield.

"I guess it's the *how* I'm confused about."

"I wish I could attribute it to all the reading I did about the occult, but I can't help but feel there's maybe something more to it." He stared ahead at the rain gushing down the windshield for several moments before he continued. "That demon, that Samael, got his hands in me. I couldn't have been alive for more than few seconds after that but it sure felt a lot longer. I thought the pain would never end. When it did, I had an out of body experience, but not like the ones you read about. I didn't float above my corpse or see a bright light. I sunk into the earth."

"Was it Hell?"

"I don't know, maybe a part of it, certainly some kind of underworld, but peaceful. There were others there, dead people. They wandered aimlessly in what looked like some kind of vast cave system and I joined their numbers. I don't know how long I was down there with them, could've been hours or it could've been days. Then I saw her, Chloe's mother, Natalia."

Todd sat up. He hadn't expected that, but maybe he'd hoped for it. Les had been good to Todd when Todd was young and downright saintly when he'd sacrificed himself. He deserved a reunion with his long lost love.

"She embraced me and I felt this powerful sense of relief, and contentment, as if I'd finally arrived at the place I needed to be." He sighed, tears in his eyes. "I wanted to stay so badly, but she said I couldn't and I knew she was right. I couldn't rest while our daughter suffered."

"How did you know?"

"I saw. When Natalia touched me, she showed me, and I knew. I knew that Chloe was back in the hands of that *animal*."

On the last word, Les's tone became a growl of anger.

"Then you found me."

"Yes, because I can't help her."

Todd shook his head. "Well, fuck, man, neither can I. I failed her. The whole reason she's back in Samael's hands is because I couldn't keep her safe."

"There was nothing else you could've done. Choosing between loved ones… I couldn't imagine."

"I didn't choose. I just gave up."

"And maybe that was the right choice then, but you can't give up now. She needs you."

"What can I do?"

"Remember how you called her here in the first place. You can call her back again and free her from that pit."

"Yeah and then what? We run? Because you know that son of a bitch will come looking for her."

"So take her home."

"And where's that? Every place we've ever been is tainted by something. We've never been home before, either of us. We've just been running all our lives."

"What if you found a new home? Built a new home, maybe?"

Todd studied Les hard. The old bastard may have hit on something. Over the last few days since Anna left, his house, despite its size, had felt increasingly more claustrophobic. He could either sell it or give it to Anna. He had money saved up that he could use to purchase some land on which to build. The wheels began to turn in his head and for the first time since he left Chloe behind in the warehouse district, he felt a sense of hope.

"Yeah, I can do that. I will."

"Good. I'll be watching."

* * *

The first place he looked into was the farmland near Potter Way, where he and Chloe had first made love. Back then, a farmhouse had stood in that field, but now it was empty. Empty and for sale.

He took a loan out through Havertown Community Bank, at the officer's preferred rate, and hired a team of builders out of the phone book. He wanted something simple, a freestanding, shotgun house. Wood-paneling. A front porch. One bedroom, one bathroom. It had to be quaint because it only had one purpose: to be the house he lived his last days in.

It took several months, during which he went through each day as if nothing was happening. He went to work, even though the anticipation for this new chance at saving Chloe sometimes drove him into fits of excitement where he could hardly sit or focus. Some nights as he tried to sleep, it drove him mad thinking that the longer the build took, the more Chloe would suffer, but he reminded himself that this was the only way to do it. It had to be a brand new place otherwise it wouldn't work at all.

Though the land was old, it only held pleasant memories. He figured that the only reason it hadn't worked before was that there'd been nowhere for her to be contained. Inside the home, she, *they*, could be safe.

The builders finished in mid-September. He moved in the day after. Since he left Anna mostly everything from their house, he'd bought all new furniture. There was very little, because that was all he needed. A couch and chair for the living room, a dining room table with a set of stools, a bed, a bookcase. The rest could wait. From his and Anna's house, he brought everything from the study: all the stacks of notebooks, his guitar, and a photo album from the old days. The new place was a downgrade from the five bedroom house he'd shared with Anna, but he needed this stripped-down life. After everything that had happened, the need to go back to basics seemed to be the only logical choice.

While he was upstairs putting the bed together, someone knocked on the front door. He raised his head, looked out of the bedroom and down the hallway. He set down the Allen wrench and got off his knees. The sound of his joints cracking reminded him that his days of putting

furniture together were coming to an end. He left the bedroom and went downstairs. There was another knock.

"Coming," he said.

As he put his hand on the knob, he contemplated not answering. For a crazy moment, a vision of opening the door to see Samael standing on the other side crossed his mind, Samael, back to take Todd to hell with him. There Todd would watch helplessly as the monster had his way with Chloe for eternity. Todd closed his eyes and took a breath to compose himself. He opened the door to see his daughter standing on the other side.

She greeted him with a hug and a wry smile. The scar on her cheek was healing nicely, but it still wasn't one hundred percent. Angry inflammation still reddened the skin around it. Todd hoped her boyfriend, Jake, wasn't the shallow type. It would be a while before she looked like herself again.

"How're you holding up?" he asked.

"I'm holding up, Dad. How about you?"

He gave a dry laugh because it was all he could do. Her sympathetic smile held. She reached out, squeezed his shoulder. Her hand was warm and it felt pleasant where she touched him. She followed him inside and he closed the door behind her. He motioned for her to have a seat and offered her a cup of coffee. She sat and shook her head. They stared at each other for a long time before either of them spoke.

"Dad…"

"Katie… I…"

They exchanged awkward smiles. The separation had luckily been drama free. Todd wouldn't have gone so far as to call it painless, it was a separation after all, but it had been mercifully quick. Regardless of how smooth it had gone, this was the first time he'd had a chance to sit and talk with Katie in a long while. He took a breath before speaking again.

"I'm so sorry about all of this."

"You don't have to be," she said. "No matter what you were involved in, I don't think you ever intended for us to get hurt."

"You've always been the most forgiving member of this family."

She dropped her eyes for a moment and shifted uncomfortably. Only one lamp shined in the room, and in the vague light, she appeared almost ghostlike, embraced by shadows. A grave expression crossed her face.

"I saw things when that man had Mom and me. Things I can't begin to explain."

Todd nodded slowly. Outside in the distance a coyote cried.

"Dad, who was he? Who was that girl?" She paused. "*What* were they?"

"I don't know if I can tell you."

"You can," she said. "You can trust me."

He examined her closely. There was something haunting about her eyes, as if her experiences had given her a much grimmer worldview. It was a look that he'd come to recognize in his own eyes since losing Chloe again. To confirm, he asked her if she believed in ghosts.

"I can't say that I don't. Not after everything I've seen."

He collected his thoughts, his memories, everything that he wanted to tell her, everything that he wanted to tell somebody. Even as he worked out what he would say, he knew how crazy it all sounded. When he looked into his daughter's eyes, he felt she was beyond judging him, her outlook now far too complex to judge anyone for what they claimed as reality. He told her everything starting with the first time Chloe walked into his life at his concert's after party, continuing with how he ran away when her issues seemed too big for him to manage. He told her how he and her mother ended up getting married according to the wishes of their parents, how after Chloe's death he buried her memories and the essence of who he was in work and building a life that he thought he was supposed to lead.

"For the longest time, I repressed those memories, but then things started to fall apart with your mom, and I found myself thinking about those days more and more. I started thinking about Chloe more and more. The day you gave me that CD was when everything really changed. She came back to life."

Todd tried to gauge Katie's reaction to that statement, but she kept a poker face. Someone coming back from the dead seemed to have no effect on her.

"With her back in my life, I couldn't let her go again. But I didn't know how to tell anyone, so I ran. I never intended for you and your mom to be involved. I love you, Katie. You're the best thing to have come out of the mess I've made of my life. I love your mom, too, but..."

Katie nodded. Her genuine understanding made her look incredibly mature to him. Flashes of the little girl she used to be danced

across his mind and faded away. She leaned forward and squeezed her hand around his.

"So what now?" she asked.

Todd opened his mouth and closed it. He had no answer for her.

"I don't know, Katie. I feel fucking lost… like…" He forced himself not to finish the sentence. What he had to say was nothing someone should ever hear from their father.

She pressed him. "Like what?"

"Like… I have nothing left to do but try to find her."

She swallowed. He had a feeling that it was anger she was gulping down. He almost wanted to beg her to get angry with him, to really let him have it. At least then it would be honest. With her, he felt like he always got off too easily.

"I don't want to see you give up, Dad. Do some soul searching. You've got plenty of time to do it now. I know you'll find whatever it is you're looking for, but please don't endanger yourself again. I don't want to lose you."

"You don't understand."

"I do understand. Trust me. You're in a lot of pain." Her hand went to the scar on her cheek and he was reminded that the wounds inflicted on her were likely much deeper than physical. "What's important is what we do in the face of the pain."

"That's why I have to try again."

Katie got to her feet and hugged him. "Do what you have to do, but be careful. Whatever you decide, I'll always love you, Dad."

Upon hearing that, warmth bloomed in his chest. He walked her to the door. After she'd driven away, he shut off the lights in his house and sat there in the darkness until he plunged into the depths of sleep.

* * *

Todd dug through his closet. He pushed aside boxes of things he knew he would never look at again. When he found what he was looking for, he wrapped his fingers around it. He relished the feel of the smooth wood and the strings on the flesh of his hand. Lifting the guitar took considerably more effort than it used to. His back and shoulder came alive with dull aches as he carried it over boxes and into his arms. Dust had collected on its body and its strings were rusted. He took it

out to the porch, set it in his lap and got to work restoring the instrument to its former majesty.

An hour went by as he polished, restrung and tuned. When he finished, the Gibson shined darkly in the cherry light of the setting sun. He set it down on his knee and leaned over it, gazing down into the cracks in the floor of the wooden porch. In that darkness, so many things lived and died, so many things he couldn't see and never would. Even parts of the world like this, that were so close and seemed so small, were far bigger than he could ever understand. Understanding this brought bittersweet humility.

He put his fingers on the fret board. It was awkward, like touching an old lover for the first time after years apart. He bent, repositioned, adjusted until familiarity returned. He was gentle when he found and pressed down on the first chord. He strummed and let it ring. Though the guitar was an electric, it wasn't plugged in. The music was soft, a subtle voice on the soundscape of the night. That was okay. He heard it; that was what mattered. Maybe she would too.

He recalled the patterns and progressions. He remembered the words. His voice cracked on the first line. Clearing his throat, he began again, from the top of "Blissfully Damaged." By the end of the first verse, he was in tears, but he continued playing. It didn't matter to him that his voice wasn't as strong as it used to be or that his hands no longer had their dexterity. What mattered was that it was all he had to give now. He transitioned into "The Lie," the inflections stronger, the emotion escalating. Minutes went by. A third song poured from him. Then another and another.

He cried for Anna and Dale, who never talked to him. He cried for Katie and her undying devotion that he didn't deserve. He cried for Chloe wherever she was now. Above all, he cried for her to return.

Eight songs and his throat hurt. His fingers burned with strain. He expelled a sigh of exhaustion and closed his eyes. When he opened them again, he raised his head to look across the moonlit field that stretched before his house. In the distance, the clearing gave way to thick woods. Crickets filled the air with their indifferent song. All of them chirped in sync with each other, unaffected by the outpouring of Todd's soul. Just another night in the mountains. Nothing worth breaking their routine.

Todd looked farther into the woods, tracing the dark outline of the hill. The moonlight made everything appear bluish gray. A strong

scent of pines hung thick in the air. He sat there, guitar over his knee expectantly, not even one hundred percent sure what he was expecting. He sighed again. For him, too, it was just another night in the mountains. Summoning her with his songs was no longer feasible. He'd lost the ability to do even that.

He started to lift the guitar off of his knee when his eyes caught a faint orange light glowing between the trees. It expanded and contracted like a fiery heart. He thought maybe there were campers on the hill. Probably not uncommon in this area. When the light grew larger, Todd sat bolt upright. From an insignificant speck, the orange expanded to a bright explosion that engulfed the side of the hill. A chorus of wails overwhelmed every other sound.

Todd's breath caught in his throat and he clutched the guitar tightly, holding it in front of him like a shield. The flames grew redder, angrier. The wailing increased in volume. Hearing the cries of tortured billions Todd wondered if Hell had grown impatient with waiting and had come for him.

His mind, still unable to accept the new worldview, grasped desperately for other meanings to what he saw. Even though Chloe had given him a different understanding of the world beyond, even though he thought that maybe through his music he could conjure her, this still felt unbelievable to him.

The fire became a spiraling tower, growing from the side of the hill and licking the dark sky. Within the column, among bright orange bursts and black clouds of smoke, bodies tried to squirm free from the torment. Even from the distance, he saw the anguish in their features. Their wailing was amplified, as if from the world's most powerful PA system, and the sounds chilled him to the marrow.

Run, a voice in the back of his mind commanded. *Run away, now!*

Quicker than it appeared, the column of fire shrunk and the crying stopped. Todd blinked several times, trying to make sense of what he'd seen. The hellish images were tattooed on his mind and the wailing echoed in his ears. Dread gnawed at him. Though he had hoped to open the door again, he now regretted it. What he'd seen made the idea of even the slightest bit of hope seem foolish.

The crickets resumed their song. The hillside was unmarked as if the flames had never been. Todd sat frozen in his chair, staring out into the night. He tried to reason that he had hallucinated the column and the tortured souls within, but the truth was that he finally knew the

hell Chloe had described. It was enough to make the furthest depths of oblivion seem attractive.

From between the trees, Chloe stepped out. She wore the same black dress he'd last seen on her. She staggered as if in a drunken daze, but she was certainly alive. Her pale skin glowed with vital energy. As she came forward, a slight inkling of hope stirred within him. Despite all he'd seen tonight, he thought maybe salvation had come for him after all. A bitter notion that maybe she'd come to punish him for being unable to save her also rose and threatened to eclipse all optimism.

She came closer. Hope and fear vied for supremacy. Todd set the guitar beside him and leaned forward. He braced to get to his feet.

Closer.

Behind her, Samael emerged, running, his hands gnarled into furious claws. He gritted his teeth in determination. Chloe looked over her shoulder as he pursued her. She quickened her pace. He was inhumanly fast, but she was fast too. She ran at the speed of desperation.

As Todd watched the scene unfold, he was sure only of the fact that the last moments of his life were upon him. Hell had come to show Todd the breadth of its power, tormenting him with one last vision of the woman he loved before Samael caught her and tore her to pieces in front of him. Then Samael would come for Todd next, because Todd had dared stand in the way.

Chloe came fast, but Samael was faster. Blood red fire burned in his eyes. He howled with the joy of the hunt, as if he knew how it would all end. Flesh and fire would meet and the fire would prevail every time. Chloe was twenty paces from Todd's porch, Samael a mere five paces behind her.

Todd had only brief moments to think. That small piece of hope apparently still lived within him. He asked himself what would happen if Chloe reached his porch, if the two of them entered his new house together.

He stood up and took his guitar in his hands. He held it over his shoulder like a baseball bat. Maybe his hope was futile, but at least he could say "fuck it," and go out swinging. *Just because the hounds of hell have you cornered doesn't mean you have to lie down and die,* words from one of his songs. Chloe was ten paces away. Samael was on her heels. He swiped forward with one arm. She ducked beneath him.

Seven paces. Panic held her face. Samael's cries tore through Todd, somehow even more horrible than the wails of the suffering in

the fiery column. Numbness spread through Todd's hands as he tightened his grip on the neck of the guitar. Four paces and Samael was practically riding on her back.

Two paces.

Samael caught her and tore her to the ground. She screamed in violent, desperate protest. Her hands reached toward the porch, toward Todd. She grasped without purchase at the empty air. Samael roped his forearm across her windpipe. Chloe's choked shrieks gouged at Todd loose from his stance.

He ran down the porch steps, the guitar raised high above his head. He screamed and felt his vocal chords shred, his chest explode. He swung the guitar at Samael's head and it connected. The body of the instrument shattered in a blast of splinters, and the strings came loose, scourging the air. Blood and teeth burst from Samael's head as the demon fell to the ground. Todd moved quickly, no thought to where the energy came from and no thought to the consequences of his actions. He jammed the last jagged piece of the guitar into Samael's chest. Ribs cracked and hot blood splattered upon Todd's face. In what felt like a single motion, he released the guitar, spun, and hauled Chloe up by the wrist.

Samael had already found his feet as Todd ran toward the porch. Blood poured from the wound on his chest. His shrieks were nonsensical, but their message was clear. He wanted Todd's blood.

Todd pressed his hand to the small of Chloe's back and forced her up the wooden stairs. Samael reached forward with ethereal fingers snaking through the air. One of Chloe's feet crossed the top step. Samael grabbed Todd by the collar and Todd's airway closed off in an instant. He fingered his throat, trying to loosen either his shirt or Samael's hold.

Samael forced Todd down and fresh pain exploded in his kneecaps. Like a vice grip Samael squeezed more of Todd's life away with each passing moment. He struggled to stay conscious. The fear of the world of torment awaiting him served as something to keep him afloat. Samael's body pressed against his back. Pieces of the guitar poked into his ribs but he barely felt it. He wondered how much longer he had. Chloe's other foot reached the top step and she fell forward, collapsing on the porch, and the grip on Todd's collar loosened. Chloe pulled a shiny object out of her dress and tapped it against the floor of the porch. A high-pitched whine filled the air and Samael screamed again.

This time, it was filled with anguish. He released his hold on Todd's collar.

Todd got his bearings and started to drag himself up the steps. He didn't stop until he reached Chloe's arms. When he looked back to Samael he saw the man in the clutches of several figures with skin like burning charcoal. Samael twisted in their hands, howling. The demons lacked distinguishable features. Each of them were lean and muscled; their eyes and mouths were brighter spots in the fires that consumed them. Beyond them a crack split the ground and spewed flames and ash. A potent smell of burning hair gushed out from the crevasse. The demons started to drag Samael's squirming body back into the hole.

"No!" Samael screeched. *"NO!"*

His body bent and folded in unnatural angles. The sounds of breaking bones and tearing organs accompanied his pain-filled screams. He scratched at the earth, hands switching from ethereal to flesh, stretching and retracting. A large, bruise-colored tentacle with hooks and suckers along its body reached up between the arms that held Samael and snaked around his broken body. As Samael sunk into the fissure, Chloe wrapped her hands around Todd from behind and squeezed. Todd couldn't take his eyes from the hellish spectacle before him. Samael jerked in the hold of the tentacle and black vomit spat from his mouth. His screaming echoed long after the earth closed over him.

Todd stared at the spot where Samael had been pulled under. The grass and dirt restored themselves to their normal state as if no split in the ground had been there mere seconds ago. The humming of crickets filled the air once again. The moon and its starry companions cast silver light over a landscape of trees and hills. It was the portrait of serenity. Chloe rubbed the back of Todd's neck.

"I made a deal, my freedom for his bondage. He can't hurt us anymore," she said.

Todd turned to face her. Inflammation burned in his chest and numbness had taken his arms. He tasted blood on his tongue and thought that maybe he'd bitten it when he fell. Exhaustion had settled over him. He knew he was dying.

Chloe smiled down at him and stroked his cheek with fingers that felt like velvet. He never bought into the saying about eyes being the window to the soul until he met Chloe. In her eyes, he almost always

saw fear and need, but now he saw only peace. He breathed her name, relished the sound of it and the way it tasted on his tongue.

She silenced him with gentle kiss on his mouth, passing her peace onto him. The world he knew began to fall away.

"Rest now," she said. "We're home."

Those were the last words he heard in this world.

***

Todd plucked the guitar strings with his fingertips for the song's lead-in. He kept his eyes closed so that he could let the melody guide him and held the pick in his mouth, ready to use when the time came. He waited to hear the ethereal chords from Chloe's synthesizer. When they entered the arrangement, he pulled the pick from his mouth and strummed a moody C minor. He let it ring out before strumming it again quickly and going to G minor. Chloe's soft vocals joined the music, singing words that she'd written before coming over. Todd made out the words, the sweeping romance, the desperation.

He didn't think it was possible to love her any more than he did in this moment. He opened his eyes and looked across the room at her. She smiled warmly in response. In the dim light of his apartment, she still glowed. Weeks had passed since the last time she used, and as a result, life had returned to her features.

They went through the song again. During the chorus, he harmonized her, adding that extra special dimension to the song. Together their voices soared, destined for each other, but also well-rehearsed, knowing what the other was doing before it was done. When they finished, Todd was breathless. The song had touched him in that deep way that only music can touch someone. He shrugged his shoulders and relaxed his grip on the guitar. She flashed him another smile.

"You want to do it again?" she asked.

He kept his eyes on her, studying the slender form of her body and her soft, pale features. Her hair hung in a loose pony tail, away from her face. He preferred her hair down, but with it pulled back he was able to see parts of her that were normally concealed: her tiny ears, her long neck, her slightly slumped shoulders as she held her hands over the synthesizer's keys. He stared long and hard, hoping his mind could permanently imprint her image.

Her eyes lit up. "What?"

"Nothing, I'm just…"

She raised an eyebrow and stepped around her keyboard. "Just… what?"

"You're beautiful."

She giggled softly. "Oh, am I?"

He nodded. "Very."

Out in the night, a bus came to a lurching, rumbling stop and let a group of people off. Their muffled conversations echoed just outside the building before fading into silence as the people made their way down the street.

Chloe crossed the room and helped Todd lean his guitar on the couch beside him. She smiled at him with her eyes and straddled him. As she plopped down on his lap, she slid her arms around his neck and planted a kiss on his lips. Her body emanated warmth and he wrapped his arms around her. They kissed again, her lips lightly teasing him before she opened her mouth and slid her tongue out to meet his. She released him and jumped back to her feet. He grasped for her, but she was just out of reach, and he felt an ache both pleasant and terrible. She skipped back behind her keyboard, locked eyes with him, and played a chord. A soft, string sound filled the room.

"Shall we play it again?"

Todd put his guitar back over his knee. "From the top."

She nodded. He kept his eyes on her, not ready to release her perfect image. She noticed his attention.

"Well, what is it now?" she asked playfully.

He considered this for a minute, stared deep into her eyes. "We're gonna live forever," he said, "aren't we?"

"Forever's a long time to put up with me, don't you think?"

"Not long enough," he said, proud of his capacity for romance.

"Sweet talker," she said, and he felt proud of her capacity for calling him on its cheesiness.

He strummed the C minor again. "From the top then?"

Her fingers danced along the keys and as he watched, his eyes drifted to her inner elbow where scars of her addiction still gave her skin an unattractive imperfection. He closed his eyes. When he opened them, her scars had disappeared.

-The End-

Lucas Mangum lives in Austin, Texas. His short stories have appeared online and in various anthologies, most recently the Fall 2014 issue of BLIGHT DIGEST and the forthcoming, V-WARS: SHOCKWAVES from IDW. He enjoys wrestling, cats, wrestling with cats, drinking craft beer, and crafting weird stories. Follow him on Twitter @LMangumFiction and visit his website, lucasmangumauthor.com.

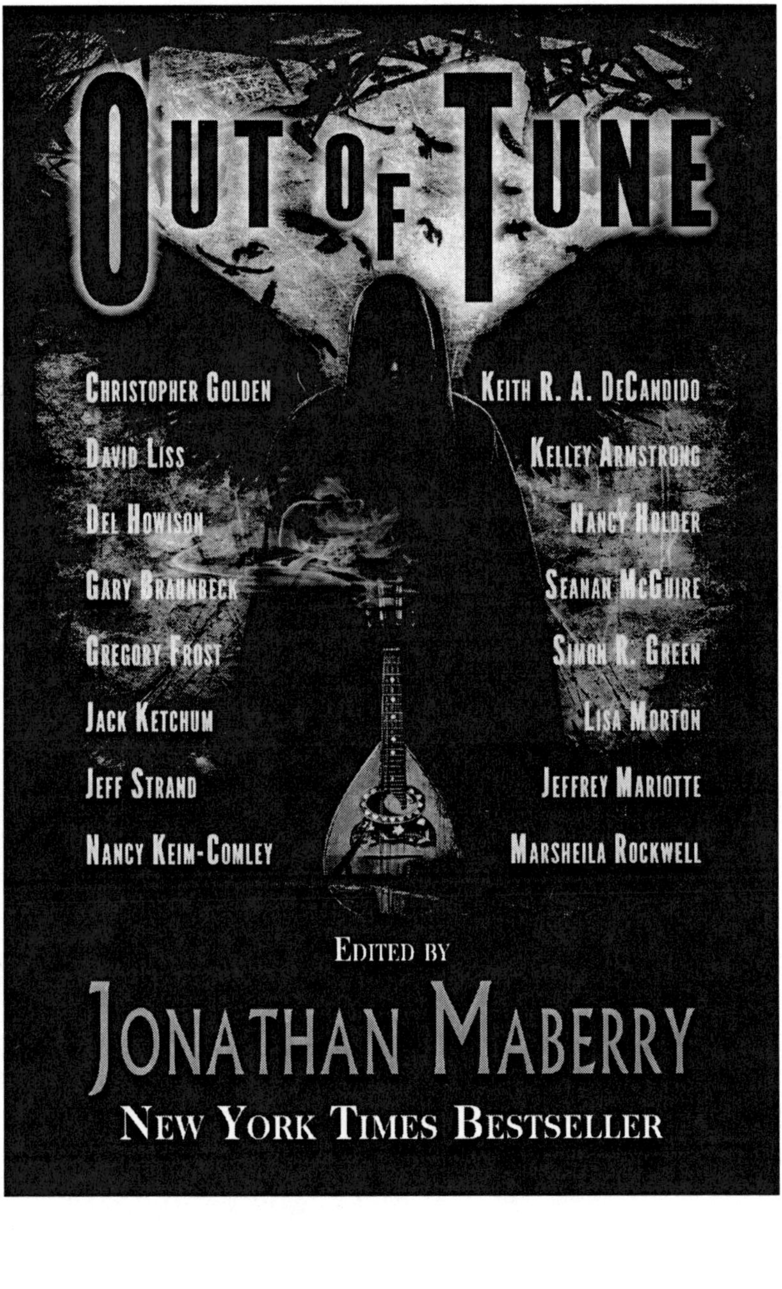

OUT OF TUNE
CHRISTOPHER GOLDEN
KEITH R. A. DECANDIDO
DAVID LISS
KELLEY ARMSTRONG
DEL HOWISON
NANCY HOLDER
GARY BRAUNBECK
SEANAN MCGUIRE
GREGORY FROST
SIMON R. GREEN
JACK KETCHUM
LISA MORTON
JEFF STRAND
JEFFREY MARIOTTE
NANCY KEIM-COMLEY
MARSHEILA ROCKWELL
EDITED BY
JONATHAN MABERRY
NEW YORK TIMES BESTSELLER